Burnt Sugar

Layne Harper

Burnt Sugar is a work of fiction. Names, characters, places and incidents either are the product of the author's imagination or are used fictitiously. Any resemblance to actual persons, living or dead, events or locales is entirely coincidental.

ISBN: 978-0-9960854-8-9

Cover Design: Michelle Preast
Editor: Missy Borucki
Formatting: Polgarus Studio

Other Works by Layne Harper:

Infinity Universe:

Falling Into Infinity

From Now Until Infinity

Finding Infinity

Infinity.

The World: According to Rachael

The World: According to Graham

Infinity Series Short Story:

Aiden's Broken Heart

ACE Series:

No Pink Caddy

A huge thank you to a few people who have made this journey just a bit sweeter . . . Christi, Nikki, Jennifer, Missy, Melissa, Jenn, Stephanie, Karrie, and Michelle. I appreciate all you do more than I can adequately express.

"One of the hardest decisions you'll ever face in life is choosing whether to walk away or try harder."

Prologue

November
(Seven hours after leaving MK's home)
Aaron

"We'll land in Austin in ten minutes, Mister Knite," a female voice says somewhere in my proximity. I don't bother opening my eyes to acknowledge her..

The sound of rain hitting the small, round plane windows mixes with the ukulele playing in my head. Jude and I watched some drama one night. She'd popped popcorn and used her pleading eyes to talk me into putting my guitar down and focusing on the TV for two hours. I think the movie was called *Blue Valentine.* It was raunchy as fuck, and there were a couple of scenes that I had to walk out of the room. That's when I learned to check Rotten Tomatoes before I watch anything with my daughter.

But there was this one scene where Ryan Gosling asks his wife to dance while he plays *You Always Hurt the Ones You Love.* It's like the saddest song ever, but the idea to lay it over the tiny, four-string, instrumental guitar was brilliant. It's cemented in my brain. Since I left MK's place, the song has played on repeat in my head.

It's a metaphor for my life. My body aches all over, but it doesn't even hold a candle to the pain in my chest. I don't know what happened. I'm so confused. I asked her to marry me, and then suddenly we were fighting and she was pissed that I did coke. In the middle of our argument, she dropped the shittiest line in the history of breakup lines: *Give me the whole and complete man I deserve.* The hell if I'll ever be that or even know what it means.

MK. She was my one chance at love.

Jude shared her blog with me long before I accidentally/on purpose bumped into MK at the bar in New Orleans. When I watched her YouTube channel, her smile got me. I loved when she messed up a recipe and laughed at herself, or when she did something spectacular and beamed with pride. She was beautiful, self-deprecating, and smart, and seemed like a girl who could love someone like me. But she was one hundred times more radiant in person.

She intrigued me enough that I gave getting to know her a shot. The way her dark brown hair covered the left side of her face, and how she rolled her eyes at something I did shot me straight in the heart. She smelled like heaven, and her heart is pure gold.

Then, like everything else in my life but music, I ruined it. *I think.* She told me how she felt about drugs. When she saw the coke I bought cut into thin lines on the bedside table, she lost her mind. She scooped it into her boot and dumped it in the toilet while she yelled. She gave enough of a damn to yell at me. That doesn't happen often in my world.

But did I listen? Of course not, because I never do, and most of the time I'm not called out on my bullshit.

I poke the sharp end of the silver shark tooth necklace she gave me that night into the pad of my thumb. *She cared enough to give me this.* She said it would help me find my way when I needed direction. Well, right now I'm about as lost as it gets.

Why didn't I put faith in this talisman instead of snorting the fine, white powder up my nostrils? I couldn't fucking cope any longer with the red gash on her face and the thought of losing her. She was mine, and I let her get hurt. I didn't protect her. It was like Jude all over again—seeing that bastard kid kneeling between her spread legs. Me ripping him off my baby girl.

My palms press against my temples and my eyes water as I attempt to make the images of my girls vulnerable and injured exit my head.

I reach over and grasp the tumbler beside me. The ice tinkles against the crystal glass as I bring the amber liquid to my lips. The contents spill down my burning throat.

I want to die. *Why can't plane crashes ever happen when I want them to?*

The wheels touch the runway with a bump. I undo the seatbelt and wait for the plane to pull into the private hangar owned by Johnny Records. The words the bartender yells at the club I own in downtown Austin ring in my head. *It's closing time. You don't have to go home, but you can't stay here.*

Coming back to Austin without MK feels like I'm visiting a foreign country and counting the hours until I can climb back on this plane and have the silver wings take me home. But my home told me to be the man she deserves, so I have everything I've ever wanted except the girl who makes it all worth something.

I can tell when we enter the hangar because the sound of the rain stops, and all I hear is the roar of the engines and, of course, the morose song on blast in my brain.

The plane comes to a stop. I stand, grabbing nothing but my phone and guitar. They're all I have. I bolted so quickly from New Orleans that I didn't bring any of my stuff with me. Seamus is supposed to be packing and closing the house.

As I step off the plane and descend the metal stairs into the hangar, my sister runs, throwing her arms around my neck. "I told you she was a witch. I told you not to meet her."

Her hug is unexpected, and I tumble backwards. My right palm slams into the metal hand railing of the stairs. Dropping my guitar case, I double over in pain. It feels as if a baseball, thrown at one hundred miles per hour, has hit my fingers.

"Oh my God. Are you okay?" Grace asks as she tries to examine my injury.

"Need some ice," I groan as I push her away.

She runs up the stairs and emerges from the plane a few moments later with a clear bag filled with ice cubes. I place it over my injury and sink my ass to the first stair. My head hangs as I stare at the yellow painted line on the grey cement. *It's really not possible for this day to get any worse.*

Grace joins me. "I couldn't believe it when Seamus called. I mean, what a bitch. She's a sorority girl that never left her little college world. She's one of those girls who will always go running to their daddy when the world kicks them in their teeth. She used you, and at least you got out of the relationship quickly." She leans in. "I mean, it was only like two weeks. Imagine if it had taken you two months or even two years to see her true colors?"

I turn towards her, feeling as if I must vindicate MK's reputation and admit the truth. "I'm the one who fucked up. She didn't." I swallow hard. "I used again."

She shrugs. "Well, that doesn't make me happy, but you're an addict. What does she expect?"

Her words clank around my head like the ice cubes in the whiskey I was just drinking. Is being an addict an excuse to get fucked up when life screws you over? I don't think MK would agree with Grace's logic, and I don't either.

I adjust the cold pack. "She's a smart girl. She doesn't want to deal with the eighteen-wheeler full of issues I warned her about. She needs a frat boy with an eight-to-five job. She needs someone who isn't covered in tattoos with long hair who makes his living playing music. I mean have you seen me? What would a girl like MK want with me?"

Grace jumps to her feet while accidentally connecting her fist with my knee. It jostles my hand and causes pain to travel from my fingertips to my shoulder as if I've been electrocuted. I grimace, but she doesn't seem to notice.

"That's bullshit, and you know it. You always tell the band how you value loyalty." She paces back and forth in front of me. "That girl wouldn't know loyalty if it smacked her upside her head. She's a rich princess who doesn't know anything about hardships and struggles. She was born with a silver spoon between her dermatologically altered lips. When the going got tough and you used, she ran for the hills. Loyalty," Grace huffs as her platinum blonde bob swings forward. "That girl doesn't even know the meaning."

"You think?" I ask with a head turn. I hadn't thought about it that way.

"I know. She could've never dealt with your touring schedule either. MK's the kind of girl that needs a boy there twenty-four/seven to hold her delicate hand. If this hadn't broken y'all, touring would have. Consider yourself having dodged a bullet."

I listen to Grace's words and turn them over to see if there's any truth to her statements. Did I dodge a bullet? I didn't know how to respond when

MK was so angry. So I did what I always do, I ran. I thought I was being a dick for using again and leaving her. It never occurred to me that I might be the one who is right.

Grace is my sister, and I know that she always has my back, but she isn't crazy about MK. Does she see something that I missed?

The flight crew walks down the steps. Standing, I let them pass.

The pilot asks, "You going to lock up?"

I shake my head. "No, we're leaving. Y'all finish up here."

I pick up my guitar case with my left hand and walk to the passenger side of my sister's car. After placing it in the backseat, I get in gingerly, fastening my seatbelt as I adjust the icepack to numb the pain.

Grace slides into the driver's seat and starts the car. As she pulls out of the airplane hangar, raindrops bounce off the windshield. We're quiet as I think about her words. Grace might be right. MK wasn't loyal. We had our first major hiccup in our relationship, and she told me to be the man she deserves. What kind of shit is that? Maybe Grace does know what she's talking about, and MK was always going to leave me—just using me for my name and the fame that could come to her blog. She's no different than the groupies who just want a piece of the image named Johnny Knite.

"Let's go drink the memory of MK away," I announce.

Grace slaps my thigh. "That's what I'm talking about."

But there's this little tiny voice in the back of my brain. An itch that I can't scratch. It keeps yelling loudly over *Welcome to the Jungle* which is what my head has currently chosen to play. The little voice says, "Maybe, just maybe, Grace is wrong, and you left your chance at true love crying on the worn hardwoods of her carriage house apartment."

Chapter One

MK
February

I've waited . . .

I've waited long enough to share this news. Here goes nothing . . .

Hi! For those of you who are new to my site, and if my blog stats are correct, there are a bunch of you, my name is Mary Kay Landry, MK for short. I hope you spend some time here reading and watching the years' worth of posts. If your social life is more hopping than mine so time is an issue, here's a brief synopsis: I began No Pink Caddy more than seven years ago. It was a way for me to connect with other single girls who were also in their early twenties and disappointed by the real world. Over the years, it's grown to be a place where I've shared my dating woes, thrift store finds, sold the repurposed furniture I've breathed new life into, and taught you how to make some rockin' Cajun dishes.

Damn. There's that word—rockin'.

I also fell in love with a rock star, who the world calls Johnny Knite, and tumbled into the corner of my fabulous marble coffee table, suffering a concussion and a nice red gash from my cheek to my eye socket.

Let's pause this story here. I was completely sober and, honestly, just had a bit of a spill. Contrary to what you may have read, I was alone at the time and found by Bella (faceless, snarky voice you hear off-camera).

If I'm being completely honest with you, and I always strive to be, I wasn't sure I was going to continue this site. My accident was just that—an accident—but because the man I love is famous, my little oops turned into headline-making news. What I also have come to learn is that I'm more well-known than I ever believed.

I must admit, that's taken some getting used to. Before I began my relationship with Johnny Knite, I considered myself to have an online presence. Now, I feel as if I'm the Lion Fish in the New Orleans Aquarium, and you are the school children pressed against the thick glass watching my every move.

I've taken some time away from No Pink Caddy to evaluate my personal and online life. Here are my conclusions, in no certain order:

1. *I will continue this site. Robin Roberts (good Southern girl) says to turn your mess into a message. That's what I intend to do. I'm going to share my vulnerabilities and flaws, but I'll also share my joys and triumphs. What I've come to realize is that I can't NOT post here. No Pink Caddy is my metaphorical child. Abandoning it would be like cutting off my arm, and goodness knows, I don't need any more medical bills.*

2. *Alis volat propriis. It means with her own wings she flies. Yes, the influx of followers of this site were not gained through my hard work, but well, you're here. I do believe that in this crazy world sometimes people come into your life when you need them the most. Maybe you and I were meant to find each other for purposes yet to be defined.*

3. *I am taking more precautions. As it was pointed out to me, I live a free-spirit lifestyle. I believe the term he used was vagabond. It seems everyone in North America now knows my address, and I no longer feel safe in my own home. This is crazy to even type, but I have a privacy fence installed around my wonderful carriage house. So far it's working well keeping the creepers out.*

Notice to Johnny's Fans: Johnny Knite is NOT *here and even if he was, he's probably doing something very normal like watching a movie or eating a bowl of cereal and doesn't want to be interrupted.*

I walk over to the closest window, peering through the slats of my plantation shutters. Every single day, rain or shine, the same reporter is outside. His name is Stan. I tried politely explaining that Johnny Knite will no longer be visiting my home. He picked up his black camera, which hangs around his neck, and snapped my picture. Hopefully, this post will finally convince him to take a hike.

It would also be nice if the hordes of Johnny Knite fans, especially female fans, would lose my address. I've been woken up in the middle of night by their knocks on my front door, chants of his name, and rocks thrown at my windows. Fortunately, nothing has been damaged, but it's only a matter of time.

There's no need to detail the horrible insults that have been hurled my way by his "biggest" fans. Somehow the anonymity of a screen name makes it okay to call me a whore, bitch, troll, and to dissect every appearance flaw I have.

But for every Tweet that made me want to quit No Pink Caddy, there was a positive comment. Girls from around the world found my site and sent wonderful, encouraging messages about how they could relate to my journey or tried a recipe. One of my favorite connections is a girl who emailed me from Nicaragua. She's opening the first Cajun restaurant in her town using my recipes modified with local ingredients. I inspired her to follow her own dream. That gives me goose bumps.

Walking back to my laptop, I sit down on my only barstool and review what I've written so far. Sigh . . . That wasn't so bad, but now comes the hard part. Staring at my screen, I wonder if I'm able to type the rest. A stirring in my stomach compels me to reach out to him one more time, to give him one last chance to renew my faith. I open the messenger app on my Mac.

Me: *How are you? It's been so long since I've heard from you that my worry has turned to the realization that whatever we had is no more. I'm no longer carrying my phone everywhere I go in the hopes that you'll text. I'm writing a post letting my readers know that we're over. It feels like a lie to keep pretending we're something that you obviously don't think we are. If you'd like to read it before it goes live, let me know or have your publicist contact me. I'm sorry we turned out like we did. You'll always have a place in my heart.*

After hitting *send*, I begin making excuses why I need to give him a few more minutes to stop me from publicly breaking up with him. He's in the shower. He's in a meeting. His phone battery is dead. After a while, and longer than I care to admit, the regret sets in. Why can't I see my time with Aaron for what it was? He's a musician who lives in a world nothing like mine. We were each other's two-week distraction. The sex was epic, but that's it. *MOVE ON.* All of this would be so much easier to accept if he hadn't shared his new album and cover art. His songs were written about our relationship. Him, on the cover, wearing the necklace I gave him to help him find his way, and my name tattooed on the fist squeezing the anatomically correct heart over his own heart. My name placed next to his daughter's.

But it's been three months since I learned he was using again and asked him to get help. Nothing. Not a text or phone call. Thanksgiving, Christmas, and New Year's have all passed without so much as a *thinking of you* note. Valentine's Day was three days ago. Not even a half-eaten, red satin box of drug store purchased chocolates.

The man who I once refused to Google now is a daily Internet search. I have an alert set up for his name or Jude's. Not a morsel of information has made it online.

Taking a sip of wine, I know it's time. If Aaron still wanted me in his life, I'd be by his side. He's not one who takes no for an answer. What hurts the most is that he didn't even give me the courtesy of a breakup text. His silence has been deafening.

My fingers tremble as they dance across the keyboard.

With all the housekeeping stuff taken care of, I also need to share the change in my personal life. Johnny Knite and I are no longer a couple. Please don't jump to conclusions. Basically, everything the media reported surrounding us and my accident was FALSE. I have the utmost respect for him. His heart is pure, and his soul is beautiful. For reasons, I will not elaborate on, we feel it's best to go our separate ways. I still love him, and just writing these words makes me sick to my stomach.

And they do, but that's why I must share this post. It's time to move on. I can't keep hiding in my apartment. I need my life back. And this is an important step in making that happen.

We've been over for a while, but I couldn't share with you until I could find a lesson in my time with him. Here it is . . . He showed me what it felt like to be loved and return that same emotion. I throw the terms love, chemistry, and connection around this site like birdseed at the park. But I experienced the meaning behind those words, and instead of being bitter that they've been taken away, I'm hopeful that one day I'll have the opportunity to experience those emotions again.

Love is not for the faint of heart, but I'm brave enough to keep trying.

Muah,

MK

Without checking *Messenger*, I hit *publish*. Relief washes over me in waves, turning my bones to Jell-O. I pick up my glass of wine, toasting my computer screen. The smile on my face is not one of joy. It's like I'm seeing my old life in the rearview mirror. This moment ends the chapter on the first thirty and a half years I've existed on this planet. Tomorrow when I wake up, I will begin a new one.

My time with Aaron and after he stormed out of my carriage house has fundamentally changed me as a person. The old, carefree, fiercely independent girl, with the motto of *Alis Volat Propriis,* is gone forever.

Over the last three months, I've dealt with days so black that Bella would come over, forcing me to eat. I quit filming videos and sharing pictures of myself because I looked too ill. Christmas Day was the worst. I dragged myself to Bethany's home to watch my nieces open their presents. The mask I wore, I thought, was a joyful one. After the gifts were unwrapped, my precious four-year-old niece crawled in my lap and kissed my cheek. I asked her if she'd gotten everything from Santa that she asked for. She replied, "Auntie MK, I asked Santa to give you your smile back, but he forgot to deliver it." Her fingers drew the corners of my lips into a grotesque smile. She giggled. "There. You look pretty again." I couldn't keep the tears from falling down my cheeks and spent the next five days in bed.

Mourning a lost relationship in the privacy of my apartment was one thing, but every single time I step foot outside, I'm reminded of him as the reporters and fans scream his name. If it hadn't been for Grandmother paying to build the fence, Bella's unrelenting support, Tripp's handyman skills to keep the carriage house from looking vacant, and my mother finally dragging me to a psychiatrist, I wouldn't be the stronger woman that I am today. What's the saying? *It takes a village . . .*

With my own wings, I no longer fly. But, I hope by making this post live, I'll begin healing and discovering just exactly who the new Mary Kay Landry is.

It's officially over.

We're officially over.

Closing the screen, I stand and walk into my kitchen to fix a late dinner.

I pull out a white container of leftovers from supper last night. Grandmother and I checked out a new restaurant by her home. This is sort of a pastime of ours. We love exploring new places that pop up all over our beloved New Orleans. The Ginger Rose is Asian fusion. We shared an order of tiger prawns, so when my red curry chicken arrived, I barely touched it. Leftovers are the best.

Grabbing a spoon, I dump a blob onto my teal ceramic plate and stick it in the microwave. Normally, I'd heat in the oven, but laziness is prevailing tonight.

Punching in sixty seconds, I lean against the counter and watch the plate turn in a circle. It's hypnotizing. As usual when my mind is unoccupied with details, it drifts to a long-haired, blond boy. Tall. Toned body with asymmetrical tattooed skin. His full lips and sparkling blue eyes which could drive me wild and make me shake my head in disbelief. My very own Peter Pan. My lost boy who never grew up.

My stomach growls as if it's telling the microwave to hurry up. Throwing my hands over my belly button, I laugh, shaking me from a path that I don't need to walk down for the millionth time because I've started a new chapter and all. The joyous sound exiting my mouth is not one that my ears have heard in a long time.

My whole body feels lighter, as if I could float, or maybe I'm deflated like a balloon after the party has long ago ended. It's over.

A loud dinging noise draws my eyes to the countdown clock on the microwave. Still six seconds left. Then I hear it again and realize it's a Google alert.

Walking over to my computer, I open the message. My eyes scan the words. Any chance of me enjoying my leftover curry flies out the window and is replaced with the crippling feeling of dread.

Austin, Texas: In a surprise move, Johnny Knite and the band ACE just released the long-awaited and rumored album Alis Volat Propriis. *This new music confirms that the band has not broken up despite reports to the contrary after Johnny's run in with the law and then time spent in rehab for drug abuse. Right now, it only appears to be available on iTunes.*

Seconds later, another Google alert flashes across my screen.

Austin, Texas: Johnny Knite and his band ACE have announced a forty-date arena tour to promote their new album Alis Volat Propriis. *Tour is set to kick off in April in Boston. Check their website for more details.*

Then another alert appears.

New Orleans, Louisiana: MK Landry, blogger and girlfriend of Johnny Knite, has announced the end of their relationship. The reason is listed as, "We feel it's best to go our separate ways." Knite's publicist has issued a statement stating that she does not comment on her client's personal life.

Alert after alert pours in and my phone begins ringing and chiming with those trying to reach me. It's just like it was after my accident. I ignore them, turning off all my electronics. I open the microwave door and dump the contents of my uneaten dinner in the garbage can before I crawl into bed and bury my head under the covers.

I would like to believe it was a coincidence that I shared with my followers that we were no longer dating and his album went live only minutes later. But I'm no fool. He did this to prove a point—maybe even to hurt me. Why though? I've done everything but take out billboards in Austin to compel him to talk to me. I've left messages for his sister and Sam. I never reached out to his daughter because, well, that just seemed a bit dirty. Why does he feel the need to torture me? What did I ever do to him?

Chapter Two

MK
July

MK Landry @NoPinkCaddy
Big meeting, y'all. If you pray, say a prayer. If you don't, that's okay. Keep me in your thoughts. #FollowYourDreams

Lacy Nutrition @LacyNutritionCenter
@NoPinkCaddy, you should be ashamed of yourself. Louisiana has one of the highest obesity rates in the country.

Lacy Nutrition @LacyNutritionCenter
@NoPinkCaddy, your recipes are high in fat and sugar. Promote #HealthyEating instead. #SocialResponsibilty

"We love you. Like we love you so much we'd marry you," the bright, bubbly blonde says with so much enthusiasm that I cringe a bit. It's been awhile since I've been around anyone that is so happy. For the last eight months, I've avoided people like her because as the saying goes, misery loves company.

Her laugh carries through the small café, and I glance over my shoulder to see if anyone is staring at us. Fortunately, no one seems to care. "Cindy and I read your blog and watched your videos, and we laughed." She gestures to her partner, and they exchange a smile. "Well at you, and with you. We cried when you shared your heartbreaks, and I called her and said, 'She's our next star.'"

Cindy, who looks so much like her business partner, Janet, that it's difficult to tell them apart, smiles in confirmation. "MK, you're a natural."

Picking up my glass of water, I use it as a distraction—a pause so I can have a moment to absorb their praise. Since Aaron and I broke up, life has been brutal. Then, after his surprise album drop minutes after I announced our breakup, it was like the almost-healed wound was cracked opened again. It was obvious to the world when they heard his new music that the songs were written about me. I mean his most popular song is called *Pink Cadillac.* His response in interviews has been to neither confirm nor deny it, but he gives a knowing wink or sexy little smile. That's it though. He makes no other comments about us.

Once again, I felt like I was caught with my pants around my ankles. Instead of my breakup post returning my life back to normal, he dumped the paparazzi and his fans on my doorstep for a second time. In one day, I received over a hundred phone calls, and I didn't bother to count all the emails, texts, and other messages. Everyone wanted to know my thoughts on one of the biggest names in rock essentially writing two-thirds of his new music about me. My response was to say nothing. I've never acknowledged that the album even exists. Some days I've absolutely hated him. Other days I still question why he seems hell-bent on making my life miserable. But days like today, I must thank him. Without Johnny Knite, I wouldn't be dining with two of the most successful producers of reality lifestyle programs.

Janet continues, "We left you so many messages. We'd just assumed that you were blowing us off. And then. Well, then, you called months later. And I immediately texted Cindy and told her that we scheduled this meeting, and she actually picked up the phone and called me squealing. Like she was so excited she couldn't stand it."

A smile that doesn't begin in my heart touches my cheeks. "To be honest, I wasn't at a place where I was ready to embrace this opportunity when you first contacted me. Sometimes you must wade through the trenches to come out on the other side as the person you want to be. I think I'm finally there. I can turn the mess of my life into a message."

"And it's talk like that that will make you our next star. Twenty-two minutes of you just being you." She pauses for a breath, and then adds, "Of course, we'll have story lines, and you'll work with us to make sure the content is spot-on for our viewers, but we really just want you to be you."

The linen napkin twists between my fingers as I fight to refrain from mutilating my cuticle. "This all sounds great, but I don't know, ladies. I mean, thank you, I'm totally flattered. I'm just worried people will think I'm trying to capitalize on my brief time with Johnny Knite." I plaster on another bright smile. "It's been a rough year."

And now, eight months later, I'm starting to feel like a new improved version of MK—one who's stronger, sassier, and ready to take on the world. I no longer spend hours preparing mentally to leave my home. I've learned to roll my shoulders back and smile brightly, ignoring whatever questions and comments are hurled my way. My skin has grown so thick that elephants are jealous.

I also can't continue living in limbo like I have been. My best friend is now a married woman. Even Tripp seems to be moving on. I caught him texting with his assistant, and his eyes conveyed that he was imagining dirty things. My sister is pregnant again. Everyone is advancing in their lives but me, and it's time I do something bold and brave and show the world that MK Landry is back and stronger than before.

Cindy reaches across the bistro table and motions for my hand. Reluctantly, I release the napkin and take it. It's cold and over-moisturized, slimy to the touch. "That's why we feel like now is the perfect time. You're vulnerable and real. We've all had our heart stomped on then heard songs on the radio that remind us of our ex, right?"

But how many people had those songs written about them? Sure, I'm not the first girl that has ended a relationship. But mine went down in spectacular flames in the bright lights of the media, while the paparazzi waited on my sidewalk like seagulls hoping for a morsel of food.

She continues, "Girls want to see you cry. They want you to share your vulnerabilities. You are them, except you're an exceptional cook."

The waiter appears at my side and begins clearing our plates. My salad was barely touched. First of all, I wasn't hungry, and second of all, I didn't want to spill food on Grandmother's vintage pink Chanel dress from the 60s that she loaned me for this meeting. I'll have a peanut butter sandwich once I've changed into my grubby clothes.

Janet leans in conspiratorially. "So you brought him up." Cindy and Janet exchange glances. "Tell us what's up with Johnny Knite. We've all heard the album, and it's hot, hot, hot." She fans herself with her hand. "Like I had an ear orgasm."

Cindy laughs. "An eargasm. Janet, you're too much."

"Our lips are zipped," Janet adds as she simulates the act of locking her mouth and tossing away the key.

Glancing back and forth between them, panic makes my heart tight and difficult to beat as I snatch my hand back. "There's nothing up with Johnny. It's like I said on my blog post months ago. We've decided to go our separate ways. He's been photographed with some new girl. We're really over."

Cindy rests her elbows on the table and leans in. "Sure. Sure. That's the answer his PR people told you to say. But, seriously, you can tell us. No one writes those kinds of songs and doesn't get the girl." She motions back and forth between her and Janet. "We think the model is a plant. Like a distraction to boost album sales. No one actually believes they're a couple. The world is cheering for you guys to get back together."

Janet adds, "I mean, we would like for him to make an appearance or two on your show. Can you imagine you teaching Johnny Knite how to fry beignets?"

Cindy crinkles her nose and looks toward the ceiling as if she's having a vision. "Great TV," she says with a dreamy expression on her face.

My spine straightens as my stomach churns, thankful that I didn't put food in it. "Look, ladies, I'm flattered that you're interested in turning my blog into a lifestyle show on your cable channel. Honestly, thank you for your time." I toss my napkin on the table and reach for my bag. "But Johnny Knite and I are no longer a couple. The model may be a ploy to sell more albums, but I have nothing to do with her or him any longer. We aren't in some secret publicist's dream three-way to boost album sales. He will not make special appearances, and I will no longer discuss my relationship with him. If that's not good enough for you, I understand. Hope you enjoy the rest of your day."

Standing, my pulse quickens, and I'm prepared to bolt out the door. This was a terrible idea. I received two other messages from producers interested in turning my blog into a TV show. I'll call one of them.

Janet stands, grabbing my elbow. "I'm sorry, MK." Her eyes meet Cindy's, and the business partners exchange a secret message. "We just assumed." Her laugh is awkward. "I guess we got caught up in the rumors flying around. We're still very interested in moving forward with this project if you are."

I sit back down without removing my bag from my shoulder, just in case the fight-or-flight instinct kicks in again. "Johnny Knite is a non-topic of discussion for me. I will not be introduced as his former girlfriend, lover, or any other title that indicates we had a relationship. If his name is even so much as uttered, I walk away. No Pink Caddy was a success before I had a brief fling with a rock star, and it will continue to be a success without having to mention his name."

"Yes," Janet says in a soothing voice. It reminds me of when my nieces think they're injured, and my pediatrician sister placates them with a few kind words. "But viewers are going to be interested in the girl that was Johnny's muse. And, honey, that's you."

Hearing her articulate the thoughts that have run rampant in my head for eight months is damn near panic attack inducing. My pointer finger finds the scarred cuticle skin on my thumb, and I use my nail to scrape it. "Excuse me." I don't wait for the usual politeness exchange. Tossing my napkin on the table, I bolt for the ladies' room. Fortunately, it's unoccupied.

The message Aaron sent along with the twelve music files a week after he walked out of my life, never to be seen again, echoes in my brain. *MK Landry, I'm trying to get better to be the man you deserve. I promise.* I guess his idea of "trying" was to leave me raw and exposed for the whole world to examine. For people to speculate about our brief relationship and just assume that we're still a couple because how can he write those sorts of songs and as Cindy said *not get the girl?*

Wetting a paper towel, I blot my face hoping to cool my feverish skin.

There's not a damn thing I can do about my racing heart. All the unanswered questions bubble up to the top of my brain and threaten to cripple me to the point that I'm unable to go out in public again. *If he truly felt about me like he says in his songs, how could he have completely cut me out of his life?*

Deep breathing exercises that I learned in yoga and in the psychiatrist's office come in handy and seem to help me find my center again—at least enough to finish this meeting.

"MK, don't let him steal this opportunity from you like he's stolen the last eight months," I tell the pale girl in the mirror. She seems to listen and can even slap her fake smile back on her face.

I'm composed when I slide into my chair. "Sorry, ladies." I beam. Turning to Janet, "You were saying?"

"You okay?" Cindy asks.

"Think I'm just a little nervous," I reply as if I'm letting them in on a huge secret.

"Understandable." Janet continues, "We can discuss these points when it's time to get down to the nitty-gritty details. Are you in? Are we going to do this? Are we going to move forward?"

I choose to ignore the uneasy feeling in my stomach. If I agree, I'll have to hire an agent and before I sign anything, my no-go topics of conversation will be spelled out. I remind myself of what I just told me in the mirror. "I'd love to."

The ladies clap and approach me from either side, pulling me into a group hug in the middle of the lovely restaurant. This feels surreal. I just agreed to move forward with turning my life into a reality TV show. That realization causes another tear at the delicate skin surrounding my thumbnail.

***

Later that night, my mom, Bella, Nyall, Tripp, Bethany, and I are huddled around the back-corner table in Eddy's Bar. We decided to meet here so I could give them an update on how the meeting with the producers went. Frankly, I just didn't have it in me to repeat the story a billion times.

Extra chairs crowd around the small table, and we look like we're discussing secret plans for an enemy strike.

Swallowing a sip of my rum and Diet Coke, I conclude my recap. "So what do y'all think?"

Bella, who still has the newlywed glow, speaks up first. "What do you have to lose? You've been in a funk for a long time. This at least gives you content for No Pink Caddy even if you decide to back out at the last minute. And maybe people will fall in love with you, and they'll stop being such jackasses on social media." She turns to my mom. "Sorry for the cuss word."

My mom nods and winks. "I think being a TV star would be so much fun. And maybe it'll help you find a man." She punctuates her last statement with a sip of Chardonnay.

Rolling my eyes, I quote my favorite teal and orange tank top. "A girl needs a man like a fish needs a bicycle."

Tripp shifts forward as his eyes move to his lap. He thinks he's being sly by keeping his phone in his hand under the wooden tabletop. He's not. He's checking his phone for the hundredth time in the last ten minutes.

"Well, it seems you need to find a business manager, attorney, or someone to help you navigate the unknowns," Nyall wisely advises with a twist of his wedding band around his finger.

"Yeah." I wipe the condensation from the table using a bar napkin. "I have a few names of people I can call. I've a sorority sister who's in the LA scene. She gave me some info."

As she rubs her emerging bump, Bethany asks, "Why aren't you more excited? Most girls in your position would be doing backflips." My sister has always seen through my fake smiles and quick assurances that everything is just peachy.

Visions of that terrible Monday evening play through my mind. Aaron's irrational, schizophrenic behavior. The overwhelming guilt and outrage I felt at learning of the false stories about my accident being told and retold in the media. Then moving on and thinking I was finally emerging on the other side when he published the album, and everything became so raw again. Do I want to open myself back up to the media scrutiny?

My blog is just a little speck of dust in a great big virtual world. Me committing to turning it into a television program is so much—what's the word—more.

I voice my concerns out loud. "The past months have been difficult. The breakup with Aaron and all the media attention. The loss of my privacy." I shake my head. I don't say out loud seeing Aaron with a new girl and experiencing the pain of him releasing the album he wrote about us. "I just don't know if I can rip the Band-Aid off again and show the world my bloody wounds."

"Geez, MK." Bella grimaces. "Do you need to be so graphic?"

Bethany shifts in her chair. "Look, your privacy was gone the first time you chose to post on your site. I'm not seeing what the issue is?"

Bella jumps to my defense. "Bethany, that's harsh and not entirely accurate. MK has controlled her content."

I further elaborate. "Yes, my life has been an open book, but I chose to put the details out there, and I've managed how I've been portrayed. Moving forward with a reality show leaves me vulnerable to how Cindy and Janet want to spin my life." My tongue swipes over my bottom lip reminding me of the physical injury that I caused trying to manifest the pain Aaron's drug use inflicted. "And to answer your question, Bella, yes, I need to be graphic. Because that's what I feel like I'll be doing if I move forward. My show will be scripted somewhat. I'm sure they're going to want me to date and talk about it during interviews. Looking for love is a feature of my blog."

Bethany's forehead wrinkles. "Are you not ready to date again?"

She's clueless. She's been married for so long that she's forgotten about heartbreak and how difficult it is to open yourself up to a new relationship.

"Sure." I shrug. "I'd love to meet someone who I fell in love with, who didn't break my heart into a million pieces, and then give me hope they were coming back, and then never talk to me again."

Bella adds, "And then date someone close to the age of their daughter."

I watch as Tripp's eyes cut to the floor. I know he would be that guy for me. He'd love and cherish me every day I called him husband. But it would be settling on my part, and he deserves to have a woman who loves him as much in return.

"Why do it then, honey?" my mom asks with a toss of her blonde hair. "You've had a taste of fame, and it was rather sour. Keep saving your money, and one day you'll have your store on Magazine Street. You don't need to do this."

She's right, but there's this nagging suspicion in my brain that if I don't try, I'll regret not taking this opportunity. When Janet and Cindy said they were still interested in turning my blog into a show, I was shocked. I'd waited three months before I returned their calls. I just assumed they'd moved on. The meeting had been a shot in the dark, but I'm so grateful they still think I'm relevant.

Tripp, who has been rather quiet this whole time, says, "I've known my whole life that you're special. Your smile draws people to you. Your eyes reassure them they're going to be okay. Your soul's pure. You'd be doing the world a disservice not to host your own show."

My eyes water. God, that man is incredible. "Thank you, Tripp." Smiling, I look around the table at my family and friends who love me. Having their support means the world to me. "I'm doing it. I'm going to be a reality-TV star."

Chapter Three

Aaron
July

Carly Johnson @RockerChick
Oh my Rock God! @RealJohnnyKnite is back and better than ever. #ImStillMoving

Erica Frank @FranklyIDontCare
#PinkCadillac is the best song on the radio right now. Why can't a guy love me like that?

"Are you playing *Wheels on the Bus*?" Billy asks with severe disdain lacing his voice.

I chuckle. "Guess I am." But do I stop? Of course not.

Sam joins in as she slides onto Billy's lap. Her raspy voice does its best to cancel out the hum of the plane's engines. "Up and down. Up and down. The wheels on the bus go up and down, all through the town."

Billy lifts her by her thin hips and sets her next to him. He picks up his guitar and plays along, adding bass to the classic hit. Sam's voice goes high and does an almost spot-on impression of Marilyn Monroe singing *Happy Birthday*. It's really quite impressive.

When my eyes move from watching the guitar strings, I spot Grace holding her phone up. She mouths *videoing for Jude.*

That forces my lips to curve into a smile. Because Jude spent so much time in a tour van, then tour bus, the guys and I would play her this song as if it was the only tune we knew. She'd clap and cheer, and her blonde curls would bounce around her face. I still remember very clearly the day that she came home from nursery school and realized that *Wheels on the Bus* was not written especially for her, and the other fourteen kids in her class knew it also. She was furious. Hands went to her hips. Her tiny booted foot kicked at the carpet. It was the first of many times that I disappointed her.

Disappointment seems to be a common theme in my life. As I told MK, I've ruined everything I've ever touched. It's like God blessed me with a voice, talent, fame, and a fuck-ton of luck but at the expense of absolutely everything else in my life—the woman who birthed Jude took her own life making sure I knew it was my fault, and that I'm a bastard who will never make a woman happy. MK's words resonate in my brain: *Give me the whole and complete man I deserve.* Be the man she deserves? I'll never be that. I'll never be anything more than a pretty face that stands on stage and makes people forget about their normal lives.

While you're wishing you were me, I'm wishing to have a family and quiet night on the couch, holding my wife and tickling my kids. Isn't that fucking poetic?

Laying the guitar on the tiny wood-grain table in front of me, I abruptly end our preschool jam session. I grab my bourbon and water, tilt my head back, and pour the contents down my throat. The burn does little to mask the persistent ache right under my tattooed heart.

Billy yells, "We doin' more baby songs, or are we playin' for real?"

"We should be there soon." In my best impression of a flight attendant, I stand and say, "Time to stow your belongings, put your tray tables in their upright position, and fasten your seatbelt."

Billy starts playing the opening notes of *Stairway to Heaven* as we hit turbulence causing my temple to meet the side of the plane. "Shit." I rub my head as I follow my own instructions by grabbing my glass and finding a seat at the front of the private plane, the farthest from where everyone is huddled which isn't too far. This plane isn't large.

Captain Phil comes on the loud speaker. "Sorry, everyone. Couldn't avoid that one. Came out of nowhere. We should be on the ground in twenty. Probably should buckle up."

Frank asks, "Where are we going anyway?"

"Indianapolis," Grace responds in her know-it-all voice.

We're almost a third of the way through our U.S. tour. It's easy to forget what city you're in or going to when we play a different venue every three days. Using my private plane and staying in hotels does make life on the road somewhat easier than when we lived on buses. We used to play every other night, but that killed my voice. Every three days is more manageable, but my vocal chords still get raw.

A sharp pain travels from my elbow and spiders to the tips of my fingers. I open and close my hand, trying to work the stiffness and ache out. This shit started a while ago and seems to happen more often than I care to admit.

Sam plops down next to me and replaces the bourbon in my hand with an amber-colored beer bottle. "Is Viva visiting any time soon?"

My head hangs at the sound of her name. "Why?"

"It's been a while since I've seen her."

She's prying. This is what Sam does. "She's in some country for some fashion week." Not that I care. Viva Valdez hit on me one night when I was in my club in Austin. Didn't have a clue who she was. Apparently, I was one of the only people in the world who doesn't watch the Victoria's Secret fashion show. She's hot as shit and a sweet girl, but we don't have a single thing in common.

"So I take it that's a no?" Sam's eyebrow cocks.

I growl, "She's busy doing her own thing."

"I'm tired of you being grouchy. I think we all are. Groupie time?" She takes a drink from her glass as she places her hand on my knee.

"Not in the mood to fuck." Picking up her palm, I gently rest it back in her lap.

She doesn't take no for an answer and rakes her long nails across my crotch. "I've known you since we were kids. You're always in the mood to fuck." Her laughter sounds like a cackling hyena.

Sam's right. I used to have sex to kill boredom, for cardio, because it was ten o'clock on a Tuesday, or I ran out of underwear. My brunette girl changed all of that. I got a taste of what it's like to make love and since then, the idea of random fucks seems boring, pointless, and believe it or not, a bit gross.

Trying to be cute to deflect this line of questioning, I reply, "Saving myself for the right girl."

"Ha!" Sam thankfully removes her hand. "Surely the right girl isn't the twenty-two-year-old underwear model. You know, you're old enough to be her father."

My relationship with Viva is not up for discussion with Sam. "Not doing this."

This time she's more aggressive. She reaches down and gives my dick a squeeze. It doesn't even twitch. "You know where I am if you need to play. I love when we entertain a fan."

Picking up her hand again, this time, I drop it with disgust. "Not in that place right now." I don't add that I feel like an old man.

Before rehab and meeting MK, Sam and I would get a wild hair every once in a while, and make a female groupie's day and night. That seems like another lifetime ago.

Unfastening my seatbelt, I stand up tossing the now empty bottle in the garbage and fix myself another bourbon before landing. My excuse is that I hate flying and especially hate landings. I refuse to acknowledge the real reason. When I'm buzzed, it's the only time that I don't feel like death.

***

"How bad is it?" I ask as I struggle to read Doctor Hebert's solemn face. His bushy mustache camouflages a lot of his expressions.

"Tell me again what happened." He sits on the upholstered chair in my hotel suite.

I lean back against the couch cushion and prop my feet on the marble coffee table. I do my best not to let the white and grey veined stone remind me of a certain someone and the coffee table that left her gorgeous face scarred, or that Doctor Hebert did the surgery to stitch her up. "We got in early in the morning. I'd been feeling stiff and achy from after the show so I was anxious to get here and go to sleep. I'd been out for like two, two and a half hours, and I woke unable to move my hand."

"The joints were frozen?"

I nod. "It felt like my fingers were paralyzed except it aches like I put my fist through a wall."

His head tilts. "Have you?"

I chuckle. "Fair question. Not this time."

"And your throat?"

"As if I've been swallowing swords like those guys do at the freak shows."

He leans forward, resting his forearms on his thighs. "I think it's time you see a specialist. I'm a plastic surgeon. If you want to look ten years younger, I'm your guy."

"But, Doctor Hebert, you're the only one I trust. You took care of my vocal cords when they were paralyzed. You're the reason I still have a career." I sound like a whiney bastard.

He sighs. "I was a medical student working in the emergency room of a charity hospital. I got lucky." He stands. "You got lucky."

I stand also as I drag my hand through my hair. "What do you think this is?"

"Overuse. You've abused your vocal cords most of your life. They look at bit inflamed to me, but I think you'll be fine. As for your hand, my guess is it's some sort of arthritis. I'll find a good doctor."

"I'll pay you double." I'm desperate. I don't want to start over with a new physician. Besides Jude's pediatrician, who she still sees because he's the only guy I trust with my daughter, Doctor Hebert is only doctor I'll let near my loved ones.

He laughs. "I don't want your money. Come on. Let's go grab lunch, and then I need your fancy plane to fly me back to New Orleans. I've got a practice to run."

"But what are we going to do about my hand?" At just the mention of it, I flex my fingers, hoping to work the stiffness out.

"I'm going to call a doctor friend of mine here in Indianapolis and have him come examine you."

I flop down on the couch while Doctor Hebert walks to the wall of windows and makes his phone calls. The theme music from *Wolverine* plays in my head, loudly and in stereo. That's what my hand feels like. Knives have been shoved into my joints like Hugh Jackman's character. As I stare at my right hand, I feel nothing but fear. My guitar is my life, my sanity, and sometimes the only thing that reminds me that I must keep moving forward. My goal is to die with it in my hands.

"He'll be here in an hour." Doctor Hebert stares at me with pity in his eyes. "I told him what's going on. He's going to give you a shot that will get you through the show. In the meantime, I'm going to find the best doctor in the world for you." He pauses for a beat. "Hey, Johnny?"

I look up from trying to use my non-existent x-ray vision to see through my skin.

"I promise you I'll take care of it."

Nodding, I walk over to the desk. Picking up the leather binder, I toss it in his direction. "Here's the room service menu. Knock yourself out."

Thirty minutes later, Doctor Hebert lets the guy in with our food on a push cart. He sets up the dining room table like this is a date: white linen napkins, roses in tiny vases, and silverware that could actually be silver it's so shiny. I'd normally think this was funny and give the doc a good ribbing for ordering the most expensive thing on the menu, but I'm too worried and miserable to have a sense of humor.

My cheeseburger smells damn good though. I pick up a French fry and confirm that this hotel knows how to prepare one of my favorite diet staples.

The silence is heavy. I don't have much to say and focus on eating my lunch.

Doctor Hebert spends a good five minutes preparing his plate so he can eat. Drives me fucking nuts. Therefore, I usually refuse to dine with him. If Jude was this particular about her food touching, I'd have strangled her many years ago.

"I saw the girl recently." He finally cuts into his filet and takes a bite.

"Jude?" I ask around a bite of burger. I don't bother using my hand to shield him from the view of my chewed-up food.

"No. The girl whose face I stitched up."

Fortunately, I'd swallowed, or the food would have fallen out of my mouth. Instead, at the mention of her, the burger slips out of my good hand and hits the china without a sound.

"Her cut healed beautifully. Just a small line that runs along her cheek bone. She bought some makeup I sell to cover scars."

The ache in my hand becomes damn near unbearable. I walk to the bar to fix myself a drink. I don't offer the good doctor one.

"She's really a lovely girl. Sad that she doesn't need a follow-up appointment." He cuts another bloody, rare bite. The sound of the knife scraping against the plate makes me crazy. "Her name on my schedule brightened my day. I think she's single. Might bump into her at one of her grandmother's charity events."

My back stays towards him. I have the overwhelming urge to wrap my hands around his scrawny chicken neck and squeeze.

"God, her name just slipped my mind, but I know she's a Landry. Her sister's practice is in my building. Maybe I'll bump . . ."

"MK. Her name is MK." Turning around, I walk to where my deserted burger lies. I lean over, placing both my hands on the wooden table. "Stay the fuck away from her. She'd never be interested in you, old man."

He smiles, and that big bushy mustache hides his top lip, but his bottom lip parts enough that I can see his teeth. "You're done with her. I saw the picture of you and the young model holding hands while I was standing in line at the grocery store."

That's bullshit. Doctor Hebert has never done his own food shopping, but I don't call him on it. Sitting, I drag a French fry through the cup of ketchup. "MK isn't what she seems."

"What she seems is a beautiful, gracious, kind, young lady who was in love with you. I don't know what happened, but during her follow-up appointments she was sad, pretending to be cheery, but failing miserably. If a girl like MK was in love with me, I'd never let her be upset again."

Fucking Doctor Hebert. I take another sip of my drink. MK Landry. There's a name that I tried to drink out of my mind yet she keeps rearing her beautiful brown head.

Chapter Four

MK
August

I've been relatively quiet over the past month. There's actually a very good reason this time, and it has nothing to do with an injury. Pop the champagne! Your girl has officially signed a development deal with a major cable network.

Guys, I don't even know where to begin. I was approached months ago by two producers who thought my blog would make great television material. At the time, I wasn't mentally ready to embrace such a crazy endeavor.

After lots of prayers, meditation, and good old-fashioned gut checks, I gave them a call. Thankfully, they were still interested, and the rest will, hopefully, be history.

I'm not moving to LA or New York. Because New Orleans is such a prominent feature in No Pink Caddy, it will be filmed here in my beloved city. For that, I am so grateful. My attorney had warned me that they might want to recreate my carriage house kitchen on a sound stage in some warehouse. Even as I type this, I'm making a gagging noise.

I held firm. It felt unauthentic. After lots of negotiations, the network agrees that No Pink Caddy will be more successful if it's filmed in New Orleans.

Location is still to be determined. Although, you know me. I've got plenty of ideas. I can't wait to share with you when the lease is signed. Hint . . . Hint . . .

Here's the sappy part . . . thank you! I know that following my site over the past few months has not been easy. When I go back and read the things I've posted, I pity me. I went through a dark patch after a difficult break-up and was forced into a spotlight I wasn't ready for. However, I finally feel like I can see the light at the end of the tunnel. Good things are happening again. My mood has switched to one of hopefulness.

I love you guys!

Muah,

MK

Since the initial lunch with Janet and Cindy a month ago, my life has been a blur of activity. I have a lawyer named Aiden Montgomery. He was a sports agent and is now an entertainment attorney. He was highly recommended, and so far, we don't want to kill each other even when I remember just one more thing after an hour-long conversation and text him in the middle of the night.

My manager is another story. Shannon Saks, which I'm sure isn't her real name, couldn't be any more different than me if she tried. She looked camera-ready even when I dragged her to Eddy's Bar. She has schedules and timelines and argues about everything. I don't wear enough makeup. My clothes make me look like a middle-age housewife. My Cajun accent is too thick, and no one will understand me. Bella thinks I should fire her, but Shannon's awesome when it comes to ensuring I'm happy with the decisions that are being made. There's also a tiny part of me that views her as a challenge. One day, she will wear yoga pants and a baseball cap and go out in public without her makeup on. I just know it.

"I adore this space," Cindy says. While Janet was working out the details with the cable executives back in Los Angeles, Cindy was tasked with finding a suitable location to film. I suggested a retail store on Magazine Street, a bit self-serving, but she loved the idea. She had heard of Magazine Street, but was convinced once I gave her a tour. Late ninetieth century homes are built next to retail stores from the same period. An upscale antique store catering to the wealthy of the south might be next door to an incense shop or make-your-own pottery place. It's eclectic and, in my opinion, reflects exactly why I adore my city so much.

We'd made them an offer they couldn't refuse, and just being inside these four walls gets me a bit choked up. I swallow the extra saliva. "When I worked for my ex-boyfriend's father's company, I'd walk by this location every day on my way to work and dreamt that one day this would be where I opened my retail store. It's been vacant for a really long time."

Cindy, Shannon, and I are standing inside of the old record store where I purchased my first Madonna CD when I was nine. The store faded to black when everyone switched to digital music some time ago. Many businesses have tried and failed in this location since then. My theory is that they didn't embrace the energy of the building. It's cool and chill.

Of course, I made up a backstory. Back in the 60s, this is where local musicians would bring their demos to play. People would crowd around the record player and listen to the sweet sounds of jazz. That's how the owner decided if he would buy albums from the un-signed musicians. Artists were single-handedly turned into stars or forced to keep their day jobs based on the crowd's reaction. Dreams were made or broken inside these four walls just like mine will be.

I walk towards the back of the building. "This's where I see putting in the kitchen. I think the white marble will contrast beautifully with the raw brick walls."

Cindy nods. "We'll need an idea of cost to make sure it jives with the budget, but I think it's a good idea." She walks back towards the windows. "The opening of a retail store is a great idea. It shows your creativity and will allow fans a chance to interact with you. It's going to be great."

"I agree." I'm so excited I might just wiggle out of my skin. Excitement is a foreign emotion, but it's one that I'm becoming reacquainted with. "I'd also like to hire some local artists to paint a mural on this wall." My heart warms.

"I want to make sure that the store feels like New Orleans. I'd also like to pay homage to one of the former tenants, which was a music store. Once it's open, I'd like to invite local musicians to play here on the weekends. Who wouldn't want to listen to live jazz while they shop?"

Shannon turns up her surgically altered nose. "Logistically, it's a nightmare. They would be on-camera so they'd have to sign releases, and it's not like we're going to pay them. If someone sings something inappropriate, it will ruin the scene."

"Buzzkill!" I laugh. She's so negative.

Cindy shrugs. "I think we can work all of that out, MK. But, let's do first things first. Let's hear what the contractor says, get a quote, and go from there." She checks her watch. "He should be here in a little over an hour."

Sunlight streams through the dingy windows creating the most beautiful pattern on the worn grey and mint green checked linoleum floor. If I squint, it looks like the amoebas we found in swamp water which we examined under a microscope in seventh-grade science class. Or maybe it's a paisley pattern that I've caught God doodling.

"What do you think about painting these floors instead of replacing them?" The landlord said that he'd give us a renovation budget to update. After seeing the paisley pattern, I think I'd rather keep the old and just give it new life.

Shannon shakes her head. "MK, this floor is garbage and probably asbestos filled. We could be developing lung cancer just by standing here." She makes her way to the door. "On that note, I'll be outside."

Poor Shannon. She's admitted a couple of times that she doesn't have a creative bone in her body, or at least, not the same creative bones that I have. "If you think it will be beautiful, I'm sure it will." Cindy winks. "I'm starving. Let's get some lunch."

Before I reply, she turns and joins Shannon outside.

I'm reluctant to leave my store. Technically, it's not mine, and I shouldn't get my hopes up that I get to keep it. It's leased to the production company, not me. However, there is a clause in the contract that after the show is finished filming, I can take over the lease. God, I love this space. It feels like home and where I want to spend every second of the rest of my life. My mind is already decorating it. But not wanting to seem difficult, I join them outside.

It's hotter than hell today, and the humidity must be at least at rainforest levels. I grab my long hair and grasp it in my hands, twisting it into a knot. My neck instantly feels marginally cooler. Digging in my bag, I locate two pencils and stick them through the make-shift bun.

"Shannon, don't you want to put your hair up?" Her long black hair lays board-straight against her shoulder blades. Once again, I dig back in my bag to find her a rubber band.

"No need. The heat doesn't bother me."

Maybe she's a reptile. That would be the only explanation for her not being hot and explain a lot of the facets of her personality.

Cindy, whose hair is a short, blonde, pixie cut, begins walking up Magazine. Shannon and I join her. We cross the street and stand in front of La Petite Grocery. I haven't been back since my disastrous first date with Aaron. Keeping my head down, I focus on not tripping over the uneven sidewalk.

"What about this place?" Shannon asks.

The thought of entering makes me queasy. I don't know why. Since I've been so busy focusing on the show, I've really not thought about him. Or checked the Google news alerts. Or peeked at how his album was selling on iTunes. Or replied to any of the messages or comments about the album being about me. I haven't even checked to see how he's responded when he's been asked about the album's muse. I've had my first Aaron-free month.

"Heard the food is bad."

Cindy's incredulous. "Janet and I ate here last week; it was great. MK, you should try it." She gives me a squeeze around my waist. "They're your new neighbors, right?"

My heeled sandals are attempting to imbed themselves into the concrete.

Cindy opens the door, and I manage to persuade my legs to follow Shannon in. The restaurant looks different in the daylight. It's cheerier. Memories of that night, which seems so long ago, flash in my brain. A chill overcomes me as I remember the drafty table by the windows. Aaron's searing-hot touch. A bottle of wine, and a meal that I didn't eat. Aaron's words that shook me to my core.

Following blindly, I take a seat on a bench in the front room. Shannon sits next to me and across from Cindy. They chat non-stop about anti-aging procedures, makeup, some jewelry designer I've never heard of, and other meaningless things.

I think I act normal. I think I interject in the conversation and don't reveal that I'm a mental case. I know I order and consume food, but I'm not sure what it is. My lungs don't seem to be able to inhale enough oxygen or expel carbon dioxide. Being confined in these four walls brings back a storm of emotions and feelings that I thought I had either packed away or gotten over. I didn't realize, until right this moment, just how much I miss him and how angry I still am that he cut me out of his life.

Checking my phone, I note that I've survived for a good forty-five minutes. That's long enough, right? I need to remove myself from this space.

"I'm going back to the store," I announce as I throw my napkin on the table.

Not waiting for them to respond, I rush out the front doors, now basking in the heat and humidity of a New Orleans August, instead of running for AC like the rest of the Cajuns. Leaning against the restaurant's brick wall, I find a spot of shade and sink to my bottom, finally feeling like I can breathe again. My hands lock behind my neck, and I stare at the concrete, so mad at myself for behaving this way. I repeat the words I've said at least a million times. *It was only two measly weeks. He's just another guy showing you what you want and don't want in a partner.*

Apparently, my fingers didn't get that message because without thinking, I take my phone from my bag and fire off another text to Aaron. I know it will go unread just like all the ones before. I'm sure he has my number blocked so they're hidden from view. I haven't messaged him since right before I made the break-up post live.

> Me: *It's been nine months since I've seen you. If I'd known it would have been the last time, I'd have asked for my necklace back. I know that sounds petty, and right now that's how I feel.*

I'm so angry at you. How dare you let me fall in love with you? I thought you wanted me like I wanted you. I thought what we had was real. I thought it was going to be tough, but we'd find a way to make it work.

Now, I think I've moved on. Good stuff is happening to me. Yet, I can't visit a place that we've been together without feeling like I want to die. I hope the girl you're pictured with makes you happy. If so, mail me my ducking necklace back.

I send it before double-checking. Stupid spell check changed fucking to ducking. Whatever. It's probably one of the most inarticulate things I've written, but it's honest. It's raw. I am mad at him. I'm mad that he still has such a strong pull over my emotions. They say you can only hate someone you love. God, I know I am walking that razor-sharp edge.

Feeling marginally better, I stand, brushing off any dirt from my behind. This is one of the few times in my life that I wish I smoked. It would be nice to have an excuse for hanging out in front of a restaurant when it's like ninety-eight degrees outside while I wait for my party to finish their meal.

Shannon doesn't keep me waiting. Her perfect shade of black hair is now affixed high on her head in an equally-perfect ponytail. There's not a bump or strand out of place. I should have known that she couldn't just put her hair up without a brush and mirror.

"What was that that just happened in there? Are you on something?" If her forehead wasn't so frozen, I'm sure a *V* would be between her eyes.

"Nope. I'm fine. It was just so stuffy that I had trouble breathing. Needed some fresh air."

Her hand rests on her paper-thin hip. "What does that even mean? MK, this air is so thick out here that it's like breathing underwater. I feel like a fucking fish." She walks right into my personal space and whispers in my ear, "Get it together, sister, or Cindy and Janet will walk. Do you really think that they're going to invest in you if they believe you're a nut job?"

As she steps back, I sigh. "Okay. I'm sorry. I'll do a better job. I promise."

Swallowing my pride, I feel like the bad puppy who just peed the rug.

Cindy joins us with furrowed brows. "You okay?"

"She's a bit under the weather. Maybe we should send MK home, and we'll talk to the contractor," Shannon answers for me.

I'll be damned if I let anyone else make choices and decisions about my dream. "I think I'll be fine. I apologize, ladies. Just so distracted by the show and opening a store." The saying *fake it until you make it* plays in my head. "It's like that hour on Christmas morning when you're awake, and you want your parents to wake up so you can see what's under the tree. That's how I feel about meeting with the contractor."

Cindy laughs and laces her arm through mine. "It's all part of your charm, MK."

Thank goodness. I think she bought it. Right then I vow that I will never, ever let Aaron Emerson come between me and my dreams. How I'm going to accomplish that, I have no idea, but I just am—damn it.

Straightening my shoulders, I wait for Cindy to unlock the antique door and stroll into the empty shell that will house No Pink Caddy. I tell myself that this is no different than when the paparazzi were staked outside. I survived that, and I will dominate this.

Shannon and Cindy pull out their phones and start banging away while I reach into my bag and extract a sketch pad and colored pencils. Sliding down the plaster wall, I draw what I see in my head. The vision needs to be clear so the contractor and I can work together to make this perfect—or at least my version of perfection.

Turning the red pencil to its side, I shade the wall across from me the raw brick color. Spitting on my finger, I smear the red to give it more affect. Next, I add a comfy seating area near the front of the store by a large bay window. I sketch a couch and two winged-back chairs, coloring them in different shades of red, orange and teal. It feels off so I insert a cobalt blue rug to anchor the space. On the other wall, I draw wood and metal shelving to display items for sale. The store should feel like someone is shopping in my home. I don't want ten of the same pitcher sitting on a shelf. I want one pitcher. When it's purchased, a new one will take its place. That reminds me to add a partitioned off area at the back of the space where I can store inventory and dressing rooms where shoppers can try on my vintage inspired clothing.

My dream is for girls who hate to shop to love to come to my place. They can have a cup of coffee and a cookie, and then maybe choose something to treasure from my shelves.

I'm so lost in this fantastic world that I don't register the commotion until I feel two eyes staring down at me. My mouth hangs open as I attempt to process that my favorite reality show contractor, Vince Asher, is standing right in front of me with an amused smile twinkling in his yellow and hazel eyes.

"H-h-h-i," I stammer.

He offers me his hand. Fortunately, I remember to slide my pad off my lap before I grasp it as he pulls me to my feet.

"Hi yourself. I'm Vince Asher." His face is warm and kind, and my heart does a funny little pitter-patter in my chest.

"I know." I sound like I've sucked a helium balloon. "Sorry. Yes. It's a pleasure to meet you." Then, I realize that a camera is trained on us. "Are we being filmed?"

He laughs. "All the time, sweetheart."

The funny pitter-patter turns into an ache at being called the pet name Aaron had for me. Fortunately, I realize it, and I think I keep the emotion from reaching my eyes.

"The network thought it would be a great way to cross-promote our shows. I'm going to be the contractor for your renovation."

The most amazing words that I can find to articulate are, "Sure. That would be awesome."

The cameraman hands his piece of equipment to a guy who I assume is his assistant. That's when Vince gives me, MK Landry, a hug. I could literally turn into a puddle right here on the lovely linoleum tile I was just sketching.

"I'm excited to finally meet you," the beautiful and very capable man says. "I've checked out your YouTube channel. Nice dishes you fix."

"I . . . I . . . watch you all the time." It's like once I get the sentence out, I can't shut up. "Your renovation of the old shoe factory into a multi-use building was inspiring. I've watched it like a hundred times. Especially when

I can't sleep." My hands slap over my mouth in horror. "Not that you're boring or anything. That came out all wrong."

He laughs. "I know what you meant. When all of this is done, you goin' to make me some of your famous fried oysters?"

I nod. "You betcha."

Really, MK? Let's pull it together so you aren't such a constant disaster.

Cindy joins us and kisses Vince on the cheek. "Surprise, MK."

Nodding, my face flushes to atomic levels. "Best surprise ever."

Cindy turns to Vince and grasps his arm as they talk business. They must go on and on about how good it is to see each other. I stand there awkwardly, aware that I'm not being included, but I don't know where to go or what to do.

My eyes cut to Shannon who is visiting with someone that she's obviously friendly with. Finally, I step away and pull my phone out of my bag, as if it's vitally important that I check my Twitter account right at this very moment.

No message back from Aaron, but I didn't expect one. I send a Tweet.

MK Landry @NoPinkCaddy
In a soon-to-be announced location with the famous
@VinceAsher. He's as pretty in person. #PinchMeImDreaming

Dropping my phone back in my bag, I pick up my sketches and pretend to study them while I check out Vince. He has made-for-TV good looks. He's broad and maybe three inches taller than me. His skin is the color of chicory coffee au lait, and his eyes look like they belong to a cat—a dangerous cat, like a tiger. His voice booms, echoing off the raw brick and plaster walls when he proclaims, "This space is amazing."

I can't help but feel joyous. Vince Asher thinks my retail space is amazing. This is definitely a Christmas card-worthy moment.

As soon as I see Cindy place her phone to her ear, I walk to where he's standing. "I'm honored to work with you. Would you like to see my sketches?" The cameraman has his equipment trained on me again. Glancing at Cindy, who just slipped her phone into her bag, and then to the film crew, I say, "I didn't know that this part would be filmed."

Vince's face looks less composed when he meets Cindy's eyes.

She replies, "Network execs thought the viewers might enjoy watching the storefront come to life. Kinda a behind-the-scenes glimpse. Like we want them to be cheering for your success because they've watched it come together."

"Oh. Okay." I shrug. That sounds neat. As a viewer, I'd be interested in watching someone restore and then open their first store.

I've made more than one hundred videos, but I've never made one like this. Someone who arrived with Vince suggests that I change clothes, and wouldn't you know it, she has the perfect outfit in her rental car. My tan slacks and white blouse are replaced with skinny jeans, a turquoise off-the-shoulders top, leather booties, and large, gold hoop earrings. She pulls out a small suitcase of makeup and begins working on my face. I hold very still and wait for this part to be over. Then she removes the pencils from my hair and looks at them with a bit of confusion before she places them in my palm.

Feeling the need to justify, I say, "They work great in a pinch."

Her smile is a sympathetic one. My long, dark tresses are fluffed and tossed over my shoulder. Then she pulls out the mother of all hairsprays. I thought Grandmother's friends cornered the market on hair that defies gravity. Nope. It's the Hollywood stylist.

When she hands me a mirror, I recognize me, but I'm like a glammed-up version. I look naturally effortless, but with more shading and highlighting and eye colors than I knew existed. My scar is also just a thin line the color of my skin.

She moves to Vince. He doesn't get much makeup but his bald head is rubbed with some sort of liquid. He must catch me watching because he replies, "It takes the shine off. Camera doesn't like glare."

"Oh."

Shannon fluffs me a bit more before Cindy decides we're ready for instructions. "This is super easy. Vince is going to walk MK through his vision for this space. The viewer will see computer-generated sketches as he speaks. MK, you're to listen. I know you have very specific ideas. Those are great and all, but Vince is our expert."

That sounded a bit like I should smile and look pretty for the camera without having an opinion. Never will that be okay in my book.

My eyes cut to Shannon. She clears her throat. "Before we film, why don't we have Vince and MK discuss her ideas."

Vince replies, "I've studied the blueprints for the space and have a clear idea what's possible within the budget. MK's job is to add the finishes."

Deciding to be amenable, I reply, "It's okay. I'm anxious to hear what Vince thinks. Then we can always modify." My smile is pleasant, and I'm hopeful that this isn't going to be our first stumbling block.

Someone with a black box clips it to the waist-band of my jeans at the small of my back. Then a tiny brunette-colored circle is hidden in my hair by my ear. When the man is finished, he tells me to talk.

"What do you want me to say?" I ask.

He looks over his shoulder. Another guy gives me a thumbs up, and he announces we're ready.

Vince places his hands on my shoulders. "You're going to be fine. Pretend they don't exist."

I nod. My heart does a flip with excitement. This could quite possibly be the coolest thing that's ever happened to me.

Vince's tone is confident but friendly when the camera begins to roll. "MK, I've had a chance to review the plans for this charming old space. I know you've requested a kitchen." He turns and points to the area where I thought a kitchen should go. "Maybe a large island right there." His finger draws a rectangle in the air. "Sink there. I'm thinking farmhouse style. Stove, double ovens, and dishwasher along that wall. You, of course, will use your decorating talents to choose the finishes."

I'm beaming like a kid who was just told they get an unlimited shopping spree in a toy store. "Perfect." I walk over to the brick wall where I thought my shelves for merchandise should go. "I would like a mix of bookshelves and anchored shelving for this wall."

He joins me and throws out ideas. We bat them back and forth like collaborative coworkers. I've taken his advice and forgotten that the camera is rolling and soon realize that standing still and preparing food in a kitchen or working on a piece of furniture is not the same as having to move when I turn and bump into the guy holding the camera.

"I'm so sorry." I grimace.

Cindy interjects, "We'll work on blocking, Eugene. She's never done this before."

He rolls his eyes, picks the camera up, and points it at us.

Carefully, I lead Vince to the area where I want my living room set up, then the clothing rack section, and finally the fitting rooms. Everything is possible, and it's going to be fabulous. I don't run into grumpy Eugene again.

Cindy claps her hands and turns to an older lady standing near her. "We'll need to see final numbers. Get a list of finishes from MK, and Vince's people will draw up a quote."

The lady nods and is on her phone so fast that I don't get a chance to introduce myself.

I just filmed a segment with *the* Vince Asher. I'm trying to play it cool, but I so want to text Bella and send out another Tweet. My fans will never believe this.

"Can I get a picture with you?" I'm acting like Aaron's fangirl from the restaurant, but I just can't let this moment pass.

Vince's white teeth sparkle when he agrees.

We walk outside and stand in front of my new store. Vince wraps his arm around my shoulders and tucks me against his side. I might dissolve like sugar in hot water.

Shannon takes out her phone and snaps multiple pictures from different angles.

When she's done, Vince whispers in my ear, "Can't wait to see you again. Maybe you can fry me up some of your oysters in nothin' but an apron."

Oh my God! Vince Asher just hit on me. Yup. This must be a dream.

Before I can respond with *of course, I'll make you fried oysters, you beautiful, handsome, man that knows how to use a nail gun,* he releases me and announces, "All right everyone. It's been a pleasure. We have another commitment." And just like that, he takes everyone with him but Cindy and Shannon.

As their van and three cars pull away from the curb, Cindy laughs. "God, that man is fine."

Shannon and I nod like bobble-head dolls. Understatement of the year is Vince Asher is fine, and he hit on me.

Chapter Five

Aaron
August

MK Landry @NoPinkCaddy
First meeting with my merchandise team. I'm looking for ideas. #NoPinkCaddySWAG

Lauren Long @LongLashes
@RealJohnnyKnite I'm the girl in the lacy pink bra. Tweet me for the night of your life. #BucketList

Oh fuck.

Her song is next.

My stomach feels like a shot glass shattered in it. I haven't been able to get her out of my head since Doctor Hebert brought her up.

I should have killed this album and never released it.

It's my best-selling in years.

I shouldn't have agreed to go on tour performing her songs but especially this fucking one every. Third. Night.

The tour is sold out.

Rock drums like a mad man as I hit my final note. My throat is on fire, but fortunately, my voice is strong. The crowd moves as one large organism. It's screaming and chanting, wanting more. The music continues for three minutes. This is supposed to give me a chance to have a glass of water or bourbon or whatever the poison is tonight.

The sweat pouring down my face and back turns cold, and an involuntary shiver overcomes me. My left hand taps the beat on my thigh as I appear to be feeling the music. Inside, bile creeps up my throat, and I think for a second I might be sick. Light blinds my eyes and disorientation overcomes me. I stumble, but recover.

Two minutes and then her song.

Fuck.

Turning around, I give the band the hand signal. The one that says keep playing because I need another minute or five, and then I bolt from the stage.

Grace stands behind a large speaker with her hand on her hip. "What's wrong with you?" she yells over the music.

Ripping my guitar from my shoulder, I shove it at Jose, my guitar tech. I push past her and towards the bottle of whiskey waiting for me. I embrace the burn as it hits the back of my throat.

My hand closes to a fist and then I open it again, over and over, trying to work the joints. The shot the doctor in Indianapolis gave me did wonders, but my fingers still throb during a show, and I've missed a couple of notes. It's like I can't compel my middle finger to hit the string correctly. It pisses me off. I'm a goddamn professional and shouldn't make those kinds of silly novice mistakes.

"Are you crazy? Get out there and play," she demands from behind me.

I get it. She's doing the job I pay her to do, which is to ensure my record company is run in my best interest and my shows are fucking pristine. However, she can go fuck herself right now. She has no idea what's going on inside my mind or body.

"I can't sing the next song any longer." My voice is clear and concise. There's no grey area.

"It's the number-one hit on the new album. Of course, you're going to keep playing it." She has the bitch tone that's supposed to make me not want to argue with her.

It doesn't work. I take another long swig. "This is my last time."

The whiskey numbs the pain deep in my gut or maybe my heart. Exhaling, I feel like a dragon breathing fire.

My sister places her hand on my shoulder. "We'll talk about it after the show." Her voice is softer, as if there's a heart hidden deep inside the dark hollows of her body.

Spinning around on the heels of my black leather motorcycle boots, I glare down at her. "Don't forget who you work for, little sister."

God, I'm a dick, and when I don't feel well, I'm like dick personified. Her face becomes blank. She looks like I punched her. I did, in a way. Words hurt much more than a fist. That's one lesson I learned from Miss Mary Kay Landry.

"Noted." She disappears into the blackness.

One more long pull from my good buddy, Jack Daniels, and then I reach my hand out, wiggling my fingers as if I'm the king beckoning a servant. *God, I'm an asshole.* Jose hands me back my guitar. As I take the stage again, walking back to the mic, I tell myself that this is the last time that I ever have to sing these lines. Just once more . . .

"Sorry about that brief break, guys. Needed a drink." I cock my brow, and the crowd goes crazy. "So this is a song off our new album. And I've been told that it's one of the best songs I've written in a while. Don't know about all of that, but here you are, and for the final time in concert."

My fingers glide over the strings with minimal pain as I play the opening notes of *Pink Cadillac.* Memories of the night I wrote this song swamp my brain. We'd just made love for the first time. Her in front of me, beautifully naked, with a Caribbean blue dress puddled at her feet. How she fought for us. Her bravery to open herself up to me after I tried to push her away. My hands grasping her firm breasts and tight ass. Watching the rain pressed against her back. Her. Everything about her. Her smell. The bangs that cover her eyes. Her innocence and ferociousness. I wrote this song, giving her the pink Cadillac that had alluded her for so long. But it's really about me giving her the only thing I've never given another woman—my heart.

My voice cracks as a sharp pain shoots down my throat. Cold sweat soaks my white T-shirt. The world goes black with just a pinpoint of blinding light.

My head swims. It's like the worst kind of high. I can't sleep it off. I'm standing on a stage in front of twenty thousand fans.

Gripping the mic stand, I try to pull myself together. Fuck. What's wrong with me? I attempt to push MK into the vault where she was nicely locked away until Doctor Hebert's visit. During Malcom's guitar solo, I do my damnedest to focus on the crowd and use their energy to get me through the last verse. Their hands are thrown in the air, and they sing my words back to me. This crowd is on fire. *What city is this again?*

Just one more time. Then never again.

I start the stanza strong. My voice is damn near perfect. *Maybe I can do this.* I'm on autopilot. I focus on doing what I do best, and that's giving my fans a fan-fucking-tastic show. Then I sing the line that kills me. "I knew she couldn't be anything but mine."

My middle finger cramps as I try strumming the string. It's not possible for me to continue as my vocal cords seize. I do the trick where I hold the mic towards the crowd and act like I want them to sing my words back to me. My heart's beating so fast and hard that I swear someone slipped me speed. It's just got to end, and soon. Fortunately, the next song is heavier and has nothing to do with MK.

Fifteen more seconds . . .

Ten . . .

Five . . .

Fucking over.

As the final note sounds, my vocal cords relax, and I'm able to swallow and even breathe again. My finger relaxes and can fly over the strings with ease.

The rest of the show goes as it should. We finish the last encore and leave the crowd screaming for more. This feeling is better than any artificial high. Back in the beginning, when we were playing small clubs and venues, we didn't have contracts that assessed fines if we went over a certain time. We'd play sometimes until the manager would turn on the lights and kick us out.

Those were the days. It was just me and the band and us sneaking underage Grace into the clubs with us, telling the owner she was our manager. Then she actually started doing the job. Jude came along. Mom would watch her when we played. I'd get woken up in the morning to Jude's sweet face and special daddy kisses. That was when we were clawing our way to the top of the music food chain. That was when life was simpler.

Rock slaps me on the back as we head to the backstage gathering room to meet fans. "Great show, but what the fuck happened in the middle? We aren't playing *Pink Cadillac* anymore—the fuck?"

Shrugging it off, I chuckle. "Tired of that song, and I just needed a drink, like I said."

He pushes me against the cement brick wall and throws his solid arm over my chest as people continue to stream past us. He's taken me completely by surprise. His cold, dark eyes see through my lie. "Bullshit. You don't have to tell me, but don't fuckin' lie to me. We've been brothers way too long."

Holding up my hands, I meet his squint. "Noted. Fine. Then I don't want to talk about it."

He lets me go, reminding me of a Mastiff puppy. The guy is huge but has no clue what to do with his size. About ten years ago, he traded his cocaine habit for the gym. It's worked for him. "Cara and I are here if you need to talk."

I nod. We continue to walk in silence before I ask, "How did you know that Cara was the one?"

The two have been together for what seems like forever. She's a freelance tattoo artist who's done most of my ink. They seem like they were made for each other. She tours with us in between trips back to Austin for work.

He's quiet for a moment before replying, "She cared enough to call me on my bullshit."

MK called me on my bullshit.

He continues, "Look, man. I can't give love advice or any of that shit, but what I can tell you is that Viva is not the person you're supposed to be with. She's too young, but she's a smokin' hot distraction until you find the right girl." He punctuates his statement with a laugh.

I don't reply. Viva is a very sweet girl and hot is a good way to describe her, but I don't miss her when she's not around. I don't check my phone hoping she's called or texted. And I certainly never count down the days to seeing her again. I don't track her on *Find My Friends* or worry about her when she's not around.

The noise from the gathering room greets me when I'm still far enough away to know that tonight, everyone is in the mood to party. Not feeling it at all, I walk past the entrance and to my dressing room. Pushing the door open, I close and lock it behind me so I don't get any unwanted visitors. I flop down on the couch and hold my head in my hands as I stare at the ceiling.

"What the fuck is wrong with me?" I ask the universe. I'd like an answer that covers both my mental and physical fucked-upness. A year ago, I was preparing to enter rehab, not believing that I needed help. It was a deal to keep me from serving jail time. The prosecutor didn't want the publicity of an assault trial against someone famous who did what most dads would do in the same situation—beat the shit out of the guy who tried to rape his daughter. I thought six to eight weeks of vacation sounded sweet. Chose a place on the beach. Had no idea when I stepped off the plane that this small island in the Caribbean would fuck my world. As much of an asshole as I was, they still made me meet with the doctor who ran the program.

Then the doc mind-fucked me. He's the one who pointed out I had never had a healthy relationship. He's who suggested that I open myself up to more than just fucking women. He's the bastard who planted it in my head to try dating and maybe even falling in love.

Here I lie, after a huge show, staring at the ceiling thinking about chocolate brown hair brushing against my thighs as she rides my cock instead of getting a meaningless blowjob from a female willing to donate her mouth for my masturbation needs.

Fucking MK.

Pain travels through my wrist and down the bones in my hand. I flex, hoping to find some position that relieves the throb.

MK.

When I needed her the most, she tossed me out like a piece of trash. No, she melted and then burned me like a marshmallow forgotten in a campfire.

I fell in love with someone who doesn't have a clue how to stand by their partner for better or worse. She's a good-time girl.

My right fist tightens, imbedding my nails in the hard skin on my palm.

Standing, I grab the bottle of Jim Beam from the counter and walk out of my dressing room to join the party. Time to dull the pain.

Chapter Six

MK
August

Happy 31st birthday to me! I appreciate your calls, messages, videos, and tweets, and I even received a Hallmark birthday card in the mail from Grandmother with a $20 bill inside. The tradition continues.

So I have some news. . .

It's official! You're going to be able to visit me whenever you wish. The lease is signed on my store. Y'all, it's simply fantastic. I've admired the space since I was a kid. Truly this is a dream come true, and I keep pinching myself that this is really happening.

More later. I'm off to meet Bella.

Cheers,

MK

The dingy yellowed shade flies up, hitting the top of the window, causing me to yelp. My hand covers my racing heart, and a giggle escapes my lips. Staring through the dirty floor-to-ceiling window, I make a mental note to find someone who can clean the outside of these puppies regularly.

Grasping the bottle of blue liquid, I mist the pane of glass as I pray it will come clean. Nothing is more depressing than not being able to see outside. Wadding up the back-to-school sale circular, I smear the droplets over the pane, put a little elbow grease into it, and step back, admiring my work.

Mercifully, I can see clearly through the window and note a couple holding hands walking by. They're cute. The girl and I make eye contact, and she smiles.

It's Sunday afternoon. Tomorrow, the pre-production team arrives. Shannon says the day will be long so I should get a good night's rest. I don't think that's possible.

"It's getting there," Bella says as she rests her hands on my shoulders.

We've gotten a lot accomplished. The dirty linoleum floors have been bleached and scrubbed. They're marginally shinier than they were before. I still love them and feel committed to giving them new life.

I look into her dark eyes and smile. "Thanks. I'm happy you're here."

"I know." She sprays blue cleaner on the window next to mine and begins wiping it. "I'm so proud of you, MK, and besides, there's really nothing I'd rather be doing on a Sunday than cleaning floors and windows."

She's so cheeky sometimes.

Scrubbing a smudge that looks like peanut butter, I internalize her words. I've been overly emotional—even weepy lately. The enormous endeavor I'm about to begin is finally becoming real. I'm Mary Kay Landry, and I'm about to open my store on Magazine Street and have a lifestyle reality show. My wildest dreams are coming true. No. That's not true. It never occurred to me to dream this big.

"Have you thought about how different my life is this year as opposed to last?" Pausing for a second, I add, "Both of our lives."

She grabs the stepladder and sprays the tops of both of our windows and scrubs. "I'm married. You're going to be a TV star. I mean it happens every year, right?" she teases.

"Maybe next year, at this time, I'll be married."

She adds, "And I'll be a mom."

"Yours is much more plausible." I laugh.

Silence falls over both of us as the sounds of scrubbing glass fill the large space. "You know we've been trying since the wedding."

I can read my best friend like a book. Her muscles are taut with tension.

"It's only been like three months. You're fine." How do I know this? I don't. But I feel the overwhelming need to reassure her.

She steps down and moves the ladder to the third window. "I probably am. Nyall and I are just so anxious to become parents."

"I know you are. It will happen when the time is right. Then, I'll be an aunt, and you'll be a mum, and we'll spoil your baby rotten." Because Nyall is British, Bella is determined that the baby will call her mum instead of mom.

I walk over to the small refrigerator I purchased for the space so the crew will have cold water tomorrow and pull out a bottle of wine. Red Solo cups are stacked on top so I grab two. Opening the bottle, I pour us each a cup.

Bella disposes of our used newspaper and leans the cleaning supplies against the brick wall. Then she walks over to the center of the shop and sits down on the worn, but clean floor. I join her, handing her a glass.

"Have you thought anymore about appearing on camera?" Cindy and Janet suggested that my fans would love to meet Bella on-screen. She's been the snarky voice off camera for so long. They offered to pay her on a per-episode basis. So far, she's been noncommittal.

After taking a chug of wine, she leans back on her palms and says, "Nyall and I've discussed it, and we don't think it's a good idea. I love you, MK, but you're about to become a celebrity. I saw what your life was like after your relationship with Aaron became public. That's not something either of us want."

God, her words hit home, and I trace the star tattoo on the inside of my wrist. It's not the life I want either, but I want my store and something new and different, so this is the price I must pay. Plus, my existence has already been headline making news. Like the saying goes, I can't put the genie back in the bottle.

I guess my silence makes her feel the need to justify her response. "Like, I'm super happy for you. You're going to handle it just fine. You've already had experience. Maybe I'll be your personal assistant."

My face lights up. "I'll pay you as soon as I can and look, Bella, I get it. You don't have to be on screen, but I felt I would be a really crummy friend if I didn't at least offer."

She smiles, crinkling the star scar on her cheek. "Always lookin' out from me, chica. Love you."

"Love you too."

"So as your new PA, the first order of business is firing Shannon. She's awful."

I laugh, and the noise echoes around the empty space. "She's really not so bad. A little uptight, but I think we can break her." I change the subject because Shannon might be difficult, but she's a necessary evil. "I really do appreciate you helping me clean up around here today. I know that part of the show is getting the store ready, but I just couldn't have company show up and not even be able to see outside."

She holds her Solo cup up, and we toast. "Have you talked to Tripp lately?"

"We've texted back and forth about silly stuff, but no. Why? What's going on?" My voice rises with worry.

"He slept with his assistant."

My mouth hangs open. Tripp is not the type who sleeps around. In fact, Tripp is the guy who's like *It's only been three dates, of course we aren't having sex.* Clapping my hands, I say, "Do tell. I need details."

She turns towards me, and we revert to our fourteen-year-old selves. "They've been flirting and stuff for a while."

"Yeah. I know he was texting with her last month when we all met at Eddy's."

"So, he had an evening meeting at his office. She offered to stay. Meeting canceled at the last minute, and they did it in the conference room." Bella's cheeks are glowing. She's as excited as I am.

"That's so dirty," I squeal. "Love it."

"So now she's wanting a relationship, and he's freaking out."

My head turns to the side. "Why?"

Bella's expression changes to a pained one. She hesitates for a moment and looks to the ceiling before replying, "He's not sure he's over you."

My shoulders slump. We're childhood friends who tried dating. I adore him, find Tripp to be very handsome, but there's no attraction. He's a great human being and wonderful friend but he doesn't stir the sort of emotions in me that say, for example, Aaron did. I've made it very clear that we're just friends, and I thought he had quit carrying the torch for me. Apparently, I was wrong.

"Should I talk to him again? I can state for the thousandth time that we will never be anything more than friends." I sound more frustrated than I actually feel because I'm so tired of this being a part of our friendship. I'm not that incredible. The boy needs to move on for goodness sake.

Bella's head moves back and forth. "I think this is something that he's got to work through on his own."

My heart aches and falls into the pit of my stomach. Guilt is such a crummy feeling, and it's one I attempt to avoid at all costs. I know this is Tripp's issue, but it's hard to turn a blind eye or cold shoulder when a friend is in pain and you're the cause.

"Well, while I'm already feeling guilty, I might as well meet the family for church." Standing, I dust off my behind and slam the rest of my glass of wine before tossing the cup in the white garbage bag lying on the floor near the fridge.

"You make mass sound so appealing." Bella laughs as she finishes her Solo cup and disposes of it.

"I don't mean it like that. I get something out of church. If nothing else, it's a ritual I've performed every Sunday for most of my life. I find it's a place I can meditate and concentrate on what lies ahead for the upcoming week. This week is going to be crazier than others." I lock the front door and hug my friend before we part ways.

"Let me know if you need me tomorrow. Your PA is ready to report for duty." She does a silly salute before turning around and walking the opposite direction that I'm headed.

It's so warm today that my lightweight shirt sticks to my body. My short-shorts do little to keep me cool. It's days like today that I wish I had a car. Not because I mind walking, but I hate when it's this hot and this still. It's miserable.

Whistling Willie is nowhere to be found on his street corner and I don't blame him. Playing the bongos takes a tremendous amount of cardio, and it's too dang hot for that. Even the trees seem to be beaten down by the heat. The leaves hang on their stems and the branches sag over the cracked sidewalk.

I let myself in through my locked gate and then into my cottage house. After a quick shower and half-hearted attempt to blow-dry my hair, I throw it up in a messy bun with the thought that God doesn't care what I look like. But my mother does, so I slide a form fitting, yellow, sleeveless dress over my curves and a pair of silver designer sandals on my feet. Normally, I cover my scar with special concealer purchased from the Geraldo-looking plastic surgeon, but it's just too hot outside. Light powder will have to do. It does little to hide the ugly red line, which now looks like I've been scratched by a cat. I've learned to accept it as one learns to accept the bump on their nose or uneven eyebrows. My scar is a new feature of me.

Opening the Uber app, I summon a car, grab my bag, and race out the front door to meet my ride. It's still sweltering even though the sun has begun to set. I carefully make my way down the brick path with the goal of not getting the heel of my sandal stuck in a crevice. I'm so focused on not tripping that as I open the gate, I run into a very strong, male chest.

His hands grasp my biceps to stop me from tumbling backwards. *Why in the world do I own shoes that I can't walk in?*

"You okay?"

I look up into the eyes of Vince Asher. "W-w-what are you doing here?"

"Stopping by to say hi. Don't have your number." He ends his statement with a gorgeous smile.

I couldn't be more shocked. "But you had my address?" Why do I say this? I wish I was like the characters in movies that always have a quick and witty comment.

This time he laughs. "As you said in your post. Everyone in the world knows where you live."

My eyes grow wide. "Well, that's just fantastic. I'm going to wind up on one of those damn walking tours of the city. Everyone is going to point at the house where dumbass MK lives. The girl who was stupid enough to date a rock star." Then it occurs to me that Vince Asher is standing outside my gate, and he might have a good reason, and probably doesn't care to listen to my ramblings. "I'm off to mass."

The Uber pulls up. My eyes dart between the driver and the hot male specimen standing in front of me.

Vince throws up his hands. "My mama would kill me if I kept a good southern girl from going to church. I was hoping I could take you to dinner before we start pre-production tomorrow." His smile could be used to sell toothpaste it's so pretty. "But we can do it another day."

Is he kidding? I turn to the Uber driver. "Sorry, but I don't need you after all."

He nods and drives off.

Then I grab my phone and send a text to the family telling them that something came up. Vince Asher hit on me, and now he's ready to take me to dinner, even if it's to talk shop. He's exactly the kind of man that I need to get back on the dating horse.

"Ready." Am I acting desperate? Probably. Is Vince used to women who are smoother and know how to play a good game? I would guess so. But this is me, and I'm just a mess.

He steps back as his eyes move from the top of my head to the points of my toes. "You look gorgeous."

I shrug. "Thanks." My hands smooth over the linen. "My mother and grandmother insist that wearing jeans in church is an insult to Jesus. I don't know about all of that, but I do know their raised brows and judgy smirks compel me enough to slap on a dress."

Vince makes a fist and brings it to his mouth as if he's trying not to laugh.

"It's okay. My sister and I quote *Steel Magnolias* frequently. If you don't have anything nice to say just go sit by Grandmother and her friends." Pausing for a second, I adjust my bag. "That's not exactly the quote, but you get the idea."

A trickle of sweat rolls down my cheek bone. "Want me to take you to the muffuletta shop, which is next door to Eddy's Bar and the dry cleaners? Sandwiches are good, and I'm hot and could use a cold beer."

Vince makes a sweeping hand gesture. "Lead the way, my dear." Then he takes my hand, and I melt. It has nothing to do with the heat.

Chapter Seven

Aaron
August

Latoya Carren @BeautifulCarren
I'm looking for you @RealJohnnyKnite. Tweet me where you're partying. #KissKissBangBang

Michelle Lou @BlackEyes
@RealJohnnyKnite I'll show you my #PinkCadillac and I don't mean the car.

Rock Star Groupies @RockStarGroupies
@VivaValdez was photographed leaving the Miami airport. @RealJohnnyKnite is in town for a show. #CoupleWatch

Candy McKay @ACERocks
@RealJohnnyKnite don't let us down. We want #PinkCadillac and the other songs from #AlisVolatPropriis

"I hate all these girls propositioning you." She shakes her head in disgust as she scrolls through Twitter. Before I can acknowledge her comment, she asks, "You want sammich?"

I'm so irritable that I feel like I've been electrocuted. Every nerve ending is on high alert. I just want to be left alone with my guitar, notebook, and fucked-up head. "No. I'm good. Order whatever you want." My eyes never leave the corner of the gunmetal coffee table.

"I surprise you, and you don't even give me attention." Her voice is whiny, which further adds to my irritation. My daughter doesn't whine and neither should a grown-ass woman.

Sighing, I quit strumming the guitar strings. "I'm sorry. It's just that you surprised me, and I wasn't prepared for a visitor."

We're in Miami. I was hoping to check out some local talent—always scouting for my label—and meet up with some friends. Viva's surprise visit has put me in a shitty mood, and I can't figure out why. It's like as soon as I opened the suite door and saw her standing there, the ache in my hand hit new, off-the-charts levels. Like even though I haven't so much as taken a Tylenol, I was about to hit up the narcotic pain relievers Billy keeps in his backpack.

As she walks over to where I'm sitting, her peach silk robe falls open revealing her dark olive skin, taut abs, and small, but firm tits. She's stunning. I should be buried deep inside her feeling like a new man. Instead, I feel like I'm ninety-years-old.

She sucks on her forefinger and drags it over each nipple making them stand at attention. "I'm good surprise?"

No. She's a distraction and right now. I just want to be miserable. "You're beautiful. Really, I'm a lucky guy to have you, but I'm not feeling good. Run down from the tour, and I just need to be alone. You know, to like, regroup, and shit."

She crosses her arms as her bottom lip curls down, brushing her chin. "I'm calling my friends then."

Oh! Thank God.

"That would be nice. I'm sure you could use a night out. Have fun . . ." I stop myself. I almost called her sweetheart. That word should never exit my lips again. "Viva," I finish. "I'll give you my credit card."

She stands, fastening her robe so quickly that I don't get the one last look at her boobs that I was hoping for. The door slams as she walks into the bathroom.

Picking up the guitar, my shark tooth necklace MK gave me the night I bought coke slips from the confines of my t-shirt. Tucking it back, I begin to strum the opening notes of *Pink Cadillac.* Playing this song is like thumping a bruise. Yet, I can't seem to stop myself. We haven't played it since my meltdown, and the fans have noticed. I make it a point to stay off social media, but it's Grace's job to keep me abreast of what's going on with my businesses. She's pointed out at least ten times how I'm disappointing the fans. They're posting comments about how good the show is but are mad we aren't playing our number-one song.

Why does it cause my vocal cords to freeze up and for me to have a huge freak-out? Is it MK? I don't think so. Over the years, I've written many songs about people in my life. None of them have affected me like this one has. It's got to be just a coincidence.

Slapping the smooth wood, I fling my guitar across the couch as rage bubbles in my gut. I need a doctor or someone who can fix whatever is fucking wrong with me. I'm Johnny Knite, not some fucking, fucked-up, pussy, soft rock star who can't handle his shit. I purposely live in Austin to avoid the primadonna rock star pricks who live indulgent lifestyles. I'm a hardcore motherfucking rocker who lives his songs. I need to man the fuck up.

Grabbing my phone, I text Doctor Hebert.

Me: *Find me a doc yet?*

Doctor Hebert: *Where are you going next?*

Me: *LA*

Doctor Hebert: *He'll see you there.*

The bathroom door opens, and Viva comes prancing out in very high heels, tight jeans, and a white sheer blouse revealing a black bra.

"Viva, look, I'm sorry," I begin. I am sorry. I'm sorry I'm an asshole to a very sweet girl.

"Don't apologize, Johnny. I don't want to hear your empty words. I'm meeting some girlfriends. Don't wait up, and while I'm gone, figure out what your problem is. I don't have many days off, and I don't want to waste them on a . . ." She gestures at me as if I'm a piece of trash. "On a man that doesn't know how to love me both mentally and physically."

My head falls in my hands as she leaves. Tugging at my hair, I yell, "What the fuck is wrong with me?"

"I don't know. But I deserve better." The door slams behind her.

The word *deserve* causes a bolt of energy to travel down my spine. MK's words are set to a hard driving tempo *Be the man I deserve.* It's so loud in my head that I can hear nothing else.

I grab the half-drunk bottle of scotch in front of me and gulp it down. The more I drink, the clearer it becomes. It's MK Landry's fault. Even though I'm so goddamn angry at her that if she was in front of me, I'd . . . I'd—what would I do?

Staring down at my cock, I'm completely perplexed. It's the first time I haven't had to work to get my dick hard since I stormed out of MK's carriage house. "Really?" I ask it, as if it might respond. "Her mean-as-shit words play in my head, and somehow that causes you to get hard? That's fucked up."

I've got to quit this bullshit. If I don't find Johnny Knite soon, I'm going to lose my mind. That's not a stupid mom saying like *you're making me pull my hair out.* I literally think I'm going to wind up in a straitjacket in a padded room somewhere.

After tugging on my boots, I make my way to Sam's room. I've barely knocked when she opens the door. She looks down the hallway. "Where's Viva?"

"Out with friends. Want to go get shitfaced like old times?"

***

Four hours later we're in the hottest night club on Miami beach. I recognize about a third of the people in our VIP section. Women are dressed in tight Spandex dresses so short that the bottoms of their ass cheeks are showing. Sam's entertaining a young pretty-boy on one side and gorgeous blonde girl on the other while Billy stands about ten feet from her with lusty eyes. I once thought their sex games were fucked up. Now, I've come to realize that it works for them. Besides Rock and Cara, they're the happiest couple I know.

Taking a sip of beer, I lean back against the plush, plum velvet cushion and hope I'm giving off the aloof rock star vibe. My legs are crossed, and my arms are stretched out, making it difficult for anyone to sit next to me. I'm out of the hotel room and in public. This is a huge step since my life got fucked up.

My mind starts calculating dates, and I soon realize that today is the one-year anniversary since I left for my stint in rehab. I take another sip of beer as if to spit in the face of the place that fucked with my normal, calm, simple, easy, life.

A tall, thin blonde straddles my lap shaking me from my thoughts. "Hey, Johnny. Want to go back to your place?"

Before I answer, she leans down and sucks on my neck. My hands grasp her waist, moving her to my left side. "Not interested."

The music is in my head switches from the normal tempo I hear to the theme from *Fatal Attraction.*

Not to be deterred, she leans down and bites my cock through my jeans. I hate to do it, but I motion for my bodyguard, Zed. He's performed this same drill more times than I can count.

I point toward the girl. Zed taps her shoulder. She looks up, and he says, "Ma'am, come with me."

He helps her to her feet and escorts her out of our section.

Grace flops down on the other side of me, away from where the girl was sitting. The radio in my head switches to *Ding-Dong! The Witch is Dead* sung in the Munchkin voice. "See you're staying true to Viva tonight," she yells over the electronic beat.

Oh shit! I completely forgot to invite her. "Somethin' like that."

Should I text her? I left my phone in the hotel. I could probably find a way for us to get in touch, but I don't feel like bothering. This is why I stay in my room. Here I am in a club with great music playing, and yet I'm on a couch all alone wishing my sister would take a hike.

Maybe I need to do coke again. I haven't touched it since the blow up with MK. Maybe a couple lines of it would fix whatever is wrong with me. It always did the trick before.

Standing, I give Grace the brush-off and grab Zed. Twenty minutes later, the two of us are in a town car driving back to the hotel to meet my old hook-up. I've spent this time convincing myself that cocaine is what I need to feel like me again. I won't do a lot. Just enough to get back in the right place mentally. Then I can focus on whatever is wrong with my hand.

Zed makes the exchange and brings it to my room.

Here the empty baggy sits on the metal coffee table with me leaned over it and a rolled twenty-dollar bill resting in my right hand. Staring at the snow white powder, I reflect on this year, since I completed rehab.

Jude went off to college. It was hard leaving my baby in another state, but she seems to be doing well at Vanderbilt. Maybe after the incident and my legal troubles, she needed to get away—a fresh start.

I met MK. She was the best and worst thing that's ever happened to me. I found love and heartache in a short period of time. I also wrote a lot of ACE's new album.

I've reestablished myself again in the music world. Instead of being a songwriter and executive, I've spent this year performing. Touring is shit, but rocking out on stage with my band makes the travel and hotels worth it.

So why do I sit here staring at the coke? It's not like I've ever been reflective before I snorted it up my nostrils. There's a pain deep in my chest that wasn't there before I walked out on MK. It's an old war wound. I've come to appreciate it as a new fixture of me.

MK.

Was I happy before her? I thought I was, but I was really just living. I was a dad to Jude. I was running a very successful label and writing music. Every couple of years, I was touring, but I had taken four years off when Jude was in high school. What MK gave me was someone who made me care about myself. She made me feel alive and scared the shit out of me.

Putting the rolled-up bill to my nose and sniffing the fine white powder somehow feels as if I'm cheating myself. I certainly haven't been a saint since rehab, but MK kicking me out of her place made me realize that someone in this world did give a damn about a guy named Aaron—not just Johnny Knite.

And that's when I conclude that what I want isn't divided into neat, little, white lines. I don't want to get fucked up. Instead, I crave the intense feeling of being cared for, worried about, and loved.

My body seems to wilt at this powerful revelation. The ache deep in my chest kicks me in my ribs. Lying in the fetal position on the hotel suite couch, cold sweat causes tremors to seize my muscles. My heart races so fast that if I could, I'd call an ambulance. Instead, I fight to breathe and pray that whatever this is, it passes soon.

Then is hits me. In rehab, they talked about this superfluous term *rock bottom*. It went in one ear and out the other, but this is what they described. *I've physically reached fucking rock bottom.*

My mind reviews all the times that I thought I had experienced the worst days of my life: Jude's traumatic entrance to this world and her being born drug addicted, the woman who birthed her overdosing while blaming me for ruining her life, the son of a bitch positioned between my screaming daughter's spread thighs, not being able to find out why MK was in the hospital, and no one confirming if she was alive or dead. I realize that I've found the lowest point that I can mentally reach. If I don't take control of my life, it will kill me—the ache in my chest will kill me. I can't orphan Jude. As crappy of a father as I've been, I'm at least her father, and she knows that I love her unconditionally.

Time passes and eventually the tremors stop to the point that I'm able to scrape the powder back into the baggy, and I crawl to the toilet—my legs too weak to carry me. As I pour the one thing that's gotten me through every really shitty period of my life into the water, a bright light moves through me, opening my eyes. Coke also cost me the only good thing I've ever had besides my daughter. Coke took my MK away.

My stomach contracts and heaves as the drinks I had at the club splash into the drug-filled water. It's a purging of sorts. My body rids itself of the demon inside that keeps sabotaging anyone who dares to love me.

I want MK back.

No. That's not correct. It's not a want, it's a need. I'm ready to be loved and wanted. I need someone to cherish me. I crave someone in my life who is there because they have intense feelings for me, and I'm not just a paycheck.

Standing, I flush the toilet and rinse my mouth. I feel better than I have in years. But if I'm going to do this, I'm going to do it right.

I call the concierge and request a room for Viva. Gathering up her stuff, I have Zed move it to her new room. Before we leave, I scratch out a note on the hotel stationery and leave it on her pillow.

Viva, it's been great, but I'm not the guy for you. Sorry. Enjoy the rest of your stay in Miami.

Sincerely,
Johnny

Only MK calls me Aaron.

Chapter Eight

MK
August

MK Landry @NoPinkCaddy
You'll never believe where I am. Dinner with Vince Asher. Notice I didn't tag him. #HesSoPretty

Pilar Gomez @CookIsAlwaysRight
@NoPinkCaddy is a fraud. I found one of her recipes in an old New Orleans Junior League cookbook. #YouShouldBeAshamed

Rock Star Groupies @RockStarGroupies
@VivaValdez is dancing @HautNightclub with an unknown guy. @RealJohnnyKnite is not here.

A drop of olive oil dribbles down his chin. Laughing, I lean forward and use my napkin to wipe it. Vince's chuckle fills the tiny space. "You didn't tell me how messy these are."

"But they're good, huh?" I reply with a wink.

"That they are. So tell me why a pretty girl in a bright yellow dress would tackle such a messy food? I said I'd take you anywhere you wished." A couple of black olives escape the confines of the bread and fall to his paper plate.

I love Vince's voice. He uses it like most people add hand gestures to a conversation. His inflection and how he turns a phrase is something special. I wonder if he developed this for his TV show or if it's just a God-given talent.

My eyes grow wide, and I turn my head. "This is where I wished." I take a sip of Diet Coke. "But seriously, would you have ever tried this place if I hadn't brought you?"

He tries pointing but his sandwich degrades to a wonderful pile of meats, veggies, mangled bread, and oil. "I'm grabbing a fork and at least two rolls of paper towels. Need anything?"

Shaking my head, I take another bite of my quarter of a muffaletta while I watch him walk to the counter. His plain orange T-shirt skims his sculpted physique effortlessly. It's tucked into a pair of lightly-dyed denim jeans that also do a great job of showing off his legs without looking uncomfortable. He wears a ball cap, protecting his bald head from the New Orleans sun.

When he sits down, I ask, "Who's the team on your hat?"

His brows raise for a second before he replies, "San Jose Sharks. You not a hockey fan?"

"No. In fact, I don't think I've ever seen a hockey game."

"We can rectify that. Season begins in October. I'll take you to one." He wipes his face and hands, turning them over to ensure he got all the mess.

I finish swallowing my bite. "That would be fun. So why are you in town?"

He leans back in his chair, pushing his plate away. "Tomorrow they're going to start shooting B-roll. It's my show, my brand, my name. Not much happens that I'm not a part of."

I like that. I need to remember those words. My show. My name. My brand. "What's B-roll?"

He chuckles, but not in a demeaning way. "In a movie, it's like a flashback scene or something similar that quickly gives the viewer important background. In what we do, it's a little different. B-roll is filmed without sound. If you're ever watching a show and there is a voice-over or music on top of footage, then that's B-roll." Lacing his hands, he leans forward resting his elbows on the table. "From what I understand, I think they're going to set up a time-lapse camera to capture the transformation of the store, shoot some of the New Orleans sites, and probably find an alligator or two to add for local flare."

So full that I can't take another bite, I push my plate away. I'm quickly realizing I don't know what I don't know. "I'm curious why it's important for you to supervise the B-roll footage. You won't be in it, right?"

Vince taps the table as if he's punctuating the statement. "Here's why, MK. Nobody knows who the camera guy or the director is, but everyone knows Vince Asher. My show gets canceled or looks sloppy—guess whose neck is on the chopping block? Everyone associated with my show will move on to other jobs. It's my reputation. It's my name."

All of a sudden, the food in my stomach doesn't seem to be settling well. "I'm just blindly trusting Janet and Cindy and all their people that they will do a good job for me."

He stands, gathering up all the trash on the table. "You've an agent and manager, right?"

"I just have a manager, Shannon. She took the pictures of us outside the store."

He dumps everything in the big, red garbage can by the door and sits back down. "Right, but you have to have an agent. How did you get this gig?"

I probably overshare just how I went about turning my blog into a show.

Vince shakes his head. "You just might be the luckiest chick I've ever heard of. Want to get out of this restaurant, have a drink, and I'll try to impart five years' worth of knowledge in one evening?"

"Please."

He offers me his hand, and I take it. His working-man's touch instantly reminds me of Aaron's hard, callused hands. I picture two long arms pushing a Pinocchio version of Aaron into a large metal door like they have in banks. Mentally turning the lock, I tell Aaron to stay in there. He's not ruining my night with Vince.

We walk hand in hand next door to Eddy's Bar. I greet Eddy and introduce him to Vince. As usual, Eddy is unimpressed and doesn't bother making eye contact. All part of his charm. Vince orders an Abita Amber, and I yell for Eddy to make it two.

We take a table in the back. I say hello to the regulars who greet me also, but I don't stop to visit. Vince is mine tonight, and I don't want to share.

"This place is nice," he says as he checks the bar out. It hasn't changed a bit in all the years I've been coming here.

"It's a great neighborhood dive. Not many tourists stop by, and we sorta have a family thing going on here." I pause for a second spying Doctor Jared looking remarkably well sitting at a table with a pretty blonde about his age. "See that guy in the gold LSU shirt?"

"Yeah." Vince nods.

"He's the doctor who took care of me when I got this." I point to my scar.

With a frown marring his features, he reaches across the table and traces it. "I thought this was a scratch."

I can't help but lean into his touch. "No. Some girls get fake boobs when they turn thirty. My plastic surgery was because I fell into the corner of my coffee table." And it led to the end of what I thought was my happily-ever-after.

"MK." He sighs. "I'm sorry." He takes my hand, giving it a squeeze.

"It's all good. Really." I change the subject. "I'm ready to be educated about showbiz."

I'm sad when Vince leans back in his chair and replaces my hand with his beer. I was hoping he could play professor while we touched. He spends the next thirty minutes sharing some great advice. While peeling the label on my bottle, I try to absorb every word that comes out of his mouth. "Can you be a mentor for me?"

"I don't know about that." He looks down at the floor, and I think he might be a tad embarrassed by my question.

"Sorry. That was probably too much to ask." I stand, heading to the bar to order us another round. Why do I push? My whole life I've just assumed that everyone is like me—an open book. I hate it. You'd think by the age of thirty-one, I would have learned.

As I set the bottle in front of him, I apologize a second time.

He thanks me for the beer and then says, "You're a smart, talented girl. You don't need me, MK. I'm just a contractor. You and your show are going to far surpass what I can offer."

That's when I realize that the great Vince Asher, the contractor whose show I watch religiously, is intimidated by me.

We finish our beers and leave Eddy's Bar. As we're walking back to my place, he stops and points at a house. "Why does that home have Mardi Gras lights strung around their porch. It isn't until February, right?"

"A lot of people keep theirs up year-round." It's funny how I just accept that this is a feature of my neighborhood, but how strange it is to a visitor.

"Isn't it tacky? In my neighborhood, Christmas lights come down on December twenty-sixth."

We start walking again. "No. I'm sure some people think they shouldn't be lit when it's not the season, but most of us just kinda accept it for it is. I think it would be boring to live in a place where all the houses look the same, and you can only decorate with lights Thanksgiving to Christmas."

He stops and looks up at utility lines that pass over the street. "Did people purposely throw beads up there?"

"Sort of. Parades don't come down this street. So yeah. Probably kids tossed them up there."

We continue. "The person who owns this multi-million-dollar house." He gestures at the large antebellum mansion near my place. "They don't care that faded beads hang so close to their property?"

"You know when you move to the Garden District of New Orleans that there are no zoning laws. You must preserve the original architecture, but you could easily live next door to a crack house, and Mardi Gras decorations up all year round are just par for the course."

We stop in front of my locked gate. After exchanging phone numbers, he brushes a gentle and sweet kiss on my cheek and tells me he'll see me tomorrow. That's when I go into the carriage house and fall into my bed convinced that this must be a fantastic dream that I never want to wake from.

Chapter Nine

Aaron
August

Carl Jacobs @Jacobsoverandout
Dear Baby Jesus @RealJohnnyKnite just got off the elevator in a speedo. #SureHeIsntGay

Sun, sun, sun, here comes the sun plays on repeat in my head as I cut through the water. At some point during the night, I remembered the conversation MK and I had about my high school swimming days. I also recalled how much I enjoyed swimming laps after she suggested it. Then the Monday happened, and everything good seemed to wilt and die.

The hotel has a lap pool so I've decided to give it a try. The concierge found me a swim cap, goggles, and a Speedo with the hotel name scrolled near my cock. I'm sure this is a story he'll share over a beer with friends—the night he let a rock star into the lap pool after procuring swimming gear at four in the morning. My head lifts from the water, and I check the time. It's close to five. I've been swimming for almost an hour. My muscles and tendons in my hand feel great—like nothing has ever been wrong.

My head goes back into the water, and I start the song again. *Here comes the sun.* What I soon realize is that just the Beatles song is playing. There's no static or other noise. My head hasn't been this quiet since the last time I made love to MK. That leads me to playing *Pink Cadillac* in my brain. I find that it slows my pace which is good because my muscles are fatigued. I don't feel like I might die. Even the one line—the one that almost killed me—plays nicely without incident.

One more lap, and I can finish the song.

Slap! Something hits against my shoulder causing my feet to go to the bottom of the pool. As I stand up, a boot whizzes by my head. Yanking off the goggles, I yell, "What the fuck, Viva?"

A black, silk night gown is bunched just above her matching panties. Her dark brown hair is wild around her makeup-smeared face. She's yelling at me in Spanish, and I'm only picking up a few words like *bastardo, vete al carajo,* and *te odio.* I took four years of Spanish in high school. Today, I couldn't conjugate a verb to save Jude's life, but the Spanish I learned playing bars around the Austin area will stick with me forever.

My mind turns as I'm trying to figure out why she's so pissed. Pushing off from the coping, I stand and walk over to the stack of white hotel towels. She follows behind and hurls another boot in my direction. *Where do they keep coming from?*

"Stop it," I yell. "What's your problem?"

Mascara tears pour down her cheeks. "I love you, and you break up with me with a note when I surprise you." Then, she reverts to Spanish.

She said she loved me? My forehead wrinkles. "How can you love me?" Wrapping the towel around my waist, I look at her as if I've never seen her before. "I have another woman's name tattooed on my chest."

Viva balls up her fist and hits me over my heart. I let her get one punch in because I deserve it. When she goes for the second, I grab her wrist, and then the other, as she swings with her left hand. I pull her against me as I stare into her blood-shot eyes. "Tell me why you think you love me." My voice is not one that I recognize. It's deep and troubled.

Her bottom lip trembles. "I thought we had something."

My head turns. "Viva, we've only spent maybe a week together since we began dating months ago. I just don't understand why you think we're something more than what we were?" That nagging voice in my head reminds me that MK and I said we loved each other in less than two weeks.

"You're a rock star. You're supposed to be . . . what's the word?" Her eyes travel to the ceiling and then back to mine.

"Difficult? Aloof?" I suggest.

"No." Her head shakes back and forth causing some strands to slap me in the face. "A bastard."

The alcohol is strong on her breath. "Go to bed. Sleep it off. We can talk more later, but I'm done for tonight."

Letting her go, I bend, picking up my boot and notice the one in the pool along with my credit card. I grab the pole with a net attached to the end and fish my belongings out of the water.

As I turn to exit the pool area, Viva says in a small voice, "Can I have just one night to make you see how good we can be together?"

Turning around, I lean against the doorjamb, feeling much older than my thirty-eight years. "You're a great woman, Viva. Don't settle for a guy like me." Then I say the words to her that MK said to me. "I'll never be the man you deserve." They just slip out of my mouth, and MK's voice is so strong in my head that I swear she could be whispering in my ear: *Give me the whole and complete man I deserve.*

Feeling like the dick I am, I turn and walk out of the natatorium leaving her crying in her hands. There's nothing I can do to console her. She's upset over something that never existed—at least in my eyes.

Knocking on Sam's door, I wait for her and Billy to finish whatever they're up to. After standing there for a few minutes, I leave, assuming they're already asleep.

From behind me, I hear, "What's wrong with you?"

I stop, turn around, and say, "Need to talk."

Her smile tells me she's pleased that I asked. A Disturbed song blares in my head as I let us both into my room.

Collapsing on the couch, I pick up my guitar and begin playing *Pink Cadillac.* I think better with it in hand.

"So we don't play it any longer in concert, yet you sit here shaking like a leaf and playing that song looking like a junkie trying to stay sober." She crosses her legs and leans in like she's the mind-fuck doctor, waiting for my response.

I start the song over. That's when she snatches the guitar out of my hands, standing over me with her legs spread and hands on her hips like the dominatrix she likes to be.

Sighing, I sprawl out on the couch, freeing the words that are torturing my soul. "I'm still in love with MK." The bile creeps up my throat, and I swallow hard, willing myself to calm the fuck down. It's the first time I've said it out loud. It's not nearly as therapeutic as I had hoped it would be. In fact, it's so fucking scary I want to hide under a pillow.

The smile on Sam's face is a told-you-so one that makes me want to tackle her and pin her arms down like I used to do when we were kids. "What're you going to do about it?"

Using my elbow, I shield my face. "I don't know. I'm sure she wants nothing to do with me. I've been an ass, but she gave up on me. She kicked me when I was down." I peek one eye out. "You know how I value loyalty."

The next thing I know, Sam is the one straddling my waist and pinning my arms above my head. Her eyes are dancing with happiness. "You're such a dumb shit."

"Hey," I yell using my hips to buck her off.

"I'm so sick of you being miserable. Either get MK back or start doing coke again. Pick one because this morose bullshit has got to stop. It's affecting the tour, and most of all, I miss my best friend."

That makes me quit fighting her and smile. "I miss being happy."

She sits back on my hips, yelps when her behind touches my wet towel, and climbs off. Standing over me she gets her joker smile. "Well, genius, there's your answer. You were happy with MK, and you were happy doing coke. One makes Jude really damn angry and scared, and the other makes her giddy."

"I bought coke tonight," I admit in a solemn voice.

Sam drops to the floor and sits in a folded position. "How was it?"

I'm not sure I have the words to articulate what happened. "I swam instead."

Her head cocks like a confused puppy. "What?"

"I got into the pool and swam laps like I did in high school."

"And?"

"And I didn't do coke. Then Viva found out I ended things, and she flipped her shit."

"No more Viva?"

"Nope." Sitting, I put my head in between my knees. "I haven't told anyone this, but when MK ended things she told me to become the man she deserved." I make eye contact with Sam. "And I basically used those words when I broke up with Viva."

Swallowing, I continue, "It made me realize just how much I still love MK and how I'm not even close to being a decent partner. Hell, I can't even love a supermodel who demanded nothing of me. She didn't want me to be a better person. She was willing to take my mood swings and shitty personality."

Sam crawls on the couch and kneads my shoulders. "You're a good person. You've raised a phenomenal daughter who is down to earth, smart, and independent. And you managed to do that in this crazy un-real world we live in. You and MK had a fight—a spat. Billy and I've had plenty of them. But you don't know how to fight with a lover so you got scared and ran. Maybe you should give MK a call."

Just the thought of talking to her causes my stomach to revolt. No. I can't do that. My shoulders tense under her palms, and I swallow hard. My head shakes. "No. No. I can't call her."

Standing, I pace back and forth behind the couch. "She might hang up on me. You should read her messages. She's fucking livid, Sam. Like she's not one for cussing, and she's sent me texts where calls me lots of fucked-up words."

"I'm sure she is. You stormed out. Left her hanging. Teased her with an album written about her and never contacted her again. If she didn't want to cut your balls off and make them into a necklace, she wouldn't be the right woman for you."

I stop pacing. "So you think if I give her a ring, she'll answer?"

She shakes her head. "I wouldn't."

My arms fly up in frustration. "Then why are you setting me up for failure?" Women. They've got to be the most confusing creatures on the planet.

"You're going to have to fight for her. You're going to have to convince her that you still love her, and she should give you two another shot. She's probably not going to be real pleased to hear from you. In fact, I bet it's going to take a lot of groveling. You're going to have to put your heart on the line, and you're going to have to do things that you'd normally refuse to do because you have to prove to her you can be her partner."

"How in the hell do I do that?"

Sam laughs. "It's certainly not by writing her another album."

Chapter Ten

MK
September

MK Landry @NoPinkCaddy
This is really happening! In LA meeting with my potential agent. Say a prayer I don't make a fool out of myself.

Barbara Lloyd @SouthernStyleDishes
@NoPinkCaddy is a hack. Her dishes are no more Cajun than #PopeyesChicken. Visit my site instead.

Viva Valdez @VivaValdez
I hate men! #ThereIsAReasonICouldBeALesbian

"Welcome to LA," Holden Grayson says as he extends his hand. He's in his mid-thirties, slightly overweight, and has curly auburn hair with freckles sprinkled across his nose. There's something about him that I found endearing when we chatted on the phone. He was warm and friendly. Maybe he could even be described as a bit goofy. He also seemed to be the opposite of the Los Angeles stereotype, which I hope is a good thing. He didn't seem pretentious or feel a little show being filmed in New Orleans was beneath his firm.

The guy is supposed to be the best reality-star agent in the business. I think the only reason he took my call was because he's Vince's agent also, and Vince made the introduction.

We're in Holden's corner office located in a mid-rise building on a crowded street somewhere between downtown LA and Beverly Hills. If I had to find this place again, I couldn't.

I'm trying hard to avoid looking out the floor-to-ceiling window behind his desk which features a perfect view of a billboard advertising ACE's world tour and the show tonight. I also do my best to not notice the naked torso of Aaron wearing my necklace and my saying *Alis Volat Propriis* scrolled in the font Cara designed for me along the bottom of the board. And, of course, my eyes never scan along the tattooed fingers clinching the heart to read my initials. *Damn you, Aaron Emerson.*

"Please have a seat on the couch." He gestures at the white leather sofa with chrome metal accents. Much too modern for my taste, but that seems to be the LA aesthetic. "Would you like a drink? Scratch that." He grabs his phone and hits a button. "Bring Miss Landry a glass of red wine. I think she prefers Cab."

I do as he says and sit on the very hard couch. It was obviously not purchased for comfort. Holden takes the seat across from me. It looks equally uncomfortable, but I notice that he's sitting higher than I am. I wonder if it's some sort of psychology mind trick. Not that I'm a psychologist, but I enjoy playing one. I've heard this is a thing people use to feel more important.

No sooner does he take his seat than the door opens and a young man dressed in a grey suit enters with a glass of wine. He hands it me and disappears in a flash. The words, "Thank you," stumble from my lips, but I'm not entirely sure he heard me.

It's ten o'clock in the morning, and I've just been handed a glass of wine. As I take a sip, I reason that it's noon in Louisiana, so a glass of wine would be appropriate if I was home.

"So, Miss Landry," Holden begins. "First of all, happy late birthday. I hope you had a nice celebration."

He seems insincere, and I sense this is nothing more than a formality statement. Where is the nice guy I chatted with on the phone? The whole vibe of this office is wrong. Taking another sip of wine, "Yes. My birthday was a lovely one." And just because I can't help myself, I continue to rattle off details that he doesn't care about. "My best friend took me out to a three-hour lunch. Then, Grandmother hosted a small party at her house. You wouldn't believe all the characters she invited because you see, even though it's my birthday, I don't get to make the guest list."

"Good. That's wonderful to hear." He crosses his legs and leans back. "Let's talk about your show in the works—No Pink Caddy?" He raises his eyebrow at the name, I think. "From what I can tell, the entertainment lawyer you hired did a good job negotiating you a very fair contract. I know Cindy and Janet, and they have a great reputation in the industry. Usually we get involved before the client has a show and contract in place, but Vince explained the unique circumstance you find yourself in."

Resting my glass on the chrome coffee table, I lean forward and turn a bit towards Holden, hoping to relieve the pressure on my tailbone. I think the ground would be softer. "I'm so new at all of this. I'm sorry if I did things out of order. Between my sorority sister and Vince, I think I'm starting to figure out what I don't know yet."

"Rebecca?"

"Yes, Rebecca put me in contact with Aiden Montgomery. He visited with Cindy and Janet's production company, and before I knew it, I had a FedEx envelope on my doorstep."

Holden doesn't respond to my statement. "After reviewing the content on your site and looking over the contract, I think my agency can be of use to you." He leans forward with a glint in his eye. "A book deal seems obvious. Of course, your name-branded cookware will sell well. Probably that will be an exclusive deal with a retailer. Furniture line with a regional company. Maybe we can even swing a clothing deal." He looks me up and down. "You have a unique style."

I glance down at my vintage St. John Knit navy suit also borrowed from Grandmother and wonder what he means by unique style. I also laugh in my head at the idea of a furniture deal. I still haven't replaced the Robin's egg blue couch, over-stuffed chair, and marble coffee table Aaron sent to a landfill somewhere on the outskirts of New Orleans. But as the saying goes, the cobbler's kids have the worst shoes. "Umm . . . that's really great and all, but aren't we putting the cart before the horse?"

He smiles, but it's patronizing. *This man is not polite at all.* "The details will take months to work out. If I've read your contract correctly, you've already begun preproduction and will start filming in a couple of weeks."

"Well, yes. The first season—"

"Will focus on getting your store open for business while mixing in segments where you show off your talents," he finishes.

I nod.

"Air date of January."

Nodding again, I question why he even had me fly out to LA to meet with him. He seems to know everything and has a clear plan for my career.

He adjusts in his seat so he's now leaning forward. "I brought you here to discuss changing the name of the show."

My heart plummets to my stomach as his statement answers the question in my head.

"I noticed in the contract the name of the program is listed as *to be determined.* My public relations team hates the name No Pink Caddy. It's shit to brand. It doesn't make sense to most of the United States, and it says nothing about who you are."

Now it's also clear why I'm having a glass of cabernet sauvignon wine at a business meeting in LA at ten o'clock in the morning. I should have brought Shannon. She advised me to let her come, and even stomped her pointed-toe Jimmy Choo, but I told her that I could handle this. "No Pink Caddy has been the name of my blog since it began. See, it's a play on my name, Mary Kay."

He crosses his legs. "Yes. I get all of that, but it doesn't mean it's good." Holden gestures as if the name is an annoying butler who brought him champagne instead of wine. "We want the initials MK to become synonymous with living a Southern lifestyle. We want twenty-somethings to run to their local Target to purchase MK's dishes because they're turquoise and she uses them on her show. Since Michael Kors has branded MK, we're thinking of changing your name to MKL. When pronounced fast, it's Michael." He adds, "You know, male names for females are all the rage."

My eyes grow wide with disgust at hearing the name of my ex-boyfriend who I worked for for years. Quitting that horrible job is one of the highlights of my life. I'd rather be called anything than the name of that troll. "No." I shake my head to further emphasize just how much I hate the idea. "No. My name isn't Michael. It's Mary Kay or MK. If that's the direction you want me to go, this might not be a good fit." I grab my purse and rest my glass back on the coffee table. Why is everyone trying to make me into something I'm not?

He waves his arms. "Just a suggestion. You seem to focus a lot on the colors aqua and red. Maybe we can do something with that. My marketing team would love to throw some ideas at you. It's so important that we brand you well from the beginning. Having to make changes when you're already a household name is costly and confusing to the public."

I'm a brand? Is this what I want to be? Do I want cookware and books and a clothing line? Do I want to no longer be associated with the name No Pink Caddy? My head is swimming in doubts. I'm being pushed out of my comfort zone by someone who I'm hoping to hire to be on my side.

This is too much, but I'm here. Vince says that Holden is the best in the business. *Ughhh . . .*

Before I can fully process what's happening, Holden's office is transformed into a No Pink Caddy rebranding meeting. A guy in an over-tailored suit is flanked by two young girls who look fresh from the sorority house. It turns into a Monty Python skit. *Why didn't I bring Shannon with me? Stupid, MK. Very stupid.*

"What about Southern Sass or Southern Spice?" the overly tailored guy suggests as he slides a piece of modern artwork to the right, revealing a whiteboard. He uses a red marker to write down *Southern Sass* and *Southern Spice.*

"Ummm . . . but I'm No Pink Caddy." I still am not understanding why I need to change my name and take another slug of wine. It's gotten me this far, hasn't it?

The guy in the tailored suit smiles as if I'm a child who doesn't understand why I can't eat the whole tub of ice cream. "Yes. And you can still be No Pink Caddy any time you want. However, for branding, you need a new identity. I think I like Southern Spice." The two girls nod. "What do you think H-Man?"

"Not bad. What about GRITS? Girl Raised in the South," Holden throws out.

Tailored Suit adds *GRITS* to the board.

"Do you make grits?"

I nod as my pointer finger picks away at the tender skin surrounding my thumb. "I do teach viewers how to make an excellent shrimp and grits dish, but let's back up. I've been very successful with No Pink Caddy." I gesture towards Holden using my left hand. I think I might have drawn blood on my right cuticle. "You couldn't believe that I landed my show without your assistance. Maybe that's a sign that we shouldn't mess with what's working."

His smile is patronizing. "Michael, you're a . . ."

"It's MK," I correct.

He drops his chin and rolls his eyes. "MK, you're a sweet girl who has made your career out of being naïve and having a wee bit of talent." His fingers demonstrate just how little talent he believes I have. "That's gotten you a production deal. Let my team carry you to the finish line. We can take that naivety and talent and make you millions. But you just have to trust us."

I remember my southern manners. "I appreciate all the work you've put into this. I can tell you really care about my future." Smiling at Holden, "I look forward to hearing more name suggestions. For right now though, I'd just like to focus on getting my store opened and my first season in the books. We can talk about the other things at a later date." I stand to leave. I'm meeting Shannon in an hour to pick out items for the store. That seems like much more fun than discussing how my new agent is going to rebrand me.

"Wonderful. Just a few papers we'll need you to sign," Holden smiles. "But your name must be decided before production begins."

"I'm sorry," I say as I glance around the room, and then I'm instantly mad at myself for apologizing. I should never apologize for being me. My eyes find

Aaron's across the street and lock with his. An inner strength grips my chest, and I use it to reclaim this meeting. "You see, y'all have thrown me for a loop. Imagine finding out that the name you've had your whole life is something different. I wasn't prepared for this. This is like burning sugar. If you burn it, you can still use it, it just has a different taste, and you make it into something else." I punctuate my statement with a huge smile. "I was prepared to remain MK Landry and my show to be called No Pink Caddy. Now, you're telling me . . ."

"That's it." Holden jumps to his feet as I cringe. "Your show should be called *Burnt Sugar.*"

I stare at him. His team is silent.

Holden continues, "That's what you've done. You've lived your metaphor. You thought you'd marry your college boyfriend right after college and have a couple of kids." He snaps, "Your line . . . *the life I'm living is not what was promised in the college brochure.* Or something like that. You took your life, the sugar. It got burnt, the life you live now. Now it's burnt sugar that you use to make . . ."

He motions for me to continue. "Umm . . . I use burnt sugar to make pralines."

He jumps on the couch cushion next to me, and I flinch. "Yes. Pralines are damn good, right?"

"Sure." I shrug.

"Burnt Sugar. Think about it, MK."

I glance at Holden's team. They seem to like it also.

Tailored Suit adds it to the white board.

"I'll consider it."

A stack of papers is placed in front of me. I sign them not because I like Holden, his team, or their ideas. Mary Kay Landry scribbles on the dotted line because I have no other choice. Vince talked highly of Holden. He's supposed to be the best in the industry. As I scan through the pages, I feel as if I'm on a speeding train with no brakes. This out-of-control chaos inside my soul tells me that I'm way out of my comfort zone. Between seeing the billboards for ACE's tour and the rebranding of MK, I can't wait until tomorrow when I get on a plane back home.

After I sign my life away, Holden shakes my hand. "I'll set up a meeting with Janet and Cindy to discuss naming the show *Burnt Sugar.*"

Do I like *Burnt Sugar?* I don't even know anymore. I've lost my way, and I need a good night with Bella to help me find myself again. I reach up and grasp for my shark tooth necklace which as always helped me feel grounded. It's as if I try to touch my leg which is no longer there. Loneliness grips my soul, and it's all I can do to exit the glass doors before tears spill down my cheeks.

I want to go home, and I know that home is much more than just a destination.

Chapter Eleven

Aaron
September

Jude Emerson @HorseGirl4Life
In LA to visit my dad. Hopefully he realizes I've been to the zoo a million times and just want to shop. #DadsRLame

Jude Emerson @HorseGirl4Life
Happy late birthday @NoPinkCaddy. Congrats on your show and store. Can't wait to visit.

"Oh my God. That's her." The words tumble out of my mouth in a whisper, which completely contradicts my nerves. Every hair is at attention as if a bolt of lightning has passed through my body. My heart refuses to beat, and I think Rock sucker-punched me in the gut.

"Who?" Jude asks as she throws herself across my lap to see out of the window. "That's MK," she yells, and then taps the driver's shoulder. "Pull over."

"No," I command, this time much louder. I'm not ready to talk to her yet. I don't know what I would even say.

"Yes," Jude says with just as much conviction. "This's stupid and ridiculous. I mean, what are the chances that we would see her in LA?"

Yeah. What are the chances? It's like fate is kicking my ass.

It's horrible Los Angeles traffic, and we're stopped at a light. Like a fool, I click the lock on the town car as if MK is the boogeyman and might open the door and kidnap me. But then again, maybe that wouldn't be so bad. It would force me to talk to her.

She's walking along the sidewalk dressed in a navy, figure-hugging dress. Her ass looks luscious. Board-straight brown hair touched by the summer sun swishes back and forth along her back as she walks in heels that make her legs look lickable. At the corner, she greets a female leaving a Starbucks. She doesn't hold a candle to MK. The two continue to cross the street, heading away from me. Again.

"Dad, it's like some sort of cosmic collision. Maybe even fate." God, it's amazing how much we think alike sometimes. "This is the universe telling you that you should dump Life—"

"Viva," I correct.

She rolls her eyes. "And beg MK to take you back."

"What's so wrong with Viva?" I haven't told Jude that Viva and I ended things a week ago. Never crossed my mind to mention it. It surprises me she even cares enough to bring up her name.

The car begins to roll. I look down, realizing this is the first time I've been completely sober in six weeks. I knew I had to dry myself out for Jude's visit, or she would worry about me. I'm also supposed to see the doctor before my show tonight. I'm not looking forward to a lecture about alcohol.

She leans back against the black leather seat and looks every bit the teenager she still is. Hair the color of straw falls around her face. "Where would you like for me to begin? Her age? Her lack of intelligence? The fact that she's as tall as you? What do you see in her?"

She was a distraction. "She's a very nice person, Jude. You shouldn't be so judgmental." My dad voice is spot-on.

"I'll consider it while you consider telling the driver to pull over so you can chase down MK, scoop her up in your arms, and carry her back to your hotel room *Pretty Woman* style."

I chuckle, but it isn't sincere. If only life was so easy. "You've watched too many of those shitty romantic movies."

"You know she's going to be a reality TV star. I don't get why you ruined stuff with her, and because of that, I can't be on her new show, and we can't be friends?"

Finally, we creep through the light. My eyes sweep along the sidewalk, hoping to catch one more glimpse of her, but she's gone.

Jude has kept me abreast of everything MK has posted on her site—even when I asked her to quit sharing. I am happy for MK if being a reality star is what she wants. I'm sure the world will fall in love with her just as much I did. She'll be successful in whatever she does. Her personality draws people to her like lightning bugs on a warm summer night.

Doubling over in the car, I pretend to screw with my shoe while I try to get my breathing under control. I remind myself of the bad things MK has done. She kicked me out of her life when I needed her the most. Loyalty is a damn important trait, and MK doesn't know the meaning of the word. *How many more times can I say that?* I sound like Grace.

When we get back to our hotel suite near the Staples Center, I kiss Jude's cheek. "I have an interview. See you later." So far, Jude's made it nineteen years staying relatively out of the public eye. I'm sure it helps that her last name is Emerson and not Knite. She doesn't give a damn what my profession is, and she seems a bit surprised when others do.

"Great. I think I'm going to find Sam and see if she wants to watch a movie or go shopping in the hotel gift store."

"Sounds good. Have fun." I watch my life bounce down the narrow hall.

Grace's hand catches the edge of the door before it closes. Her brown business suit seems silly and out of place, it's as if she's trying too hard to be a businesswoman and the suit somehow gives her credibility. I quit trying to explain this long ago. Clothes don't make the man. "Mandy Jean will be here in ten. Sasha has approved the list of questions." Grace picks up a pair of Jude's sandals, opens the other bedroom door, and tosses them in. She continues tidying up the living room which I don't think looks out of order. "You've been featured in *Rolling Stone* before, but this is still great publicity for you. It puts the final nail in all the haters' coffins who said that your career was over after the incident. I know you despise the word comeback, but that's essentially what it is, and you're killing it." She picks a piece of lint off the back of one of the dining chairs and drops it on the floor. "The doctor will meet you in the dressing room at Staples. Sound check went well. I know you like to do it yourself, but I think it was important to spend some time with Jude. She's really growing up."

Grace walks over to where I'm leaned against the wall and starts fiddling with my hair. I slap her hand away with a scowl as I make my way to the minibar.

"Brush your hair. It looks like you've been dragging your fingers through it."

Ignoring her, I pull out the bottle of Jameson from the fridge. Fuck sobriety. Seeing MK has screwed with my head. The white quartz counter is littered with the tiny liquor bottles I pulled out to make room for the larger one last night. It was my "just in case" or back up plan.

"What's your problem?" my darling sister asks.

Popping off the lid, I take a long pull from the bottle. The burn down my throat and into my stomach does its job numbing some of the pain in my right hand. My middle finger is curled in a *C* position. I can straighten it, but it feels like there's a rubber band that's too tight pulling it back into the awkward position.

I debate if I'm honestly going to answer Grace's question. Then I decide that Jude will probably tell her so I might as well beat her to the punch. "Saw MK today."

Grace's eyes grow wide. "Oh God. Did you fuck her?"

My face screws into the Jesus-Christ-do-you-hear-what-comes-out-of-your-mouth look that I've been giving my little sister for most of her life. I shake my head. "She was walking down the sidewalk. Do you think I asked Jude to hop out and get Daddy a soda while I banged MK in the backseat of a town car? God, Grace."

Her hand goes over her heart as she exhales a long breath. "Thank goodness. You should have told the driver to swerve."

My fist clinches and pain travels down my arm, reaching my fingertips with such force that my hand splays out as if I've touched something hot. I fight to keep from doubling over. "What did she ever do to you?" My lip curls. "Fuck, did she kill your puppy? Burn your house down?" I lean against the cabinet for support. "She was polite, respectful, and in no way fucked with your life. Whatever you have against her, you need to let it go. This kind of hatred towards someone will eat away at your gut and eventually kill you." Shaking my head, I continue, "I'm so fucking disappointed in you." I turn my back to her because she literally at this moment disgusts me.

There's a loud knock on the suite door. Instead of going to answer it, Grace rests her hand on my shoulder. In a soft, sincere voice, she says, "It's hard watching your brother get his heart trampled on."

I should let it go. I should answer the door and let the interviewer in. *Jesus, I've already forgotten her name.* But I can't not finish this conversation. Turning around, I say, "You were cold to her the day you met her. She'd done nothing. Why? Tell me why MK was such a problem for you."

Grace ignores me and walks to the door.

My voice booms, "Don't open it until you answer my question." A thought crosses my mind. A terrible thought. One that I can't even believe I have inside my head. *Grace is jealous of MK.* "Will you ever accept that one day a female may be more important to me than you?"

She giggles but doesn't turn around. "Of course. Jude is."

My bottom lip catches between my teeth as my head shakes back and forth. "No. Not Jude. And you know that's not what I mean." I pause for a second. "The reason you liked Viva is that you knew it wasn't going anywhere."

There's another rap on the suite door. The world shifts a bit more in focus. I turn around, grabbing the bottle of Jameson and head into the bedroom, slamming the door behind me. I need to think.

That terrible last conversation with MK plays through my head. I didn't know what to do or how to handle MK's words. Having no relationship experience, I was like a teenager with my first broken heart. Grace was there for me. She told me I was lucky to see what kind of person MK really was. Grace said that MK had no idea how to stand by anyone when life got tough because she was a princess, raised by a wealthy family. She's not like us, born poor as mice, struggling for every single dime we have. MK didn't have to claw her way to the top. Her life has been spoon-fed to her. She thought she was using me to promote her site. She said that MK wanted my money and name.

I sink to the beige carpeted floor in front of the king-sized bed.

And I listened to every word.

Because I took her advice, I believed that MK was the problem. Grace made me feel that I, once again, made a bad choice in who I decided to fuck. The woman who birthed Jude was probably the first girl that I could have possibly fallen for and look how horrible that decision was. Yes, I have a daughter, and I wouldn't trade her for anything, but her mother was a terrible, sick person. I believed Grace because I don't trust my own judgement when it comes to women.

The blinders are off, and I see Grace for the first time as she really is. What does she know about love? She's been married to my career. She's afraid of losing me—losing what we've built. She has nothing to fall back on. I am her life. The band and Johnny Records is all she has.

Pulling out my phone, I begin reading the texts MK's sent since we ended things. Rubbing the shark tooth charm on her necklace gives me a strange sense of peace. It's as if there's a piece of MK's soul imbedded in it. I've never removed it from around my neck, and I insisted that it be on the cover of *Alis Volat Propriis* even while Grace protested loudly.

I read her last text first. It makes me laugh. I can picture her sending it: hair all in her face, pushing her bangs behind her ears. I can see her punching away at the phone screen as if it's her mortal enemy. I love her typo *ducking* as she asks for her necklace back.

"Not a chance, sweetheart," I tell my phone screen.

Another gulp from the bottle as I scroll down, reading her words of love.

I love you. Please let me know you're okay.

Her messages from when we first broke up are too painful for me to read even when I'm getting self-medicated. That's when I thought if I shared the album with her she'd see how much I loved her, and she'd just love me for who I am and not make me change. Not make me stop being Johnny Knite.

Another slug from the bottle.

That was never going to happen. She's MK who wants her husband to fit in her perfect mold. A flawed, selfish rock star, who gets fucked up to deal with problems is like a round peg for a square hole.

But you swim laps now instead of using. Am I strong enough to keep that up?

More of her messages. More of my bottle.

Then just to torture myself a bit more, I pull up the naked picture I took of her the night we made love for the first time. My nail traces the dress, like an ocean at her feet. I knew I already loved her. I knew I would ruin us. I warned her off. I told her I would fuck us up, and I'd die a bitter old man, and look at me. The pain in my hand reminds me of just how old I've become.

"Fucking look at me," I command myself. I'm sitting on the floor in a hotel room hunched over my phone reliving the two most perfect weeks of my life. I've become what I despise the most—weak and pathetic.

I open the *Find My Friends* app. "Oh, MK," I say to the phone screen. "You've got to be more careful with your personal safety."

Staring at her tiny profile picture, her broad smile cheering me up. It looks like she's in a car moving toward a destination. I set an alert to let me know when she arrives.

Standing, I walk into the bathroom and splash cold water on my cheeks to clear my head. Then I run a brush through my long hair just like my sister asked.

I'm a rock star. It's expected that I keep a reporter waiting. As my hand turns the knob, I push all thoughts of MK Landry away and slip into my alter ego, Johnny Knite.

Two heads turn at the sound of the door opening. Grace rushes over to me with an apology written in her eyes. I brush past her, walking over to the reporter. She's a pretty girl in that hot librarian sort of way. Her eyes are framed with thick, black, plastic glasses. Her hair is of a similar shade. It contrasts with her pale complexion. She's dressed in a brown, flowery dress with a tie at the waist and black Dr. Martens. Her hand goes out. "Mandy Jean."

I shake it before I sit down on the couch. "Pleasure to meet you, Miss

Jean." My interview voice is thick with my Texan accent. Tucking my right leg under me, I get comfortable for the forty-five-minute scheduled meeting. "Grace, please fix me a drink."

Out of my peripheral vision I see her scurry into the bedroom. Mandy takes the seat across from the couch.

"You like LA?" she asks as she grabs her orange notebook and feather pen. Her iPhone is in her lap.

"It's all right. Never mind coming to play here, do a little business, soak up some sun, maybe catch a couple of waves, and then head back to Texas."

Grace says that I sound like Matthew McConaughey when I let my accent slip out. As I'm talking, I hear myself selling Lincolns.

"But you're not, are you? Halfway through your comeback tour." She holds up her phone. "I'm going to record this interview. Mind?"

Shaking my head. "It's not a comeback if you've never really left. I've been doing my thing out of the spotlight in Austin. Running a record company. Signing acts. Writing music. I even opened a bar. Just because I haven't toured in a while doesn't mean I was home twiddling my thumbs."

"Raising your daughter?" Her eyebrow cocks in a way that tells me she's reaching. "I do believe she's nineteen now. You quit touring when she entered high school."

"I do not discuss my daughter in any interviews."

"She just completed her freshman year at Vanderbilt." It's a statement, and one I don't feel the need to confirm. "I've heard she's quite the equestrian. Makes good grades. From everything my sources have told me, she's really a very normal girl."

And the reason she's so normal is because she's been kept out of my spotlight. "I'm sure your readers don't care where my daughter goes to college or that she makes good grades and likes to ride horses." *Where's that drink, Grace?*

"Look. This is off the record, but I'm curious why you don't share more of the triumphant story of raising Jude. I mean, you're a single dad who found a balance between rock god and diaper duty. From what I can dig up, she's an accomplished kid in her own right. Equestrian team at Vanderbilt is nothing to sneeze at. You could be a real inspiration to our readers. Just think of all your single parent fans out there."

Grace enters to my right, handing me the glass before taking the other chair.

I give Mandy Jean a pointed look. She's not the first and probably will not be the last reporter who's brought this to my attention. I smile. "Still off the record?"

She nods.

"Say it," I demand.

"Yes. Still off the record." She leans forward as if she's about to get the scoop of the century.

"You know why she's such an amazing human?" I pause for effect. "It's because I've kept her out of the spotlight and raised her to be her own person. I'm lucky enough to have a mother and a sister that gave up their lives so I could follow my dreams and still be a parent. Most single fathers don't have the kind of support that I did. Jude is not my triumph. She's the product of three people who have devoted their lives to her and a band that didn't mind having a baby, toddler, child, or teenager hanging around." I swallow a gulp of my drink. "Now, I know you submitted questions to my publicist, and I know for a fact that my daughter was not on the topic list because if she was, I'd fire her ass. Now, shall we discuss the success of my new album, *Alis Volat Propriis*?"

Miss Jean's cheeks pinken just enough that I know I've made my point. She smiles and replies with a shrug, "Can't blame me for trying. Just one more thing though. I really do admire you. I'm a single mother, and it's a very trying job. I'd love to buy you a beer." She looks at my high ball glass of whiskey. "Or a bourbon and get some tips."

"Maybe one day." There's no need to tell her that I have no advice to give. I think Jude is more of a product of my luck then any sort of parenting strategy.

"Back on the record." Her next questions are of the standard fare. What do I contribute my longevity in this business to? How have I kept the core members of my band? The same questions I've gotten asked in every city on this tour. I'm disappointed in Miss Jean. I thought a reporter for *Rolling Stone* would be a bit more creative.

Then she asks the dreaded question. The one they all ask, yet I despise it all the same. "This album seems to be deeply personal. Much more than your others."

I take a sip of my drink as if I'm pondering the answer, but really, this has become boring. "As a writer, I'm influenced by the world around me. Even guys like a good, sappy love story every now and then." I punctuate with my killer half-grin.

She scribbles furiously in her notebook. Without looking up, "Yes, but it seems that the timing of this album coincides with your breakup with MK Landry. Was that planned?"

Mandy Jean has done her research. It's the first time I've been asked about this coincidence between the album release and MK's break-up post. The public has a short memory. My relationship with MK made a few gossip mags. There was one week of speculation that I was the one who caused her injuries, but as soon as the police confirmed that I was not a suspect, and it was an accident, the public got distracted by a pop star pregnant with twins and a model over-dosing. The beauty with tabloid gossip is once you're out of sight, you're out of mind. "Pure coincidence." A larger sip of whiskey slides down my throat.

"Let's see. Miss Landry posted the breakup news at . . ." She scans her notebook. "At six thirty-seven in the evening, and you dropped the new album and announced the tour at seven oh-four." She takes off her glasses. "I'd say that's a bit more than luck or coincidence."

Shrugging, I reply, "Not sure what else to tell you."

"Be honest with your fans, Mister Knite. If MK is the muse behind your most critically acclaimed album to date, they want to know that." Her eyebrow cocks, "You do have a number one song on the charts that's called *Pink Cadillac.*"

I look to Grace. Her face is passive, but her eyes are wild, darting back and forth and blinking as if she's trying to communicate via Morse code. The last thing she wants is for me to be linked publicly with MK Landry again. The allegations that I caused MK's injuries caused a shit-storm for her and my publicist. "Artists don't owe it to their fans to discuss why or who a song is written for. I think it's best to let my fans decide—to let them imagine that my songs are written for them and about their lives. I wish there was a story here, but there's just not."

Mandy Jean pulls a folded-up sheet of typing paper from her notebook. "We've reached out to MK's manager. This is what her statement says, 'Although Miss Landry and Mister Knite were a couple once, they haven't been together for some time. Miss Landry has moved on, and it seems Mister Knite has also.'"

What does that mean? MK has moved on? I checked her site a couple of days ago. There was no mention of a date or a guy in her life. I haven't read anything about her seeing someone else. Suddenly, the whiskey isn't settling right in my stomach. Sweat beads on my forehead. "Grace, can you open the balcony door?"

A small smile appears on Miss Jean's face.

"The statement is correct. I've been publicly linked to Viva Valdez. Why aren't you asking if the album is written about her?"

A gust of wind blows into the suite sending a little chill down my back. "Because Viva isn't associated with a pink Cadillac."

Leaning forward, I readjust, resting my elbows on my knees. "Look, you're really barking up the wrong tree here. Do you have other questions, or is this interview over?"

"Mister Knite, when you agreed to this interview did you not think these questions would come up? *Rolling Stone* is known for provocative interviews. I don't want you to feed me the same answers that you've given every hometown newspaper. Our readers want something they can sink their teeth into. They want details they can't find other places. Just as you would never want to play a crowd and half-ass it, I don't want my name associated with another fluff piece about how great it is that ACE is back on top."

She stands and begins packing her things. "*Alis Volat Propriis was* clearly inspired by your time spent with Miss Landry. The album is very different than your past ones. You invited your fans into your bedroom when you released it. They want more info. They want to know if you get the girl." Her bag slips over her shoulder. "Your publicist has my number. If you change your mind and want to actually consent to a real interview, I'll be happy to meet you anywhere in the world. But today has been a waste of both of our time."

Grace leaps to her feet. "Mandy, he's very sorry. Would you like to try again tomorrow?"

Now, I'm standing also. I address Grace first. "I'm not your puppet." Then, I turn to Mandy Jean. "You're absolutely correct. I'm not ready for this sort of interview right now. And I'll not be ready tomorrow. Just so we're clear, I'll never discuss my daughter or about being a single father, but the album I will. I just need some time." What I need is closure with MK. I either need to say the final words that I've needed to speak for a long time, or I need to fuck her brains out and remind her why she shouldn't have ever given up on us.

Mandy Jean nods. "I respect that. Hope to hear from you soon."

Pulling my phone out, I have an alert. MK is staying about five minutes from here. I know exactly what I'm going to do.

"Where are you going?" Grace asks as I climb into the elevator with the reporter.

As the doors close, I answer, "To finally find some peace."

Chapter Twelve

MK
September

MK Landry @NoPinkCaddy
Help! If you could rename my site, what would you call it? #NoPinkCaddyNeedsAFacelift

Mandy Jean @ReportersRock
Shaking my head. Need unspoken prayers. So frustrated right now.

"Southern Style. Taste of the South. Cajun Princess. Southern Spice." I rattle off the names that Holden's firm sent me. I purposely don't mention *Burnt Sugar*. It's still growing on me.

Shannon takes a sip of her wine as she props her feet on the eggplant purple ottoman. "God, those are so bad that I'm suddenly craving a bottle of Southern Comfort." A look of disgust distorts her appearance, and she shivers.

I laugh at her very appropriate joke. She's still movie star perfect, but I've changed into grey cotton lounge pants and the over-sized purple LSU t-shirt that I slept in. Vince and I have a date tonight. He wants to take me to dinner at one of his favorite restaurants. He said it's a bit of payback for the muffaletta. I can't imagine what type of food it is, but I'm excited to go. Shannon and I are working until it's time for me to get dressed.

"Do you think No Pink Caddy is bad? I mean honestly. You're taking a nice cut from whatever I make. Give it to me real." I'm propped up on pillows with my legs crossed.

She's quiet for a bit while her eyes check out the ceiling. Finally, she says, "I see their point. I didn't understand what No Pink Caddy meant and had to ask you. It's a very southern thing."

Nodding, I reply, "That's fair."

"But you've also been using it for a long time. I can see why you want to call the store that. But it's not a good name if someone hits the guide button and is looking for something interesting to watch. It says nothing about who you are."

Now it's my turn to be silent as I contemplate what she said. She's right. No one would choose to watch *No Pink Caddy*. It doesn't make sense. I will not compromise on the name for the store, but maybe I can be open to a different name for the show.

My head falls back against the headboard as I open my mind to let ideas flow. Words like hurricane, cayenne pepper, crawfish, mint julep, and bourbon ping pong around. I flip and try to piece them together.

Shannon throws out jazz terms playing on New Orleans's love of that style of music. I counter with some of our famous dishes like jambalaya and etouffee. We both agree that etouffee is a terrible name for a show.

"This is harder than naming a baby." I throw my hands up in defeat. Then I toss out the name that Holden and his team liked. "What do you think of *Burnt Sugar*?"

Shannon wrinkles her nose.

"You use burnt sugar to make caramel and pralines. Holden felt it was sort of a metaphor for my life. Like it was supposed to be sugary and very sweet, but it wound up like burnt sugar. Dumped by the college boyfriend, working for his family's company, batting zero in the love area, but I didn't give up. I took the sugar that I thought I couldn't use and turned it into something new and different. That's my blog and now, after my breakup, the reality show."

Her head turns to the side and her mouth twists as if she's contemplating what I'm saying.

I continue, "Pralines are darn tasty. There's nothing wrong with pralines but they aren't light or fluffy like cake. They're dense." I burst out laughing. "And a little nutty."

It's as if the smooth plaster of her face cracks, and I catch a glimpse of the real Shannon. Her smile is gorgeous. "Burnt Sugar is you—hardheaded and crazy."

Picking up one of the hotel bed's throw pillows, I toss it at Shannon as we both giggle.

A knock on my hotel door disrupts our light-hearted moment. "Coming," I yell. I tell Shannon, "They shorted me washcloths."

Crawling off the bed, I walk to the door, grabbing some wadded-up ones out of my wallet to use for a tip. My hand grips the door knob, turning it to the right.

In an instant, I'm sure I've slipped back in time—ten months exactly. My mind doesn't have a chance to register who is standing there before I'm pushed up against the wall just inside my room and his mouth slams into mine. His tongue, not asking for permission, swipes over my clenched teeth. He uses one arm to pin my hands over my head as the dollars tumble to the carpet just like my defenses. His knee works to spread my thighs. He's frenzied and wild and smells of whiskey and sweat. His hair gets trapped between our lips, and his free fingers yank it angrily away.

Stunned is an understatement. I never thought I would see or hear from Aaron again, let alone find his tongue attempting to persuade my jaw to unclench.

This feels surreal and unbelievable as if I'm watching this happen to someone else. I'm numb. Did I fall asleep while brainstorming? Is this the equivalent to a wet dream? The warm breath tastes of Aaron. The lips feel like Aaron's—soft and full. But surely this is not him. He's ignored me. He's done things to purposely hurt me. He's a bastard who turned his back, leaving me in his cold, dark shadow.

Finally, my brain registers that yes, this is indeed Aaron manhandling my body, and I'm not okay with it. My head jerks to the side, breaking our kiss. "Get off me. What do you think you're doing?" My voice is high-pitched and cracks as I try to catch my breath.

His eyes meet mine as he steps back but not far enough that I would call him out of my personal space, and he doesn't release my hands. "I can't help myself," he pants as he drags his fingers through his much longer than when we were together blond hair.

Wiggling my hands free, I push him further away as my eyes glance to Shannon. I think I may have shocked the woman who's seen it all. "Everything okay?" She's got her cell phone in hand as if she's not sure if she should call the police.

Aaron turns to the door apparently just now realizing that there's someone else in the room. His face is flushed.

"Is everything okay?" Shannon asks again.

That's a great question, and I have no idea. "Shannon, why don't you head home? I'll meet you at the airport tomorrow. Thanks for all your help today."

Aaron remains facing the doorjamb as if he's put himself in time out.

She mouths *That's Johnny Knite.*

Nodding, I roll my eyes. I'm not sure why. It feels childish, but right now, I just can't seem to process anything so I blame it on the Aaron affect.

She shakes her head as Aaron keeps his back to her as he walks over to the hotel room window, looking out at my view of the parking garage.

As soon as the door closes I ask, "Are you crazy?" My voice has lost the squeaky effect, and it's dropped an octave sounding as if I'm a monster in a horror film. "We aren't even friends, acquaintances. You have a girlfriend, and I have a new life. What're you doing here?"

His hands clasp behind his head, and he leans forward pressing his forehead against the glass. Back muscles strain against the thin cotton shirt. In a deep, soft voice, he gulps, "I can't move on."

My blood pressure must hit stroke levels because my face feels as if it's on fire. My heart is beating loudly in my ears. I want to hit him. I've never in my life so badly wanted to throw a punch, breaking his straight, perfect nose. "Lucky for you, I have," I reply through my clenched jaw with nails imbedded in my palms. "I waited, Aaron. I messaged you. And called you. I gave you chance after chance and made excuse after excuse as to why you walked out of my life and never returned. You told me you were working to fix yourself. You . . ."

He turns around, shoving his hands deep into the pockets of his worn jeans. His chin almost touches his chest. Blonde strands of hair shield either side of his face. "You abandoned me."

Licking my lips, I reply, "I don't have time for this or you. Get out of my hotel room, and stay out of my life." My body vibrates with anger. Aaron's reappearance is the absolute last thing I need right now.

"You're shaking." When he picks his head up, his cheeks are flushed, and he looks as if he's aged five years since I saw him last. He takes two steps toward me, but my hand flies out in front.

"Stop." Tears slide down my cheeks, and I'm furious with myself for crying. I've shed enough tears over Aaron Emerson. He doesn't deserve any more.

"Sweetheart, I didn't come here to make you upset." His forehead forms a *V* as if he's completely confused.

The back of my hand swipes under my eyes. "Well, you have. Go. Get out of my hotel room. Whatever we had is dead and buried. Go pour your heart out in a new album about the new girlfriend and forget I ever existed."

He throws his arms up. "But that's just it, MK. I don't understand this, but whatever we had or have hasn't gone away. I don't want to think about you. I don't want to almost puke every time I have to sing the songs I wrote about you. I want to move on also, but I can't. I'm stuck in MK purgatory where you haunt my nights and fill my days. Where there's no one else but you. It's like I was able to push you away, and then all of sudden one little reminder, and I'm fucking obsessed."

"Ha," I scoff as I walk over and flop on the seat abandoned by Shannon. My feet rest on the ottoman as my arms cross over my chest. "Does your girlfriend know you feel this way? If I was her, I'd punch you in the balls. You're pathetic."

He rolls his eyes as they cut to the floor.

"Get out, Aaron." I sound as drained as I feel. "My life and my heart are closed. The door with your name on it has been nailed shut." Swallowing hard, I tell the biggest lie ever told. "You were two weeks that ultimately meant nothing. A good fuck, and that's it."

My heart threatens to break again along the fissures that were just beginning to scab over. His shoulders slump, and his head hangs. I feel as if I've kicked a poor, pathetic beast turned out into the streets who once knew love and affection and then cruelly had it removed.

"I don't believe you," he says as he toes an imaginary spot on my carpet with the blunted end of his motorcycle boot. As he moves, my necklace slips from the confines of his blue brushed-cotton shirt. The light catches the silver shark tooth, making it glimmer.

Before I can stop myself, I charge him like a crazed bull seeing red. My feet move without my brain's permission. My hand clasps around the braided jute cord. He grasps my forearm, preventing me from yanking it from his neck. His other arm wraps around my back as his lips brush over mine. This time his kiss is chaste, sweet, tender. He repeats the word *mine* while his soft lips dot my jaw.

My muscles relax as my body accepts what my brain cannot. My heart recognizes its other half. I melt into his torso. He releases my arm and weaves his fingers into my hair. His groan bounces off the hotel walls when I bite his bottom lip.

"See, sweetheart? I was so much more to you than just a good fuck," he whispers in my ear.

His words snap me back to reality. I step away and smooth my rumpled shirt. "This changes nothing, Aaron. Go back to your tour and your girlfriend. But give me back my necklace first."

That smile. The one that makes me want to melt. Well, he gives me that smile. "Never." He kisses the silver charm. "Come to my show tonight."

One would have to be blind or deaf to miss the billboards and buzz in the LA air about ACE's show tonight. Two sold-out nights. I've been doing my best to ignore the billboards, signs, commercials, and fanfare about ACE's comeback tour. In fact, I didn't even see the sign right outside of Holden's office window. Nope. Never saw it.

"How did you know I was here?"

He smirks. "You live life like a vagabond."

"You used *Find My Friends*?" I'm indignant and have the overwhelming urge to slap that smug look right off his face.

He shrugs. "You never deleted me."

Of course, I didn't. Never occurred to me to do so. And now I'm just angry at myself. "Stalker." My arms cross over my chest. "So all this time you knew exactly where I was but just chose to not find me . . . Return a call . . .Text . . .Nothing." Turning away from his penetrating eyes, I find an interesting spot on the wall. "Get out." Although I don't sound like I want him to leave at all.

His hand brushes my hair over my shoulder as he stands so close behind me that I can feel the magnetic pull between us. Kisses dot the base of my neck. "I'm an asshole, MK." He works his way to my ear. "Does it make you feel better to hear me say the words?"

With barely a shake of my head, I reply, "No. It actually doesn't."

The fire in my gut returns. My eyes narrow as I spin around and into his sculpted chest. He doesn't step back so I do. "You say a lot of words. Sing them also. You left me to deal with the onslaught of media. You left me in limbo. You made me a fool. I've spent too long hating you. Now, I nothing you."

"What the hell does that mean?" His penetrating glare feels as if it's boring into my soul.

I open the door inside my chest where I've stored all the unhealthy feelings I have towards him and let the words flow. "It means that I realized to hate you as much as I did was because I still harbored some sort of love. I've reached the point that you mean nothing to me. I don't hate you. I don't love you. I don't like you. I nothing you."

His smirk is cocky, but the crack in his voice lets me know that he has some doubts. "You responded to my kiss, MK. I felt you."

"You left me confused and alone. You sent me the album then never responded. You told me you were trying. I had so many reporters in front of my carriage house that the New Orleans police had to come. I've been called horrible names, had my reputation slandered, been harassed by your fans, and my privacy violated. And the whole time you could have done something to stop it all, but you didn't." Shaking my head, I add, "I wouldn't treat my worst enemy how you treated the person you were supposed to love."

I watch the man that I once thought I knew transform before my eyes. He changes from the mild-mannered, funny guy who was quick with a provocative comment, eating a bowl of cereal, who always seemed a bit unsure of himself when it came to me, and into the big bad wolf. I got a taste of this side of Aaron at the dinner with his band, but he never turned that anger in my direction. He grows to seven feet tall and bends over me as if his arms are tree branches caught in a raging storm. Then he bellows like a wild man, "You. Gave. Up. On. Me."

I back down to no one. Standing toe to toe with him, I poke my finger into his breastbone. "You were high and not rational, even schizophrenic. You'd just gotten out of rehab. I wanted you to go back to your house and sleep it off." My fingertip bends at an odd angle, hurting like crazy from pushing too hard into his chest. The pain feels raw and real, and I cling to it as proof that this isn't a dream. "I wanted you to call your doctor and seek his advice after telling him you'd used. I thought we were taking a twelve-hour break, maybe even a day. I had no idea when you left that the next time I saw you again, you'd be releasing an album written about me, and then having to see pictures of some girl draped all over you." I swallow the too much extra spit and fight to keep the tears from falling down my cheeks again. "I thought we'd hit our first pothole, but we'd work through it."

He's still just as fierce. His blue eyes are almost black. "You told me to be the whole and complete man that you deserve. What'd you expect me to do? Hang around so I could continue disappointing you?"

I see something new in Aaron's twisted expression, and my stomach does a funny little flip. For the first time, a tiny crack appears in the metal door protecting my soul from him. "I hurt you," I whisper. This is a new revelation. In all the time I've spent analyzing what went wrong, it never occurred to me that I was the problem. That I was the one who pushed him away.

He drops to the edge of the bed and buries his face in his hands. I walk to him, positioning myself between his spread thighs, wrapping my arms around his back. His left cheek presses against my worn LSU shirt. "I'm sorry," I tell him as I kiss the top of his head.

His arms lock around the small of my back, and he embraces me as if he loosens his grip, I might disappear.

Our moment is ruined by the vibrating of his phone.

"Answer it."

"No," he replies with a sigh.

The phone stops buzzing for a moment, but then starts up again.

"Fuck," he mumbles as he releases me, and I walk over to my own phone left on the bed-side table.

"What?" he angrily asks the person who dared to call interrupting our moment.

I open the *Find My Friends* app on my phone and go to delete Aaron but pause before confirming. Closing the app, I open my messages. There's one from Vince letting me know that he's picking me up from my hotel at seven o'clock. It's six-thirty, and I still don't know what I'm wearing.

Trying to ignore Aaron's side of the conversation, I walk over to my bag and rummage through the clothes I brought. I can't help but overhear Aaron growling. "Fine. Then send a car here. I'm sure the over-paid wardrobe girl has another shitty shirt and worn pair of jeans."

I extract a white eyelet sundress from my bag.

He pulls the phone away from his mouth and motions with his pointer finger. "Awesome. Wear that one." Aaron's tone is much gentler. Then his phone returns to the side of his face. "Tell the doctor not to leave. I'll be there shortly."

When he hangs up, I ask, "Why are you seeing a doctor?"

He rolls his eyes at my question. "No panties under the dress."

I drape the article of clothing over my arm. "You're giving me underwear advice for my date? Are you crazy? Did you not just hear when I made it clear that I don't want a damn thing to do with you."

"Yeah, but you don't mean it. You get annoyed with me, and then you forgive and forget. I'm going to play the whole show with a raging hard on." The expression on his face can only be described as lusty. His eyes are heavy, and his smile says he thinks he's going to get to remove this dress.

"Oh. You think I'm going to your concert." My head shakes back and forth, and my laugh is rueful. "Not on your life. I have a date tonight, and it's not with you."

His face screws into a crazy contorted Picasso-style expression. "Who in the fuck are you going on a date with?

"None of your business. Go do your show. Sing the songs you wrote about me." Then I lie just because I'm still angry at him, and I want to inflict pain. "I'm going to assume that you showing up here is nothing more than you hoping to get laid."

"Come on, MK. Don't do this." He pulls me to him and throws the dress on the carpet. "Ditch the guy. Come to my concert. I swear to God I will not molest you one little bit after it's over. We can go get ice cream and watch a Disney movie."

Shaking my head, I sound resolved when I reply, "I'm glad you came by, but, Aaron, there's nothing left for us. Give me back my necklace, and you can move on just like I have. I'm sure your girlfriend wouldn't be pleased that you're here."

"We're over. We have been." He drags his hand through his long hair. The last bit of sun pours through the hotel window, highlighting his body with a yellow hue. *He really is the golden boy.* "I need you back in my life. It's not about the sex; it's about something in here." He touches his heart as he licks his lips. "Please don't go out with this guy. Please come to my show. Please stay up all night and just talk to me. Please help me to feel whole again."

Like a coward, I distract myself from his pleas by picking up my dress. Looking towards the wall because my heart will not allow me to see the hurt in his eyes, I reply, "I can't. I. Nothing. You."

I run into the bathroom, closing and locking the door behind me. When I hear the hotel room door slam with a loud bang, I sink to the edge of the bathtub and have myself a good, old-fashioned meltdown. My chest heaves with sobs as I gasp for air. Trembling hands make it difficult to grab a tissue from the box, and I wind up using the hem of my shirt.

I was over him. I'd picked up the pieces of my shattered world and reassembled them into something better and stronger, or so I thought. Then, one surprise visit from my rock star, and I realize that I love him just as much as I did ten months ago. My feelings never faded. I just learned how to bury them deeper in the dark confines of my heart.

Once I've physically expunged the tornado of emotions that escaped through the crack in the metal door, I'm completely mentally and physically dead. I pick my withered body up from the cold hotel tile.

It crosses my mind to cancel on Vince, but I quickly determine that's letting Aaron win. Seeing him is only a setback in reclaiming my life. I refuse to spend a lonely night in this room shedding more tears over Mister Emerson. So instead, I pull myself together, clean my face, get dressed, and meet Vince in the lobby only thirty minutes late.

Chapter Thirteen

Aaron
September

MK Landry @NoPinkCaddy
Goodbye LA! As always, you never disappoint. I'm so ready to be home.

Rock Star Groupies @RockStarGroupies
Rep for @VivaValdez has confirmed that her and @RealJohnnyKnite are no longer a couple. #LookOutSanFran

Johnny Knite @RealJohnnyKnite
Hey San Francisco! Y'all ready for ACE? Let me hear you tonight. #LoveThisCity

"Hi, MK, this is . . . ummmm . . . Aaron. I don't really know what to say. I . . .ummmm . . . haven't left a voicemail for anyone ever. I think. Well, maybe Jude, but it was more of a you-were-supposed-to-be-home-thirty-minutes-ago-and-now-I-think-you're-dead sorta message." I cup my hand around the phone so the guys will not overhear. "I've texted you, and you haven't responded. It's been a week and—"

The robotic voice asks if I'd like to review my message. Delete.

Picking up my plastic Solo cup filled with bourbon and a splash of water,

I take a sip before I start again. "MK, fucking return a message. I saw you deleted me from *Find My Friends.* Why? Call me back."

Sighing, I hit one and erase that message also.

Rolling my shoulders and stretching my neck to let the tension out, I try again. "I hate that you went on a date, and I hate that you will not call me back. I can't accept that you nothing me. I'm not sleeping or eating. I just need to talk to you. I just need to figure out how I can make you see how good we can be together. And . . . I'm a pathetic fucking creeper."

I delete that one too. We're in San Francisco tonight and taking the stage in ten minutes, but I can't seem to find any peace. Seeing her. Kissing her. It's left me completely out of sorts.

The crowd chants "ACE" so loudly that the cement walls vibrate. The band members are each doing their own thing to get pumped up. Billy has Sam pushed against a speaker with his hand up her short leather skirt. Rock is doing push-ups where he claps in between, and I'm . . . well, I'm being a pathetic fuck.

One more try . . .

"Hey, MK. I'm about to take the stage, but I thought I'd leave you a message. Call me, and I can talk after the show. K. Bye." That was good. I sounded upbeat—reasonable and not neurotic.

"It's time," Jose says as he hands my guitar to me.

It slides easily over my head and across my body. I flex my hand and have a silent conversation with myself, willing me to get through this show without any craziness. The doctor I saw in LA had his nurse do x-rays and take all my blood. Fucking vampire. I should have the results in the next couple of days. He asked the best question though: *Have I been under any stress?* I wanted to laugh. Where should I begin? Rehab? Breakup with MK? First tour in five years? Having to sing her songs? Being constantly asked about my muse in every new city we arrive in? Jude in one ear begging me to make things right with MK? Grace who still isn't really talking to me? The fact I haven't fucked anything but my hand in months? That my fingers feel as if they've been electrocuted? That I was brave enough to visit MK, and she blew me off and went on a date?

What would I have to be stressed about?

Handing Jose my phone, I take my position. The crowd chants "*ACE*" even louder—if that's possible. The air is electric. Sam and Billy finish their thing, and the rest of the band runs out on stage. A giant screen-printed image of the cover of our album acts as a stage curtain. Lights illuminate the image, and I smile when I see the shark tooth necklace. Reaching up, I run my finger over the sharp edge of the tooth, thinking of nothing but her.

As the curtain falls, the opening hard-driving notes of *Forked Tongue* are served up raw and edgy for the crowd. They lose their collective mind. It's a get-the-party-started sort of jam. No matter how many times we've begun a show with this song, it never gets old. My heart beats in time with the drums, my hands shake, and I bounce on my toes in anticipation of greeting the screaming masses. This will always be my drug of choice. Quickly my brain adds *and MK,* but I push that thought away.

On cue, I stroll onto the stage, strumming my guitar. As soon as the crowd spies me, there's a loud roar. Nodding, I take my place in front of the mic stand.

For the next two hours, I own the crowd's heart, soul, and mind. I play for them like my life depends on it and in some ways, it does. This is the only thing that isn't fucked up in my world.

I sing to the crowd. They return my words—the words I've written. I tell them I love them, and they yell it back. I've had fans say that my music saved their lives, and they conceived their children while listening to my voice. It's a high, and one that I never want to come down from.

For one hundred and twenty minutes, we are one, and my life is perfect. But like all good things, it must eventually come to an end.

I hand my guitar to Jose, and take a towel from someone, using it to wipe the sweat that runs down my cheeks and drips off my chin. My fingers beckon for the device I've become tethered to.

Jose hands me my phone, and I immediately check for missed calls and texts like I'm a high school girl waiting to be asked to the prom. My heart skips a beat when I see I've a missed call from MK.

I let the guys continue walking towards the dressing room as I duck into a doorway to listen to her voice. Eagerly, I type in my password because my hand is shaking so that the finger-reader can't recognize my thumbprint. I hit the voicemail button and bring the phone to my ear.

"Aaron, I've gotten your messages and voicemail." Her voice is like a song to my ear. I catch myself smiling when she says my real name. "I didn't want you to think I was purposely ignoring you. My life is complicated right now, and I'm only focusing on No Pink Caddy. I think it would be best if you and I didn't talk or see each other for a while—or ever." My stomach clinches at her words. "I'm really glad you came by my hotel room. It was nice getting proof of life and wishing you well. Give Jude a hug from me." She pauses for a second. "And please send my necklace back."

Staring at my phone in disbelief, I save her message. She can't blow me off that easily. I didn't get to be the front man for one of the most successful rock bands of all times, named after me, by taking no for an answer.

I want to call her, but I know it's the middle of the night in New Orleans. Contemplating, I decide that I don't give a damn. The phone rings three times before she says in a sleepy voice, "Hello."

"Fuck you," I tell her as I walk to my dressing room. "Tell me, MK, that seeing me hasn't fucked your world. Tell me that you haven't thought about me every waking minute and reminisce about the time we shared."

She sighs. "Aaron, it's after two in the morning. If I hadn't been asleep, I wouldn't have answered your call. Go have sex with a groupie and leave me alone."

I let my dressing room door slam behind me. The banging sound reflects my pissed off mood. "You're frustrating me." My hand drags through my sweat-soaked hair. "If it's your goal to drive me crazy, well, it's working. I don't want to fuck anyone else. I want to hold you and kiss your neck and watch you roll your eyes at something I say. I want to cook dinner with you and laugh at some dumb sitcom we agree to only watch together. Why can't you believe that?" Pacing, I hang my head.

"Because when you want those things you don't leave the other person hung out to dry. You don't purposely inflict pain on them." She sounds very awake now. "You don't leave them because you got mad and took your toys and flew back to Austin. You certainly don't leave them to be tabloid gossip and to deal with the storm of media that descended on their front lawn. People went through my garbage, and paid my second-grade teacher for a tad bit of gossip about me." She pauses for a heartbeat. "You released the album written about me and then forced me to read all the speculation that circulated on Twitter about who the girl is."

"Dick move." I kick an imaginary ball, and then pull my wet shirt over my head, tossing it on the ground. "So how long are you going to punish me for being an asshole?"

"I'm not punishing you. This isn't some sort of test where I'm going to make you walk through hot coals to earn your way back into my life." She pauses. "I know this is going to come as a huge shock to you, but you don't get everything you want by stomping your booted foot."

There's a knock on my door. "Hold on," I tell her. Then to the door, I yell, "What?"

Grace's muffled voice says, "They're ready for you at the meet and greet."

"Be there in a minute," I reply not planning on going anywhere until I get MK to understand that she's being pig-headed. Then, into the phone, I tell her, "I just want you to give us another chance. I fucked up and so did you." She coughs and I continue, "I might have fucked up worse than you. Whatever. Don't slam the door on us."

"Pumpkin, there's not a door for me to slam. When you left me alone to deal with the public mess you created, you showed me the kind of person you really are." I've never heard her so cold and angry.

"When I saw you in LA, you felt it too. I know you did. You melted into my kiss, sweetheart. You can say we're over, and you can fly your single flag all over your site, but we'll never be finished. Your heart still belongs to me. You just have to come to that conclusion on your own." I end the call and toss my phone on the cushion next to me.

Fucking MK. Why can't she just move past me being an asshole and embrace the new and improved version of me? I'm different this time.

Chapter Fourteen

MK
September

LE @ LEFlyGirl
Fucking just admit it @NoPinkCaddy you're who @RealJohnnyKnite wrote #AlisVolatPropriis about.

LE @ LEFlyGirl
@NoPinkCaddy you're a fraud. You only share the sugary parts of your life. #SoOverYou

MK Landry @NoPinkCaddy
Filming more B roll today. I'm going to be out and about around #NOLA. If you see me, give me a wave.

I never went back to sleep last night. After he hung up on me, I thought about firing off some nasty texts. In my mind, they were freaking gold. I even added extra exclamation points and everything to make him understand why I'm so over him.

Instead of typing my hateful words into my phone, I got up and went for a run. I'm not an exercise kind of girl, but sometimes my feet slamming against the concrete mimics the feeling of punching a certain someone in their smug grill and releases a bit of the tension.

"Okay, MK, we want a shot of you dancing down this block of Bourbon Street," Cindy instructs. "The camera will start at Saint Peter and follow you to the corner of Toulouse. This will probably be used for the opening credits so ham it up."

It's a Thursday in the French Quarter, and the sounds of jazz mixed with *Turn Down For What* blend together in the most interesting sort of way. It's kind of like gumbo. I can't explain why it's so good, it just is. "Got it." I give her a thumbs up.

Grumpy Eugene motions with his hand, and I sashay my way down the black asphalt. It's early so the people surrounding me are mostly sober tourists. I know this because they stop and stare. Native New Orleans folks could care less if there's a camera. Ignoring them, I do a little turn and shuffle step when I reach the middle of the block.

Margo, my stylist, has me dressed in skinny jeans, an aqua blouse that ties right above my belly button, and black heels that are like five inches tall. This outfit was not designed for dancing.

When I reach the stop sign, I do a little shimmy that drops my behind just above the nasty concrete but not touching it. That would be disgusting.

Cindy yells, "Cut." Then she turns to me. "That was awesome, honey. I especially liked the twerk at the end."

Wrinkling my nose, I tell her, "As if."

We both laugh.

"Okay, I want a shot with you and a Lucky Dog cart," Cindy says and the crew of people follow her to the next block. Fortunately, the hog dog vendors are a dime a dozen on Bourbon Street. They're so popular that John Kennedy Toole featured them in his book *Confederacy of Dunces.* He called them Paradise Hot Dogs, but any good New Orleans girl knows who he was referring to.

The gentleman signs the waiver and three different cameras get shots of me ordering and taking a bite out of the Bourbon Street staple.

"Next we're going to film you around Jackson Square. Sound good?"

Nodding, we begin walking the two blocks towards the river.

Bella catches up with me. "Remember that old show we used to watch at

Grandmother's when she thought we were 'napping' at like the age of nine?"

"*The Mary Tyler Moore Show*?" I ask.

"Yeah that one. You filming walking down the street reminded me of the opening credits where she tosses her hat," Bella says as she locks her arm with mine.

"Ha. That's a compliment. We loved that show." We walk around a chunk of sidewalk that's missing. "Guess who called in the middle of the night?"

She hip bumps me. "Your life is so much more interesting than mine. Rock stars chase you down and profess their love. Instead, I sleep next to boring old Nyall who snores just a wee bit."

"Trade you my neurotic rock star for your stable, practical minded Brit any day." We both scoff at my absurd statement. "He's so adamant that we should get back together. He says all the things that a girl wants to hear, but let's be real. He's made his fortune writing and singing songs that make women throw their panties at him."

"Are you one of them?" We turn left on Chartres and continue walking towards the square.

"I want to believe him. Like if I could look into the future and know that he's sincere, I'd probably at least be able to have a conversation with him without wanting to squeeze and twist his balls."

She lets go of my arm. "They say that absence makes the heart grow fonder. Maybe you guys needed to break up and go through those awful months to arrive in a better place. Like maybe you'll look back at this time as the best thing that ever happened to you instead of the worst of times."

I pick my hair off my neck and pray for a cool breeze. "Maybe. He's on tour for the next four months so I figure I'll just continue blowing him off. If he's still adamant about us giving this relationship another try, I'll deal with it then."

"Jesus, MK, he's not a disease. You make him sound like he's cancer or taxes or the mortgage payment."

"I guess he kind of is. I'd moved on. Then, once again, he barrels into my life, and I realize after seeing him, that yes, I still have strong feelings for him. I'm just not sure I'll ever be able to forgive him for what he did to my life."

Our crew arrives at Jackson Square. There's a jazz band playing in front of Saint Louis Cathedral. The iron fence surrounding the green space is hung with art by local artisans hoping for a buyer. Horse drawn carriages border the opposite side of the square, waiting for eager tourists to pay for a ride.

Bella says, "I was there for every horrible day. I pushed through the crowds outside of your home, and I've read the nasty things said about you. I forced you to eat and shower and get out of bed. He indirectly caused all that heartache, but he didn't intentionally inflict that on you. It was part of his eighteen-wheeler full of baggage that he warned you about."

We stop walking about twenty feet from the crew and move into the shadow created by the Cathedral. I want to finish this conversation and hold up one finger to Cindy asking for a moment. "I can buy that argument for when we broke up, but dropping his album on the same day I posted we were over was intentional."

She brushes her curls from her face. "Yes. Might be true. But he didn't call the media organizations and say, 'Go over to MK's house. Her life was just getting back to normal.'"

I look at the ground wishing he'd never put me in this position to have to think about him again. Until LA, I thought I'd moved on. Now, I stand in one of my favorite places in the city with my stomach in knots because Bella's words have penetrated the wall built in anger around my heart, and I admit that her points are valid. I need quiet, time, and probably a bottle of wine to figure out exactly where my head is when it comes to Aaron Emerson. "Let's join the crew."

"All right, gang." Cindy claps her hands to get our attention. "First, I want MK to get read by a fortune teller. MK, I'll let you choose your person."

My heart flutters. I've never gotten read before. These ladies have always seemed like quacks. It's a service they perform to pay their rent by scamming tourists out of their dollars. Plus, I've been warned my whole life to stay away from the occult. I don't think Mom or Grandmother would be okay with me doing this. "What about if I look at art instead?"

Cindy scratches her chin. "That's tough. We must pay the artist for the rights to show his or her work. It gets tricky." Her eyes cut to the side. "A fortune teller would really be best."

Nodding, I become resolved that this is what my job is requiring of me.

I don't walk to the lady who is closest to our group. Instead, I scan the faces of the women at card tables in front of the cathedral. Two are in costume—what you would think a fortune teller would look like. The third lady appears as if she got dressed in the dark. She's wearing a New Orleans Saints football jersey, brightly colored head wrap, brown feather earrings that dust along the tops of her shoulders, bright yellow leggings, and black combat boots. There's something about the boots that pull me too her.

"Hi. I'm MK Landry, and I'm filming a reality show. Would you mind telling my fortune on camera?"

The lady is older than me, but I can't tell her age. Her skin seems prematurely wrinkled by the Louisiana sun. "You gonna pay me?"

Cindy is at my side. "We'll pay your fee plus one hundred dollars if you'll sign this sheet of paper." She extracts a single piece of white computer paper from her bag and a blue pen.

"I'm Ruby," she says as she sticks out her hand. "Sit down right there, young lady." She motions at the orange and lime green folding chair in front of her card table.

Then she hands the signed paper to Cindy. "Keep your cameras close. This reading is going to blow your mind."

Glancing at Bella, I see she has an apprehensive look on her face. You can't grow up around New Orleans and not be exposed to the supernatural. It's been called the most haunted city in the country. We have vampire and ghost tours that run nightly. People pay to visit our cemeteries. We bury our dead above ground. To natives, that's what we must do because of the high underground water level. To outsiders, it's different. Also, I'm a good Catholic girl. We don't play with Ouija Boards, evoke the name of the devil, or invite spirits into our lives.

I say a quick prayer.

Dear God,

I know that this is wrong, and I'm sorry that I'm doing it. Please forgive me and know that Cindy made me do it.

Amen

"Give me your hands," Ruby instructs as a gust of wind blows the scarf covering her hair revealing a couple of rust grey strands.

I place my hands on top of her chapped skin. The cameras are on either side of us, and I can tell by their angles that they're concentrating on our connection. The third camera is further back getting a wider shot. She leans over, examining the lines cutting across my palms. Then she sits up, drops her head back, and hums.

I patiently wait for this nonsense to be over.

"Someone you had thought was dead has recently turned up in your life again," Ruby says as her eyes fly open, and her back goes stiff as a board.

Shaking my head, I reply, "Nope. I don't think you're correct." No ghosts in the carriage house last time I checked.

Her hands grasp mine, and her eyes seem to pop out of her head. "Yes. I see him clearly. He looks like a famous person. Long blond hair that touches the middle of his neck and blue eyes."

I was the topic of conversation by the media on and off for five months. She could easily recognize me from the tabloids. My scar is a distinguishing characteristic. But my heart still skips a beat at the crazy idea that she could possibly have a gift. "I don't know anyone that fits that description that has passed away."

Dropping my hands, she does this mystical or jazz dance where she crosses her fingers in front of her face. "He could have been dead to you, and now, he's reentered your life."

Rolling my eyes, I don't care how good this is for TV, I'm annoyed. I lean back. "We all know I dated Johnny Knite for a brief period. We broke up and have moved on."

She leans in very close and motions for me scoot forward. I do as she asks. "Is he the soul that is next to yours? Don't discount him so quickly."

My head snaps to Cindy. We agreed that Aaron would not be a part of my show. My voice is high-pitched mirroring my racing heart. "You paid her to say this for ratings."

Cindy shakes her head and mouths *I did not.* Then says, "You chose the fortune teller."

I face Ruby again. Her eyes roll back in her head and for a moment I think she's having a seizure. "The one you fight is the one you will ultimately choose. But it's not your choice, really. He's the one who has been chosen for you."

My shoulders tighten. "My biological grandfather died before I was born. Surely you can relay a message from him."

Her head falls forward and in a strange, deep voice she says, "He told me to tell you to quit being difficult like Grandmother."

I fly away from the table knocking the chair over in the process. It's like one minute I'm sitting, and the next, I'm thirty feet away panting and hunched over like I've run a marathon. "We're done," I yell to anyone who can hear.

Then, at that very second, my phone buzzes in my jean pocket. Taking it out, I read his words.

> Aaron: *I was so mad at you last night. You make me fucking crazy. But my soul seems to find yours in sleep. They tangoed across an Argentinian graveyard. I woke up more resolved than ever to make us right again. XXXOOO*

Shoving my phone at Bella, I announce to the crew, "I'm done with the French Quarter."

Chapter Fifteen

Aaron
September

Vince Vasquez @RockGod_69
@RealJohnnyKnite be a man, and own your shit. Just confirm that #AlisVolatPropriis was written for that pink girl.

MK Landry @NoPinkCaddy
Filming around #NOLA. Look for me. I'm the girl wearing the uber smile. #LifeIsGood

Betty Frankin'Berry @FrankinBerryChompChomp
Why? Why can't ACE play their newer stuff. Oldies but goodies are fine, but give me #PinkCadillac

Me: *Answer your texts. You're driving me crazy.*

Me: *I'm sorry. You're probably working. I just send you something straight from my heart, and then you ignore it, and it makes me crazy. Tell me to fuck off. Okay. Don't tell me that. It would piss me off. I miss you.*

Staring at the phone screen, I wait for her response. The seconds tick to minutes, and I decide to go for a swim. Ten minutes later, I'm in my trunks headed to the hotel's lap pool with my goggles and towel draped over my arm.

I dive into the water, my hands cutting through the liquid as if they're a knife to warm butter. The lyrics to *Runaway* by Bon Jovi play in my head.

Ten laps.

Fifteen.

Twenty.

Thirty.

My head breaks the water as I grasp the side of the pool. I pull myself up and sit on the edge. Drying my hands, I check my phone. I have a text from MK. Eagerly, I swipe to read her words.

MK: *What makes this time different? How do I know that the next bump in the road you use again and dump me?*

Me: *Stop it. Quit looking to the past. I've told you that I won't do that to you again. Why can't you just trust me?*

MK: *Bella made me see that the aftereffects of our breakup were part of your eighteen-wheeler. I just don't know if I can do this again.*

Me: *I'd give anything to rewind time and change the past. I can't. Please just give me another chance.*

I sit there for longer than I care to admit to waiting for her response before I rest my phone on my towel and dive into the chlorinated water. Never in my life have I had to work so hard to convince another human being to spend time with me. It's like pulling teeth. *Why can't I love someone who's simpler?*

Choosing another song to play in my head, I jam out to *Little Miss Can't Be Wrong.* I lose count at lap twenty-two and just wear myself out to the point that I can barely drag my tired bones out of the pool. My body flops on the cement as a towel hits my wet back. Looking up, I smile at Sam's evil grin. "Get out of the pool, hot shot. Grace is screaming that we have a fan thing in twenty."

"Fuck," I reply as do my best to blend into the tile.

"Lose track of time?" she asks as I fold my body into a seated position.

"Can't lose something that you don't keep." I wrap the towel around my shoulders. My finger is too pruned to log into to my phone so I type the passcode.

MK replied.

> MK: *You're wearing me down. Do you want me because I'm tired of fighting? Please just leave me alone.*

I walk back to my hotel room to change. After I'm showered, dressed, and have a stiff bourbon in my hand, I text her back.

> Me: *I want you any way I can get you. I prefer you compliant.*

Reading what I wrote, it sounds stalkerish. I don't want to be the creepy fucker again.

> Me: *I don't mean it like that. I just feel like if you gave us a chance, you'd see that I'm going to work really hard to make us okay. I've tasted life without you, and it's bitter. I now know what's on the line.*

Holding my phone, I will her to reply. I need her response before I must smile, shake hands, and kiss the cheeks of all my biggest fans.

Finally, as I'm walking out the door, I hear the ding of my phone.

> MK: *God, I so want to believe you. Unfortunately, the security fence around my carriage house reminds me that I must protect my heart.*

Her words are like a knife in my chest. Hitting the phone icon next to her name, I wait for MK to answer.

"Why do you doubt me?" I ask with a furrowed brow.

She sniffs. "Let me tell you about my day. I had to dance down Bourbon Street, hold a baby gator, eat oysters on the half shell, and get read by a fortune teller. I know that probably sounds great to you, but I'm tired, Aaron. Do you have any understanding what it's like to open myself up every single day to a camera crew while I have you texting me pleas that make me feel raw?"

With a smirk, I reply, "I'll make it easy on you. Just agree to give me a second chance, and we can cross off one of your perceived problems."

Grace texts me a nasty message telling me I'm needed downstairs in the ballroom ASAP. I ignore it and continue talking to MK.

"You're like the bird dog my step-grandfather had when I was a kid." She pauses and clears her throat. "He would take him hunting around rural Louisiana. The dog could retrieve a fallen dove like no other, but he was a jerk to live with. Grandmother would lock him in a kennel in the backyard when we came over because he would try to grasp us in his jaws and bring us to my grandfather. The dog found no pleasure in life other than retrieving."

I laugh. "You're comparing me to an animal."

"Don't be dense, Aaron. You want me because I'm a challenge. You like the thrill of the hunt just like the bird dog. You won't care about me once you think you've conquered Mount MK." Her voice is harsh.

Shaking my head, I stare at the phone. "I guess you've got to at least give me a chance to spend time with you to see if that's true. Right now, you're so dead set that I'm wrong for you that you can't entertain the idea that I just might be your happily ever after."

The phone is silent as another text from Grace comes through.

Grace: *Get your ass down here. We've got a line of people out the door waiting to meet you.*

Me: *Coming*

"Aaron," MK says in a solemn voice. "Please just give me some time." She pauses and then whispers, "You scare me."

"MK—"

She cuts me off. "My brain says to run far, far away, but you're right. My heart wants to believe you so desperately that I'm influencing fortune tellers to whisper exactly what I want to hear."

"What?" I ask as I close my hotel suite door.

"Never mind," she sighs. "I need space to think."

"Grace is texting. I'm late for a fan event." Swallowing, I reach deep into the pit of my stomach and rummage around until I find the courage to make my boldest move yet. "I want to see you again. After my show, I'm going to take my plane to New Orleans. Don't tell me no. Just give me a chance to spend some time showing you how great we can be again."

The line is silent, and I feel like my life hangs in the balance. I'm a man walking a tight wire over Niagara Falls. I'd like to order her to just do what I say. It's how I've managed my career. I bark and people jump. MK doesn't take orders. I must compel her to give us another chance—prove to her that we can be better the second time around. "Don't tell me no, sweetheart. Don't look back on this moment and have huge regrets."

Then, the most beautiful word that I've heard in a long, long time reaches my ears. "Okay."

Chapter Sixteen

MK

September

MK Landry @NoPinkCaddy
Tomorrow we begin filming. Crazy excited. Watch out world. Here comes #NoPinkCaddy

Kyle Reid @NOLALove_143
@NoPinkCaddy move your shit. I can't find a place to park. Too many damn people on Magazine Street.

Shannon: *Your call time is 8:30 am. Don't be late! I'll meet you at your trailer.*

Oh my God! I have a call time and a trailer. I read the text for like the hundredth time. I've been up since five because I was too nervous to sleep, and then when I did doze, I dreamed that I was being held against my will by pirates who wouldn't release me, and I missed my call time. I've showered, blown out my hair, put cream on my scar, and made coffee. Now, I'm sitting down at my trusty Mac to share the beginning of my day with my fans.

Short and sweet . . . Today is the big day. Today, we begin transforming my dream location into my dream store. I'm nervous, like first-day-at-a-

new-school-and-you-don't-know-anyone-and-have-never-been-inside-the-building nervous. I'm excited. I've dreamt of this day for so many years. It never occurred to me to dream about a lifestyle show to go along with it.

I pause for a second and dab at my eyes.

I'm also weepy. I try to not live my life in hyper drive, forgetting to stop and smell the roses. Today, I'm going to try to remember every detail and absorb every second of it. I want to look back on this day when I'm one hundred years old and still recall every moment. At my funeral, my grandchildren should be able to retell the story of the day that Granny turned her dreams into a reality.

Taking a sip of coffee, I reread what I've written, laughing at my granny reference.

I'm going to do my best to post pics and updates as much as I can, but who knows? I may be sworn to secrecy. All new to me.

Here's something fun for you guys. No Pink Caddy will open its doors in three short weeks. The grand opening will be filmed for the show. Local to New Orleans? Fill out this form, and you just might win a chance to be the first to check it out.

Muah,

MK

I look at the clock on the microwave; it's a little before seven. I get the brilliant idea to make a couple of batches of cookies. The first meeting I presided over as president of my sorority, I baked cookies and made sure that every girl got one. How can you be mean and negative when your stomach is filled with ooey-gooey chocolatey goodness?

I always have ingredients on hand. Grabbing them from the cabinet by the refrigerator, I pour the flour, chocolate chips, caramel chips, baking soda, sugar, and already beaten eggs into my aqua Mixmaster.

Turning on the Britney Spears Pandora station, I sing, ". . . *Baby one more time,*" as I dance around the kitchen. My bottle of cooking spray turns into a bedazzled microphone. My hip swing spins me around, and I punch in three hundred and fifty degrees, setting the oven. I'm on fire. Seriously, I should film myself and campaign to be one of Britney's back-up dancers.

I don't remember a buzzing sound in the song? When I hear it again, it dawns on me that it isn't my phone. It's the call box on my gate.

Pausing the music, I answer, "Hello."

"Flowers for Miss Landry," a male voice says.

"Ohhhh," I squeal. "Just a second."

I turn off the mixer and walk outside.

The delivery guy is shielded by the most obnoxious display of flowers I've ever seen. It looks to be an arrangement that would be sent to a funeral, definitely not a good-luck-on-your-first-day bouquet. After opening the gate, I sort of balance it on my hip while I sign his paperwork. We wish each other a good day, and I carry the behemoth thing into the carriage house being extra careful not to drop it.

After resting it on the counter, I dig through the baby's breath, green fern, pink carnations, pink roses, and something else pink that I've never seen before to find the card.

My dearest MK,

Good luck today! Just know, I'm your biggest ducking fan. I'll be at your place at 8:00 tonight. We're going to dinner, and the rest of the night is up to you. Thanks for agreeing to give us a second chance.

Love,

Aaron

I laugh at the ducking reference. That was cute, clever, and funny but also tells me he received all the texts that I sent.

Staring at the card and then the flowers and then at the card again, I wonder if I'm making a huge mistake. His timing couldn't be any worse. I'm in the middle of filming the renovation of my store. I've got merchandising meetings and employees to hire. My focus should be one hundred percent on that. I don't have the time or energy to deal with the needy rock star.

Grabbing my phone, I type . . .

> Me: *Look, I shouldn't have agreed to seeing you. I can't focus on my career and a relationship right now. I'm sorry. Let's reconnect when your tour is over, and I'm further along in filming.*

I don't send it. I can't quite compel my finger to hit the up-arrow button. Instead I leave my phone resting on the counter.

Grace's words flood my brain. *"You'll see, my darling. I'm warning you right now—you're his play-thing, his new addiction. He'll tire of you when life gets rough—when the honeymoon is over. When you're no longer the new hotness. A new one will come along, and you'll be like the rest of us—lost in his shadow."*

Am I the new toy that he wants and can't have? Will I once again give in to him and then be thrown away when life hits a speed bump? The difference is now I'll be forced to discuss it on my show.

Looking back at the funeral spread, I shake my head. I don't have a clue what to do with it so I take a picture and send it to Bella.

> Me: *Flowers from Aaron. Drop by my place, and get rid of this. Nursing home? Hospital? Cemetery? Your choice. I'll leave the card for you to read next to it.*

I go back to making my cookies and try not to think about tonight. I have the most important day of my No Pink Caddy life so far, and I will not be derailed by Aaron Emerson and his date and the text telling him to go away and the hideous flowers.

After the dough is in the oven and the timer has been set, the nagging mother voice in my head reaches a fever pitch. I grab my phone deleting the text I had written.

Me: *Thank you for the flowers. I have no idea what my schedule will be today. If your only reason for coming is to see me, you might want to reconsider.*

It's much more passive-aggressive than what I had previously written. Part of me is kicking my own behind. But there's this tiny speck in my heart that wants to believe that Aaron's sincere. It's the part that remembers what it's like to be adored and loved by him, and it craves those feelings again.

The timer dings, and I pull the two cookie sheets from the oven. I let them cool while I pack my laptop and make my bed. Making my bed is a task that doesn't always get completed, but new career equals better habits.

Once the cookies are cooled enough, I place them in a pink Tupperware container and set them by my bag. Checking my phone, it's seven-forty. I could kill another ten minutes here before I need to leave, or I can just be a little more than early. Yup. The ants in my pants tell me it's time to go.

As my phone falls into my bag, I hear the text tinkling noise. Wouldn't you know it, it's Aaron.

Aaron: *Of course, the only reason I'm coming is to see you. I got you to say, "Okay." That was ducking huge. What I HATE is you dating someone else. What I HATE even more is this indifference you seem to have towards us.*

As I'm reading it another text arrives.

Aaron: *I hate autocorrect. If I want to say fucking, I should be allowed. That's not all that I hate. I hate not seeing you and hearing your laugh. I miss you. I miss your smile and how you roll your eyes at me. I miss our conversations. I miss seeing you first thing in the morning.*

And then another.

Aaron: *I know you're headed to your first day. I'm so proud of you. Knock'em dead. Can't wait to hear about it tonight.*

Staring at my phone, I don't know how to reply. In three texts, he was angry, sweet, and encouraging. That familiar stirring in my gut happens. It's the one that I had every time my rock star kept me guessing and on my toes. My lips draw into a smile that I'm ashamed of. I should be stronger than this. I'd be so disappointed in Bella if Nyall had treated her like Aaron treated me and she let him back into her life.

Me: *Okay.*

Aaron: *I send you three nice texts and I all I get back is "okay." SMH*

Me: *Leaving now . . . Go to sleep.*

Aaron: *Already did the sleep thing. I'm a new man.*

Me: *It's like 5:45 there, and you've slept and woken up?*

Aaron: *Your text woke me. Now I'm wide awake.*

Aaron: *All of me is wide awake if you want to know.*

Rolling my eyes, I type my response.

Me: *When isn't all of you awake?*

There's a pause long enough that I pick up my things and begin walking to my first day filming. As I pass Whistling Willie's empty corner, my phone vibrates in my hand.

Aaron: *I know you think I'm an asshole and full of shit. But believe this. You're the only girl for me . . . all of me.*

Aaron: *I can't wait to see you tonight.*

Chapter Seventeen

Aaron
September

Rock Star Groupies @RockStarGroupies
Didn't play #PinkCadillac. What's up with that @RealJohnnyKnite? Number one song and not playing live.

James Core @GuitarGuy
Huge #ACE fan and love @RealJohnnyKnite. Last night he was off. Screwed up some cords. #disappointed

"You're going where?" Grace asks as I watch her jaw tighten. This is probably her attempt to keep it from dropping open in surprise.

"New Orleans." I bought a duffle bag from the hotel gift shop. It's bright blue with a white outline of Mount Rainer printed on the side. Shoving in a clean pair of jeans, I think what else I might need for an overnight stay. One of the perks of being me is that I have someone who travels with us that takes care of my clothes. Having to pack myself is something I haven't done in a long time.

"Oh," she replies.

I've always been able to read Grace like a book. After our blowup in LA, she's been acting weird—like she agrees with me and hasn't been a bitch one single time. Most people would probably think this is a good thing, but it's odd.

"You aren't going to lecture me? You know why I'm going." I have to prod her just a little.

I crumple a red Blink-182 shirt and stick it in the bag. Her hand reaches in and extracts it. For a split-second I think she's going to throw it back on the bed and begin one of her infamous Grace tirades. Instead, she runs her hands over the wrinkles and folds it neatly. Then, she places it back in.

"Make sure you're back in time for sound check."

God, I hate the weirdness. "I'm going to try to persuade MK to give us another chance. That means she's going to be around."

My strong, confident sister sinks to the mattress. She proceeds to fold a pair of khaki cargo shorts, two pairs of gym socks, and my swim trunks before she says, "You aren't happy."

I nod and wait for her to continue as I reach up instinctively and run my thumb over the cool point of the tooth.

She takes a deep breath and exhales while she tears a loose thread from the hem of my shorts. "Touring used to make you happy."

Leaning against the dresser, I cross my arms over my chest while I calculate whether her statement needs validation. Journey's *Faithfully* plays in my head.

Fortunately, Grace keeps talking. "This tour has obviously been rough on you. You're miserable." Her eyes meet mine before she swallows and continues, "MK is not my favorite person. I think she's immature, naïve, and will never fully be able to immerse herself in this life."

My biceps tense as I prepare for another battle.

"At the time, I thought she was a couple of weeks' distraction. But, I can see that you believe that you fell in love with her, and you think she's your key to happiness." She stands and looks at me with the same bright blue eyes that she used when she was little to convince me to let her sleep in my bed when she was scared at night. "You may not believe this, but all I've ever wanted is the best for you. Maybe no girl will ever be worthy of you in my eyes." She shrugs. "But as long as she makes you happy then that's all I need."

"Thank you." I want to reach out to her. My brain screams to give her a hug or rumple her hair, but I don't. We've never had a particularly affectionate relationship. So instead, I change the subject. "I heard back from the doctor."

Concern spiders around her eyes and her bobbed blonde hair shades the sides of her face. "And?"

"And he says that I need more testing, but he's pretty sure this is some sort of arthritis." At just the mention of the word, my hand flexes and then balls into a fist. "He said that I need more X-rays and additional bloodwork to figure out what sort of arthritis it is."

"So when are you going to do those tests?"

Shrugging, I shove my hands in my pockets. "I guess whenever I can get back to LA."

She stands throwing her arms towards the ceiling. "You're Johnny Knite. The doctor comes to you and if he won't, I'll find you another one. Don't be stupid. This is your career. You're a corporation. Because of you, we have ninety-three employees who put food on their table. You can't just blow this off. Your health is vital to you being successful. But by your logic, instead of flying to LA and getting this diagnosed, you're traveling to see MK instead."

I hate her words. Turning away, I toe a patch of carpet. She doesn't understand that making things right with MK is vital to my health. "Okay. Set something up for whatever city we're going to next."

Wanting to end this conversation, I head to the bathroom and shut the door behind me. The bottle of Tylenol rests next to my electric toothbrush. I pick both up and throw them into my toiletry bag. I add my razor, deodorant, and brush.

When I walk back into the bedroom, Grace is placing the rest of my folded items in the bag. I toss in my black toiletry bag.

"I'll have Jennifer take care of the rest of your things."

Nodding, I stand feeling the tension travel back and forth between us as if it's electric bolts. I'm so tired of this weirdness.

She zips the hideous tote and hands it to me. Her eyes soften, and a little smile draws her cheeks. "I love you, Aaron."

It's the first time she's called me by my real name in so many years that it sounds foreign coming off her tongue.

Taking the bag from her, I drop it on the floor and pull my baby sister into a deep, true hug. It's probably the first real affection we've shown each other in more years than I can count. It feels good to not be employer and employee and to finally feel like brother and sister again. "I love you too, Gracie."

Chapter Eighteen

MK
September

MK Landry @NoPinkCaddy
Sorry #GardenDistrict. I didn't realize we'd take up so much room. #Thanks4YourPatience

MK Landry @NoPinkCaddy
I have a dressing room and a stylist. Poor Margo, she has no idea what she signed up for.

MK Landry @NoPinkCaddy
Vince Asher just walked into a meeting. I'm fanning myself. #NoticeIDidntTagHim #FanGirling

I grab a pen and begin spinning it around my fingers as I do everything in my power to leave my poor abused cuticle alone. Janet is standing at a white board and writing times with a one or two-word description of what they mean to our production schedule.

Because I don't know enough to have an opinion, I sit here quietly sipping on a glass of lemonade while Vince, Shannon, Cindy and the older lady, who I've come to learn is named Robbie, debate the schedule.

Vince leans forward on the card table, and I think for a moment that it might collapse under his enormous arm muscles. It creaks and groans and I guess decides to do its job and stay erect. "I understand what you're saying, Janet, but it's unreasonable to think we can paint the floors in the design MK has asked for in one day. There is such a thing as drying times. And if you haven't noticed, paint dries slower in this swamp."

Cindy replies, "We're on the clock. Each day we lose to drying floors costs us ten thousand dollars. Let's just scrap them and put in hardwoods."

Shannon speaks on my behalf. "MK's design is part of the approved budget and renovations. The painted floors are important to her."

Every head in the cramped trailer swings in my direction. I swallow hard before I reply, "I really think I can paint them myself. I can start as soon as production ends on Friday. They'll be ready for Monday."

"Quit being stubborn," Vince admonishes with a head shake. "What's wrong with us installing wood floors? They're very New Orleans after all."

All the eyes are trained on me again. The plate of cookies I made this morning are in front of me, and I push it in their general direction. My cookies helped diffuse many of a situation when I was president of my sorority. "I had a vision." Standing up, I walk to the board and grab a purple dry erase marker. I begin sketching the paisley pattern I'd drawn on my pad in what seems like so many months ago. In reality, it's only been about five weeks. "See, the dirt from the glass cast this sort of shadow on the floors. A voice inside my head told me to save the old floors and to paint the pattern. It's my passion. It doesn't need to be filmed,"—I swallow hard—"but I will not be okay with getting rid of them."

Janet looks at Vince. "If she's good with spending all weekend doing that back breaking work who am I to argue?"

"Thank you." I walk back and take my chair, melting into the metal, relieved that I won this battle. Now, I just have to figure out how I'm going to paint the floors and have them dry in essentially forty-eight hours. I might have to call in some favors.

Janet caps the marker that I used and looks at Vince. "If you can give us a minute."

Vince stands and pushes in his metal chair. On the way to the door, he pauses, squeezes my shoulder, and then shuts the door behind him. I do my best to ignore the butterflies his touch stirs in my stomach. I don't have time to dwell on the fact that Vince is here and seems to have feelings for me while Aaron is leaving his tour to take me on a date tonight. As the saying goes . . . when it rains, it pours.

Cindy and Janet exchange one of their speaking-without-words glances and Janet sits down while Cindy assumes the position in front of the card tables. "We need to finalize the name of the show."

The butterflies in my tummy feel like they've been doused in acid.

Janet joins us at the table and pats my hand. "MK, Cindy and I understand what it's like to be told that the name that you came up with isn't good enough. I named my son Francis and I refuse to acknowledge that he has his friends call him *F*." Her head shakes. "I mean, who in God's name wants to be known as a letter."

Cindy clears her throat, and Janet's face morphs into a horrified look when she realizes what she said. "I'm sorry. MK is a lovely name."

Cindy takes over for her flustered partner. "I think what Janet is trying to say is that the store can be named *No Pink Caddy*. You can refer to you blog as *No Pink Caddy*, but we all agree and after speaking with Holden, we're even more convinced that *Burnt Sugar* is the perfect name for the show."

Robbie hands me a blue binder. A label on the cover reads *Burnt Sugar*. The font is bold, and the letters have cute little scrolls at the top of the *B* and at the end of the *R*. It's southern, girly, and strong.

"Inside is the market research we've conducted. I think you'll see that our target demographic thinks *Burnt Sugar* is a relatable name."

I don't bother opening it. Looking around the room, I see four women who seem to only want me to succeed. Holden's firm still believes that *Burnt Sugar* is the perfect choice. And from the two-inch-thick binder in front of me, the public does too. "*Burnt Sugar* it is."

***

A parking lot two blocks from the store has been transformed into white trailer city. *I'm one of the Hollywood assholes the neighbors complain about.* One building is my dressing room. I didn't know what to expect when Shannon told me I'd have my own space. Thankfully, I didn't spend too much time dreaming of how lovely it would be because it's not glamorous at all. There's a maroon couch made of cracked leather with two matching chairs, a tiny bathroom with a shower that I can't bend over in, two racks of clothing, a curtained off corner for me to change behind, and a makeup/hair area with twelve bright lightbulbs. The carpet is grey, stained, and threadbare.

Bella sits with her legs crossed in one of the chairs eating a bag of popcorn while Margo my hairstylist, makeup, and wardrobe assistant fluffs my tresses.

Shannon leans against the wall, reminding me of all the things that I'm not supposed to do on camera. Some of the favorite no-noes include not turning my back to the camera, not eating anything, watch out for the camera man, and if people peek in the windows don't acknowledge them until the cameras are off. Oh! I also shouldn't sneeze, wipe my nose, or bend over at the waist. If I drop something, I must squat with my knees together to pick it up.

"Got it." I give her the thumbs up.

"And for the love of everything holy, don't drool over Vince."

Catching Bella's reflection in the mirror, I see her eyes roll. "God, Shannon. You treat her like she's a moron." They've been at each other since Bella arrived about an hour ago.

Shannon replies, "It's my job to shepherd MK through this. And what's your job?"

"My job is to . . ."

"Stop it," I tell both of them. "I'm nervous enough without you two bickering and stressing me out."

There's a knock on the trailer door. Bella yells for whomever it is to enter. As the door opens, she gasps. Vince strolls in looking like the fine male specimen he is. "They're ready for us."

Margo douses my hair with half a bottle of hairspray, steps back, nods her approval, and warns, "Walk quickly. I'm not sure that hairspray will hold in this humidity."

Bella stands, tossing her curls over her shoulder and sticks out her hand. "Bella Conner. I'm MK's best friend and assistant."

Vince shakes her hand and then turns, walking over to me. Behind his back, she mouths, *God, that man is fine.*

Nodding, it seems that everyone can agree on Vince's Hollywood good looks.

He offers me his arm which I'm quite thankful for. These heels Margo put me in are ridiculously high. We head out of the trailer park, past the security guard, and walk the two blocks to my store. When we're out of ear shot, he asks, "Have plans tonight? We could celebrate your first official day on set."

I have plans, but I'd be fine if bad weather kept Aaron's plane from landing, I've told myself. Because there isn't a cloud in the sky most likely, I'm going to see him tonight, and what I hate to admit to myself is that I can't wait until eight o'clock. "You're a brave man for asking. After that LA sandwich shop you took me and then forced me to eat a meatball sub, I'd be scared of where I might take you." My eyebrow cocks. "You haven't had to peel a couple of pounds of the spiciest crawfish known to mankind. They're messy, good, and make grown men cry."

He pretends his knees are shaking, as his mouth hangs open in mock terror. "I ain't afraid of those bugs." He laughs at his joke and then asks, "Did the marinara come out of your white dress? Which was not a smart thing to wear when you knew I was going to seek revenge for the muffaletta." Then he adds, "But it sure looked great on you."

"A soak in bleach and it was good to go." We walk around a man who is sitting against a wall asleep. He looks like he might have had one too many drinks last night. "I can't believe your solution to my stained dress was for me to wear that hideous Venice Beach tourist shirt over it." We both laugh. "I'm sure people thought I was crazy."

He deadpans, "It's LA. They probably thought you were on the cusp of a new fashion trend." Pausing, then he asks, "So what about that dinner tonight? I could go for crawfish."

I like Vince. He's easy on the eyes and a boatload of fun, but I think even if Aaron wasn't in the picture that dating him would be a bad idea. His show films mostly in Los Angeles, and I really don't want to do the long-distance thing. *Aaron's long distance and you're seeing him tonight.*

Pushing all thoughts of Aaron from my head, I reply, "I'm sorry, but a friend beat you to the punch."

He takes my hand, giving it a squeeze. "No worries. Maybe tomorrow."

"Yeah. Sure."

As he opens the front door to No Pink Caddy, Vince says, "Pause a second and take all this in. You're walking on the set of your reality show and into the store of you've dreamed of owning. MK, own this moment."

Looking up at the sky, I do my best to keep the tears from streaming down my cheeks and ruining Margo's hard work. But one slips down and lands on the concrete making a clean splash on the dirty sidewalk. Pulling out my phone, I take a picture of the front door of No Pink Caddy and attach it to my tweet.

> **MK Landry** @NoPinkCaddy
> When one door closes, another opens. Welcome to
> #NoPinkCaddy #BurntSugar

Chapter Nineteen

Aaron
September

Rock Star Groupies @RockStarGroupies
@RealJohnnyKnite is in Seattle tonight. Keep an eye out for him. Post if you know his location. #SingleJohnnyKnite

A thousand horses are racing in my chest.

Seamus puts the car in park and opens the driver's door. I'm assuming he's getting out to open mine.

"No. Give me a sec." I stare at the tall iron fence that runs along the broken sidewalk. The sun has almost escaped this brutally warm day, casting the wrought-iron in an orange glow, making it look like it's on fire. Behind the fence, everything still looks the same—same white clapboard siding and same black railing leading to her front door. But it's not the same. She has the high fence installed because of me. She has the gate with a call box because I led the paparazzi and my fans to her front door. I put her in danger. It's ironic that I used because I couldn't protect her, yet I left her so vulnerable she felt the need for the fence. *My vagabond, free spirit is now contained.*

I feel like such an asshole. It's one thing to hear her tell me about the pain I've caused. It's another to see the evidence in person.

I've never in my life wanted so badly to rewind time. My muscles twitch with the need to race out of the car, scoop her in my arms, and carry her back to Austin—to the safety of my little house in the middle of my vineyard. Cameras don't reach us there. The media can't get close. It's where Jude learned to ride a bike and played in her now abandoned treehouse. It's where MK could restore the antiques she loves so much and cook in my Tuscan-styled kitchen until her heart is content.

Taking a deep breath, I try to slow my shallow breathing. I want to play this cool. I don't want MK to know just how much these next hours we'll spend together mean to me. I'm not that well versed in relationships, but even I know that girls don't like needy, pathetic guys.

Before I open the car door, I tuck the necklace into my shirt, grab my straw fedora, and pick up my duffle. "Seamus, just keep your phone with you."

"Have a good evening," my New Orleans employee wishes me.

Yeah. Let's hope it is.

My hands drag along the rough denim of my jeans. I don't want to greet MK with sweaty palms.

Pushing the button by the gate, her sweet voice causes my stomach to do a flip. "Hi, Aaron. I'll let you in."

"Uh . . . thanks," I stammer sounding pathetic. *Shit. Get it together.*

A buzzing noise lets me know that it's okay to push the gate open. I walk into MK's personal space with a tiny prayer that I'm walking to my destiny.

Her front door opens, and when she steps out onto the small landing, I think I forget to breathe. Brown hair seems to swirl around her firm breasts. Erect nipples push against the *R* and *A* of her tank top that reads *A girl needs a man like a fish needs a bicycle.* I feel pretty confident that this top was chosen specifically to send me a message.

"Are you going to walk and get out of this heat or are you just going to stand there staring?" she says with a strong Cajun accent. I love when it escapes.

Shit. I forgot to walk.

I couldn't keep the smile from my face if I tried. "It's hot out here? I haven't noticed." A bead of sweat trickles down my back.

Her eyes roll as she turns around and walks back into her home. I follow like the love-sick fool that I am.

Words swirl in my brain—things I want to say to her.

You are the most beautiful woman I've ever seen.

You make me feel complete just by being in your presence.

I don't want to ever be without you.

Let's leave this all behind. You and me can be perfect together away from all the distractions.

Marry me.

Instead of telling her phrases that she won't believe, I step into her living room and ask, "Where in the hell is your furniture?"

Her head whips around and her hair flies like crazy, sticking to her cheeks. "You." She marches over to where I'm standing and pushes on my chest. "You got rid of my furniture. You tossed my things without asking my permission. You're the reason that I work at my kitchen island sitting on an old, uncomfortable barstool."

Dropping my bag just inside the door, I grab her hand because frankly her pushing on my sternum hurts. "Yeah. I did all of that, but it's been like ten months. Why haven't you bought new stuff?"

Her eyes narrow as her head turns to the side. "Do you think money grows on trees? I had to ask Grandmother to pay for the fence and gate out front." She turns and walks away which makes my chest tight. "After you left me raw and exposed to the world, it took me some time before I could write or make videos again. Advertising dollars were pouring in, but I had to save that money. I didn't know how long it would last or what my future looked like. I couldn't spend money on furniture, not even thrift store finds."

She grows quiet as she opens the refrigerator and pours herself a glass of wine. I watch her throat move up and then down as she takes a large gulp.

This is not how I had planned our reunion, and I hate myself for being such a careless asshole.

"I'm . . ." I start before she cuts me off.

"Don't say it, Aaron. I don't want your apologies. But this is another reason why we shouldn't be together. We're too different. You don't have any concept of what it's like to struggle. You can toss furniture just because it gets dirty. I live month to month. My savings account has twenty dollars in it.

How did you think I could afford to replace the things you tossed?"

Well, this is a role reversal. "Yeah, I have money now, but I didn't. I worked my ass off for it. I mopped floors and sometimes didn't eat so Jude could. I've known a kind of poor that you've only read about in books."

Her hands go to her hips. "Then you should have been more sensitive to my struggles when you had my furniture hauled off."

She's infuriating. I had her couch, chair, and coffee table taken to the landfill because they were stained with her blood and vomit. I didn't want her to have a reminder of that terrible night. I thought I was doing her a favor. It never occurred to me that she could still be this pissed. "Are you always going to punish me for my shit behavior? Because, if so, maybe you're right, and we shouldn't be together." I can't believe the words come out of my mouth. Immediately, I wish I could grab them before they reach her ears and shove them back inside.

Tears fall down her cheeks as she takes another slug out of the glass. "Today was the best day of my life. Please don't ruin it. I don't want to fight with you. Can we not talk about the past and just try to enjoy the moment? Please don't make me regret turning down a date with Vince."

At the mention of the other guy's name, I feel as if a knife has been shoved into my side. I walk past the spot on her worn hardwoods where I made the biggest mistake of my life by letting her give up on me.

Taking the wine from her hand, I rest it on the counter and pull her warm body into my arms as I kiss her forehead. It's the first time I've had a chance to examine her scar up close. Doctor Hebert did a beautiful job. I'm sure it's easily covered with makeup, but it's still a physical reminder of one of the scariest nights of my life. I push the thoughts away and try to focus on the present and the fact that I'm competing with another guy for her heart. "I know you don't want to hear my apologies, but please just let me say that I'm so fucking sorry for everything. I wouldn't have gotten rid of your stuff if I had known how much it meant to you. I'm sorry I didn't pay to replace it. I'm sorry I did coke, and I stormed out of your place and didn't come back. I'm sorry I released the album without giving you any warning, and I'm especially sorry that my thoughtlessness and carelessness made your life difficult. I'm sorry I abandoned you and left you struggling. But what I'm most sorry about is that I turned my back on the one woman I've ever loved and left her raw and exposed to my world."

Her body quivers, and I hold her so tightly that I think I might squeeze her to death. The smell of her soap lingers on her olive skin and it reminds me of the ocean breeze. "You, MK, are right for me." Then I say the words that I used to hate. "Teach me to be the man you deserve."

She pulls back, reaching up, and removing my fedora. She tosses it on the island before she runs her hands through my hair. Feeling her fingers against my scalp gives me chills. "I'm sorry I told you that. It was a crummy thing for me to say. I promise to not bring up our fight if you promise to never say those horrid words again."

Kissing the tip of her nose, I reply, "Deal."

"I'm going to have to find a way to live in the present and leave the hurt and pain in the past, or we'll just keep torturing each other."

"We'll work on it." She picks up her glass and says with a little side smile, "Want to buy me dinner and in exchange, I'll tell you all about my day?"

Warmth spreads from my chest outward. "I guess I could be persuaded to buy you dinner, and if you must tell me about your day, I could possibly listen."

My sarcasm makes her laugh. It's the finest piece of music I've ever heard. She balls up her fist and punches me in my right arm. A bolt of electricity travels to my hand, and it takes everything that I have to not double over from the pain and remain passive. My middle finger twitches and rolls inward against my palm.

"Let me change tops, and I'll be ready to go."

When her bedroom door shuts, I race to my bag and dig with my left hand until I find the Tylenol. I throw a handful in my mouth and use MK's left over wine to wash them down. My whole hand aches but my finger hurts the worst. Using the thumb on my left hand, I manually straighten it and then press my palm against the cold marble of her kitchen island to keep it from curling back.

I'm not sure if the Tylenol kicks in or if my muscles decide to relax, but fortunately, by the time she walks into the empty living space, I can act normal. I'm not letting whatever this is come between me and my future.

***

I've never seen her so animated.

"You should see my shop. It's crazy. Like there are lights placed on ladder-looking things suspended from the ceiling. And there's Murray, who's a camera guy. He's really funny and sweet. Eugene doesn't like me because he says I don't understand blocking. And well, I don't. This is all new to me. And there's Kat. She holds this xylophone looking thing around her neck. She mixes the sound while we're filming. Is that not crazy?"

The waiter places a bowl of pad Thai in front of her, but she barely seems to notice. "Then there's this other camera guy. I don't think he likes me very much, but I just said in my head, 'Self, don't let him rain on your parade.'"

She picks up her chopsticks and uses them to grab a piece of chicken.

We're in the back corner of some Asian fusion restaurant that she said was good. We could be eating paper for all I care. I just love watching and listening to her share her day.

Grabbing the spoon, I take a sip of the soup I ordered. "Is he an asshole?" One phone call and I could have him fired. Janet and Cindy work with the guy who I got hired as the network head of the cable company. So MK's boss owes me some huge favors.

She shakes her head. "No. He's just grumpy."

"Have they started the renovation?"

She's beaming. "Yes. I helped Vince and his crew build the kitchen cabinets today."

There's that name again, *Vince*. "So who's this Vince guy?"

MK rests her chopsticks on the side of the plate. "He's Vince Asher." She says this like I must be dense. "Famous contractor. Has his own show. Janet and Cindy produce his also. They thought it would be good promotion for my show if he was the contractor. So we're kinda like filming both at once."

I make a mental note to get Zed to run a check on this Vince Asher. Then I ask the question that I don't want the answer to. "Are you seeing him?" Now that I'm putting two and two together, I think he's the one she ditched me for in LA.

"Seeing? Like he's my boyfriend?" She shakes her head as she picks up her chopsticks. "No. We've gone on a few dates."

"Like how many is a few?"

Her head turns to the side causing her hair to form a curtain around the left side of her face. "More than one." She stares at her plate like the food is really fucking interesting. "Enough about me. How's the tour?"

I don't want to talk about me. Or my tour. Or anything else. I want to hear more about these few dates with the contractor. Reminding myself to not be an asshole, I reply, "Fine. It's going well."

Her laugh is gorgeous. "Okay, man of few words, can you tell me a little more than fine?"

Pushing my bowl of soup aside, I lean forward. "Do you really want to hear the boring shit? That's what touring is. It's boring. It's two hours of the best experience ever and then three days of boring."

Her nose crinkles. "How can traveling to different cities, or even countries, be called boring?" MK's voice changes to one that can only be described as patronizing. "Poor little rock star has to sing his songs on stage while thousands of people imagine themselves either being him or being made love to by him."

Then before I can stop myself, I reply, "You're the only one who knows what it's like to have the poor little rock star make love to them."

Our eyes lock across the table. There's a moment. There's something between us. She's into me also. Her mouth forms a perfect little *O*. Her eyes slant and an audible gasp escapes her cherry-red lips. I'm so hopeful that I'm not making up this chemistry. She swallows hard and then stares down at her plate of noodles.

Silence falls over the table before she breaks it by asking about Jude.

"She's great. Sophomore at Vanderbilt. She's set her eye on qualifying for the Olympics in equestrian jumping." Shrugging, I add, "Who knows if she'll make it."

"That's wonderful," MK says. "I'm sure you're so proud."

"What dad wouldn't be?" Talking about Jude to someone who has only met her a few times is still a rather foreign concept. I've actively avoided mentioning her name to anyone but the band and family for so long that I've kept Jude partitioned off in my heart. Changing the subject, I ask, "How's your family?"

"My sister's pregnant."

I barely know her sister. She's a pediatrician who asked my angel foundation for a grant. I gave it to her hoping it would give me an in with MK. "Planned?"

Her face twists. "What kind of question is that?"

Taking a sip of water, I state, "She's got like two already. I just can't imagine with her practice and her organization that she would have time for a third kid. I mean, I could barely keep up with one."

My explanation must have made sense because her face relaxes a fraction, and I think she was about to yell, but changes her mind. "I don't know if the baby was planned, but they're happy. She's having another girl. She's even floated the idea of naming her after me."

That seems bizarre. "Right, but you're Mary Kay. Your grandma and mom are Mary Katherine and Mary Kate. Isn't it your job to carry on the naming trend?"

Before she can respond our dinner is interrupted by a fan. The girl looks sheepish as she approaches us. "You're Johnny Knite."

I nod.

"I thought so. I told my friend that it was you. Mind if we take a selfie? I have tickets to your show here next month."

MK's doesn't look upset so I use the white napkin to wipe my mouth before I turn towards the girl. She bends down and places her face next to mine. Before I know it, she's kissing my cheek as the flash goes off, momentarily blinding me.

"Thanks," she calls over her shoulder as she walks back to her table.

Then, it's like nothing happened, MK responds to my question about her name. "Yeah. I guess it's sort of my job to keep the naming trend going, but let's check reality. I'm thirty-one, not married, not seriously dating anyone.

The chances of me getting married and having a child—girl child at that—are slim. It's okay. I was kinda flattered."

My fist slams down on the table surprising even me. "That's bullshit. It's your name."

Her mouth hangs open. "Um . . . I don't particularly like Mary Kay. Hence, why I go by MK. If my sister wants to take that burden from me, I'll gladly let her."

I have no idea why I'm so pissed, but I am. How dare Bethany just assume MK isn't getting married or having a baby girl. It isn't her right to take this privilege away from the girl that I love.

Tossing my napkin on the table, I lean in. "Tell your sister that's our decision, not hers. We'll choose if we want to keep the Mary K. tradition going."

She laughs. "That's awfully presumptuous of you, Mister Emerson. As far as I'm concerned this is a two-old-friends-catching-up kind of evening. I don't think we're at a place where you're naming our children."

"Then let's get to that place. I've been without you, and it was shit. I tried dating, and it was also shit." I toss my hands up in the hair. "Just quit being a scaredy cat and ditch the Vince guy and be mine until we're ghosts. And maybe then we'll be lucky enough to haunt the same house."

The waiter walks up to the table right as I end my rather poetic plea. I ask for the check hoping to get out of this public place and back to where the outside world doesn't exist.

When he walks away, she leans forward resting her elbows on the table. "It's that easy for you?"

"Fuck, yeah." I lean back crossing my arms.

"What if we try again, and we screw us up? I mean we did sabotage us after only two weeks."

"I'm sure that's some kind of record. We just won't fuck us up again."

"But I'm starting a whole new journey. You're on tour. We'll never make this work." I think she's trying to convince herself that she should not give us another chance. I'll have to work on her negative thoughts.

With a half-smile, I lean forward and take her hand. Her warmth spreads through my chest. "Pessimist."

"No, I'm a realist, Aaron. You're going to be leaving for Europe and Asia. I'm here in New Orleans filming my show. You and I both know that long distance relationships don't last."

Swallowing, my head screams *tell her you'd give it all up for her.* Instead, I reply, "Cara and Rock make it work. We can also. Look, I'm not going to pressure you into anything. This is supposed to be a congratulations dinner. Let's just see where it goes." I also add in my head *and don't see the contractor again.*

She seems to like my answer because she replies, "I can do that. Ready to go?"

I've never been more ready in all my life, but I don't think she means it like I interpret it.

Chapter Twenty

MK
September

Rock Star Groupies @RockStarGroupies
@RealJohnnyKnite spotted at the nightclub @VibeSeattle. Back off girls, he's mine.

Rock Star Groupies @RockStarGroupies
False alarm! @RealJohnnyKnite where are you hiding?

Laurie Smith @AccountantsHaveMoreFun
@RockStarGroupies Pic of me with @RealJohnnyKnite. He's in #NOLA with @NoPinkCaddy

He sits on one side of the SUV, and I push myself so tightly against the other door that a particle of air couldn't fit. "I've an eight a.m. call time tomorrow."

The city is dark. Rain clouds blanket the sky not letting the moon do its job. Seamus is driving. I expect him to turn on the street where Aaron's house is, but he doesn't. He passes it and turns on mine.

"We aren't going to your place?"

"I didn't have Seamus get it ready."

"What? I didn't know you had to get houses ready. What does that even mean?" I turn towards him.

"No one's been in it since it was cleaned and locked back in November." Aaron's voice is soft. When he talks, sometimes it sounds melodic. I love it.

"I thought the bands signed on your label sometimes recorded there."

He chuckles. "Only with my blessing."

"So you didn't allow them to record there?"

The car stops in front of my gate. He doesn't answer my question.

"Thanks, Seamus. I'll see you in the morning." He opens the car door and slides out.

"Yes, sir. Text if you need anything."

Aaron climbs out first and offers me his hand, and I take it as I slide out from the backseat. "You're crashing at my place?" I'm not entirely sure I'm okay with this. When we're together, the chemistry is off the charts. My hormones suffer from short term memory loss and think a good night of Aaron loving is just what we need. Fortunately, my brain is still in control and told them to take a hike.

The street lamp gives off just enough light that I can see his shadowed face as I use my key to let us through the gate. He continues, "If that's okay with you. If it's not, I can go get a hotel room."

"It's fine, but I feel like this was planned," I reply as Seamus pulls away from the curb.

"I'd planned to sleep on your couch."

Rain drops splat against the sidewalk. I squeal and laugh. "I love the rain."

"Race ya," Aaron yells over his shoulder and takes off down my brick path. We run up the stairs, through the front door, and go crashing into my living room. Our combined laughter bounces off the walls. Without me having soft furnishings to absorb the echo, one last reminder of our happiness sounds when we're both quiet.

He brushes the damp strands of hair from my face. His tongue swipes over his thick, full lips as he spreads his legs making us close to the same height. "You're beautiful," he whispers as his finger traces my scar.

Before my brain can tell my hormones to back off, my hands lace around his neck as his wet hair brushes my knuckles. "You must have a thing for wet girls."

Realizing what I said, we both laugh at my inappropriate comment.

"I do like my girl wet." His smile is dirty.

Pulling his face to mine, I can't resist his filthy mouth. A moan sounds deep in his throat as he presses his body against mine. His arms wrap around my back securing us together. My tongue finds his and our sweet, soft kiss becomes more fevered as his hardness presses into my stomach.

I step back. "We're not doing this again. Last time, we made everything move so fast. If we have a chance of surviving your tour and my crazy filming schedule, we've got to do this the right way."

He smirks, looking sexy as hell. "You're the one who kissed me."

"Jerk," I call over my shoulder as I walk into the bedroom. That kiss was too good, and my body is begging for one more round.

He follows behind, carrying his bag.

"So just to make sure I'm clear . . . Making love is moving too fast." He sits down on the edge of my bed and slides off his motorcycle boots.

Choosing a modest over-sized T-shirt that I received for volunteering at church and pair of workout shorts, I head to the bathroom to change. Through the closed door, I yell, "Sex complicates a relationship. Plus, you're on tour. I'm not naïve to what goes on out on the road."

I take off my clothing and lay each piece over the lip of the tub to dry.

The door flies open just as I slide the fresh shirt over my head. Tugging on the hem, I make sure it covers my lacy thong—one always needs to be prepared. His eyes are wide, and the scowl on his face lets me know that he's not the least bit happy.

"Do you think I'd cheat on you, MK?" His shirt is off revealing the swirls of colors on the left side of his upper body. Denim jeans hang on his hip bones. Bare feet go toe to toe with mine.

Not wanting to bend over because he would clearly see the white lacy strip of my panties, I try to do this weird little move where I use my foot to grasp my sports shorts.

"Oh for God's sake," he booms as he bends down and picks up the material. He hands them to me and then turns around as he drags his hand through his damp hair. "My tongue has tasted every bit of your body, but by all means, I'll give you your modesty."

I pull them up my legs not really sure how to respond to that comment. "Thank you. I'm dressed."

When he turns back around, his lips are turned down and his shoulders slumped. "I'm trying here. I'm trying to be the man . . ." He stops himself before he says the ugly word *deserve.* "You're who I want. No other woman compares. I'm the one who should be worried. I'm the one who shouldn't want a relationship with you. You're seeing someone you work with yet you're standing in your apartment bathroom with me."

My eyes narrow at his accusation. "That's not fair, Aaron. Vince and I have gone on a few dates. We're not exclusive, and I'm certainly not cheating on him. For all I know, he could be standing in another girl's bathroom right now. Dear God, I've told you this already. Quit bringing him up." Swallowing, I reach out and place my palm on his stubbly cheek, and he leans into my touch. "I'm trying to make this fresh start easy for you. When we can swing it, we'll see each other. I can't leave New Orleans. You'll be in town in a couple of weeks. We'll go to dinner and text and just play it by ear."

He removes my fingers from his cheek, placing sweet kisses on my knuckles. "We'll do this however you want. But you need to know that there's no one else. There aren't fan girls or groupies or models or actresses." The back of his hand runs across my cheek and over my scar again. "There's only one girl who I want, and I'll wait for her to realize that she can't live without me either."

With those powerful words, he turns around and walks back into my bedroom leaving me feeling very much like an impulsive teenager. As I brush my teeth, I wage an internal war with myself. I should have asked him to go to a hotel. There's nothing good that's going to come out of him in my bed. I go over all the reasons that I should kick him out, and there are many. The most important one being, I don't have the ability to cater to him. As I found out last time, he's demanding of my time and attention. Everything I have inside of me is completely focused on *Burnt Sugar.* I can't stop filming to hop on a plane to see him because he's bored. If I decide to cautiously take the next step with him, will he be okay with having to take a backseat to my career? I have a feeling that's a lot to ask.

Also, I know that while he's on tour that he's constantly surrounded by temptation, and it's not just the women. We've yet to talk about what ultimately drove us a part—his addiction.

Flipping off the bathroom lights, I walk over to my bedside table in the dark and turn on the lamp. A clap of thunder causes me to jump, and I grab my heart with a laugh. The storm is getting closer.

Aaron's laying on top of the new comforter my sister bought me for my birthday. She said that the salesperson called it boho chic. She laughed and said she didn't know about me being chic, but it looked like something I'd love.

"Do you want to change out of those jeans?" I grab my hand lotion and lather my palms.

"Since we're doing this whole modesty thing, I was waiting for you to get out of the bathroom." He stands and picks up his small bag disappearing behind the door.

I could point out that he got my comforter wet, but I don't. I just mentally cringe and will myself to move on.

There's no doubt how attracted I am to him. A younger version of me would have followed him behind the shut door and helped him undress. I'd have thrown caution to the wind and just enjoyed a one night stand. Sighing, I flop against the thick pillows on my bed reminding myself that he's much more than just sex. He's everything, and that's what's so damn scary. I can't open myself back up to that level of pain.

"Are you okay with me sleeping here? I really can get a hotel room." He exits the bathroom and drops the bag at the foot of my bed. He has on a pair of red soccer-styled shorts and nothing else. My necklace rests on his right collar bone. I'd love to snatch it off, and then it would be mine again, but I decide to let it go—for now.

I pat the mattress next to me. "You're fine. Nope. No hotel for you, but I do have to go to bed. Morning is going to be here soon."

He slides close to me, but we don't touch. I want to hold his hand and bury myself against his side. Instead, I lie next to him paralyzed by my desire and terrified to trust him with my heart again.

It's so awkward. Finally, I get the nerve to ask, "Do you mind if I rest my head on your chest?"

Aaron leans up on his elbow. "I want to ask a question, and I don't want you to go all MK on me."

Wrinkling my nose, I ask, "What does that mean?"

"It means that I just want you to answer and not include a five-minute lecture along with it."

"I don't do that." I shake my head.

His head turns and slanted eyes tell me that maybe I do.

Swallowing he asks, "Do you still nothing me?"

I don't reply immediately because I don't know what to tell him. I don't nothing him, and the truth is, I never did. Even when I was purposely ignoring all the media attention about ACE, I still had feelings. They were just ragey and stabby emotions. I also don't want to let him in. My life is simpler without Aaron Emerson.

"Your silence is scaring the shit out of me, sweetheart." The way he's gnawing on his bottom lip confirms his confession.

"I don't know what you want me to say." I stare at the ceiling for guidance. "It's not as easy as a yes or no answer. I mean . . ."

"Stop it, MK." He cuts me off with a single finger placed over my lips. "Do you still nothing me?"

Taking a deep breath, I reply, "I kissed you, didn't I?"

"I've kissed girls who I didn't even know their names. Do you think that means shit to me?"

His words are shocking, but I know they're legitimate. And if I'm honest with myself, I've done the same thing, just not in the same numbers as him. I think about the football player that I had a one-night stand with, and we had sex on his balcony in the Quarter for anyone to watch. I'm sure I kissed him, and it meant nothing.

He grabs a piece of my hair and twirls it between his fingers. "Just say the words. Just tell me that you no longer nothing me."

I admit the truth. "Aaron, I no longer nothing you, and I never felt that way."

His smile lights up his whole face, making his blue eyes twinkle. "That's what I thought." He smirks and says, "Of course, you can lay on my chest."

He flops back against the mattress, and I sit, examining his tattoo in the lamp light. I've seen it on his album art. I've also seen it on billboards, signs, and images on the Internet. Now, I get to see my name inked on his sculpted chest in person.

I've always admired the fist gripping the anatomical heart tattooed over his real heart. The letters *MK* are a beautiful shade of reddish-pink. They're on the fist's ring finger. Leaning down, I kiss the ink. When I look up, he's staring at me with the softest, most gentle expression on his face.

"Cara asked me if I was sure at least ten times before she'd do it. She even made Rock examine me to make sure I was sober," he chuckles.

"Were you?" I ask as I rest my ear on top of the tattoo. He combs my hair with his fingers pausing each time at my scalp to give it a rub.

"Stone cold sober."

"Speaking of sober . . ." I hate to have this talk now, but if he's still using, then I need to snatch my heart off the chopping block before we get any further.

His hands pause still wrapped in my hair. "Are you asking if I'm doing coke?"

Am I asking if he's still doing just one drug? I don't think I am. I need to know what I'm getting myself into, and I must trust that he's going to be honest with me. This is test number one. "I'm asking who or what else I have to compete with for your attention."

The bellowing sound comes from his toes. It's so body jerking that my head bounces off his rib cage. He sits, bringing me with him. "That's about the best way that I've ever heard addiction phrased."

Bright light flashes through my bedroom as a loud boom rattles the pictures on the wall. Then the side lamp goes out. "Ugh, we've lost power."

"So," he replies. Awkwardly, we try to fit together. I don't want to press too tightly against his side because I don't want him to get any ideas. I grab the quilt and cover us both. "It just means that I get to keep you safe."

He doesn't answer my question and silence falls between us. The sounds of the rain against the roof and window fills the void of him not responding.

My eye lids grow heavy and begin to fall.

"I swim," he says as his arm tightens against my back. "I probably drink more than I should, but I swim instead of using anything else. I can thank you for that."

Rain splashing mixes with his baritone voice as he sings *Pink Cadillac* as I relax in his protective embrace. His fingers run down my ribs lulling me to a beautiful place that I haven't found since the last time I was in his arms.

The final words I hear before sleep overcomes are, "I knew she couldn't be anything but mine."

Chapter Twenty-One

Aaron
September

Talk Magazine @TalkMagazine
@RealJohnnyKnite was spotted in #NOLA. He was dining with @NoPinkCaddy his rumored muse.

Talk Magazine @TalkMagazine
@RealJohnnyKnite we want more hot albums like #AlisVolatPropriis

MK Landry @NoPinkCaddy
Second day on the set of #BurntSugar. Did I mention that the show has been officially named? #ForeverNoPinkCaddy

Digging through her makeup drawer, I find a tube of bright pink lipstick. It's fucking hideous. Hopefully my beautiful girl wouldn't mar her sweet lips with this Pepto Bismol shade. Maybe it was purchased and used for a Halloween costume.

On her bathroom mirror, I scroll *Until next time, sweetheart.* Putting the cap on the tube, I toss the lipstick in the garbage. It shouldn't be worn again.

MK's been gone for a couple of hours. I pretended to be asleep when she left because I couldn't bring myself to say the word *goodbye.* Sleep never found me during the night. I stayed up holding her, breathing in her scent, and writing a new song in my head—tapping the beat on the curve of her shoulder. As soon as I heard the front door close, I got up and sang it into my phone. It's about her. She's my muse.

The thought of leaving her again makes me crazy, but I have a show tonight. Grace is right. I am a company. If I don't step onto that stage, the show doesn't happen, and everyone who works for Johnny Knite doesn't get paid.

The only reason I find to put one foot in front of the other is the draw of adding instruments to the lyrics. My guitar is waiting for me in Seattle and calling my name like the siren she is.

Checking my phone, I note Seamus should be here any moment. I straighten the sheets and tuck them around the mattress. Pulling and adjusting, I can't seem to get the flat sheet right. Taking a picture, I send it to Grace with the message *Help.*

Grace: *Run your hand over the wrinkles and get your ass back to Seattle.*

Me: *On my way.*

Her trick works and once I have the comforter evenly placed so it hangs correctly on both sides of the bed, I grab the eight pillows and toss them against the headboard. Stepping back, I admire my work. It's probably been twenty years since I've made a bed. It looks good if I do say so myself.

Reluctantly, I pack the blue bag and then set it next to the front door. Checking my phone again, Seamus is still about five minutes away. I'd sit on the couch and wait, but, well, there's no couch which makes me feel like an asshole.

Opening her kitchen cabinets, I find a box of some healthy twig and berry cereal. Just the smell tells me that it's way to healthy. Shoving it back in its place, I make a face and quickly attempt to forget that anything so bland actually exists. In her refrigerator I spy a plastic container of hummus. Perfect! Next to the horrible cereal, there was a box of crackers. I plop down on her bar stool and enjoy my breakfast feast. It's no Lucky Charms in a mixing bowl, but it'll do.

Just as I'm finishing the last of the container, I receive a text from Seamus letting me know that he's out front. I toss my garbage because I'm a good house guest.

But before I walk out her front door, I'm drawn to her bedroom. The perfumey smell of MK tickles my nose as my heart clenches. Suddenly, I don't care about getting back to my tour and guitar. I want Seamus to drive me to her set and hang out all day watching my girl make her dreams come true, and I can also ensure the contractor knows that MK is mine. Fuck. I find it hard to compel my feet to move. Then, without considering my actions or giving it a second thought, I walk over to the bed and dig through the throw pillows to find the pillow she must normally sleep on. It smells the strongest like her. Bringing it to my nose, I inhale her scent before slipping off the aqua case. I know it's a little creepy, but I don't care. An involuntary smile spreads my lips. I walk out of her bedroom and shove the thin, satin material in my bag. I lock her door behind me and say a little prayer that she's already missing me as much as I'm missing her.

***

The crowd begins chanting something over the final notes of *Time Stand Still.* It starts off sounding like jumbled garbage. Glancing over at Sam, I check to see if she understands. She gives a little shrug as she continues playing. Then it grows louder, and clearer. It hits me. They're screaming for *Pink Cadillac.*

Giving the signal for the band to stop playing, I step closer to the mic. "What do you want?" I yell over the roaring crowd.

"*Pink Cadillac*"

"*Pink Cadillac*"

"*Pink Cadillac*"

"Well, I'm in the business of giving the people what they paid their good, hard-earned, money to hear." Turning around I nod to the band.

Sam mouths *You sure?*

I catch Grace's smile out of the corner of my eye. She's beaming as she claps like a fool.

Turning back to Sam, I nod. I'm happy. My sister seems happy. This moment feels so damn good.

Then to the crowd, "We haven't played this song in a couple of weeks in concert, but I've heard it's a favorite. You asked for it. Here's *Pink Cadillac.*"

As I sing our number one hit, I relive last night in my mind. The crowd thinks I'm singing to them, but I'm not. I'm holding MK against me while she snuggles into my bare chest. I love how she can find just the right places on my body to conform to.

When the song ends instead of feeling crazy and like I'm going to be sick, I'm energized.

Imagine the band's surprise when I signal that we'll perform more songs off our new album.

The crowd loves it and hopefully realizes they're getting something out of the norm. I've heard that fans Google our set lists so they know what song will come next. Imagine their surprise when we toss the set list and just play like the old days.

After the show, I race for the dressing room. I want to talk to MK. I want to share with her how great the show was and how I sang her songs, but before I call, I look at the time. We're two hours behind New Orleans so it's a little after two in the morning there. Last time I woke her with a call, she was less than thrilled, and it didn't go particularly well. I'm one to learn from my mistakes.

Sighing, I sink into the couch deciding to text her, but when I click on her name, I discover that she's already messaged me. Butterflies kick up in the stomach. This is progress. When I saw her in LA she ignored me for a week and then left me the brush-off voicemail.

MK: *Dude, what's with tossing my favorite tube of lipstick in the garbage? You owe me $22. But I liked my message. Hope you're rocking their faces off. Thanks for the visit.*

About an hour later . . .

MK: *The pillowcase you stole is $18. I'm not entirely sure that the cost is correct, but that amount should cover it.*

MK: *My hummus? Now what am I supposed to eat for a late-night snack? Damn you . . .*

And a few seconds later . . .

MK: *And while we're on the subject, I think you should replace the things we're no longer mentioning that you destroyed.*

MK: *And I want to be reimbursed for the security fence.*

MK: *You know what? I'm requiring a security deposit before you're allowed to visit again.*

Smiling at my phone, I shake my head. God, I love this girl.

Me: *You're expensive. Want to meet me in Vegas Friday after you're done taping? I can be yours until Monday morning. Until then, I'll enjoy my expensive pillowcase and hummus filled stomach and dream of you.*

I catch myself whistling in the shower. When the band decides to go to an after-hours club, I happily agree to their surprise. It's crazy how hearing from her without me having to make the first move makes me giddy.

Chapter Twenty-Two

MK
September

Rock Star Groupies @RockStarGroupies
@RealJohnnyKnite put on every fan's dream show. Played whole #AlisVolatPropriis album. #I'mDying

Johnny Knite @RealJohnnyKnite
Thank you, Seattle. You were on fire. Great show and great fans. Can't wait to see you again.

MK Landry @NoPinkCaddy
Grand Opening of #NoPinkCaddy will be in just over two weeks. Want to attend? Register HERE. #YouKnowYouWantTo

I dial his number. This is going to be an interesting conversation and give me a bit of insight on how exactly a relationship might work with us never being in the same city. It's a test of sorts. I brace myself for the call. I never know which version of Aaron I'm going to get.

"Sweetheart," he says sounding out of breath.

"What are you doing?" I ask surprised. I had prepared for somber Aaron, moody Aaron, diva Aaron, or even demanding Aaron. Exercise Aaron never entered my mind. "You sound like you ran a marathon."

"Just got out of the pool. I swam to *Scent of a Woman* by Cheap Trick. You were on my mind."

I don't know if I've ever heard the song so instead of trying to sound informed and falling on my face, I disregard the comment. "Cool. Well, I guess you got a good workout by the sound of your breathing. Do you have a sec?"

"Anything for you. Just give me a moment while I drink some water." Heavy breathing and chugging sounds fill the line before he replies, "Okay. What's up?"

Exhaling, I share the speech I'd rehearsed. "I got your message about me coming to Vegas. I appreciate the invite, but I must work at the store this weekend. See, they can't pay the crew to paint my floors. They were going to force me to accept hardwoods which probably meant laminate, and I just couldn't agree to that so I volunteered to paint them myself." I hop on top of my kitchen island and pick bits of jambalaya off the plate using my fingers.

"Okay," he replies. "Want me to come there instead?"

He sounds so reasonable. I'd prepared for diva and demanding Aaron. I figured there would be hurled threats if I didn't acquiesce. "If you want." I shrug even though he can't see me. "I'm going to have to spend time at the store, and you're going to have to help me do some painting."

"Hold a second. I'm putting you on speaker." His voice sounds more distant. "That actually works. One of my latest acts signed is performing at a club in New Orleans on Saturday. We can knock out whatever you need at the store, and then, if you want, we can go listen to them play."

I actually move the phone away from my ear and stare at it for a moment. Shaking my head, I pick up a few more bits of rice and put them in my mouth. "Okay. I adore live music."

"I'll text you the details. Probably I'll leave right after our Vegas thing so it will be early when I arrive. That work?" he asks sounding like he's chomping on gum.

"Yeah. Just whatever is best for you. What are you chewing on?"

"Some fucking hippie protein bar that Grace left in my room. She says I'm pushing forty and have to quit eating like a teenager."

Laughing, this might be the first time his sister and I have seen eye to eye. "That's some truth if I've ever heard it."

"Fuck both of you," he chuckles. "A crap diet has gotten me this far. No reason to change now."

"I'll fix you some heart-healthy shrimp this weekend and toss them with fresh, spinach leaves, Brussel sprouts, and artichoke hearts. If you're lucky, I might even drizzle a teaspoon of olive oil over it." Imagining the look on Aaron's face makes me smile.

"Well that meal guarantees that we're having takeout." I hear a rustling noise. "All right, sweetheart. I've got to get showered and head to a meeting dinner thing and then do a walk through with the facilities manager at the casino. Trust me, I'd much rather chat with you."

I'm still in shock that this is such a reasonable conversation. "Okay. Have a nice evening."

"Hey, MK . . ."

I hear my name just as I'm about to end the call. "Yeah?"

There's a hesitation. "Is it shitty of me to ask what's up with the contractor?" It's truly a question and not a statement demanding an answer. "I just need to know where I stand."

"I haven't gone out again with him since Los Angeles. We see each other on set and work closely together, but that's it." I grab a piece of sausage and pop it in my mouth.

"And if he asks you out again?"

Ugh. I have no idea how to answer. The truth is that I don't have time for any new relationship and that includes one with Aaron. Every waking moment is spent doing something for No Pink Caddy. Even in my dreams, I can't relax. Last night, I dreamt that no one came to the grand opening, and Shannon was paying homeless people to come in and shop. My full-time relationship is an eight hundred square foot, old building which requires every bit of my focus and my site that's been pretty neglected.

Instead of telling him all of this, I reply, "I won't go."

He sighs. "Thank you, sweetheart."

After we hang up, I text Bella.

Me: *You're not going to believe this. I told Aaron I couldn't come to Vegas so he's coming to NOLA.*

Bella: *No temper tantrums?*

Me: *None. It's been a long time since I've been this surprised.*

Bella: *Guess he's got more tricks up his sleeve.*

***

"Plans tonight?" Vince asks as we walk from white trailer city to No Pink Caddy.

He's asked on Monday, and I blew him off. He asked on Tuesday, but we all went out for a crew dinner so I was off the hook. Wednesday, when he asked, I had already made plans with Bella. Today is Thursday, and I'm feeling like a real jerk.

"Well . . . Umm . . ." *Even though Aaron and I aren't officially dating again, I'd feel like a piece of gum on the bottom of a shoe on Bourbon Street if I go to dinner with you. Plus I told him I wouldn't.* "I've got to get caught up on laundry."

He takes my elbow and helps me navigate around a huge crack in the sidewalk. They've got me in like five inch heels again. It's ridiculous.

"I'm beginning to think that you're avoiding going out with me." He stops walking right before we turn the corner to the shop.

Stopping also, I run my pointer finger over my thumb cuticle and decide to trace my star tattoo instead. I don't want to tell Vince about Aaron. I'm not entirely sure there's anything to tell, and I don't want Janet and Cindy to know that we're talking again. I saw their reaction to the idea that I could teach him to fry beignets. Just the thought causes a shiver to run down my spine.

"Vince, I feel like my life has been turned upside down and then put in a blender. You and I, well, I think we would have been great if we'd met under different circumstances or if I was more settled with this new life." His face remains passive as I speak. Taking his hand, I give it a squeeze. "I think we're a victim of timing."

He lets go and pulls me into a hug. "I wish you all the best in your show and personal life. You're a great girl."

"Thank you," I reply with a dip of my chin. "Shall we go stain cabinets?"

We continue walking. "You're working in those heels?" He laughs.

"Margo promises I can change after we do our joint interview and then my individual. I snuck a pair of blue-jean overalls onto one of the clothing racks. I'm so hoping she says I can put on those with a pair of Chucks."

He holds the door open as I walk into my favorite place on earth. "I love the smell of sawdust."

"We should bottle it and wear it as cologne."

***

"You're going to show MK the problem with the cabinets," Janet instructs Vince. "I get that it's an easy fix with some nails, but we need a bit of drama. This project is going too smoothly."

She turns to me. "The camera is going to film you dropping by the store to check on Vince's progress. You're going to walk through the door and find him in the back of the store trying to solve the issue. He's the expert. Let him give you the answer."

Then back to Vince, she says, "Remember, I need drama."

"Got it," he replies as he walks over to the cabinet doors that are balanced between two saw horses. The rest of the kitchen is built, and it looks great. The marble for the countertops should be here later today. I'm so hoping that the design assistant, Marcy, picked out pretty slabs. I'd wanted to join her, but there just wasn't time.

He hired local carpenters to do the wood work. What I've come to realize is Vince doesn't do much on a project when the cameras aren't on. I don't either. Janet explained that it's our jobs to look pretty and take directions. There's a beehive of people who never have camera time that actually make the job happen.

All the worker bees scatter. I've been told there's a trailer they go to for drinks and food. The multiple cameras get in place. The sound girl has Vince and me test our mics. This whole process takes around thirty minutes.

Then I'm sent outside with a cameraman.

He films me walking about thirty feet, opening the door, and entering the store.

"Hi!" I greet Vince. "I just finished lunch with a friend and thought I would stop by to see how it's going."

He's standing near the saw horses holding a piece of white trim. Looking up, he calls, "Glad you did. Why don't you come over here and take a look at this?"

The camera follows me until I reach Vince's side. "What's going on?"

"The wood glue is not wanting to stick to the glossy paint finish that you chose. See . . ." He demonstrates how easily it is to remove the trim from the cabinet door.

The whole time I'm thinking *this is the drama problem? Use a trim nail and counter sink.* Instead of solving the issue, I play along. "Oh. I do see. That's a huge issue. Do I need to change the finish?" I hate making myself look incompetent.

He gives me, the camera, and the female viewers at home a gorgeous smile. With a wink, he says, "You know I'm in this business to please my clients. I think we can use trim nails."

Gee, why didn't I think of that? "Great. I'm really committed to the high gloss white on the traditional style cabinets. It adds an updated flair." I caress the shiny surface as if it's the cheek of a newborn baby.

Janet yells cut and then starts giving out orders. "Group interview time." She positions Vince and me against the raw, red brick wall. "I need you two to discuss the progress on the remodel of the store and tell the viewers what's next."

I've only been doing this for four days, but I think I get better with each interview. I feel more comfortable in front of the camera and seem to have found my pace. Vince and I play well off each other. This is actually the most fun I've ever had in my life.

Next, we have what is called the producer interview. Janet stands off camera and asks me questions. She said she'll be edited out so the viewer will just think I'm giving them the inside scoop.

After I'm finished, I'm sent back to my trailer to change into work clothes. Vince and I are going to install the shelves on the brick wall where I'll display items for sale.

When I walk into my dressing room on wheels, Bella is sitting on the couch, flipping through a magazine. "Your phone's been going crazy."

Margo says, "I've pulled two outfits for you to choose from."

"Thank you," I reply to Margo and walk into my makeshift dressing area. Then to Bella, "Who's been trying to get ahold of me?"

"Don't know."

"You're my assistant. You're supposed to take care of these things," I sigh as I notice that my overalls didn't make the final cut. I have two tank tops. One is a stretchy blue lace and the other is green ribbed cotton. My pants choices are blue jeans or blue jean shorts.

I slip the sky-blue tank over my head.

"Fine," she replies, and I feel the floor vibrate as she walks. "It's like ten messages from Aaron."

My head flies out from behind the curtain at the mention of his name. "Give it to me."

She mouths *I could have read them out loud.*

She knows that I'm keeping Mister Emerson a secret and can be a such a brat sometimes.

I slip on the jean shorts and exit the confined space. After doing a little twirl, Margo approves.

Taking the seat across from Bella, I scroll through Aaron's texts.

> Aaron: *I can be there as early as five a.m. on Saturday morning. Too early? I can get Seamus to prepare the house.*
>
> Aaron: *Here's the deal. I don't want Seamus to prepare the NOLA house. I mean I don't care if he dusts it, but I want to spend time with you. Can you wear something other than a baggy shirt and soccer shorts?*

Then, about twenty minutes later, he sent another message.

> Aaron: *I didn't mean it like that. Okay, I did because you're all I think about and well, I'm a guy and you're a beautiful girl. Therefore I want to have sex with you, but what you wear won't change that.*

Pausing, I laugh. Thankfully, Margo asks if I'm hungry and offers to go to the food trailer for me. I gladly send her off.

When the door closes, I tell Bella, "I'm going to read you these texts because you're my best friend."

She nods and tosses the magazine she'd resumed reading. Clapping like a fool she says, "Yay. I love love."

I start over and catch her up on what I've already read. "Okay, so the next one says, *but I want to make love to you not fuck you. That's kinda crazy for me. I don't just want in your panties. I want all of you. I only want to make love to you if you're making love back.*"

Continuing, I read the next text. "He says, *why hasn't someone invented a way to take back sent text? I'm sorry I sent the last one and, well, all of them. Fuck, MK. I miss you. I haven't painted floors ever in my life, but it sounds like fun. It's a great way to relax on my day off.*"

Bella jumps to her feet. "You've got him, MK. He's yours for the takin'. That boy is panting for you." Her victory dance is uniquely her own.

"Sit down." I roll my eyes. "You remember what his sister told me. I'm his play thing. His new hotness. He has a short attention span and will grow tired of me. Then, I'm once again going to be poor, little MK dumped for a second time by the rock star."

She shrugs. "Or you're MK, the rock star's girlfriend and gets every bit of his attention, devotion, and love and every girl is green with jealousy."

My head falls between my knees, and I once again wish that our paths had never crossed and he never reentered my life. He makes things complicated. Filming a reality show is enough of a leap out of my comfort zone. I don't need to add dating one of the most famous men in the world to my plate.

"MK." Bella snaps her fingers near my right ear. I sit up, looking at her. "*Burnt Sugar* is the name of your show, right?"

I nod.

"Maybe burnt sugar is also a metaphor for your relationship with Aaron. Is he the knight in shining armor you've wished for? No. He has a rocky past, a teenage daughter, and, as he told you, enough baggage to fill an eighteen-wheeler—which you've witnessed—but he's crazy about you."

"And how is that burnt sugar?"

"You're still hoping for a guy like Tripp. You want someone who looks like they could model for J Crew and has a normal, high income job. Tripp is your sugar. He's your ideal, but you're not attracted to him. You're attracted to the guy who is burnt sugar. He wouldn't be caught dead wearing a pink collared shirt and light blue striped shorts. Aaron would rather poke his eye out than own a chain of carwashes. But he's who makes your heart flutter." She pauses and offers me her hands, pulling me to my feet. "You thought I was reading that gossip rag, but I was watching you read his messages. Did you know you were smiling? Did you know that your face was lit up like a Christmas tree? Give yourself permission to give him another shot, and this time quit letting your head get in the way of your heart."

"That's why you're my best friend. You know the words that I need to hear and when I need to hear them." I throw my arms around her neck. "I love you, Bella Boo."

Grabbing my phone, I settle back into the maroon leather chair.

> Me: *I can't wait for you to help me paint the floors. You can be my assistant. I think working off your pillowcase debt is a good idea. I miss you too.*

"Bella, what if he dumps me again and I have all those crazy people camped out on my front lawn?"

She kneels next to my chair. "You've been down that path. You'll be ready. Plus, you're no longer the scared girl who quit her job in a fit of rage and then decided to focus on NPC full time. You're an established woman with your own reality show. Honey, you've got scoreboard. Johnny Knite didn't make you. You made you. You pulled yourself up by the bootstraps. He's the lucky SOB who gets to bask in your glow. He chooses to screw that up? His loss, but then you at least know that he's not your ever after instead of being left with lots of question marks."

Chapter Twenty-Three

Aaron
September

Johnny Knite @RealJohnnyKnite
What's up Vegas? Two sold-out shows. Who's ready to party?

MK Landry @NoPinkCaddy
Kitchen is in! Who wants to take a cooking class from *moi*?
Stay tuned. We're getting close. #BurntSugar

I hate Vegas. It's where I got alcohol poisoning and arrested. It's opulent. It's over the top. It's basically everything that's wrong with this world.

"We're honored to host you and your band, ACE," the owner of the casino says pulling me out of my dark thoughts. His name is Robert Haines. He's in his mid-forties and inherited this place from his old man. Lucky bastard. My dad didn't even acknowledge that he knocked-up my mom.

"Thank you for opening your casino to us and our fans. We were excited and honored when we heard we were invited to play here." Total bullshit. I told Grace to cancel. There are too many of my vices at my fingertips in this town. The alcohol is free, and my former dealer lives half a mile up the strip. I was hoping MK would come and keep me occupied, but instead I'm going to her.

I can't let her down. I can't use again.

We're in a private dining room inside a posh restaurant located on the second floor of the casino. Grace set this dinner up and insisted that I come. I'd have been happy hiding in my suite until it's time to play my sst and head to the private airstrip.

Bottles of alcohol are being passed around like bags of chips at one of Jude's high school slumber parties. I met with the doctor today and, after taking x-rays of my hand and drawing more blood, we discussed my alcohol consumption. I'm trying to do better. I really am, but then the waiter pours me an aged fifty years' bourbon and all bets are off.

The second and third highball glass taste just as good as the first. My bandmates get rowdy and begin formulating plans for making the strip our bitch. Robert places a call and gets us set up in a VIP section in one of the top night clubs in Vegas.

The feeling of being bullet proof and twenty-two again starts pumping through my veins. I haven't torn a night up in a long time. Tonight is beginning to look promising.

My phone vibrates in my pocket. I pull it out and smile when I see it's a text from MK.

MK: *Long day on set. I'm about to go to bed. I miss my pillowcase, but I miss you more.*

I smile like the fucking Joker. My girl misses me. Maybe she's coming around. This is the most promising message yet.

And then just because I'm a glutton for punishment . . .

Me: *What are you wearing?*

To my surprise, she replies quickly.

MK: *A certain someone's Def Leppard shirt.*

Me: *Lucky shirt.*

Jesus Christ, I'm getting a boner in the middle of a private room in one of the most expensive restaurants in Vegas while surrounded by my band and sister. How fourteen-years-old of me.

MK: *What are you wearing?*

I contemplate making up something sexy like I'm lying naked on the bed with my legs spread holding my gigantic, throbbing cock. Instead, I decide to go with funny.

Me: *A shark tooth necklace . . .*

MK: *JERK*

Me: *Shouty capitals are rude. BTW, my band is looking at me like I'm crazy. We're in the middle of dinner with the owner of the casino while I'm typing on my phone, smiling like crazy.*

MK: *I lick my finger and thumb massaging my nipples, bringing them to hard points. They push against the soft cotton. The bit of friction making my . . .*

Oh God. I know she's fucking with me, but my dick can't seem to make that connection. I should put the phone away and ignore her, but when have I ever done what I should?

Me: *Your pussy is wet . . . Fuck! Stop this right now. The owner and I are about to have a private chat about the band doing a year of residency here when the tour is over. I need to concentrate not be sitting here with the hardest dick in Vegas.*

MK: *Oh. That's really cool. I hope the talks go well. Good night.*

"Why are you staring at your phone like that?" Grace asks.

"Uh . . . Sorry," I reply. "I'm going to step out and make a call. I'll be back in a moment."

I must adjust myself before I stand and make my way out the private entrance. I'm in a long, narrow, beige hallway. It contrasts with the over-the-top décor of the casino. At the end are two stainless steel doors with windows indicating that the public area lies beyond.

After exiting, I realize that I'm in the restroom hallway near the restaurant. There are two club leather chairs with a black granite cube table in between. I grab a chair and give her a call.

She's laughing when she answers. "That was fun."

"Fuck, sweetheart," I sigh as I remove my grey fedora and drag my left hand through my hair.

"I thought you had a meeting," she says in a sing-song voice.

"I do. I stepped out to regroup. It's not fair to sext me."

She giggles again. "I was just teasing you. I mean not really. I am wearing your shirt and my nipples are hard, but it could be because I have the AC turned down to sixty-nine. It's hotter than hell today."

"You're lucky that I don't get on a plane, fly to New Orleans, kidnap you, and bring you back on tour with me. I'd tuck you against me, and spend every moment making sure you knew how much I wanted you." Well, that was very stalkerish. I blame the lack of blood in my brain.

Her little sigh causes my dick to jump. "How should I respond to that?" The sweet, upbeat voice has been replaced with one that sounds unsure and frustrated. "Aaron, you say these words, and I believe you mean them, but I'm so afraid that you're going to get bored with me. I'm going to give myself to you, and you're not going to find me good enough. Some pretty little thing in a leather bustier is going to sashay up to you after a show and you're going to be like 'MK, who?'"

Wow. This conversation took a ninety-degree turn. I didn't want anything serious or heavy. I was calling to tell her goodnight. My fist digs into my thigh. "How many times do I have to tell you that you're what and who I want? I fucking asked you to marry me. You think I did that because I was coked up. Nope. I asked you because you're it. You're the whole ball of wax. You're the one. I knew it then. Got stupid for a while. And now have been clearly reminded."

The phone line falls quiet before she replies, "Then if all of that is true, how could you abandon me?" Quickly, she says, "Never mind. I don't want to rehash that again. I just wish I could believe that's the truth. Time will help. Go to your meeting. I'm going to bed."

I feel like we take two steps forward and one step back. It's beyond infuriating. "Good night. I'll text you when I'm getting on the plane." Sniffles cause my heart to skip a beat. "Why are you crying, sweetheart?"

The sniffles turn into sobs. "I want this to be easy, Aaron. Why can't you have an eight to five job and wear a suit to work? Why do you have to be rock star? Why can't you be vanilla ice cream? I like vanilla ice cream."

My stomachache reminds me that this is an issue between us. I'll never be her ideal guy. She's never going to be okay with me touring and my crazy life. Her freak out when the media showed up at her doorstep tells me she'll never be able to handle a red carpet lined with reporters screaming questions and asking her to model. Her life is limited to a small store on Magazine Street in New Orleans. She wants to live within walking distance to it and go to church every Sunday with her family. This will eventually become a problem because my career is worldwide. We'll have to resolve this together.

My princess MK hasn't quite come to terms with the fact she's not going to live her sorority girl dream life if she runs away with me. I decide to go with a humorous response. "That life is boring. Who wants to wear a suit, although I do look quite dapper in one? And vanilla ice cream is shit. I mean who wants vanilla when you can have pralines and cream? There's nuts . . ."

"And burnt sugar," she laughs through sniffles.

"I don't know about burnt sugar. There's caramel."

"Never mind. I'll explain this weekend. Goodnight, Aaron."

I hate hanging up with her. "Are we good, sweetheart?"

She sniffs. "I'm okay. We're okay. I'm just super stressed, and this has been a tiring week. I'm feeling overwhelmed, like I can't get everything that needs to be accomplished finished. Do you know that I didn't pee at all today while I was on set?"

"I hope not. That would have been awkward."

"No. Like I peed when I got up this morning, but I didn't go to the bathroom until I got home at seven tonight. That's not healthy."

I agree. "That's not good. You've got to make time for you. Sometimes you have to tell everyone to fuck off and give you a minute."

"Easier said than done," she scoffs.

"You've made a couple of comments about me being a spoiled rock star. I get it. I'm sure I am in a lot of ways, but I've had to put limits on what I'll do because as we skyrocketed to fame, everyone wanted a piece of me. I couldn't breathe, and I had a toddler at home, with no mother, who needed her parent. If I hadn't put limits and been demanding, I'd be dead now. This business would have literally killed me."

"Thank you," she replies. "That's great advice, and I appreciate it. Any other pearls of wisdom, send them my way. I'm just ready to do what I do best, and that's bringing new life to the old. All this other stuff is superfluous."

"We have the weekend. Just you and me and bucket of paint." I smile as I say it and warmth travels down my limbs.

"That sounds dreamy."

"Goodnight, sweetheart."

"Rock your meeting."

"Always."

I slip my phone back in my pocket feeling high on MK. The girl is like a drug. I don't even have to taste her to be a lovesick fool. I have this feeling in my gut that we're going to be okay. We'll figure this out, and we'll find our happiness even if it kills us.

I place my fedora back on my head before I re-enter the private dining room. The waiters have broken the room back up into individual tables while I was gone. Apparently, the band left. Only Grace and Robert remain.

I make my apologies as I join them at small table in the corner. "Sorry about that."

Grace looks perplexed. "Everything okay with Jude?"

"Oh yeah." I'm curious why she thinks that was my daughter who I stepped out to call. "I mean, I guess. I talked to her before we came down for dinner. She has a test and a project due next week."

I watch Grace's face change when she realizes who has kept them waiting. I'll give her credit there's only a brief flash of annoyance before she replaces it with a polite smile.

Turning my attention to Robert, "I'm anxious to hear your ideas. I know it's kind of become the thing for artists to do. Residency in Vegas and the fans come to us."

He takes a sip of his bourbon and motions to a waiter. "Yes. We've watched our competitors do it with much success. They're selling out every show, plus getting revenue from the rooms, gambling, dining, etc. We have Stan Upton whose illusionist show has done well for us. Plus, we have the comedy lounge that seats two hundred and fifty. Our guests love to watch the up and coming comics. When we've hosted concerts, they've always sold out. My investors and I feel it's time that we have an artist take up residency here."

A glass of bourbon is placed in front of me. I take a sip. "We're a rock band though. I'm not interested in a Broadway style production. That's not who ACE is."

Grace interjects. "Robert's people and I've been kicking around some ideas. Here's one we think is interesting. What about you, alone on the stage with just your guitar, mic, and a stool?" She pauses for a second before she adds, "Like the night you played at the bar in New Orleans."

I've relived that evening in my mind at least a thousand times. It was the first time I'd been on stage since rehab. I was pissed at my band and MK. I just wanted to play. Zed drove me to Eddy's Bar. I took the stage with my guitar and sang my heart out. Then I realized my girl was in the crowd, and it made the whole experience fucking perfect.

"Just an empty stage and me? I've played like that in small clubs, but doesn't Vegas want the glitz and glamour of a choreographed show?" I take a sip of bourbon as I play the theme song to *Mad Max* in my head.

"Garth Brooks did something similar, and it was hugely successful. You'd tell a story through your music. Talk about the meaning behind your songs.

Since you've written them, fans will get a kick out of hearing about their origins. You can cover other's tunes as well." Robert holds up his high ball glass as if to toast.

I don't join him in celebrating quite yet. "What about my band? These guys are family. We've been together since high school or the early days of playing in clubs around Austin. You want me to just ditch'em?"

Grace replies, "It would be no different than you taking years off from touring like you did when Jude was in high school. They'd be free to work on separate projects. Even if they just decided to sit home in their underwear, they have royalty checks paying their bills and the bills for future generations."

Slamming my drink down, the liquid sloshes back and forth. "I'm not sure this is a good idea. We've taken hiatuses before, and they've done their own thing, but I never performed for payment without them."

"We don't have to pay you," Robert interjects with a laugh.

My smile can only be described as sarcastic.

Getting us off this topic because I'm going to have to think long and hard about my band, I ask, "How many shows are you thinking?"

Grace replies, "Probably five a week. Like maybe Thursday night, two on Friday and two on Saturday nights. You'd do that for three months and then take three months off."

"So I would only have to be in Vegas Thursday through Sunday morning?"

Robert answers, "There would be some publicity things we'd ask you to do, of course. But yes, we'd give you a permanent residence in the hotel. You could use it every day or whenever you perform. It would be up to you."

The thought of performing without traveling from city to city does sound tempting, but we're in the middle of a world tour. I offer him my hand. "Thank you. I appreciate the offer. I'm going to have to spend some time thinking about it."

As we shake, he says, "Don't take too long. I've got other artists very interested in the gig. You're my first choice though."

How kind.

As I turn to leave the restaurant, I hear Grace tell Robert, "That went better than I expected."

Robert replies, "He'll come around."

I'm buzzed, and my head is filled with thoughts regarding Robert's offer. I text Sam that I'm not joining them at the club and head up to my room to change. I've had just enough alcohol that a night surrounded by temptation would be a recipe for disaster. I'm choosing the be the kind of man that MK deserves.

Twenty minutes later, I'm diving into the hotel's lap pool. Cutting through the water, I reach the edge do a flip-turn and head back in the opposite direction. I repeat my conversation with Robert over and over until I lose count and the chaos in my head is replaced with *Sun, Sun, Here Comes the Sun.*

My muscles scream with fatigue and my lungs ache, yet I keep going. Eventually the music in my brain ends also, and all I hear is the sweet sound of emptiness.

I have no idea how much time has passed, but my muscles are so fatigued that it's hard for me to pull myself out of the water. Draping the hotel provided bathrobe around me, I drag my spent body upstairs to my room.

As I fall asleep, it dawns on me that this is the first time I've been in Sin City that I've gone to bed alone. But I really haven't. MK's pillowcase covers the hotel one, and she spends the night dancing through my dreams.

Chapter Twenty-Four

MK
September

SuzyQ @SuzyQNews
Spotted #ACE at Tao Nightclub. No @RealJohnnyKnite.
#WheresWaldo

MK Landry @NoPinkCaddy
Sometimes you have to take matters into your own hands.
#ILoveToPaint #FamilyRocks #BurntSugar

MK Landry @NoPinkCaddy
Having nightmares about no one coming to #NoPinkCaddy grand opening. You're going to come right?

"Please consider hardwoods," Bella pleads as I compare two paint samples. One is called Purple Haze the other is Orchid Sunrise.

Ignoring her, I place the small, square colored chips on the dingy, dark cement of the paint store. "I think I like Purple Haze because it has a cooler sounding name. The Orchid Sunrise sounds like a special drink the country club would serve at Easter brunch to get the members nice and toasted, but I think it will look better against the mint green checkered floors. What do you think?"

“Oh look. Over there. There’s the hardwood flooring section. I bet I can con an employee to change the name of some lovely oak to Orchid Sunrise.” Bella’s arms are folded and she’s leaning against aisle cap as if this is the worst torture she’s ever experienced.

“If you’d said Purple Haze for the name of the oak flooring, you might have been able to convince me.” I carry the paint chip to the counter and ask them to mix it for me. Then, we grab a shopping basket and fill it with all the supplies we’ll need for my painted floor project. “This will be so much fun.”

As she grabs a roller, she asks, “How do you talk me into all these crazy ideas? It’s like you hypnotize me, and I just dumbly nod. ‘Sure, MK. It sounds like a great idea to give up my Friday afternoon and evening to do manual labor.’”

I kiss her cheek. “You love me. It’s a function of our deep and everlasting friendship.”

A mom and her daughter are walking towards us as we meander down the aisle. The child looks to be maybe three or four years old. As they pass, she says, “Mommy, I wish I could have a star on my cheek.”

Glancing over at Bella, I trace the star tattoo on my wrist. She’s smiling. “Kids are so innocent.”

Nodding, I reply, “They sure are. I bet she goes home and draws one on her cheek so she can be just like you.”

Bella grabs my arm. “I mean look at you. I’ve rocked my star scar so well that you had to be a follower and get one on your wrist.”

“Yup. We’re star sisters.”

That makes us both laugh.

Ten minutes later, we’re loading the trunk of Bella’s car with everything that I’ll need to transform my store’s floors into the vision in my head.

***

“Okay. Guys, thank you for coming. I can’t tell you how much it means to me that you’ve given up your Friday night on the town to help me. I love you all.”

Bella, Nyall, Mom, Dad, and Grandmother all arrived a few minutes ago to help make this project go faster.

"I've created templates." I hold up the amoeba shapes cut out of thick cardboard boxes. "The idea is to make the floor look like a paisley fabric. I did a sample area over here." Walking to the back of the store, I motion for them to follow. "It's not dry yet, but this is the look I'm going for. I think we should start back here and work our way forward."

Grandmother says in her thick Southern accent, "Darlin', why don't I get my yard guy and have him send some people over to do this? I'll pay."

"I wish it were that simple. It has to be dry and ready for the crew on Monday morning. I really don't think it will take that long with all of your help." I was shocked when Mom said that Grandmother was pitching in. She has a staff that takes care of everything around her home. I didn't know she knew how to hold a paint brush.

"Well, I do have a minor in art," she drawls. "I'll be happy to put it to use and be a stenciler." I watch my grandmother do something I've never seen before. She takes off her diamonds, putting them in the pocket of her Chanel bag and drops it on the floor. "Let's get started."

Mom and I exchange a look that says *Are we sure an alien hasn't kidnapped Grandmother and replaced her with a clone willing to mess up her weekly manicure?*

We work in teams. Grandmother stencils, and I paint.

When we're in a corner away from the rest of the gang, she says, "I got a check for a substantial sum of money."

"Hmmm . . ." I respond as I fill in the trace with the lovely shade of purple paint.

"It was from Johnny Records. Strangely enough, it's close to the sum of money I gave you to install the fence and gate around your carriage house." Her probing eyes try to meet mine, but I'm smart enough to focus on my roller.

"That was generous of him considering he was the reason it was installed."

"Mary Kay Landry, look at your grandmother," she demands.

I pick my head up and give her a sheepish smile. "We've been talking."

Now, I know where I get my eye rolling from. It's genetic. "I make it a practice to not meddle in your love life, but do you think he's a good choice for a future husband? He's more of a really great summer fling."

My mouth hangs open. Grandmother can be dirty. "We're just getting to know each other again. It's all just a bit of fun we're having."

She tsks. "A bit of fun and then you have a bun in the oven."

Oh my God. This conversation must end and soon. "So, Grandma, how's the charity ball planning coming?"

Fortunately, she takes the bait and gets me caught up on the plans. My phone vibrates in back pocket about five minutes into the conversation. It's a message from Tripp.

Tripp: *Headed your way. Need anything?*

"Tripp is coming. Want him to bring dinner?"

To my surprise, Grandmother says, "Have him pick up that Mardi Gras pizza and some alcohol. This is a rather lame party."

I think my mother's eyes might bug out of her head.

"Okay." I text him back with our dinner pick up request.

Calling our favorite Italian joint, I order the Mardi Gras pizza. It has purple onions, yellow squash, green zucchini, pepperoni and garlic on it. It's a rule. Everyone must eat a slice so we can't smell the stench of garlic on each other.

Thirty minutes later, Tripp knocks on the locked front door. I place my paint roller on the tray and race to let him in. To my surprise, a beautiful, dark haired woman is with him.

"I'll take those." I reach out my arms and he places the warm pizza boxes on them.

Tripp and the girl step inside, and he turns the lock behind him. Everyone stops what they're doing and stares at the pair. It's been ages since anyone has seen him by the side of a girl that isn't me.

Tripp clears his throat and says, "I'd like y'all to meet my girlfriend, Roseanna."

Bella and I lock eyes. She seems to be pleased so therefore I smile. I turn to the beautiful brunette and say, "Welcome, Roseanna." She's holding a brown paper bag and wearing a warm smile. "Thanks for coming. It's nice to put a face with the name."

"Yes. I've heard so much about all of you." She has a hint of an accent. It might be Puerto Rican, but I'm not sure.

I grab the paper plates and red Solo cups from my beautiful kitchen cabinets. We haven't filled them yet with the ceramic dishes I ordered.

Once we all have our pizza and either a glass of wine or bottle of Amber Abita, we sit down on the floor leaning against the brick wall.

"Your store is beautiful," Roseanna compliments.

"Thanks. It's my dream come true," I reply as I take a bite of the floppy slice.

"Tripp said that you've wanted to do this for a long time. And a reality show on top of it. We can't wait to snuggle into the couch and watch you on TV."

Hmmm . . . Roseanna and Tripp are close enough that she's his girlfriend, and they're going to watch my show together. I couldn't be happier for the two of them, but she better be good to my friend or I'll sic Bella on her.

Grandmother asks how filming is going, and I spend the rest of our picnic dinner educating everyone about how a reality show is filmed.

Nyall says, "The place really looks fabulous. What's left to do?"

"Well, we don't have all the shelving installed. I want a mural on that wall." I point to the plaster wall across from us. "It'll probably have to wait. I used most of my budget on the kitchen. I need it for the show and to demo recipes, but I also want a place to teach cooking classes and just prepare things for shoppers to sample."

Roseanna replies, "I've never been in any store like that. I think it will be great."

"Thank you." I smile at Tripp, pleased that he has chosen a woman that seems to be classy, polite, and worthy of his attention. "Okay, dinner break over. Everyone, back to work."

"MK, I've got to run to my truck and get a tool box. I was going to install something for you," Tripp says as he tosses his and Roseanna's plates into the stainless-steel garbage bin.

"Ok." I shrug.

He returns looking like the complete stud he is. Dark hair is swept away from his face and his deep brown eyes contrast perfectly with his olive complexion. His body fills the door frame. Dressed in a designer plaid shirt, it's tucked in neatly to his expensive jeans. Carrying his shiny, red tool box, he looks more like he's posing for a sexy book cover or Playgirl Magazine than helping me paint floors. I appreciate his beauty for what it is. His eyes connect with Roseanna, and she stands up, joining him by his side. Tripp is the definition of what I thought I always wanted in a guy. Maybe my tastes have taken a walk on the wild side.

"We got you a little gift." He pulls a thin, wrapped present from the back waistband of his jeans.

Handing it to me, I remove the green paper. It's a vintage, rectangular sign that reads *Come In, We're Open.* The writing is old, and it's made of metal with hints of rust around the edges. It's so gorgeous and perfect that I gasp. Hugging it to my chest, I feel as if I've won the lottery. "I love it."

"Roseanna and I found it at an antique store in Mobile. We both thought that your store couldn't open without it. Want me to hang it for you?" Tripp's cheeks are blushing.

I hand Bella the sign and throw my arms around both of their necks, knocking poor Roseanna off balance. She recovers, and we both laugh.

Roseanna helps Tripp hang the sign while the rest of us get back to work. At some point, Bella's phone finds an 80s-pop station on Pandora. Our painting chore turns into a karaoke dance party while we work. Even Grandmother gets into it and joins Bella and me in performing *Jessie's Girl.*

Around midnight, I get a text from Aaron.

Aaron: *About to go to work. Private show for some of the casino's VIPs. My plan is to walk off the stage and straight to a car to take me to the air strip. Counting down the hours until I get to my MK.*

Me: *Rock their faces off.*

Aaron: *Always.*

We're working our way towards the door. The floor looks exactly how I imagined it. "It's beautiful guys. Thank you."

"What's left?" Bella asks.

"Well, I need to finish this bit right here, and then let it dry. Tomorrow, I'm going to use a combination of black paint and paint pens to add the paisley details so it doesn't just look like amoebas."

"Need help with that?" Dad asks.

"I don't think so. I . . . ummm . . . I'll take care of it." I'm not quite ready to share with my parents that the guy who made my life miserable might be back in the picture.

"Well, okay," Mom says. "If you change your mind give us a call."

After cleaning up, Grandmother extracts the diamonds from her bag. The flecks of purple paint which remain on her paper-thin, loose skin contrasts next to the shiny, brilliant rocks. Her hands tell the story of an aging, fabulous woman who would do anything for her granddaughter—even manual labor. "All right, kids, let's go have a night cap at Eddy's."

I follow my family and friends out of the store after finishing the spot by the front door, feeling so blessed to be surrounded by such a fantastic group of people. As we walk down the sidewalk to our favorite neighborhood watering hole, I let them get ahead so I can take a moment to appreciate how fortunate I am. They've had my back through the good times and bad. They've loved me when I've been unlovable. I don't know Roseanna well and she doesn't know me, but she showed up and she helped her boyfriend's friend in need.

As we pass by the dry cleaners, I yell to my gang, "I love you people."

Bella turns over her shoulder and replies, "We must love you too because I'm covered in paint and my back is aching, and I haven't thought about murdering you once."

Chapter Twenty-Five

Aaron
September

MK Landry @NoPinkCaddy
Check out the floors #NoPinkCaddy. More work to do, but I'm seeing hearts. Love them so much.

MK Landry @NoPinkCaddy
We're so close to being ready for you to visit. Join me at the grand opening. Enter here. #BurntSugar

"Hi." She yawns as she leans against the doorjamb dressed in short lavender silk shorts and a matching sleeveless top. Her nipples tent the material in the cool, breezy September morning. The glow from the sun just greeting the day highlights the peaks, casting them in a darker shade of purple. Her hair is a mess around her face. Sleepy eyes tell me that I woke her.

"Hi," I reply standing on the next to the top step. "It's early. Like six in the morning, I think."

"Yeah." She grins. "But this is when you're going to bed."

I don't want to stand out here and make small talk. My lips tingle with the desire to brush them over the curve of her chin. Before I can reason if it's a wise idea to maul her, I drop my bag and guitar case on the front porch, closing the gap between us, kicking the door closed behind me. I scoop her in my arms as her hands clinch my biceps. She yelps in surprise, but then snuggles into my chest as I carry her through her empty living room and into her bedroom.

Placing her gently on the bed as if she were an infant, I strip off my rough denim jeans and pull my shirt over my head. I leave my underwear on only because I think if I get completely naked there will be no stopping my dick from finding where he longs to be, and there's also the weirdness about modesty when I was last here.

I watch her face carefully to see if she's going to reprimand me for being too forward. I'd told her that we didn't have to make love. I think I even said I'd be okay with watching a Disney cartoon. That's all entirely true, but that doesn't mean that I can't have hope.

To my relief, she just looks dreamy. Sliding under the covers, I pull her to my chest. The silk material over her nipples, brushing against my pecs causes an involuntary moan to escape my throat.

My lips kiss her hair, forehead, ear, cheek, neck, and the beautiful little dip of her shoulder right before I reach her collarbone. She's pliable in my hands—relaxed as if she recognizes that her proper place is in my arms. I push my luck, slipping one of the straps from her shoulder revealing the swell of her breast. Creamy olive skin, just a shade lighter than her chest, greets me as a beam of sunshine slips through the partially-open shutters. The throb in my cock is painful.

Ignoring it, I take my time kissing the skin touched by the summer sun and just the line that hasn't seen its rays. I don't move past that barrier afraid she's going to stop me or give me another one hundred reasons why we'll never last. My heart can't take being shot down, at least not right now. Intimacy is what I crave.

I beg her to respond. I need her to give me a little sound or action that lets me know that it's okay to keep going. I want her. I want to make love to her more than anything else in the world, but when I told her that I needed her to make love back, I was serious. I'll wait forever for her to be ready, but God, I hope it doesn't take that long.

Leaning on my forearm, I use my other hand to brush her tangled brown hair from her eyes. They're shut, and she looks happy and peaceful. "Good morning, Miss Landry. Did you have sweet dreams?"

Her smile is so enticing that I fight to keep from kissing her lips. "I dreamt of a rock star. He showed up on my front porch, swept me off my feet, placed me in bed, and has made me feel like the most cherished girl in the world."

Those words . . . Well, they touch me right in my heart. "Not a dream, sweetheart. Your rock star did all of those things to make sure you knew that you are indeed the most cherished girl in the world."

MK's hand strokes over her name, tattooed on my chest, leaving a trail of fire where she touches. "I love this," she says. "I feel like no other girl can love you because you've chosen my name on your heart."

"That's my girl. You're finally getting it. I'm yours and only yours."

She wraps her arms around my neck pulling me on top of her. My mouth slams against hers completely unable to resist her full lips any longer. Our tongues begin a sensual, erotic dance. This is what I've written songs about. This feeling has caused wars between countries and taken lives. I now understand. Those lips are mine and will never touch anyone else's.

Her nails rake down my back as my tongue laps over the pulse point on her neck. Then I almost lose my shit when she arches up pressing her pussy against my cock.

"Fuck," I groan using every bit of will power that I possess to keep from ripping her silk shorts off and having my way with her.

She takes my face between her palms. "Look at me," she orders.

My eyes travel from the top of the headboard to her gorgeous smile.

"If we do this, Aaron, tell me I'm yours. You have to promise me that there will never be anyone else but me."

"Sweetheart, there's only you."

Her grip on my cheeks tightens. "I mean it, Aaron. Be man enough to get out of my bed and walk out my door if you aren't in this with everything you've got."

I pull back, sitting on her thighs, as I stare down into the only eyes I've ever let see my soul. "Mary Kay Landry, I'm yours. You couldn't get rid of me if you tried. You kick me out. I move to the couch. You change the locks.

I sleep on the porch. All I want in the world is to be yours like you're already mine."

There's a hesitation to her smile and hardness in her eyes. "You doubt me?"

"It's not a doubt." Her tongue swipes over her teeth. "It's that I want so much to believe you. I think right now, you're absolutely telling me what's in your heart, but I want to make sure that you will still feel that way once I've given myself to you."

Frustration wrinkles my forehead. Once again, this is our dance . . . two steps forward and one step back. I make sure my voice stays level. "I can't look into the future and tell you what lies ahead. My magic eight ball is broken. Love is a leap of faith." I shrug. "I'm jumping in with both feet, and you must do that also."

She scoots out from under me and leans against headboard. I flop across the foot of the bed preparing to hear more concerns and reasons why we shouldn't be in a relationship. Instead, she surprises me. "I got read by a fortune teller."

Looking up, I ponder where this conversation is going. She'd mentioned something about seeing a fortune teller in a past conversation, but she didn't elaborate.

"It was for the opening credits of *Burnt Sugar.* We were just filming stuff that's New Orleans. We went to Jackson Square, and Cindy thought it would be good TV to have images of me getting read by a psychic. Like here I am, MK who's lost in the world, so I seek out supernatural guidance."

I roll on my side and use my arm to brace my head. I'm completely intrigued where she's going with this. "Did you learn anything interesting?"

"First, do you believe that people can see into the future and stuff like that?" The way her head turns tells me that this conversation is very important to her.

Instead of giving her a flippant answer, I think about what I do believe. "The human mind is more complex than we can decode. I'm willing to believe that there are people who can connect with souls that have died, and that people, especially moms, can have premonitions about things about to happen. Do I believe that someone can tell me what I'm going to be doing a week from Tuesday? No, I think that's dumb. But I believe souls are energy and that they're not necessarily tied to our human form and sometimes people can tap into that energy."

She swallows. "To be honest, I've never given it much thought. My mom said to stay away from the occult and the church backs her up so I have. I was leery of the reading."

Nodding, I get that. I don't think I'd want to meet someone who could potentially tell me things I didn't want to hear from my dead father.

"Anyway, she got all weird, and then said that someone who I thought was dead has re-entered my life. Then, she freaking described you." Her voice speeds up as she tells me the story. Her eyes are wide, and she's wringing her hands. "She said that our souls are together. She may have used the word destined. I don't quite remember." Her tongue swipes over her bottom lip. "I got scared and accused her of recognizing me and even said that Cindy had paid her to tell me that stuff."

"Okay." I nod. "That seems likely. It makes better TV if she reads you accurately."

Her head moves back and forth. "Here's the weird part, as if that wasn't odd enough. She made a comment about my grandfather. He died way before I was born. Everyone always comments how alike Grandmother and I are. The psychic said that Grandfather told her to tell me to quit being difficult like Grandmother. My mom said that he'd always tell Grandmother that she was being difficult. Like both Mom and the fortune teller used the same word."

She shudders. "I got out of there. I ended that nonsense because it was so freaky."

"Do you believe that our souls are together?" If this fraud is helping convince MK to take me back, I'll be happy to pay her also.

"You texted me at the exact second I ended the reading. You had a dream about our souls tangoing."

I crawl to MK and rest my head in her lap, tired of fighting the overwhelming need to touch her. Immediately, her fingers go into my hair.

"That was such a real dream. It was like I knew you were in New Orleans, and I knew I was asleep in a hotel, but our souls met in dreams so we'd never really be apart."

"That's beautiful." She smiles. "I'm going to believe that's true. No matter where your career takes you across the globe and even if I'm never able to join you, our souls will stay together."

Her eyes get the dreamy glow that I've come to associate as my MK feeling loved. Her pointer finger starts at my Adam's apple and makes its way to my heart. She traces her name. "Aaron Emerson, make love to me."

I keep my composure on the outside, but on the inside, I melt into a little pile of sentimental goo. Scooting off the bed, I tell her, "Sweetheart, lay back and let me love you." A knot builds in my throat, and I'm surprised that I can get the words out around it.

She complies with a beautiful, sweet smile.

"Hold on." She looks perplexed so I explain, "I left my stuff outside. There's something I need."

If I could fly, I would. I fling the door open with such force that I check to make sure the doorknob didn't dent the wall. My tab with MK seems to be growing. I don't need sheetrock repair on my list. Grabbing my things, I drop my bag in the living room and rest my case on her kitchen island. After unsnapping the locks, I remove my guitar and walk back in the bedroom.

She sits up.

"I wrote this song when I was here Monday night. It's still rough, and I'm working on it, but I want you to hear it." I sit down on the edge of the bed at her feet and place the guitar in my lap.

"Really?" She laughs. "I just told you I want to make love to you and you want to play me a song?" This might be the number one thing I love about her. She's always this southern belle, such a lady, but then she gets demanding and I feel like I get this side of MK that is only mine. It's the one she keeps locked inside her carriage house.

"It's worth it." I sit with my legs crossed in front of her while resting the guitar on my lap. I begin strumming the opening notes to the song. "You see, I didn't have a name for this when I wrote it, but after talking to you Thursday night, I realized you knew the name without hearing it. I give you your song, *Burnt Sugar.* But this is really me giving myself to you."

The lyrics are sweet. They're about me thinking that I wanted a single life, living like a lone wolf, and then long brown hair and chocolate eyes stole my heart, teaching me that what I thought my life would be like was completely wrong. The music I composed over the words is my nod to the city she adores. I've written a part for the sax and I even asked Sam what she thought of adding a bit of a Zydeco flair. Of course, that doesn't translate well to me just playing and singing along to my guitar, but it's not important now. I want her to hear what she means to me. My music says what it's difficult for me to express sometimes.

Her eyes become glassy as she leans forward with a smile the size of Texas. "It's perfect. Have you thought about adding a bit of NOLA to it?"

"Yeah." I nod and regale her with my ideas.

She suggests speeding up the tempo so it's more upbeat. "I think that might be theme music for *Burnt Sugar.* Are you willing to share?"

Am I willing? It never occurred to me that she'd need music for her show. "Fuck yeah. You think I'd let someone else write anything for you?"

She leans forward and takes the guitar from my lap resting it next to her. Her eyes are hooded as her tongue swipes over her bottom lip. "Play my body like you play your guitar."

Best. Invitation. Ever.

My initial thought is to dive on top of her and be inside in like fifteen seconds flat. I could go ahead and blow my load then spend the next forty-eight hours ravishing her body.

Deciding against that plan, I scoot to the end of the bed and begin sucking each of her pink polished toes into my mouth as I massage the arch of her right foot. Her pleasure moans tell me that I'm doing a badass job.

After moving to her left foot, I kiss my way over the bump of her ankle and I notice a tiny freckle next to her rounded tendon. It's so cute that I run my tongue over it and give it a long suck.

When I start traveling upward, she taps the back of my head. I look up and see that she has a scowl on her face. "What's wrong?"

She says with a sheepish grin, "You see, I forgot to shave before you arrived."

"And?" I ask her. No clue where she's going with this train of thought.

"Well . . . I have dark hair, and it grows fast. The prickles may cut your lips and tongue, and that would be kind of awful. You'd be singing on stage and everyone would wonder why . . ."

I roll my eyes. "Shut up, MK. Lie back and let me love your gorgeous body. Do you think I give a fuck if you have stubble on your legs?"

She crosses her arms and flops back down on the mattress. Only she can find a way to be difficult during this time.

"Would you rather that I just went straight to eating your pussy? I mean I'm trying to have some foreplay here."

Her hand slams against the mattress. "You don't have to be crude. I was being polite by giving you a warning. You're a grown ass man. You do what you wish. But you can't say that I didn't warn you." Her Cajun accent is thick. I picture her threatening me with a frying pan.

"What I wish is to slam my dick inside of you and make you fucking forget all the dumb shit that passes through your brain while I'm trying to take you to the place of Bliss you've told me about."

She wiggles her hips and places her hands on her stomach. "Okay. I'm ready to find Bliss," she replies in a cutesy voice.

Standing up, I run my hand through my matted hair. "See, now you've confused me. Should I start back where I was before I was rudely interrupted by your inner thoughts, or should I start with where I was headed?"

She kneels on the edge of the bed placing her boobs tantalizing close to my lips. Her lips touch mine and all my confusion and frustration fades away. "I want you to show me how much you've missed me."

Looking up into her large eyes, I give her my cocky smile as I grab my dick through my underwear. "It's evident right here, sweetheart."

Playfully, she hits my left arm. Then she makes things much easier by removing her silk top and shoving a nipple in my mouth. Thank God, this woman was made for me.

"You taste like the sweetest treat," I tell her as I move to the other breast.

She's a fine delicacy. She's dessert with whipped cream.

Her hands give my hair a tug when I bite her nipple. The touch of pain mixes with the extreme pleasure of feeling her body pressed against mine. It's hedonism at its finest.

Each breast fills up a hand. They're perfect—not too big and not too small. I hold them as if they're the most precious treasure ever. "I love your tits. They're perfection just like you."

Nails drag down my spine. With a groan, my head falls back and her breast pops out of my mouth. Her lips covers mine as if she's trying to absorb my sounds of pleasure. Our tongues tango just like our souls did in my dream, and I wrap my arms so tightly around her that she's sure to know just how much I need her.

Placing her on the bed, I pull the silk shorts down her legs and toss them over my shoulder. "No panties? Were you planning on seducing me?"

"I might have hoped that we would reach this place." Her look is mischievous, and I adore it.

Spreading her muscular thighs, that beautiful pink pussy which has starred in both night and daytime fantasies, is ready and waiting for me. I reflect on how far we've come in such a short time and how grateful I am that I'm getting a second chance to love her.

"Why are you looking at me all weird?" she asks with a scowl.

"I'm not, sweetheart." I run my hand up and down the inside of her leg. "Just taking a second to appreciate how fucking lucky I am."

Her features relax as I move between her thighs. Using my tongue, I lap up every bit of sweetness my girl will give me making my way to the place I crave the most. Spreading her lips, I suck and teethe her clit.

Moans and cries of pleasure mix with the sounds my mouth makes as I devour her. It's a beautiful sonnet that we're creating together.

Her hips buck up from the mattress as she frantically taps my head. "I want you." Her voice is breathless and needy.

I look into MK's eyes. "I'm all yours."

Kicking off my underwear, I position my cock at her entrance. Taking one last look at her lean, tanned naked body, I prepare myself for just how good it's going to be when I finally have made her mine once again.

"You need a condom," she groans.

I shake my head. "Why?"

"I saw the pics of the model. There's some in my bedside drawer."

Crawling off her, I stand next to the mattress. "Why do you have condoms in your bedside drawer?"

"Does it matter? Just get one." She sounds as frustrated and frantic as I feel.

Reluctantly, I open the drawer and find the box. I tear open the package and roll the little fucker down my dick. It's as unhappy as I am. "This is bullshit."

"Do you want to argue about it or do you want some of this?" She drags her finger through her short pubic hair and shows me the moisture.

Who am I to argue? Crawling back on the bed, I drive into her with one solid push. Her body opens itself up to accommodate me. She whispers, "Aaron, you feel so good."

"You too, baby. You too," I breathe as I keep still, feeling her tightness envelop me. Her warmth makes me feel safe, and that I'll always have a place to call home. My head is clear. There's no music playing. I'm experiencing instead of being numbed to the world.

Slowly, I pull back and then slide back in. Over and over and over again. I'm lost in her. I quit worrying about making sure that I'm doing a good job and pleasuring her. Instead, I revel in our bodies becoming one.

"This is what I missed the most," she says through tear-filled eyes. "I wanted this connection."

I pull back and ease in again.

"This is making love, and it's so fucking sweet." The only good thing about the condom is that it keeps me from coming in like two seconds.

She grips my forearms, and I love that she'll probably leave a bruise her hold is so tight.

We're a solid perfect mass of sweaty bodies.

I grab her around her back and pull her on top of me as I lean back on my hands. Her arms wrap around my neck as she bounces on my dick. Her taut nipples rub against the hair on my chest. MK's head drops back and a delicious sound exits her throat.

My mouth finds hers, as her teeth imbed in my lips. She rides my cock finding her bliss. I follow her a few seconds later, and we both tumble to the sheets. I pull her against me and hold on with everything I've got. I never want this moment to end.

Chapter Twenty-Six

MK
September

Music Times @MusicTimesMagazine
Sources close to LV casino mogul Robert Haines are reporting that he's in negotiations with @RealJohnnyKnite

Music Times @MusicTimesMagazine
@RealJohnnyKnite would have residency at @CelestialPalaceCasino.

Rock Star Groupies @RockStarGroupies
@RealJohnnyKnite OMG! @CelestialPalaceCasino do it. Sign him.

He rolls the condom off, ties the end, and drops it on the ground with a plop. I'm totally grossed out, but I fight the overwhelming urge to ask him to toss it in the kitchen garbage. Instead, I suppress the crazy and snuggle against his tattooed arm trying to be present in the moment.

I might be certifiably insane, but God it feels great to be wanted by this man. His body feels as if it was made for mine. I love the silence and ease between us.

His hand taps a rhythm on my bicep. It's a slow lazy beat.

My eyes grow heavy and for a bit I think I might doze off.

"So what do I have to do to ditch the rubbers?" he asks, as my eyes fly open.

Stretching, I yawn as I sit up. "You have to get tested for everything under the sun, and then I'll consider it." My voice is content like we should be chatting about running through a sunny meadow filled with daffodils instead of venereal disease.

"You in Bliss?" He rubs my bent knee.

"Yup. Don't ruin my moment by talking about VD." I lay back down snuggling deeper into his side and kiss his pec.

Aaron sighs and the beat he taps is more up-tempo yet the silence that hangs between us feels heavier. "Why do you have condoms?"

I sit back up in bed, completely naked with my legs tucked under me. "Fine. Okay. Let's have this very awkward conversation then."

He leans against the headboard and drags his hand through his messy hair. "Sorry. I just can't clear my mind until I replace the thought of a train of guys moving through here with the truth."

Pulling the comforter over my hips, I cross my arms over my breasts. "I haven't slept with anyone since you. I'm not a whore, and I take issue with you imagining that I am. I mean a train of guys? That's just crude, Aaron."

He grabs for me, but I resist. His forehead forms a *V*, but he doesn't push it. "I don't think you're a whore. I just get crazy at the thought of anyone else touching you." He audibly swallows. "The condoms were a surprise."

"They shouldn't be. I'm a thirty-one-year-old, single female. It would be odd if I wasn't having sex." Kicking the blanket off, I stand, walking towards the bathroom. "And if you must know they were a bachelorette party gift from Bella as a joke." I stop at the doorway. "Aaron, why do you do this? Why must you ruin a lovely moment with such harsh words?"

His head hangs. "I don't know, MK. I'm a man with my heart on my sleeve. I'm just worried that you're going to realize that I'm not good enough for you, and you're going to leave me." We make eye contact, and I try to give him a reassuring smile. He continues, "I need to know that I'm yours for the rest of our lives. That it's just you and me. That you accept that I'm not or ever will be a lawyer, doctor, or Indian Chief. I'll never wear shorts with tiny alligators on them or collared golf shirts."

He stands and walks to me. "I say fuck a lot and I probably drink too much on occasion. I'm staying away from drugs, but well, that's a day by day process, and I may screw up. You can't kick me out of your life just because I disappoint you. You have to love the perfectly imperfect man that is me."

I caress his cheek as he leans into my touch. "I love the perfectly imperfect man that you are. Are you who I always pictured I'd fall for? Nope. I've never been the girl lusting over music men, but we didn't choose each other." Placing a kiss on his heart, "Our souls found their other half."

"God, sweetheart," he says, wrapping his arms around my waist. Nuzzling into my hair, he takes a deep breath. "I fucking love that you smell like sex and me."

Leaning back, I laugh. "That means I need a shower." I drop my arms, stepping into my bathroom. My bare behind feels the sting of his palm.

"I like my scent all over you," he says peering around the door.

I blow him a kiss, and he turns around, giving me the bit of privacy that I like.

I splash cold water on my face and look in the mirror at a girl who is completely smitten with the boy in the other room. But I have no idea why. He's crass, unrefined, a bit insane, and sexy as hell. The only thing I reason is that it's like I told him, we didn't choose each other. Sometimes you find your other half in the person you least expect to fall for.

"Viva and I didn't have sex," Aaron says from the other room.

I watch my serene expression morph into mouth-hanging-open shock in a millisecond. Sticking my head around the doorjamb, I roll my eyes. "You think I was born yesterday? The rock star always has sex with the Victoria Secret's Angel."

He smirks and shrugs. "This rock star didn't. We were never in the same place long enough. We weren't really together like staying with each other. She was busy, and so was I."

As I walk back to the bed, his eyes hood and his mouth goes slack as he tracks me. I feel like I've had my body worshiped without him laying a finger.

When I get close enough, he pulls me on top of his chest with his already hard penis trapped between our bodies.

He kisses my scar. "I never got on a plane between shows to see her. I didn't hold onto my phone hoping for one little smart-mouthed text. Feel my dick against you?"

I nod.

"I didn't get hard at just the sight of her. Only you, sweetheart. Only you make me this crazy."

My thoughts exactly.

He smirks. "Congratulations. Welcome to the rest of your life."

"I'll feel properly congratulated once that rubber is over your dick." I wiggle off him and hand him another condom.

His eyes squint. "You think I'm lying."

Shaking my head, I reply, "No, I don't." I curl up next to him and play with the fine, blond hair that sprinkles his chest. "I will just feel better once you've been tested."

He throws the condom, still in its wrapper, on the floor as he rolls on top of me. His chin rests on my chin. "I swear on Jude's life that you're the only person I've been with since rehab."

My eyes shut. It's not that I didn't believe him when he said that he's been celibate. It's just a tad shocking considering his track record.

"Come on, MK. Tell me you believe me." He kisses my lids.

My eyes meet his. "Fine. I believe you. You don't have to use a condom."

His knee spreads my thighs, as he slips inside without a problem. We spend the next however amount of time truly making love to each other. I don't care that my legs need a shave or that I probably have morning breath. We tenderly kiss and our slow, lazy rhythm says that neither one of us want this to end. As we climax together, he throws his leg over my hip and whispers as if it's a prayer, "This forever."

***

"You sure you'd rather paint than go pick out living room furniture?" he asks looking so darn cute in a pair of faded denim jeans and a white shirt that reads

Waylon, Willie, and the Boys. I could easily go for another round between the sheets.

"Yes." That's not entirely true. I've gotten over my need to find something vintage and fabulous to fill the blank space in my place and have concluded that I just need something. I'm tired of not having a place for guests or me to sit. But when have I had time? Since my initial meeting with Janet and Cindy, all I've done is work. I feel like a horse racing around the track. It's hard to stop because something always needs my attention.

Plus, shopping takes money and patience. Both of which, I don't possess.

Aaron leans against raw brick wall in my store, posed as if he's a model at a photoshoot. I grab my phone and snap a picture while he looks out the window. He catches me, flashing a sweet smile as he closes the space between us—walking like a predatory cat.

"You think I'm fuckable," he says as he slips my phone in my overall's back pocket and places his arms around my waist as if we're going to dance.

"I think you're handsome." My face heats.

His cocky smile and narrowed eyes are hot. "You're wishing I'd take you again up against that wall."

The burn between my legs says that I do indeed wish he would take me against the wall and do all sorts of other dirty things to my body. Instead, I reply, "That would be super fun, but right now, we have to turn these purple amoebas into paisleys. Then, we're going to watch your new band. Maybe later . . . if you're lucky."

"Don't force me to make you beg." His cocked brow says maybe that's exactly what I want to make him do. He continues, "Sweetheart, I'm a musician. I don't have a drop of artistic skills in me. Want me to fly Cara down here? She could give you kickass paisleys while we focus on other things that I'm much better at." His hips move suggestively.

"No. It has to get done today so that it can dry overnight and be ready for Monday." I place my hand on his chest. "I'm sure you'll be a great artist. I have faith in you."

Grabbing the paint and pens, I walk over to the corner. I sit down next to one of the blobs. Aaron joins me at my side with his dark leather motorcycle boots inches from my calf.

"Okay." I demonstrate with a thick black paint pen. "I want you to be creative. Trace the inside of the purple, leaving about half an inch between the edge and the black. Once you're done with that, then fill in the middle. You can do flowers like I'm doing or just geometric shapes. Whatever. As long as it looks like paisleys."

When I meet his eyes, he's scowling and flexing his right hand. "What about if I ask Jude to come down?"

The rage bubbles to my mouth as I toss my arms in the air. I told him I had to paint this weekend, and he agreed. I didn't spring this job on him. "Look, don't help me," I yell. Then in a more resolved tone I say, "I'll see if Bella can give up another night. I mean really, Aaron. Just go. I'll text you when I'm finished."

Turning my back to him, I take out my phone and press with too much force on Bella's name.

He places his hands on my shoulder and catches my eyes which are trying their damnedest to avoid his soft baby blues. "It just seems like a lot of work, and I was going to get someone to help who knows what they're doing. I'm not trying to bail on you."

Nodding, my chest relaxes at his explanation. "Great. Then let's get started."

He uses his phone to turn on his Pandora station. The reason I know this is because one of his older songs plays first. I'd recognize that deep voice anywhere.

I look up from drawing wavy lines. "How humble of you."

He's about three feet away working on his own paisley. "Thought this time might be used having an ACE appreciation class while we work." His smile is sexy. "If you're my girlfriend, you should actually know some of our music."

After finishing, I butt-scoot to the next one. "I know some of your songs, Aaron. It's not like I'm a music idiot." Okay. I am, but I hate having this flaw pointed out to me.

"You were the one who called yourself a music idiot. Not me." I can hear the smirk in his voice.

"Damn. I really need to think before I speak." I laugh at myself.

As his songs play, he tells me about them. I get a history lesson of ACE and, I must say, I appreciate his music so much more knowing the origin of his biggest hits. I learn what he was thinking when he was writing the song. Sometimes he shares how shocked he was when a certain track became a number one hit. He tells me one of the songs he wrote in fifteen minutes and tossed on an album because his producer was being a jerk and kept insisting the album needed one more song. Critics have called it one of the best songs he's ever written.

We take a break after we've been working for two hours. I open a bottle of wine and offer him a red Solo cup. He accepts with his left hand. We sit down, leaning against the plaster wall.

Our fingers lock while sipping our wine and listening to his music. This moment feels so perfect that I ask, "Will you come to the grand opening party here at No Pink Caddy?"

Turning towards me, Aaron's eyes are soft and just the corners of his mouth turn up. "It's going to be filmed for your show?"

The invite was spontaneous. I haven't spent any time thinking a couple of steps ahead. It will confirm that we're dating again. I think we're so new that it might be a horrible idea. Fresh relationships don't need the pressure of the media and the bright spotlight that follows him.

Before I can start back-pedaling, Aaron continues, "I've never been asked by a girl to be her date to anything." He looks so pleased that you'd think I just gave him a million dollars, but I guess that's a bad analogy. He already has plenty of money.

My nail finds my cuticle. I should tell him that it's a really bad idea, but I don't. I can't disappoint that face. I take his cup and rest it next to mine. Then I crawl in his lap, dotting tiny kisses on his neck. "I want you there. It's like the biggest evening of my life so far. If we're going to be a couple, then of course you're going to be there. Aaron Emerson, will you be my date?"

I feel like a fraud because the whole time I hope that he has a show that night, and we can keep us private for a bit longer.

He doesn't say *thank you* or tell me how much my words mean to him.

Instead he shows me. He wraps me in his arms and buries his head in my chest. There's not a doubt in my mind that if he's willing to appear on camera at my side at this pivotal event on my reality show that he's committed to us. The bit of time I spent with his daughter, I learned just how private he likes to keep his personal life.

When he raises his cheek, I think I might catch a glimpse of shiny eyes. He turns and picks up his cup of wine, and I grab mine also.

"Your bathroom working?" he asks as he stands.

"Yes. It's functional at this point but not very pretty."

"That's all I need." He leaves his wine on the island and disappears into the restroom.

I whip out my phone and post a Tweet.

> **MK Landry** @NoPinkCaddy
> Floors are almost ready for your pretty high-heeled shoes. Who wants another chance to win an invite? #NPCGrandOpening

I so want to share the beautiful picture I took of Aaron, but he's like my special little secret. I get him to myself for just a couple more weeks. The time will come soon enough when I'll write a hearts and flowers blog post, and we'll be inviting the paparazzi to the sidewalk outside of my carriage house once more. Right now, he's mine, and I'm enjoying every second.

When he exits the bathroom, I look up to see him standing over me. "How much do we have left?"

Surveying the store, I reply, "We can split this up over two days as long as we work on it in the morning. Maybe spend another hour and see how much we can get done?"

His smile doesn't touch his eyes. "Okay."

I don't have time to analyze what could be wrong with him and go back to making my paisleys beautiful. And I must say that Aaron's doing a fine job even if he's not enjoying it. His designs are masculine. I love that in one of the blobs he drew music notes in a great pattern. I might not have gotten my jazz mural I dreamed of, but my music man added something important to him to my space. That's the kind of things that will make No Pink Caddy different from all the other stores that line this street.

As I'm sketching interconnected daisy flowers, a terrible sound exits Aaron's mouth. My head snaps in his direction, and I see him doubled over lying on the floor.

"Are you okay?" I yell as I place my paint brush back in the tray and race to his side.

He's curled up in a tight ball and loud moans echo off the store walls.

My hand grips his shoulder. "What's wrong?"

He's shaking, and my heart is beating double time.

He sits back on his heels. "Take the brush from my hand." There's black paint smears all over his white shirt. It looks like a child finger-painted it.

Grasping the handle, I give it a tug. "Aaron, you've got to loosen your grip."

Through clinched teeth, he grinds, "I fucking can't."

I spread my legs, leaning over at the waist. I take hold of the stained bristles and give them another pull. It slips from his hand as I tumble backwards, falling on my behind.

"You okay," he yells with his strained voice.

"Fine." I scamper to my feet and rush back to his side as I pick up a paper napkin to get the paint from my palm. "What do we need to do? Hospital? Ambulance?"

"Get my phone. Call Doctor Hebert." His words are slurred as he's talking through a tightly clenched jaw.

I reach into his pocket and take out his phone. "Code?"

"Spell *Pink*."

I type in the number seven, four, six, five and scroll through his contacts until I find Doctor Hebert. Hitting the call button, I wait for the doctor to answer.

"What'd you do this time?" A jovial male voice answers.

"Hi. This is Mary Kay Landry. I'm with Aaron Emerson. Umm . . . Johnny Knite. He's in a lot of pain." As if on cue, Aaron moans so loud that I'm sure the doctor hears him. "He asked me to call you."

"Put me on speaker." This time his voice sounds controlled and professional.

I do what he asks.

Aaron groans, "In New Orleans. Can't open my hand. It hurts like a motherfucker."

"You need to get to an emergency room. I can't help you." The doctor tells him. Then he adds, "But I'll meet you there as a friend."

"Thanks," he gasps as he uses his left hand to end the call. Next, he hits the icon next to Seamus's name.

When the man answers, Aaron says, "Car to MK's shop ASAP. It's an emergency."

I hang up on Seamus and put Aaron's phone in my bag. Rubbing his back, I ask, "What's going on?"

"Been having problems with my hand. It'll be fine." The skin around his eyes is pulled so tight that wrinkles spider web from the corners. The deep *V* on his forehead makes him look ten years older. His complexion is ash grey, and he swallows hard as if he's trying to keep from being ill.

Feeling completely helpless, I kiss his shoulder as I pray to God. *Please let Aaron be okay. Please take away his pain and help me to deal with whatever this is. Help me find the strength to be an advocate for him. Help me comfort him and help us both be strong. In Jesus's name, Amen.*

When I spot the black SUV arrive out front, I help Aaron to his feet. He doesn't walk to the car, it's more of a hunched-over stagger. I follow behind him locking the front door to the store and crawl into the backseat with my guy.

On the way to the emergency room, he leans over in the backseat of the SUV holding his right hand and moaning over the sound of the road noise. I scoot next to him and do what I can to comfort him. I tell him that we're almost at our destination and that everything will be okay.

I text Bethany to tell her that we're on our way to the emergency room. God bless my sister. She doesn't ask why I'm with Aaron or have I lost my mind. She replies that she's on her way and will meet us there.

Next, I text Bella. I hate calling in favors, but my floors must be finished by Monday morning.

Me: *Long story . . . On the way to the hospital with Aaron. He hurt his hand. Anyway, can you round up some of the gang and get them to finish the paisleys? I understand if you can't. I'm asking a lot.*

Two minutes later, she replies . . .

Bella: *Of course. Take care of Aaron. We're headed up there now. Tripp and Roseanna will be there after they finish dinner. We've got this.*

Me: *Thank you. I love you more than I can fit in this text.*

I don't ask him all the questions that are swimming in my head like *how long have you been in this kind of pain? Why in God's name did you paint for hours if you're having hand trouble? Are you a complete moron?* It also crosses my mind that we should let Grace know that her brother is on the way to the hospital. I keep that thought to myself, and determine that we'll cross that bridge when we come to it.

Seamus pulls into the patient drop-off, and I help Aaron out of the car. Fortunately, we both spy Doctor Hebert about the same time. He rushes to Aaron's side and helps us into a room. Apparently, it pays to be a celebrity because we completely skip the waiting room, and there just happens to be an open, private room in an ER in New Orleans on a Saturday night.

A nurse greets us, immediately starting an IV in Aaron's left arm.

Doctor Hebert instructs Aaron to show him his hand. He has kept his right fist dug into his belly this whole time so I haven't seen it either. With much effort, Aaron moves his arm to rest on his thigh. I know that it's been, at the most, thirty minutes since he collapsed in pain, but his hand looks atrophied as if he lost the use of it long ago. It's curled to the point that his pointer finger touches the skin just below the palm and the angle of his wrist looks as if he broke it.

Gasping, I kiss his shoulder blade, as I continue to rub his back.

"She's giving you something for the pain and a muscle relaxer. It's going to take a minute to work though." Doctor Hebert walks closer and examines Aaron's hand without touching it. "What were the results of the x-rays and blood work?"

"Normal," Aaron replies without removing his gaze from his lap. "Need more testing."

"I made a call to a neurologist."

At that news, Aaron looks up and states, "This is bad."

The doctor nods and turns towards me. "Have you called Grace?"

Shaking my head, I stroke Aaron's cheek. "Do you want me to let your sister know what's going on?"

He nods and drops his chin.

I've kept Grace's number in my phone. The thought occurred to me more than once to delete it, but I guess there was always a bit of hope that maybe she'd reach out, and I'd know Aaron was okay. I didn't want to not answer her call.

Brushing a kiss on his stubbly jaw, I wrap my arm around him, giving him a side hug. "I'm going to step in the hallway and call Grace. If you need me, yell."

He tries to smile, but it looks more like a pained grimace.

We're at the end of a long corridor. I go into the stairwell and do some breathing exercises before I dial Grace's number. She made her feelings regarding me quite clear, and she warned me off her brother. I'm sure I'm the last person she wants to speak to, and the feeling is mutual.

Inhaling and exhaling one more time, I hit the *call* button. After four rings, it goes to her voicemail.

"Grace, this is MK. I mean Mary Kay Landry. Anyway, Aaron and I are in a hospital in New Orleans. He's okay, but he's in extreme pain with his hand. Doctor Hebert is with us, and we're waiting to see a specialist. Please call back on this number."

I'm almost ashamed to admit how happy I am that she didn't answer. Next, I call my sister just catching her up on Aaron's condition and letting her know where we are. She's almost here.

After letting out a deep breath, I walk back into Aaron's room. The medicine must be working because his shoulders no longer brush his ears, and he's leaned back against the stack of pillows.

Doctor Hebert excuses himself.

I pull up a chair next to the bed and sit, holding Aaron's left hand.

When the door closes, Aaron squeezes my fingers. "What did she say?"

"I left a voicemail."

He swallows and nods.

"You seem to be feeling better."

"Feel fucking high as a kite. It's like I'm lying here, but I'm really floating above us watching you hold my hand." His voice slurs a bit. "You're pretty."

"Thank you." Shifting to the right, I ask, "How long has this been going on?"

"A bit."

I lean down and kiss his forearm. "How long is a bit?"

"Longer than a few but not as long as some time."

Well, this is going nowhere fast. I have a feeling that maybe this is his attempt at humor. He's answering my questions evasively like I replied to his at dinner on Monday when he asked about Vince. "My sister is on her way."

"Did you tell her that I'm not OD'ing?"

Now he's slurring like crazy. He sounds like he could be overdosing. "Not when I first texted her but I just talked to her so she'd know what's going on."

"Great. She's going to think I'm a loser." He releases my hand and holds up his pointer finger wagging it back and forth. "No rock stars for MK. They forgot to say no to drugs."

"Stop it, Aaron," I warn as I take his palm and press it against mine. "She now knows this isn't drug related. Plus, she's not like that. Bethany is a doctor first and sister second."

As if on cue, she opens the door and walks in dressed in black slacks and floral pregnancy top. "MK," she greets me with a feathered kiss on my cheek. "Aaron."

He gives her a childlike wave with his left hand.

"Start at the beginning and tell me everything."

Aaron is pretty much no help, but I tell her again what I know and every once in a while, he contributes a tidbit to the conversation. She agrees that if Aaron is correct and his x-rays and bloodwork are negative that it's time for a neurologist. She excuses herself to find out which doctor will be seeing him.

As her hand takes the doorknob, Aaron says, "You can't name your baby MK."

Bethany stops, turns around, and lets the door close.

My stomach flutters as my heart clenches. I'm mortified that he would mention it to my sister. I love her very much, and I want Aaron to stay out of this.

"It's MK's privilege to name her baby girl Mary K something or another. Not yours." His eyes are shut as if he's sleeping. He's clearly not.

I squeeze his hand trying to get him to shut up as I contemplate grabbing one of the many pillows behind him and using it to cover his face so he can't breathe. Murder is not on my mind. Maybe I'll hold it there just until he passes out. "Remember? We talked about this. I said that I was honored that Bethany is considering carrying on *Mary* as a family name. It takes a lot of the pressure off me."

Aaron opens his eyes and drops my hand, pointing at my sister. "Just don't do it, okay?" He's slurring his words so hopefully Bethany will write this conversation off as the ramblings of a guy high on pain medicine.

She turns to me. Her shoulders are rolled back, and I know my sister well enough to know that she's furious. "Do you feel the same way?"

"Can we not discuss this right now? I'm terribly worried about him." I motion to Aaron as I grimace.

Bethany leans against the door. "If you have an issue, you need to speak up, MK. We're thinking of revealing her name next weekend."

My high rock star yells, "*Alis Volat Propriis* with MK's own wings she flies."

Tilting my head, I look at him wondering what he means and silently pleading for the drugs to take effect. Then he adds, "And that goes for naming our baby Mary."

I motion for Bethany to leave as I shake my head. Aaron doesn't need to anger those who are trying to help him.

She says, "Going to check on his doctor." Her eyes are wide and back stiff as she walks out of Aaron's room.

Admonishing him, I lean over and whisper in his ear, "The way to get people to help you is by not being an asshole. Remember that."

He turns his head towards me, opening his eyes revealing dilated pupils. "I want a baby girl named Mary something or another. What about Mary Fred? Then we can call her MF." Aaron thinks this is the funniest thing he's ever said, and I do my best to find inner strength so I don't grab the pillow.

When my phone rings, I'm relieved, which is a completely new revelation, to see Grace's name on my screen. It gives me an opportunity to ignore Aaron for a moment. "Hello," I answer.

Her voice is panicked. "Where are you? I'm in a car on the way to the airport."

"We're at Tulane. He's doing okay. They gave him pain medicine and muscle relaxers." I look at him and note that it looks like he might have finally found sleep. "He's better because they're working, and we're waiting to see the neurologist."

"Neurologist?" she yells so loudly that I pull the phone from my ear.

"Yes. He told Doctor Hebert that his tests were all negative. My sister is here also, and she agrees it's time for a neurologist."

"Fuck. What have they said about his show on Monday?"

I know she's his right-hand woman as well as his sister, but damn, it annoys me that she's worried about his concert right now. "We haven't discussed it."

"Okay. Text me every little thing they say. I'm taking the casino's plane and will hopefully be there in four hours."

"Great," I reply not exactly excited to see her, but realizing that it's important that Grace be here for her brother.

When I end the call, Aaron, whom I thought was sleeping, says, "Hurricane Gracie is expected to make landfall in four hours. Everyone take cover."

Chapter Twenty-Seven

Aaron
September

Rock Star Groupies @RockStarGroupies
@RealJohnnyKnite is at #ClubNowhere in @CelestialPalaceCasino right now.

Rock Star Groupies @RockStarGroupies
@RealJohnnyKnite is making out with a blonde. I don't recognize her from our group.

My head is so cloudy that I'm not entirely sure where I am, but I know that I'm not pressed against MK as I should be. My eyes are heavy and just want to stay closed, but then I hear her sniffle. *She's somewhere near.*

Rolling on my side, I compel my lids to open so I can see MK's pretty face. Her hair is disheveled and purple shades the puffy skin under her dark brown irises. *Why is she not next to me?*

When I'm able to focus and see past her, I spy my sister leaning against the wall with her arms crossed over her chest.

Oh yeah. I'm in the hospital. The memory of the extreme pain of the muscles contracting last night makes my heart race. In a panic, I flex my hand to make sure it's there. Feeling it still attached, I let out a deep breath.

"Hi," I say to both of them.

MK brushes her palm over my cheek and smiles her sweet smile. "Good morning, sleepy head."

"Am I okay?" I try to sit up, but she places her hand on my chest and grabs a remote control, raising the back of the bed. Looking down, I see I'm in a hospital gown, and I have a blanket draped over my legs.

Grace steps forward and leans against the foot of the hospital bed. "You're going to be just fine. I've found a specialist. He's the best in the world, and other famous musicians have used him. He's had lots of success, and he's willing to meet with you."

My eyes cut to MK as the panic returns with such force that I'd swear my insides have been tied into knots. "What's wrong with me? Why do I need a specialist?"

Her fingers tickle the short hair on my forearms, leaving heated tracks where she's touched. "You were a little spacey last night, but your sister had all the medical information from the doctors you've seen along your tour. The neurologist thinks, and Doctor Hebert and Bethany agree, that you have something called musician's dystonia."

"The fuck is that?"

She licks her bottom lip before she replies. "This is how I understand it." Her soft touch morphs into pressure as she clings to my arm. "After the doctors left, I Googled and read what I could on it. There's nothing wrong with your hand or fingers. That's the good news."

"That's awesome." My stomach unknots in relief. I can play my guitar.

MK scowls, and my heart plummets into my stomach. "It's actually something in your brain." She pauses. All I can think of is the ugly word *cancer,* and I grip her hand, preparing for the worst. This is my curse. I finally convince MK to give us another chance, and I'm the happiest I've been since before we broke up. Now, I'm going to die. "It's a movement disorder. For some reason your head is sending the wrong messages to your hand and more specifically your middle finger. Musicians get it. They aren't sure why, but it usually affects the area of the body that does the most repeated motions. It would make sense that it has affected the fingers that you play guitar with."

"Not cancer?"

Her head shakes as her eyes soften. My bones turn to jelly in relief. "No, baby. Not cancer and not life threatening. However, you're going to have to take some time away from playing."

"But my life is music . . ." My heart does a nasty flip as my career passes before my eyes. I see me getting my first guitar as a kid and teaching myself to play. Memories of working at the radio station come tumbling back. That's where I interned sweeping floors to learn the business. Sam and I playing guitar in my garage and on the navy blue plaid comforter where we'd experiment with our sound, and then with each other. Our first time when we played a live show and how I was so nervous that I tried coke to get me through it. It worked and became rocker's little helper.

My guitar. It got me through the shunning and death of my father. It was with me when the person who birthed Jude was pregnant. And my daughter's traumatic entrance into this world. My guitar put food on the table, and Jude in horse riding gear. It got me signed to a label and even bought me out of my contract and into my own record company. But most of all, it's saved my life. That's not a flippant statement. My guitar has been the reason that I've kept going, when it would have been easy to take just a little more of whatever I was snorting.

"My hand feels fine now." I make eye contact with Grace. "Let's get out of here. We have a show tomorrow." My instincts kick in, and I just want to run away from this dystonia thing. It's like maybe if I leave New Orleans it will stay here. Logically, I know this doesn't make sense, but I'm not in a logical place right now.

She walks around to the other side of the bed from MK. "The band is on the way to New Orleans. We're meeting at the house. The specialist is flying in and will also be there."

Releasing MK's hand, I try to get out of the hospital bed until the IV in my arm reminds me that I'm still physically tethered to this place. "Tell the band not to come. Why? So we can waste a day off? I'm playing tomorrow. We're coming to the end of the US leg of this tour. Then we have Europe and Asia. I'm not disappointing the fans."

Grace's business face slides firmly in place as she rolls her shoulders back.

"We have decisions to make that affect not just you and your recovery but the band and our business. While I go tell the nurse that you're awake and ready to leave, you need to quit thinking like an artist and start thinking like the CEO of a record label." She walks to the door and opens it. "And remember the fact that a lot of people depend on you for their paycheck."

As the door closes with a thud, my arm covers my eyes as I try to process what's going on. I still feel a bit drugged. Everything MK and Grace have said is swirling in my brain like a tie-dyed T-shirt while *Helter Skelter* by The Beatles blares as if it's being played on an eight-track.

MK's gentle touch stroking my ribs keeps me from completely falling into the dark abyss. "You're going to be fine, Aaron. Is your hand feeling better?"

"Yeah. It feels great, like nothing is wrong."

"They gave you Botox injections in the muscles. That helped them to relax." She giggles. "I told them you're almost forty so it's about time. I asked if they would also hit the worry lines around your eyes."

When I don't respond, she continues, "Sorry. I know this isn't funny, but I'm just trying to lighten the mood. There's a therapy the neurologist who saw you last night told us about. It's helped other musicians train their brains to work with their fingers again."

"Why can't I do this therapy while we tour?" I say the word *therapy* as if it's dirty and ugly.

"You might be able to. I guess that's a question for the doctor. He's flying in from New York."

I meet MK's eyes as I confess to her just how scared I am. "This is my comeback tour. I fucking hate the term *comeback* because it implies that I left, but it is. This is my proof to the world that I'm still relevant. It can't be canceled."

"That's what you guys are going to figure out." She leans, kissing my forehead. "Grace is right. You have to do what's best for you and the band. I saw you last night, and Aaron, that can't happen again."

"Fuck. I can't think. I feel like I've been drugged." I rub my eyes hoping to clear the chaos.

"You have," she chuckles. "You were all kinds of messed up."

"And you didn't bolt." I don't know why I say it. Maybe I'm in a shitty mood and lashing out at her. Maybe I still haven't fully forgiven her, but I'm an asshole and I need to learn to keep my mouth shut.

"Of course, I didn't. We promised each other that we're in this through the good and the bad. I took that vow really freaking seriously." Her forehead creases, and her lips tighten into thin slits.

"Sorry, sweetheart. Working on my asshole tendencies."

The door opens and Grace walks in followed by a nurse. In minutes, my IV is removed, and MK hands me the clothing I was wearing yesterday except now the shirt is stained with black paint.

Once I'm in the bathroom, I take a moment to work my hand. It feels normal—like categorically normal. I stare holes through the skin as I watch my muscles contract and release. There's no fever in it, and I think I could play for hours. If the injections worked this time, why can't they just keep shooting me up with the Botox?

I throw on my clothes and splash water on my face. It's time to face the music, literally. When I open the bathroom door, MK and Grace are engaged in a hushed conversation. I pause for a second, trying to listen to what they're discussing.

MK's body language appears relaxed but guarded. Her arms aren't crossed, but I do notice her finger tracing the outline of the star on the inside of her wrist. She does this when she's bothered.

Grace appears to be explaining something, and I catch a few of her words . . . trust, work together.

MK smiles, and her hands relax. She replies, "Thank you. That means a lot to me. I think we both want what's best for Aaron."

I can't be positive, but I think Grace and MK might not necessarily be friends, but they've become allies.

Clearing my throat, they turn towards me. Grace says, "Seamus has the car out back. Hungry?"

"I want a chorizo, egg, and cheese taco," I reply as I grab MK's behind. "With some salsa and sour cream."

MK yelps, before she replies, "This ain't Texas, cowboy. How about we stop at a store, and I'll let you pick out any kind of breakfast cereal you want?"

"Deal."

Chapter Twenty-Eight

MK
September

Rock Star Groupies @RockStarGroupies
@RealJohnnyKnite sighting was a false alarm. Blonde said it wasn't him, but might be an imposter. #StaySharpOutThere

"Here's your mixing bowl." I place it in front of Aaron who's seated on my lone barstool, looking disheveled with a stubble beard, and sexy as hell.

He pours half a box of Fruity Pebbles, adding just enough milk to wet the cereal.

Leaning against the counter, I ask, "How do you stay in such good shape and eat like that? My God, I think I've probably added cellulite to the back of my thighs just by looking at that bowl."

He takes a huge spoonful, chews it, and swallows before replying, "I guess good genes. Performing live is a damn good work out too. And then there's the swimming."

"Yeah. You mentioned the swimming. I'm glad that's working for you." Turning around, I walk towards the bedroom. "I'm going to get in the shower while you eat."

He stands, grabbing his bowl with one arm, tucking it into his chest. He reminds me of Winnie the Pooh with a honey jar. "I'll come with you."

Shaking my head, I start the water as he puts the lid down on the toilet.

"Save your lecture about this being unsanitary or whatever else is racing through your head. I don't care. I'm not missing my strip show."

Sexy is not how I would describe how I'm feeling. Worried, exhausted, scared, are all adjectives that would work. I walk over to him and take the bowl out of his hands, resting it next to my sink. Wrapping my arms around his neck, I hug him and kiss his hair. "I'm so sorry this is happening to you, Aaron. All I want is for you to be happy."

He nuzzles between my breasts. "I'd be happier if you were naked."

Stepping back, I tilt his chin up so he's looking in my eyes. "I know what you do. You revert to a sixteen-year-old boy when you're nervous or frightened. It's okay. I'll let you, but remember that I'm here for you."

His hair falls over his cheeks as he grabs his bowl of cereal and begins eating again. I take that for what it is. In some ways, he's so good at expressing his emotions that it's hard to believe he's male. He was cocky enough to show up at my hotel room. I certainly didn't knock on his door in Austin after we stopped talking. But then I look at him now. I know he's scared to death, and I know he wants me by his side, but he doesn't want to discuss it so he cracks a joke. That's okay with me as long as he doesn't push me away.

Grace's nagging words don't seem capable of being expunged from my brain. *"He'll tire of you when life gets rough—when the honeymoon is over. When you're no longer the new hotness. A new one will come along, and you'll be like the rest of us—lost in his shadow."*

I unhook my overall straps, and they fall to the ground. I've been in them for so long that they're becoming part of my skin.

"That's what I'm talking about," he heckles.

Rolling my eyes, I pull my tank off, and then bend down picking up my overalls. I stuff my things into the hamper.

"Show me them pretty titties," Aaron coaxes.

I remove my bra and panties and stand in front of him naked, raw, and vulnerable. "You like this?"

His goofy grin and overly exaggerated nod make me laugh on the inside, but my serious face doesn't crack. "Then don't screw us up. Don't forget about me because your life just got more stressful. When we made love yesterday, I gave you my heart. It's in your hands. Please don't break it." I don't add *again.*

His eyes fall as he rests the bowl on the tile next to the toilet. He reaches for me, and I let him pull me between his thighs. I place my hand on his shoulders as he kisses my sternum. "Don't give up on me because the next days, weeks, or even months are going to be shit. Stay by my side even if I'm an asshole. Love me through my shitty moods. You're my person through thick and thin."

"My person," I reply as I kiss his forehead.

The steam from the shower fills my small bathroom. Tiny water droplets bead on Aaron's temples, and I lick them from his tanned skin. A moan echoes around the small space.

He stands, picks me up, and my legs wrap around his hips as my lips touch his. He walks us until I feel the edge of my bathroom vanity just above the backs of my knees. My behind rests on the counter.

He steps away only long enough to discard his shirt, jeans, and underwear. Through the haze, I watch him as if he's a god. His brightly colored skin glows, and I'm reminded that I still don't know the meaning of his permanent ink. Damp hair strands cling to the sides of his sculpted cheeks, wrap under his jaw, and his blue eye are at half-mast.

This gorgeous man wants me. "Thank you for coming back into my life."

Aaron positions himself between my legs and takes the delicate skin, just below my ear, between his teeth, giving it a nibble then a suck. He's marking me. I'm sure Margo is not going to be very pleased tomorrow when I show up for work with a hickey, but right now, her happiness is of no concern of mine.

The pain from his bite is then soothed with the lapping of his tongue over the tender spot. My heels dig into the small of his back as my nails scratch his firm, muscular behind.

Once he's assessed his love bruise, he kisses his way across my pulse point and down to my collarbone. His tongue dips into the curve at the top of my sternum.

I lean back, placing my arms behind me as I push my breasts towards him.

His mouth pulls my left nipple between his teeth as his right-hand massages and squeezes my other one. My body feels like it might explode. Every nerve ending is on fire.

"Aaron," I gasp in a high-pitched, needy voice. "It's too much."

His left hand drags down my stomach to between my legs. His finger slides inside, filling me just enough that I drop my head back, and yell, "Yes." It's not the deep, heavy, weight of his cock that I crave, but it's a tease, reminding my body that there will be more to come.

Each time his finger pushes deeper, he pulls out, and rubs my clit. My head falls forward onto his shoulder. My neck doesn't seem to be able to support its weight any longer.

"Only you, MK. There can only be you," are the words he says as his finger replaces the fullness my body demands. Both of his hands reach around and grasp my behind as he drives inside.

I become a fiery mass of pure, hedonistic need. Every nerve and fiber of my being is raw. I want more of him. I want to be closer, and I want to claim him like he's marked me.

"You love me," I tell him as I bite just below his ear.

His hips pull back and push in with a thrust that hits the barrier inside me. He moans, "Oh God, sweetheart."

My hands slip through his hair as he picks me up and angles my back against the closed door. "Wrap your legs around me tight," he instructs. I follow his orders.

"I need this, MK." He pushes in again with a thrust that is on the verge of being painful. My hands dig into his shoulder muscles as if I could use them for handles. "Don't leave me."

My tongue laps the sweat trickling down his neck as I find my spot, the same spot I bit earlier. He yells and grips my behind with so much force that I'm sure I'll be bruised there also. Sucking, gnawing, and kissing, I leave my mark for all to see that he's mine.

With another couple of pushes, we both find our release. I hear a loud moaning sound and realize only when I ride the waves of my orgasm down that the sound was coming from me. Clinging to him, I don't want this to end.

He holds my behind as I slide down him. My feet ultimately having to support my spent body. We hold each other long after we've recovered.

Unfortunately, though, he must be at his house for a meeting soon so I break our connection.

I love the little smirk he wears when I kiss the bruise I left. "You gave me a hickey. What will my fans say tomorrow night when I take the stage and the bright lights find it?"

I step around him and walk to the shower. "Oh. I'm sure your makeup person will cover it."

Pulling back the curtain, I lift my leg over the lip of my old-fashioned bathtub. Adjusting it back, I reach for my shampoo. Just as I pour the soap into my hand, the curtain is ripped back, and he's standing next to the tub looking quite grumpy. "Why would my makeup person cover it?"

Working the lather through my hair, I come to the realization that as long as Aaron is in my life, I'll have wet bathroom floors and bowls of cereal near my toilet. Seems like a fair tradeoff. "Umm . . . the same reason Margo will cover the hickey you left on my neck."

"That's sexy as fuck. Everyone knows you've had someone be kinky and dirty with you. And at your grand opening, they'll know it's me." He points to his chest as if it's a badge of honor.

"Precisely," I reply because there's no use in arguing with him, and the fact that he's received bad news today and is facing a possible career changing meeting, and he's still into me makes me believe that Grace's harsh words were wrong. "Now, crawl your fine behind in my shower and get clean after we got so dirty."

"Jesus, MK," he says. "I love when you get all demanding and shit."

I snapshot this moment. Who knows what the next couple of hours have in store for us? Right now, though, we're perfect.

Chapter Twenty-Nine

Aaron
September

Rock Star Groupies @RockStarGroupies
@RealJohnnyKnite come out, come out, wherever you are. We're ready to play.

Cammy Tidwell @CrawfishQueen_27_
@NoPinkCaddy how did the floors turn out? Can't wait for #NoPinkCaddy to open.

"The water must be cold," she says as she sticks her head around the curtain. "Shouldn't we be heading over to your house?"

Shrugging, I wiggle my junk hoping to distract her and myself from what lies ahead. "You've left me to my own devices. Who knows how much longer I'll be in here?"

Her shoulders tense. "If you're late, they're all going to blame me. Please don't make me a bad guy."

I turn my back to her and show her just how awesome my ass is. "No, they won't. I always keep them waiting. I'm a rocker. Bad behavior is expected."

Suddenly, the water stops falling on my head. She has her know-it-all voice turned up to epic levels. "Well, you behave however you wish when I'm not around. But when you're with me, we arrive on time."

The idea of arguing crosses my mind, but instead I step out of the shower and wrap a towel around my waist. I'm thinking my best strategy with MK is to pick my battles. She seems adamant about being close to on time. I'll give her this win.

But, of course, I can't completely award her this victory so I shake back and forth spraying water droplets around the bathroom. Her head turns as she grabs a hand towel to wipe the condensation from her face. "Really, Aaron, can you try for once to be an adult?"

Kissing her cheek, I also give her firm ass a slap. "Nope. Adulting is for those not smart enough to stay a kid."

That earns me a smile and eye roll. Perfection! Then she replies, "My very own Peter Pan."

Ten minutes later, I'm dressed in jeans and a green shirt that reads *Tequila, Tacos, Lime . . . Must be Tuesday.* Jude likes to shop with my credit card on funny shirt sites. I should hire her to be my wardrobe person.

I use MK's brush to untangle my hair. It's needs to be cut like yesterday. I also use her toothbrush. I'm sure if she caught me, I'd get a lecture that included words like *gross, unsanitary,* and *childish.* What she doesn't know won't kill her.

I take a minute to focus on what waits for me a couple of blocks from here. Reminding myself that I am the boss, I vow to not let anyone influence my decision when it comes to my tour. I'm going to listen to the facts and then make the business decision that is best for Johnny Knite and the ACE brand.

Unfortunately, my brain forgot to communicate with my stomach, and I feel so sick that I don't bother finishing my cereal.

When I walk into MK's empty living room, she's sitting on her barstool at her kitchen island with her laptop open in front of her. Her eyes don't look up, and she doesn't realize that I'm watching her.

Her brown hair looks like beach waves hugging either side of her jaw and falling to just under her breasts. She's dressed in a white sleeveless top which is fitted and curves nicely over her tits and slims at her waist. Her fingers fly over the keyboard. I can tell she's concentrating because she pauses, squints, turns her head, and then the faint sound of keys being pressed reaches my ears.

She's gorgeous. Her bottom lip twists as white teeth catch the corner. She shakes her head at the screen then seems to delete something she wrote. Typing again, MK pauses and reviews her words. She must be pleased because she smiles, nods, and then hits a key with much more drama than necessary.

I want to go back to the place she calls Bliss. Fuck the band and the specialist. Fuck the fans and this tour. I've got enough money that we'd never have to work again. We could buy an island somewhere in the Caribbean, and we'd only see other humans if we choose. We'd never wear clothes. Just her and me for the rest of our lives. That's when we're perfect.

Adrenaline pumps through my veins. I could toss her over my shoulder, and we could be on my plane in an hour. Her comments about long distance relationships play on blast in my head. I don't want to believe that she's right, but I know she is. Touring has ended many great love affairs. Separation usually doesn't make the heart grow fonder. Instead it drives a wedge between two people—both unable to relate to what the other is experiencing. We can't let that happen to us. I won't let that happen. Not again.

She says spiritual shit like our souls will never be apart. That's great in theory, but the contractor is still working with her. I'm going to have to remind MK frequently who her man is.

I clear my throat.

She looks up and smiles. "You ready?"

"As I'll ever be."

***

"I've had the opportunity to review Mister Knite's medical files. They were shared with me last night. I've also had a lengthy conversation with Doctor Fontenot, who was the neurologist who examined Mister Knite. Doctor Fontenot is a colleague of mine. I believe the examination he did was thorough, and I agree with his conclusions." The good doctor looks like a douche. He's maybe in his early fifties, balding, and wears very thick, black rimmed glasses. After staring at him for a moment, I decide he resembles a penis if you put glasses on it. Then, of course, my mind travels to wondering if MK would be into dressing up my dick. The thought is so funny, I really want to share it with the band and MK, but I decide that's probably a bad idea.

Grace asks, "Do you agree with the Botox treatment that Doctor Fontenot injected?"

The band snickers, and I don't blame them. It's funny to think that I have a poison in my muscles. I'm not laughing.

He clears his throat. "Yes, yes, of course. It's an approved treatment for dystonia."

MK scoots closer and drags her nails over the tendons in my right hand. I wrap my arm around her shoulders and lean back against the sectional.

Grace speaks up again. "I guess the million-dollar question is can he continue touring?" The irony is that it's actually more of a fifty-million-dollar question.

Doctor Odom leans against the fireplace mantle and strokes his chin as if it's a magic rock with all the answers. "Well, we can do the injections for a while until they no longer work." He looks at me. "It would be best if you did not play the guitar."

My neck tenses. He's asking me not to breathe. "No."

Sam pipes up, "You play rhythm guitar. We can bring in someone else. All you have to do is sing."

My hand grips MK's biceps so tightly that she gasps. "I've never once in the history of ACE performed on stage without my guitar."

Billy interjects, "You could still wear it and even play some of the time or pretend like you're playing. It doesn't have to be mic'ed."

That sounds like a shit idea. Giving MK's body a break, I cross my arms over my chest.

Grace replies, "I think it's brilliant. His voice is fine. I know the guitar is like his security blanket so he can still wear it." She turns to me. "Just don't play."

I've had about as much as I can take. I stand, looking at each band member in the eye as I feel the tendons straining against my skin. "You go on stage, and don't play. Rock, we're going to have Auto-Tune play the drums for you. Don't worry. You can still sit behind your kit. We won't mic the drums. You can bang away if you wish. Work for you?"

Grace also stands, going toe to toe with me. "That's a bullshit comparison. We're not Auto-Tuning your voice. You're still singing. We'll hire a rhythm guitarist. Fuck, you know they're a dime a dozen. We can even borrow one from another band on our label. Hell, let's ask the kid from the opening act. I bet he'd shit his pants to get to play with you guys."

"I'm feeling minimized," I reply while re-crossing arms.

"Grow the fuck up," Grace growls. "We're in the middle of ACE's comeback tour. Venues are booked. Tickets are sold. You either make a sacrifice and have someone else play your guitar parts, or we cancel the tour and you let down all those people who have sacrificed to see you." Grace turns to the band and raises her eyebrow. "What do y'all think?"

"I didn't say I want to cancel the tour or postpone. I've never said anything even close to that. I just want to play my guitar." The solution sucks gigantic donkey balls. She's right. I know she's right. I can be an adult and remove myself for this shit situation and fully acknowledge that this is the best solution for the tour and for me. Not playing my guitar on stage is not what scares me. I'm a song man, a music writer. I've constantly got a lyric, beat, riff, or some piece of music in my head. But I can't write music without my guitar. It's what keeps me sane.

Swallowing hard, I ask, "Doctor Odom, will you come on tour with me and fix whatever is wrong with my hand?"

"I haven't discussed specifics with Grace, and I do have a thriving practice back in New York. However, you're not the first musician that my staff and I've made accommodations like this for." He pushes his glasses up his nose. "When you have a practice specializing in a disorder that only affects musicians at the top of their class, we have to be flexible with where and how the patient receives treatment." The awkward man crosses and uncrosses his arms as if they don't fit together.

Everyone begins talking amongst themselves as if the decision has been made. Then MK pipes up. I notice her hickey has been covered with makeup—probably the same one that she uses to hide her scar—and it annoys me. "Doctor Odom, I'd like to know what are the long-term issues with

Aaron continuing to perform even if he doesn't play his guitar."

Grace rolls her eyes, and there's an audible huff from the others in the room.

Doctor Odom's Adam's apple bobs up and down. "Well, there are many factors. . . I mean we could splint . . . But the audience would know . . . I mean . . ."

MK joins me in standing and wraps her arms around my waist. "You see I'm very concerned about Aaron's long term health. My goal is for him to still be playing when he's an old man. Are we sacrificing a few touring months for his overall health? I just want to see the big picture."

Doctor Odom removes his glasses and rubs his eyes. "In an ideal world, I'd suggest that Mister Knite take part in intensive therapy, a brain remapping if you will. Generally, I see only the middle finger on the right hand affected in guitarists. Of course, in Mister Knite's case, it appears to be more than just that finger and maybe muscles into the hand. We do believe that stress plays a role."

"But it can still be fixed, right, Doc?" For the first time, I question if I'll ever be okay again. Once I was assured that this isn't cancer, it never occurred to me that I wouldn't one day be fine. I'm a musician. It's the only thing that I know how to be. I didn't go to college. I have no backup plan. Sure, I own a label, and I enjoy signing new talent, but Johnny Records is more of Grace's thing. I'm a song writer. It's not just what I do. Music's the blood that runs through my veins. It's who I am. It defines me.

The rest of my life is cursed—but music is where I've been blessed. The thought of never playing my guitar again turns me into a scared little boy. I want to hide under the bed and cover my ears hoping that the bad news doesn't find me.

He pushes his glasses up his nose again. "I don't know. The Botox injections seem to be working. You might be able to rely on those until the tour is over, and then you can focus on the therapies I recommend."

Billy says, "You sure would have some pretty hands."

The band laughs, but when I look at MK, she's stoic. Once the laughter dies down, the room becomes silent. "Do you know why Aaron has this?" she asks.

"We aren't entirely sure. Sometimes there's an injury. It might have been inconsequential and unmemorable, but that along with stress, and repeated movement will cause this to happen. We usually only see what Mister Knite is experiencing in an artist performing at the highest of levels. Lots of famous artists suffer from this. It's just usually kept hidden behind the curtain."

Fortunately, no one asks if I'm stressed. I think they already know the answer. They've had to live with me during this tour.

Grace speaks up. "We have two shows in Vegas. There doesn't seem to be any reason to cancel them." She gestures to me. "Your hand is fine right now. Let's try not mic'ing the guitar." Grace reminds me of a general addressing his troops as she talks. "Johnny will sing and only play if he feels up to it. I'll find us a guitarist. Let's take this one show at a time. Sound good?"

No. It sounds like shit, but it's a good compromise for right now. All the eyes in the room are on me. "That works." I turn to address Doctor Odom. "I want to start whatever therapies immediately. You've got to get me back playing again like yesterday."

"Great." Grace claps her hands. "We're leaving for Vegas in two hours."

Doctor Odom asks me to follow him somewhere private to talk about the therapies and for him to examine me without distractions.

When I walk by Grace, she whispers, "Nice hickey. Are you a pre-teen again?"

My response is to flip her the bird with my right hand so she can see that it's working just fine.

As I lead Doctor Odom to the studio out back, I hear Rock say, "Let's see how long he can stay clean without his guitar."

A shiver runs down my spine. My thoughts exactly.

Chapter Thirty

MK

September

MK Landry @NoPinkCaddy
We're so close I can taste it. Don't forget to enter for your chance to attend #NoPinkCaddy Grand Opening.

Veronica Smith @SinnerSaint18
@RealJohnnyKnite I'm in Vegas and ready to rock out at the show tonight. #PinkCadillac

"The floors look great, MK," Vince says as he drapes his thick arm around my shoulders. When Aaron made the same gesture yesterday in the meeting at his house, shivers went down my spine. When Vince does it, it feels brotherly.

"I love them. I'm so glad I fought to save the linoleum and to add the paint. It's unexpected, and fun, and very NPC."

"We're packing up our tools today. You ready for the next part?" He drops his arm and turns toward me.

We're standing just inside the door. I look around at the beautiful work that's been done as I contemplate his question. Am I ready? The answer is an enthusiastic yes. I can't wait for the grand opening party and to officially be in business. Last night, when I had some time to think, I worked on a schedule for cooking classes. I also opened my garage and took inventory of what I have refinished and is ready for sale, what projects need to be completed, and I made a timeline for working on my pieces that I haven't started.

Shannon sent me the verbiage for the employment ad. As I read it, I had to pinch myself. No Pink Caddy will actually have paid employees besides Bella, who works for wine and quality time with my great personality.

A huge smile spreads my cheeks as I nod. "I'm so ready."

Cindy walks through the front door. "Have a good weekend, MK? The floors look great."

"I'm kinda in love with them." It's hard to be humble when I absolutely adore how they turned out. Bella and my family finished them perfectly. I especially love Aaron's music notes that he drew inside one of the paisleys, but as I admire it, my chest tightens with guilt. Why did he offer to help if his hand was bothering him? Doctor Odom assured me yesterday that it wasn't holding the paint brush that led to Aaron's trip to the hospital. But there's still a huge part of me that wishes that it hadn't happened when he was helping me.

Cindy kisses my cheek. "And I love you. You ready to tell the cameras about your hard work?"

"I took a few pictures and some video of my friends and family helping me work on them." Shrugging, I add, "I know that it wasn't in budget to film over the weekend, but I thought it might be fun to work in some raw video. I like when shows do that. It makes it feel more real."

Cindy squeals. "Oh. Let's see it!"

Vince exits out the back door giving us all a wave.

Pulling my phone from my back pocket, Cindy stands to my right side and Shannon stands on my left. We watch the video first. It's of my family and friends on their hands and knees drawing the stencil and filling it in with purple paint. "I love it, MK. Send that over, and we'll splice it in while you're describing how you painted them."

It feels so great to finally be contributing to the show. So far, it's been all Vince, and me, being the grateful client. Now, I feel like I'm the one who is actively working to make this a reality.

"Here are the pics that I took." As the words tumble out of my mouth, I show them the picture of Aaron leaning against the brick wall. I can't seem to swipe right quickly enough.

Cindy gasps. "That was Johnny Knite. Dear sweet baby Jesus, please tell me he helped with the floors."

My instinct is to lie, but I know that's foolish. She obviously saw that it's him so I need to own it and mitigate the situation. "Yes. He helped with the floors." I bite my top lip. "But it's not what you think. He was in town, and he wanted to help."

I don't think that sounds any better.

She takes my phone out of my hand and zooms in on his face. "So damn pretty. I assume you two are back together?"

Here is where I decide to not lie, but necessarily tell the whole truth. "We're talking again. Which is a huge step because I didn't care to hear a word he had to say for a long, long time."

Shannon adds, "I think Johnny needed to make peace. That's all."

I could kiss her.

Cindy's hand goes to her hip, and she turns her head giving me the you've-got-to-be-kidding-me look. "Rock stars don't paint floors on a Saturday night because they happen to be in town. That boy is in love with you."

I shrug. "Maybe he is. I mean I am pretty lovable. You did say it yourself."

"You're terrible at being nonchalant. Show me what he painted, and did you have him sign it?"

My face crinkles. "Have him sign it? Why?"

Shannon snaps her fingers. "Because his fans will want to visit the store to see his artwork."

Throwing my hands up, I exclaim, "You've got to be kidding me. He drew music notes. Not special at all. I mean that's not entirely true. I appreciate him helping, but NPC is not code for ACE's store."

Cindy laughs and gives me a side hug. "Honey, we're in this for ratings. Now, no need to tread on Johnny's name, but a little celebrity boost has got to help."

"Guess that's fair," I concede as I shove my phone back in my pocket.

"All right, sweetie. Let's get you in hair and makeup while we talk about the grand opening."

Cindy, Shannon and I walk the two blocks to the trailers. I can tell we're getting close to renovation completion because there are less people roaming around our makeshift offices. We're also down three trailers. Vince's was removed this morning. I was sad to see it leave, but it just means we're one step closer to No Pink Caddy opening its door and welcoming customers.

Margo hands me a flowy aqua blue skirt with a chevron print and a fitted white shirt when I walk in my dressing building. "I think this will work for today's interviews."

"Thank you," I reply as I disappear behind the changing curtain.

Pausing for a second, I pull out my phone and send Aaron a text. His show is tonight, and I'm worried about him.

Me: *How are you? I missed you this morning. My shower was uneventful, and my tile stayed dry. I know you're busy, but just let me know you're okay.*

Checking the clock, I note it's eight-fifteen in the morning in Vegas. Hopefully, Aaron is resting peacefully and will text me when he wakes up.

I get dressed and sit down in the makeup chair. Margo begins curling my hair while Cindy, Shannon, Bella, and Robbie take out their notebooks or phones and begin discussing the grand opening.

At the mention of the words *grand opening*, my stomach is invaded by bats. The emotions of my dream come flooding back. I experience again the sickening feeling that the lights were on and the band was playing but no one was walking through the doors. My hand grips the arm of the chair. "What if no one shows up? What will we do?"

Cindy laughs. "What makes you think no one will come?"

"I don't know," I reply as I try to stay as still as possible so Margo doesn't get mad. "I just had a dream."

Cindy squeezes my shoulder. "Attendance is not something that I'm the least bit worried about."

For some reason, those words make me feel better, and I relax a fraction of a bit. We divide duties and each take a responsibility for something. My job is to continue to promote the grand opening to my followers.

"So far, I have over one hundred people who've entered for the chance to win tickets to the party," I inform the group.

Cindy replies, "That's great. Okay. We probably need to ensure that each person is allowed to bring a guest. We want the atmosphere to be friendly not awkward with people pressed against the walls."

"I've got a jazz band in mind that I think would be awesome for entertainment," Bella says as she continues to scribble in her zebra striped notebook.

Robbie interjects, "They'll need to be informed that this will be filmed, and they must sign releases."

Bella nods. "I don't think that will be a problem."

Shannon says, "I'm going to work on the media invites."

Cindy adds, "Get with Justine. You two can coordinate those."

Shannon nods.

"I'm also going to have it catered." Bella continues to write.

I speak up. "I was planning on preparing some of my most well-known dishes."

"You won't have time," Cindy says. "Let's have it catered."

My stomach drops. "I don't want someone else serving their recipes in my store. I can start preparing stuff at night and freezing it."

Margo runs her fingers through the tight curling iron waves loosening my hair.

Shannon and Cindy exchange a look that makes me uncomfortable. I feel like the poor country mouse who just arrived in the big city.

Bella suggests, "What about if we hire someone to prepare your recipes, MK? There's that girl that Grandmother has used. She was talented."

"Yes." Clapping, I turn my head. "Perfect. Would you mind calling her and getting the lady's number?"

Bella makes a note. "Consider it done."

Margo gasps and points to my neck. "You have a hickey."

My heart clenches as my hand slaps it, and I think it becomes twenty degrees warmer in here. "Oh God. I thought I had covered it with my scar makeup."

Cindy laughs loudly and exclaims, "I told you rock stars don't just give up their Saturday nights to paint paisley." She bends down and closely examines the evidence of our love making.

I literally want to die. This would be a great time for a nuclear bomb to be dropped or for a meteor to hit the planet. There's nothing for me to say so I just shrug and smile sheepishly.

Margo digs in her makeup suitcase and finds a skin color paste. It's cool to the touch as she massages and buffs it over the bruised skin.

Cindy says, "Let's go back to the guest list. I need for you to submit to Shannon who you want to personally invite." She dramatically simulates holding a pencil and writing on an imaginary list. "I'm just going to pencil in Johnny's name as your date." She ends her statement with a smack of her lips. "Then, I'll give her a list of the VIPs that we need to include. Of course, Vince will also have some people that he needs to invite. Most of his will probably not come just because we're in Louisiana, but you never know. Folks like air time. We'll see what that count is and then you'll know how many fans you can give tickets to."

Margo motions for me to close my eyes. "I need an idea of what MK should wear. I should probably start looking today." The brushes, leaving their powder on my eyelids, is so relaxing. Every time Margo does this it's hard for me to stay awake. Not today though. I feel like a cat that's been hit by lightning.

My phone dings, but I ignore it for the time being.

Shannon replies, "I see something vintage, pretty, flowy."

Margo swipes mascara on my lashes. "How formal?"

It's Cindy that responds. "Certainly not formal. Nicer than jeans. No sparkles. She needs to look like the store."

Margo taps my cheek, and I open my eyes. Once again, when I see myself in the mirror, I note that she's performed a magic trick or maybe an illusion. I still look like MK, but a more refined, better highlighted and shaded version of me. "I'll need Johnny's wardrobe person's number. We don't want matchy prom outfits, but you two will need to look like you go together."

The tips of my ears burn, and I try to act like an adult. Yes, I'm sexually active in a newly rekindled relationship. There's nothing to feel shameful, or embarrassed about. That's what I tell myself. It does no good, and I still feel like my mom walked in my high school bedroom and caught me making out with my boyfriend.

"Date is October eleventh. We need invites sent out by Thursday," Robbie says.

Bella caps her pen. "We can do it. MK, I'll work on your list now. I'm pretty sure I know who you need to include."

With a laugh, I say, "Yes, you probably know my list better than I do."

As everyone stands and makes their way to the trailer door, I pull out my phone to see who texted earlier. It's Aaron and my sister. I read Bethany's text first.

Bethany: *First of all, how's Aaron? I hope he seeks the treatment that he needs. Second, I need to discuss the baby's name with you at some point soon. We were prepared to name her Mary Kathleen until Aaron's comment in the hospital. I need to start monogramming. I know this is of little consequence to you, but it's very important to me. Love you.*

At this point in my life, I'm so stressed that my sister could name the baby Chocolate Malt, and I wouldn't care. I don't have it in me to discuss future names of my children with the guy who has just reentered my life and is on tour. I'm in the middle of filming a reality show and find the idea of a child at this point in my life to be soul crushing. I reply.

Me: *I think Mary Kathleen is a beautiful name. I'm honored and relieved that you're carrying on the naming tradition. Hugs! Love you.*

Good. Hopefully, that's one last thing that I must deal with. Next, I focus on Aaron.

Aaron: *I hate Vegas. Have I told you that? I hate Vegas. My nose is so dry I had to send someone for saline drops. My lips are cracked. I can't play my guitar, and I miss you. I think you should ditch your show and come see me.*

Aaron: *I don't mean that. I'm happy for your success. Life is just better when you're with me.*

Smiling at the screen, I reply.

Me: *I'm sorry your lips are cracked and your nose is dry, but I'm happy that you miss me. Everyone has seen your love bite. Can you die from embarrassment? Mark Oct 11 on your calendar. It's my open house and if you're a good boy, I'll send you an invite.*

I carry my phone as I walk fast to catch up with Cindy and Shannon. Today, there is a hint of fall in the air. The temperature will stay in the eighties for the first time since May. When I was a kid, I'd be crazy hyper and barely able to sit through school when the air was like this. I'd meet Tripp after the last bell rang. We'd head to the bayou to fish or climb trees. My mom would make chili with beans for me and chili with no beans for Bethany.

My step is lighter. The humidity is lower, and the trees are thankful. Their branches hang with pride over the sidewalk instead of looking like the sun is beating them down. Even the birds are out. The most beautiful butterfly—yellow and black striped—flutters across my path and lands on the branch of a Crepe Myrtle.

In the north, they look forward to the first sign of spring and get grouchy when the trees begin dropping their leaves. Not us here in the south. The first sign of fall means we survived another hot and humid summer.

My phone vibrates when I cross the No Pink Caddy threshold.

Aaron: *I'm never a good boy, and you love it. I'm glad everyone saw it. Could you point it out to the contractor for me? It's not on my calendar because I don't keep one. You've graduated to Grace's calendar. Lucky you.*

Because I don't have any time to properly respond, I send him a smiley face emoji.

Cindy announces, "Okay, MK. Time for you to tell us how you did the floors."

I bounce to the brick wall that we use as our backdrop to film my interviews.

Today, I will make a good day.

Chapter Thirty-One

Aaron
September

> **Music Times** @MusicTimesMagazine
> Sources close to LV casino mogul @RobertHaines say that @RealJohnnyKnite is very close to signing.

> **Music Times** @MusicTimesMagazine
> @RealJohnnyKnite will sign a multi-year residency contract at @CelestialPalaceCasino.

Robert requested my presence at a meeting with him, his general manager, and a couple of his advisory board members. Grace has insisted on coming.

"I can't believe you're wearing that," she admonishes as the elevator takes us to the top floor.

I look down at the fitted black pants and black button up shirt that wardrobe handed me. "What's wrong with this?"

She gestures at my feet and then my head. "Combat boots and a fedora. Can't you just look normal every now and then?"

"When the fuck did you start caring about what I wear? I'd have on jeans and shirt if it was up to me. What's your problem?" She's been moody since we got back from New Orleans yesterday. I'm the one who was told that I can't play guitar. I'm the one with a fucked-up head. I should be the one who gets to be shitty.

Her eyes look up at the lighted metallic ceiling. "This is an important meeting. And I'm glad that the shirt's collar covers your love mark. So unprofessional." She tsks. "Don't talk about your hand for God's sake."

At the mention of the *H* word, my hand flexes and then closes into a fist. Those shots were a miracle. I'm still pain free, and it hasn't felt this good in months.

The doors slide open, and we step into a room with three-sixty views of Las Vegas. It's set up in a lounge configuration. A circular bar dominates the center. Couches and chairs with tables are placed to maximize the experience of feeling like you're on top of the strip. The colors chosen remind me of royalty. They're deep purples, rich reds, and lots and lots of gold.

It's empty except for the people we're meeting and a man standing behind the bar wiping out a wine glass. Robert walks toward us with a warm smile on his face. He shakes my hand and brushes a kiss on my sister's cheek.

She seems less tense in his presence. This strikes me as odd. I assumed the reason she was being difficult in the elevator was that she was nervous about this meeting.

He places his hand on the small of her back as he introduces us to the others in the room. The casino general manager is a sexy as hell blonde woman probably around my age. She's wearing a fitted cobalt blue business suit with silver high heels covered in spikes. Her name is Dominique, and it fits her appearance.

The other two guys are dudes in black slacks and loud shirts that look like contemporary art paintings. I've noticed the designer brand is sold in the hotel's shopping area. I wonder if they intentionally dressed alike.

A bourbon on the rocks is waiting for me, and Robert hands Grace a glass of white wine. She sits next to Robert, and I take a chair near the window.

Robert begins, "Thanks for joining us, Johnny. I know you have a show in a couple of hours, and we're looking forward to attending. The short set you played on Friday was really killer."

Nodding, I hold up my drink and then take a sip. Sometimes radio stations or venues will request me to perform a couple of songs the day before the concert. Usually it's acoustic and doesn't take up more than an hour of my time. What Robert asked was for something more than what I do for radio stations, but it honestly wasn't a big deal.

He continues, "I wanted you to meet the group that you'd be working with on your residency. Dominique, I managed to persuade away from the Hard Rock. She's damn good at her job, and she was able to successfully negotiate two big names to perform with much accolades."

Dominique crosses her legs and folds her hands in her lap seemingly pleased with her boss's praise. That's when I notice the blood red nails on her fingertips. She appears to be the kind of no-nonsense sort of person you'd expect to manage such a large operation. She looks like she could be a real ball buster. "I think you'd be very happy performing here. We'd, of course, give you much leeway in the design of your theater and work with you on the scheduling of the shows."

I'm being courted. It feels damn good to be wanted. Taking another sip of my drink, I let her statement hang in the dry, desert air for a moment. "I agree. It does make much more sense for my fans to come to me than to do another tour. We have six more months of pre-existing commitments. Then I'll need to take some time off to recover." I don't add and fix whatever is wrong with my brain.

Grace asks, "What's your time frame?"

Robert looks at his three employees and then replies, "We'd like to get a contract signed immediately. It will take some time to renovate the venue, and we need to promote and sell tickets at least six months before the first show."

I take off my fedora and run my hand through my hair. I wasn't prepared to have to make a decision this quickly. My eyes cut to Grace's hoping she can buy me some time. Instead of finding an ally, she looks like a kid who found out they get to live at Disney World. Standing, I slam the rest of my drink and place the empty glass on one of the tables. "Work out the details with Grace. I'll review them and give it some thought. But right now, you'll have to excuse me. I have a show to get ready for."

Robert stands and shakes my hand. "Of course. Grace will have something in her inbox before you leave Vegas."

As I turn away from the group, he adds, "Good luck tonight. Break a leg."

My hand goes up in a sort of wave as I smile a goofy smile. As soon as I'm in the elevator, I pull out my phone to call MK. She answers on the second ring.

"Hi, Aaron." My entire body loosens at the sound of her voice.

"Hello, beautiful. How was your day?"

"Great," she replies enthusiastically. "We planned the grand opening, finished up some of the small details on the design, and began sorting my merchandising boxes. And I filmed my segment discussing the floor renovation."

"Busy day." The doors open, and I head back to my room to change before going down to the venue. "I like they saw your mark. Did you show the contractor like I asked?"

She huffs, "Of course not." She pauses. "We can't do that again."

"Oh my, MK. You know better than to tell me that I can't do something."

"Fine. I'd prefer that you don't do that again." Then she changes the subject not giving me a chance to respond. "It's all coming together. By the way, next time you're in town, I need for you to sign the paisley with the music notes. Don't ask. I think it's dumb also, but Shannon said I must ask."

"Sure." I shrug as I slide the card key into my suite door's lock. "Have a minute? I need to ask you about something."

"Yeah. I'm just finishing making chili. Hold on one sec."

She puts the phone down while I wait. I make another drink and sit down on the chair that looks out over the beautiful casino grounds with the Vegas strip as the backdrop. My boots rest on top of the coffee table.

"Okay. I'm back. What's up?"

I tell her about the Vegas residency opportunity. I also share about it being a one man show and their other ideas. When I'm finished, I settle in prepared for her to shoot me straight. It's an incredible opportunity but a huge commitment. After the tour was over, I was prepared to head back to Austin and run Johnny Records. MK has thrown a wrench into those plans and so has this Vegas deal.

"Wow. Aaron, I have no idea what to say. This is so out of my league. I guess I don't understand why you're asking me. Wouldn't Grace or your other management people be better able to help you make this decision?"

My chest tightens as my blood pressure rises. There's fire in my gut. She's got an opinion about the hair on her legs when we're about to make love, but now when it comes to committing the next couple of years to a show in Vegas she's silent. "I'm asking you because this affects both of us. I don't know what the financials look like yet, but I'm assuming they're willing to open the casino vault. Therefore, all the people who I pay to help me increase the dollars I've made will think it's a brilliant idea. I'm asking you what you think. Do you want me to make this commitment?"

She sighs. "Here's my answer. I want you to do what's best for you. We can figure out how we can make the rest of our life work around your commitments. I've signed a contract with Cindy and Janet that says I'm committed to *Burnt Sugar* and my store for at least a year, and then they have the option to renew for the next five years. I can't imagine there would ever be a time that I'd want to ditch No Pink Caddy. I'd hope that you wouldn't try to dictate what I do with my career so I'm going to show you the same curtesy."

I don't respond. For some reason, I'm angry. Like my-heart-is-racing-and-I-want-to-punch-something angry, and I don't understand why. It's better for me to stay quiet so I don't say words that I'll regret.

"I can tell that I've said something to make you upset and I'm not sure what it is." She pauses for a second. "I'm so proud of you that they've offered you this opportunity. I want to support you in your career and to make sure that you're happy. Whatever I said that's wrong, I'm sorry."

My left fist digs into my thigh, as my right hands tugs through my hair. "I'm an asshole. I want you to demand that I take time after this tour is over and spend it loving you. How ironic." I chuckle. "I want you to be more selfish and demanding of me."

When she speaks, I can hear the smile in her voice. "Aaron Emerson, as soon as this tour is over, I demand that you never leave my side. I require your undivided attention and don't even think of going anywhere without me." She giggles. "Better?"

"Smart ass." I laugh feeling better but still just as confused.

"I do have one question. Isn't it putting the cart before the horse to think about committing to a one man show if you aren't sure you can still play the guitar?"

I realize that she voices one of things that is making me feel uneasy. "Yeah. I guess that could possibly be an issue, but I'm going to be fine. We're doing the Botox injections and rest. I'm sure that I'll be back to playing soon."

Believing in the power of positive thinking, I don't let myself question that this will not be the outcome. It has to fucking be. The thought of not playing my guitar is so gut wrenching that I can't let myself go there—especially not in my sin city. Putting MK on speaker, I fire a text off to Grace asking MK's question just in case.

"Tell me what you're wearing." I change the subject.

"I'm so sexy right now. I'm in nothing but a LSU sorority shirt from my senior year rush and pair of Gap sweatpants."

"I'd love to rip those sweatpants from your gorgeous long legs and pull that shirt over your head, kissing those perfect titties." Grabbing my cock through my pants, I'd give anything to be deep inside of her right now where the real world doesn't exist. "Take your shirt off and FaceTime me."

"No," she responds sounding shocked.

"Yes," I reply as I unbutton my pants and pull my zipper down.

"Aaron, stop it. I'm not having virtual sex with you."

"Yes, you are. Do it, MK." I end our call and dial her back on FaceTime. She answers with pursed lips and raised eyebrows. Her hair is up in a loose knot right on the top of her head. No makeup hides her gorgeous natural glow or her scar. I feel homesick.

"Do you watch the news? Celebrities are always getting hacked and their pervy pics and videos wind up being broadcast to the world. Do you think for a moment my grandmother and mother want to see video of me talking dirty to you while you jack off in your hand?"

I hold the camera so she can see my long, reddish-purple dick who is missing his favorite girl.

"Seriously, Aaron. That's all because I told you I was wearing sweatpants?"

I bring the camera so she can see my huge, shit-eating grin. "Take off your shirt. Just show me one boob," I coax.

Her arms cross over her chest. "You're out of your mind."

"Your fault. You make me crazy. We're not recording this. There will not be a video for someone to steal. It's just you and me." I show her my hand moving up and down as I grip my dick.

Then to my surprise I hear her moan as her eyes hood. "You know I think that's hot."

I believe I was able to make her late for work one day doing just this. "Show me how hot you think it is."

The phone is silent for a moment before she replies, "I'm going to walk into my bedroom." The camera shows movement as she crawls on her mattress. "I'm going to trust you that this isn't being recorded, and no one will ever watch this."

I adjust the camera so I watch her and she can see me pleasuring myself. "This is just you and me, sweetheart. No recording. Nothing for anyone to steal."

"I've never done this before, Aaron. I might suck at it so be patient." Her warning is so cute that I laugh.

"I've never done this either so we'll figure it out together. I do know that you must take your clothes off first." The camera tumbles for a second, and I see her ceiling. "Show me what I want to see," I demand.

A few moments later, I get the perfect shot of two round breasts with the prettiest light-brown nipples. "Fuck, sweetheart," I moan as I grip my dick harder. "God, I love your tits. They're begging my lips to suck them until you come from the pleasure. Slip your finger in your pussy."

The camera shakes, but then I hear a louder moan as she shows me her closed eyes and slack jaw.

"Tell me how it feels."

"Wet," she replies with a lick of her lips. "I'm so wet, and it's all your fault. It does crazy things to my body when you talk dirty."

"Show me my favorite place." My dick pulses as the camera moves down. Her finger disappears knuckle-deep, and then lazily slides back out. It's glistening in the ambient light from MK's bedside lamp. Her pubic hair is wet and clumped together in tight spirals, and my tongue involuntarily swipes over my lips longing to taste her.

"Come on your finger, but pretend it's me," I coax as my hand drops to the base of my cock and forcibly up to the head. "I'm fucking you, sweetheart. It's me that's inside you."

I need lube, but I'm not stopping to go and dig some out of my bag so I use the second best substance—spit. Her pleasure sounds are all the music that I hear inside my head. The rest of the usual chaos is quiet. "Tell me how good I feel inside you."

"Can I get my vibrator?" she asks.

"Sure," I reply as I pump myself faster at the idea of watching something else slide inside her swollen pussy. I hear the vibrating sound and watch as she positions the flesh-colored penis at her entrance. "Spread your lips, and show me it disappearing inside you. Hold the camera right by it."

The image makes me lose my mind. Her engorged clit brushes along the top of the dildo as it moves. Her muscles twitch with pleasure. Moisture drips down her lips and makes a dewy sheen on the inside of her thighs.

It's the hottest shit I've ever seen. No porn can compare to seeing the woman you love this turned on for you. "Pinch your nipples as you fuck your toy. I'm going to come with you so you've got to tell me what you're feeling." My voice is domineering and in control. She seems to respond.

The toy slides in faster. "You're so hard inside me," she moans as she writhes in pleasure on her sheets. "I want you. I want you to fuck me and make me forget about everything else but us."

"It's just the two of us, sweetheart." I grab my dick and beat off with a crazed intensity. My balls draw up tight, ready to explode. "You and me. Fuck the rest of the world. It doesn't exist. Am I hitting your clit?" I arch up ready to blow my load all over my chest.

"In just the right spot." She's quiet for a second, and her pleasure pants turn into a very loud moan. "Oh God, Aaron, I'm going to come. Like right now. Come with me."

"I'm right there. Sweetheart, I'm driving into you. My dick is hitting your sweet spot, and you're spraying it with your wetness."

"Aaron . . ." she calls as the camera goes askew. "Oh God . . . Oh God . . . Aaron, I'm coming."

"Me too. Me too." I tell her as my hot liquid sprays out of the head of my dick and onto my stomach. Looking down, I see the incredibly large mess that I've made, and I love it. My girl does this to me. "Show me your face."

The camera moves to her heavy eyes and contented smile. Brown hair is splayed in a crown around her face. My heart stops as I gasp. She's the most beautiful thing I've ever seen. "You're fucking gorgeous." I move my phone to my stomach. "This mess is because of you."

She curls into her pillow. "We're no longer virgins. I stole your cyber virginity."

I have no idea why that makes me all gooey inside, but it does. It's only been a day since I've seen her, but I miss her like I've never missed anything before.

"I've a show to do." I move the camera so she can see my face.

"You need a shower first." She smiles looking dreamy.

"Dear God, woman. The things you do to me."

Chapter Thirty-Two

MK
October

MK Landry @NoPinkCaddy
Do you ever feel like you're drowning on dry land?
#Overwhelmed #NPCGrandOpening

I'd like to say that I took Vince's advice and enjoyed every moment of the next week, but it was a blur. Kitchen is complete, the bohemian furniture I'd sketched is a reality and positioned beautifully in the store, bookshelves are in, and shelves are hung. I haven't slept much and when I have, it's been fitful. My dreams are filled with disasters—a Hurricane Katrina like storm hit and my store flooded, I was robbed and everything including my kitchen was stolen, and the strangest one of all, my store was crammed full of paparazzi chanting *Johnny Knite.*

My cuticle is so raw from picking at it, that it's now wrapped in a bandage. My stomach is constantly upset. When I do manage to eat food, I usually must visit a restroom soon after. My temper is short. I've snapped at Bella twice, and all she was trying to do was offer a suggestion. I hate me. I know I'm being difficult, but I can't seem to find any way out from this stress other than completing the store. I've worked late every day this week.

Tonight, I left at six, which is early in comparison. The lack of nutrition has caught up with me, and I feel much older than my thirty-one years. My knees and back ache, and I feel light headed when I stand too quickly. A good night's rest will hopefully do the trick.

It's Friday evening, and I'm already dressed for bed. I feel like there's not enough of me to go around.

When Bella and I were little, we'd take bubble gum and chew it until there was no flavor left. Then we'd place one side in between our front teeth and pull the other side until it was nice and thin. Our goal was to get it arm's length before it tore. I feel like the piece of gum, stretched so thin that I'm ready to rip in half.

My laptop rests on my legs. Even though my eyes are blurred, I've got a bit of work to do before I can take one of Bella's sleeping pills. I've neglected my site since we began filming, and I promised myself that I would post something, anything, tonight.

Just as I begin uploading pictures of the store, my gate calls me. When I answer, a voice says, "Miss Landry, we're here to deliver your furniture."

My lip curls. "I didn't order furniture." I'm already standing and heading outside to get to the bottom of this. I greet the delivery person in a long-sleeve shirt and cotton pants—no bra—at my gate.

He shows me a pink slip of paper. At the top is the store logo and below it in typed print reads: *couch, chair, coffee table.* There are ID numbers next to each item, but they mean nothing to me. "Who ordered this?"

"Look, lady. I don't know, but you're my last delivery tonight so can you open this gate so I can bring the stuff in?"

"Okay," I mumble as I do what he asks and move to the side.

Fifteen minutes later a linen sofa is positioned in front of my kitchen island. The most gorgeous shade of aqua velvet is upholstered on a fluffy chair made for me to spend long hours snuggled in. But, then there's the coffee table. My old marble coffee table was a thrift store shopping coup. It was fabulous and gorgeous. But my new table is truly something special. It's a slab of marble, but the corners are rounded and finished off in chrome with chrome legs—the perfect mix of modern and traditional, just like me.

I watch the delivery guys close my gate. Then I rush inside, feeling rejuvenated, and throw myself on the couch. This is mine, and I can't believe Aaron bought all of this for me.

Pulling out my phone, I send him a text.

Me: *There are no words other than thank you. I can't believe this beautiful furniture is mine.*

Running into my room, I grab my laptop and settle into my new fluffy chair. I take a selfie and Tweet it to my followers.

MK Landry @NoPinkCaddy
Happy Friday night to me! Look at how cute I am in my new chair #UnexpectedGiftsAreTheBest

A few minutes later I get a reply to my Tweet from a name I recognize.

Johnny Knite @RealJohnnyKnite
@NoPinkCaddy You look rather stunning in that chair. #GivingIsBetterThanReceiving

Oh my! Aaron is on social media, and he's acknowledging me. Does he realize that this makes it very hard to deny that our relationship is over?

MK Landry @NoPinkCaddy
@RealJohnnyKnite Is this you and not your publicist? #Dying

Johnny Knite @RealJohnnyKnite
@NoPinkCaddy don't get used to it. I'm bored and missing NOLA. #TouringMakesYouMissHome

My phone and laptop begin blowing up like it did the evening I announced our breakup, and he dropped his new album. It's mayhem. Instead of hiding under the covers this time, I sit back and note that this very moment marks the end of my old life and the beginning of the next chapter. Yes, filming *Burnt Sugar* should have marked that occasion, but only a small number of people in the world knew about it—just fans of my site and followers on social media. Aaron just chose to acknowledge our relationship in a way that couples did long ago by buying ad space in a newspaper to announce their engagement. Except the announcement is in every single newspaper around the globe.

My anonymity is gone prematurely. From this point on, I will be forever associated with the name Johnny Knite no matter what happens in our relationship.

I should be freaking out, but I'm not. We're in such a good place, even if it has been a short time, that I'm genuinely okay.

As the tweets scroll past, I see his name again.

> **Johnny Knite** @RealJohnnyKnite
> @NoPinkCaddy how's the store coming? When do we get to watch you on TV? #BurntSugarRocks

I smile at his Tweet. He's trying, and I love him for it. Relationship part one, I didn't want followers because of his fame. My motto was *alis volat propriis.* Now, I'm understanding that being in a relationship means we're partners. I can't bring him new fans, but I can stand by his side and support him in his career. That's what he's doing now. He's being a good boyfriend not doing charity work on my behalf.

> **MK Landry** @NoPinkCaddy
> @RealJohnnyKnite you kill me. Premier in January. I'll be sure to remind you. #BurntSugar #FameForGoodNotEvil

My phone rings, and it's Aaron. "I did good, huh."

Laughing, I respond, "Is that the first time you've Tweeted?"

"Obvious?" He laughs. "That was fun. I didn't upset you, did I?"

"No. Why?" I ask.

"I know you were pretty adamant about wanting to do your career on your own terms and without my help. But I just thought why not send you a bit of public love."

"That's sweet. I'm sure I'm also going get a few of your stabby, jealous fans, and hopefully, it will take a few days for the paparazzi to arrive. Thank goodness, I have my fence." I laugh.

"Par for the course."

Changing the subject, I ask, "Where are you tonight?"

"Denver, Colorado. It's cold already here. My balls are shriveled."

"Poor balls," I quip. "Did you shop online for my furniture?" My hand runs over the bumpy natural material.

"Yup. I did good." He's so cocky that I shake my head.

"You did real good." I pause for a second. "I love it. It's really beautiful, and the rounded edges on the coffee table didn't escape me."

He sighs. "I hate the mark on your face." Then be begins backtracking. "Not because it takes away from your looks because it doesn't. It's just a reminder that I should've gone home with you. I didn't, and you got hurt. Then, I walk into your carriage house, and it's empty, making me feel like an asshole. I can't repair the scar, but I can throw money at the empty living room."

Smiling, I look at the phone, my heart beating double time. "Whatever your reasoning, I'm happy. You make me happy. I can't wait to see you on Monday."

He sighs. "Oh God, you have no idea."

"How's your hand?"

He sighs again. "Shit. I had to get another round of injections in Phoenix. It did it again. I thought I was going to have to cancel the show, but the Botox worked."

This is the first time I've asked in a couple of days, and I had no idea. My heart flutters with worry. Sitting up straight up in the chair, I ask, "Why didn't you tell me?"

"Nothing you could do, and I know how stressed you are with the store. You don't need my problems."

My heart clenches. "Aaron, your problems are my problems. I want to know."

The phone is silent. "Sorry. I'll tell you next time."

"What did Doctor Odom say?" My finger goes to my cuticle, but I'm stopped by the bandage.

"Doctor Odom is back in New York. He sent one of his associates to replace him. I like him better. He has more personality."

My knuckles whiten as I grip the phone. "Why didn't you tell me that? I want Doctor Odom working with you. In my research, I found he's the best."

"I have to be in New York to see Doctor Odom, but because of the nature of this disorder, he has trained people that tour with the musician. It's all good."

Sighing, I hate this. I want Aaron to receive therapy from the best—not the guy trained by the best, but I let it go. "Okay, so what did this guy say?"

"He said to quit playing my guitar all together, so I stand on stage like a douche wearing a guitar that I don't play." He pauses. "You know what an idiot I feel like clapping my hands over my head and leaning against the mic stand like a pretentious asshole."

"But, Aaron, at least you're still performing. Those fans don't care that you're not playing your guitar. They want your throaty, haunting voice. They want to sing along and watch your lips move as the sounds that they've jammed out to on the radio and in their cars for years, move their souls."

He's quiet for a moment before he replies, "I know. It's just not the same."

"What are you doing about writing music?" I haven't wanted to ask the question. This is a sore spot, but if we're sharing then I need to know the good, bad, and ugly.

"I'm playing some," he admits. "I'm not supposed to, but I can't stop myself. I'm talking to Sam, and she's helping me. I've never asked for help before."

I'm silent as I contemplate if I should yell at him and verbally kick him in the balls or keep my mouth shut. I decide to pick the middle ground. "I must say I'm disappointed that you aren't listening to the doctor or the doctor's associate. I wish you would . . . I mean, look, Aaron, I never want you to think that I'm interfering in your career. You were a huge success before me, and you'll continue to be one with or without me. I just care enough about you to ask you to follow what the doctor orders."

"And I love you for that." He swallows. "I'm trying, MK. Balance is not something I've ever been known to find in my life. This is really fucking hard right now. I want to be with you. I want to play my guitar. I want to make my fans happy. I've got this contract for Vegas sitting in front of me, and I don't know what I want to do. Fuck, I just need the world to stop."

Resting my laptop on the coffee table, I pull my legs to my chest. "I know, Aaron. I can't imagine the stress you're under. I don't want to add to it. I'm your soft place to land. I'm sorry I even said anything." And I am. I can't imagine the pressure he has on his shoulders. He doesn't need another person adding a boulder to his eighteen-wheeler.

"And I'm your soft place to land. I talked to Bella. She said that you're not eating and working yourself until you're sick. You've got to slow down, sweetheart."

I should be furious that he called Bella, but I'm not. It's part of his stalkerish tendencies. "I'm trying. I think everything will be better once the grand opening is over." I change the subject because just the mention of No Pink Caddy makes my stomach cramp. "What's going on with the Vegas deal?"

"I think I'm signing the contract." He drops the news and lets it fester for a moment.

"Okay. Do I say congratulations?"

"Fuck, MK." Aaron sounds frustrated. "I don't know. The money is hard to say no to."

I try biting my tongue but it doesn't work. "This is probably going to come out wrong, but I'm just going to say it. How much money do you really need?"

He's quiet for some time, to the point that I check and make sure we haven't been disconnected. "You're right. I guess it's about staying relevant." He pauses, and then begins again. "I took time off when Jude was in high school, and then I dealt with the legal shit. Right now, it feels pretty damn good to be the topic of conversations and having casinos throw cash in my direction. I slipped off the radar, and it was a nice break, but I like that the fans still care enough to pay to watch me play."

This is the most honest conversation we've ever had about his career, and I'm honored he's discussing it with me. As much as I like to be the object of his sexting, I like being his partner even more. "I'm sure you'll do a great job in whatever you choose. Look, we'll figure it out. You do own your own plane after all." Swallowing, I ask, "What about your hand?"

"I texted Grace after you asked that question the other day. She says I have an insurance policy on my body parts."

That makes me giggle. "How much is your penis valued at?"

"Fucking trillions, laughing girl," he says with humor in his voice. "Seriously, though, Grace has a policy on my vocal cords and my right hand. If for some reason, I can't use one or either, then the company pays me lots of cash."

I straighten. "That's bizarre. But I find most of your life to be bizarre. Okay. So, the insurance policy would cover things if you can't fix your hand."

"Shut up, MK. Don't even let those words exit your mouth." He seems distracted and then says, "Hey, sweetheart, I'm sorry to do this, but Billy just came in. They want me to play poker. I need to give them the heads up about the casino deal."

"Good luck. Have a good night."

"You too, sweetheart."

Resting my phone on my laptop, I stand and move to my new couch. I decide I could sleep here. It's the perfect combination of soft and firm and fluffy and comfy. Aaron did well. Instead I grab my laptop and write one last Tweet promoting the invite to my grand opening, and then drag myself to bed.

Bella's sleeping pill keeps me trapped inside of my nightmares. Instead of their focus being around my store, they're about Aaron. In one dream, his hand is so painful that he severs it from his body with a sword. It's so terrible that I try my hardest to wake myself up so I can be reassured that it was just a dream, but I can't. The drug traps me and pulls be back into the horror. I wake up early Saturday morning twisted in sweat-soaked sheets with tears streaming down my face. There's not a prayer that I'm going back to sleep, so I get up, throw on whatever I can find to wear and head back to No Pink Caddy.

Chapter Thirty-Three

Aaron
October

Music Times @MusicTimesMagazine
It's all but a done deal. @RealJohnnyKnite will take up residency at @CelestialPalaceCasino. Tickets go on sale April 1.

Rock Star Groupies @RockStarGroupies
OMG! @RealJohnnyKnite is back with HER @NoPinkCaddy. Really? What does she have? #MagicPussy

"I need you to take the ball and squeeze it." Calvin hands me a neon-yellow, stress ball made of plastic and covered with soft spikes. I grasp it with my right hand and tighten my grip around it.

"How does that feel?" he asks.

"Normal. Fine. No big deal," I reply as I look out the window. We're in Oklahoma City for a show.

"Let's see if you can do that fifteen times."

I repeat the motion with ease.

"You're atypical." He studies my hand motion as he shakes his head. "You have pain associated with musician's dystonia. That doesn't always happen. Your finger posturing is also painful. Hmmm . . ." He grabs my hand and starts at the tip of my middle finger, pressing on the joints.

"I've already had to get another round of injections, and it had only been eleven days. We play New Orleans on Friday, and it's got to be a good show." I want to actually play my guitar not just stand on the stage with it hanging around my neck. My girl has never been to an ACE concert. I want to put a show on that makes her proud.

Calvin is who Doctor Odom sent to replace him. I like him. He's tall and lanky. Turns out he went to Vanderbilt on a basketball scholarship and used his free education to become a physician assistant. He thought it was great that Jude was a sophomore there and told me about some cool places to check out if Jude ever lets me visit.

"Hold your guitar for me," he orders.

I stand and walk to the case, which is leaning against the wall under the windows in my hotel room. Flipping the locks, I rescue my beloved instrument from its confines. Instead of slipping the strap over my head, I carry it, handing it to Calvin.

He shakes his head. "No. I don't want to hold it. I want you to sit on the couch and play it with a latex glove." His bag of magic tricks opens, and he hands me what looks like a clear, thick, plastic glove that a doctor or nurse would wear when examining a patient. "Put this on your right hand."

Doing what he asks, I roll the glove on almost as if it's a condom.

"Get comfortable. You want to move to the couch?"

We walk from the dining table in my suite and move to the living area. I lean back into the blue and white striped sofa, and Calvin sits across from me with a creased forehead.

"I want you to play something simple," he instructs.

The first thing that pops in my head is *The Wheels on the Bus.*

He smiles at my song choice. "I did say simple. Any discomfort at all?"

"No. I don't feel the need to stretch my hand. I'm able to hit the notes," I explain as I continue finger picking. "I will say that it feels odd playing without completely feeling the strings."

"That's the point. We're changing the touch sensation to hopefully trick your brain." He scoots to the front of the seat cushion. "Play something a bit more complex."

I switch to *Pink Cadillac.* Once again, I find it odd to not completely be able to feel my fingers on the strings, but I can play it well enough. I'd have to practice a lot wearing this thing to ever play live, but I think I could eventually get comfortable with it.

"And how's that?" Calvin asks.

"It's not perfect, but I'm playing it with no pain, and the notes I'm missing are because of the glove not my finger posturing."

He's silent for a bit as I enjoy doing what I love most: just playing my guitar. It's like being reconnected with a friend I haven't seen in forever, but we must get caught up behind a thick piece of glass that makes it difficult to speak to one another.

Calvin leans back in the chair and asks, "What's the most complex piece you know how to play? It doesn't have to be performed well like you'd play it in concert just good enough that you could try out the glove."

"That's easy. Dream Theater's *The Dance of Eternity.*" I laugh. "It kicks my ass all over the place, but every once in a while, when I'm feeling brave, I give it a try."

I can't play it. My fingers don't move fast enough that it's even recognizable, but I'm able to attempt to play it without pain and my fingers behave. About half way through, I give up and rest the guitar on the cushion next to me.

"You want to try playing with a glove tonight? Maybe keep your guitar not mic'ed. You can play your parts and see how the combination of the glove and injections do during a performance."

I stare at the glove feeling a combination of disdain and relief. "I don't know. Guitar is played by touch, and this glove is awkward, but at least I guess I could strum if I wanted to so I don't feel as stupid out there."

"Just give it a try."

***

"Good night, sweetheart," I tell my girl. We take the stage in ten minutes. This has become my pre-show ritual. I must talk to MK. We've been on the phone for an hour. Her sharing with me the candidates that she interviewed for employment at the store, dealing with merchandising screw-ups, and laughing at her and Bella's antics. She's my calm. I also haven't been drinking as much. No bottle of whiskey waits for me after the show any longer. That's her positive influence. I want to be a better man. Even though we aren't mentioning the horrible line to each other, I still think that, right now, I'm being the kind of guy that she deserves. It's the best feeling in the world.

But I'm also worried about her. I called Bella once. I was actually calling to get her to measure MK's living room so I knew what size furniture to buy. When she shared with me just how stressed MK is, I got crazy and thought about flying to New Orleans to check on her. Grace talked me down. She reminded me of my responsibilities. I would never admit this to anyone, but I have a countdown clock on my phone telling me to the second when I'll see her tomorrow morning.

"Good night. Rock their faces off." This is how she ends every call before a show.

"Always."

The wardrobe girl, Jennifer, tucks the loose end of my belt into the loop. "You've got something for me to wear to MK's grand opening?"

"I've pulled three choices for you to look at after the show." She picks a piece of lint off my shirt. The one I'm wearing tonight is a throwback to my first Poison concert.

"You checked with her assistant to make sure we match and all that shit?"

She smiles, and it's one of those annoying you're-so-cute-smiles. "Yes. I've coordinated with her assistant."

"Good." I nod. I want to make sure that I don't disappoint MK on her big night.

Calvin hands me the latex glove to slip on. I'd like to think that the crowd won't notice, but it's evident that I'm wearing a condom on my hand. Grace and I'd discussed me making up a reason to share with the audience—something funny. Instead we just decided to ignore it.

Sam slaps my back and says, "Hope it's the magic bullet."

I told the band last night that I was going to do a stint at the casino in

Vegas. We've done lots of separate stuff in the past, but this is the most high-profile. Like any family does, we fought it out and are stronger than ever before. I told them this would be like when I took off time for Jude. They're free to do their own thing, but I hope that when I call again to record another album that I can count on them. That seemed to soften the blow. I also told Grace to make sure they each get a huge bonus when the tour is over. MK's right. How much more money do I honestly need?

When the band takes the stage, Grace whispers in my ear, "Make sure you can still hold a pen. We're signing the Vegas deal after the show." I've verbally committed, but tonight is the official ink to the paper.

I salute her, beckon for my guitar, and when the curtain drops and the roar of the crowd combines with the hard driving beat of our first song, I take the stage ready to own their hearts and minds for the next two hours. Then I'm getting on a plane that will take me to my MK. I hope to own her heart and mind for much longer than that.

Chapter Thirty-Four

MK
October

Music Times @MusicTimesMagazine
@CelestialPalaceCasino has reportedly paid @RealJohnnyKnite a record amount for his residency.

MK Landry @NoPinkCaddy
All the lids to the cookie jars are chipped. Why, universe? Why? #MyPlateIsFull

MK Landry @NoPinkCaddy
Dear media, it's rude to take up so much room on the sidewalk that my neighbors must walk in the street.

MK Landry @NoPinkCaddy
Dear media, it's also rude to yell questions at me. Your momma should've taught you that you catch more flies with honey.

Eric Anderson @BeerGuitar
@RealJohnnyKnite what the hell was on your hand? #SoStrange

I race down the stairs and open the gate with such enthusiasm that no one who knows me would believe that it's five in the morning. He's standing at my gate wearing a baseball cap over his shaggy hair, dressed in a white Lone Star Beer shirt, and a faded pair of jeans. I want to lick every inch of him.

His smile is beautiful. White teeth glisten in the glow from the street lamp down the block. The press hasn't arrived yet. I'm grateful we can have our reunion without their cameras capturing every moment.

Throwing open the gate, I jump into his out stretched arms. "Welcome home," I tell him as I kiss his neck.

"Oh God, sweetheart," he replies. His arms tighten around my back, and I feel lost in him.

"Come inside," I whisper into his ear meaning it just as dirty as it sounds.

He lets me go. Bending down he picks up the ugly, blue duffle bag, and his guitar case. Wearing a devilish smirk, he says, "I plan to."

My face flushes, and I laugh at our little joke.

As soon as my door shuts, I'm on him. Pushing him into the chair he purchased, I can't wait the five extra seconds to do this on my comfortable bed. I pull my top over my head, tossing it on the floor and shove my breasts in his face like the needy hedonist that I am. He's told me to play with my nipples, but I'm a poor substitute for his callused fingers, rough against my delicate, nerve-filled skin, and his filthy mouth.

He cups each one and takes my right nipple into his mouth. "Seeing these and not being able to touch was fucking torture."

As his lips suction around the hard point, I groan, grasping his shoulders for support. My fingers remove his baseball cap, and I send it flying. I want to feel the soft strands of his hair on my fingertips. My nails scratch his scalp as he bites and sucks my nipple. Needing him more than oxygen, I reach between us and unbutton his jeans.

He smirks while he grabs my hips. "You're a bit desperate. What happened to foreplay?"

Hair falls into my eyes as I rub my engorged clit against the roughness of the denim, feeling the warm, throbbing hardness I crave. "We've had two weeks of foreplay, phone sex, and never fully getting satisfied." My hips dance on his cock as if it were inside of me, and I was bringing us both to my place of Bliss. "I need you, Aaron." My body is so on fire that just the friction against his zipper causes my head to drop back and my eyes to roll so far back in my head that I swear I can read my own dirty thoughts.

He grasps my back and pulls me to him as his mouth slams into mine. He pushes my thin shorts to the side. With his cocky smile, he states, "No underwear, Miss Landry. Such a naughty girl." Two fingers fill me, and I see stars.

"Fuck me, Aaron," I beg.

He picks me up and bends me over the arm of my couch. The delicious sound of his zipper, causes my hips to rise in eager anticipation of what's about to happen.

My shorts are pulled down, and I feel the sting of his hand against my bare cheek. It's so unexpected that I yelp. He massages the burn as his hands grasp my hips. "Your ass is gorgeous, sweetheart."

He hits the other cheek as his cock pushes its way inside without pausing to let me expand to accommodate his size. I cry out in a pleasure pain that is so intense that I must stop myself from coming. His hand positions itself in between my shoulder blades as his other hand grasps my hip.

He pulls back and slams inside again. I push against him, attempting to stand. Leaning forward, he whispers in my ear, "Relax, MK. Don't fight me. I'm going to make you let go of all your stress."

Over and over again he drives inside, hitting me at my barrier. My erect, engorged nipples rub against the raw, natural linen of my couch causing such intense sensations that I gasp for air.

His hand connects again with my ass cheek again, and I see stars. "It's too much," I plead. "I can't take any more." I try moving so that my breasts aren't rubbing against the material. Some part of me needs relief, or I think I might pass out, but Aaron stops me and holds me in place.

He hits the left cheek as he plows inside, and I come with such force that my knees give out. I conform to the shape of the arm of the couch.

He picks up my hips and rotates his dick inside as he bellows so loudly that if the press has arrived, I'm sure they're getting an earful.

I moan, letting him use my depleted body for his own selfish, wonderful needs. Nothing has felt this good. My plastic toy left me longing for the real thing—him—all of him.

"You're my everything," I tell him as he picks up my limp body and cradles me to his chest.

"Sweetest words ever." He moves us to the chair, and I could stay curled in his lap for forever. He doesn't seem interested in moving, and I don't think I'm sated yet. My sexual craving has been satisfied. But I need more of him: his touch, his scent, the sound of his beating heart.

His fingers trace down my back and sometimes pause to play a rhythm on my vertebrae. He hums a tune that I don't recognize as I beg time to stop.

"You find your bliss?" he asks after a while.

"Um-Hum."

"Good, sweetheart. Let's go to bed."

He carries me into my bedroom, and we fall asleep with my head on his chest and his leg thrown over my thighs. We're anchored to each other, and it's the most peaceful two hours of sleep I've had in eleven months.

***

"Don't you have a nice after sex glow," Bella whispers in my ear.

Blushing, I smile. No need to confirm nor deny.

"Where's the rock star?"

"I left him in my bed fast asleep." Changing the subject, "Did anyone notice that I was late?"

"The paparazzi outside distracted the girls from looking at the clock." She hands me the broken lid to a cookie jar. "What do you want to do about all of these?"

Sighing, I hold the chipped lid. "I talked to the manufacturer yesterday. They apologized and are overnighting replacements. Let's hope that we have them today."

Bella rests the white ceramic container on a wooden shelf. "Okay. I'll put a couple of these out. We can't forget to add the lids when they arrive."

"Done."

Janet, Cindy, Robbie, and Shannon are all back in Los Angeles. We aren't filming getting the merchandise set up. Cindy said people will find this boring. I'm sure she's right, but, geez, it's stressful.

It's just Bella and my two new employees helping me out today. They're sweet girls. Roxy just graduated from LSU and wants a career in fashion merchandising. She's a fan of my site so she was a natural hire. The other girl is the granddaughter of one of Grandmother's dear friends. She's twenty, very pretty, has no clue what she wants to do with her life, and thinks this job is very cool. We'll have to see how Casandra works out.

Bella tasked my new employees with steaming each article of clothing and hanging it on one of the racks that Vince built for me.

My phone vibrates, and I pull it from my bra.

Aaron: *Where are you?*

Me: *Work*

Aaron: *Why didn't you wake me? I'd have gotten the police to get you through the crowd out front.*

Me: *Grand opening in three days. I'm crazy busy. Didn't have time to jack with them.*

Aaron: *Too busy for lunch with me?*

Me: *Never*

Aaron: *Be there in thirty.*

Me: *You know when you leave my house that we're confirming us.*

Aaron: *Is that a problem? I thought that's what I was doing when I Tweeted you.*

Me: *Not for me. I agree. Just confirming.*

Aaron: *I'm golden*

Me: *When you get here, come inside.*

I take the salt and pepper shakers from their wrapping and set them next to the cookie jar. "This feels so right. He's just as in to me as I am in to him. Like seeing him this morning is the highlight of this week, and you'd think getting NPC ready would be. But then, of course, we are now going public with a relationship in its infancy." I sigh. "It is what it is."

"Things are so good for you right now. You've gotten the dream and the boy all at one time. Don't let the media rain on your parade."

"Yeah." I nod. "Easier said than done. I guess I have gotten what I've wanted. I feel like I had to go through the horrible breakup and then the months of depression to get here. Now that I've got perspective, I can see why I had to plow through the trenches to have this."

She bumps my hip. "Happy for you. You're a tough cookie."

I get another text and grab my phone.

Aaron: *There's that invitation again. On my way.*

I don't have a chance to reply because my phone starts ringing. It's Cindy.

"Hello," I answer. "How's LA?" Motioning to Bella that I'm taking a call, I walk to the back of the store.

"Well, your ears must be burning, MK."

"Why?" I ask as I hop up on the marble counter.

"Your grand opening is the hottest ticket in New Orleans and maybe all the south." She's talking fast. I've come to learn that this is what Cindy does when she's excited.

"That's good, right?" I ask.

"Should be great news for NPC and hopefully the media hype will translate to viewers in January." She pauses for a beat. "It also means that there is going to be a lot of press. So far everyone we've invited is coming. We're also preparing for paparazzi."

"I'm assuming the reason for the attention isn't because the world has a burning desire to watch *Burnt Sugar.*"

She's quiet for a moment. "No, sweetie. Your Twitter exchange with Johnny and the fact that his album is still sitting at the top of the charts with you starring as his muse has made you quite an intriguing public figure. I know you don't want him mentioned on the show, but we can't not film him if attends the grand opening."

"I know." I squeeze my temples. None of this is news. It just makes it more real when someone else tells me what I've known in my heart. "Have we confirmed to the press that he will be in attendance?"

"No. We've taken the high road and said we don't comment on your private life," Cindy replies.

"He hasn't given any hints that he wants to keep us private. He was thrilled when I invited him, but let me double check and make one hundred percent sure we're on the same page."

Cindy says, "Also, we're going to have to make a plan for how he's handled on the show. Part of your blog is your quest for love. You seem to have found it in a very public figure."

Twisting a strand of hair, I lean back, resting my head against a cabinet. "Yeah, I've thought about that also."

The dinging noise in my ear indicates that I've received a text. Pulling the phone from my ear and putting it on speaker, I read the text from my mom.

Mom: *Had to find out you were back with Aaron from the* Today Show. *Jesus Christ, MK, would it be so difficult to clue me in on your life?*

Well, that makes me feel like pond scum. I note to call Mom and give her the update as soon as possible.

"MK? You there?" Cindy asks.

I take her off speaker and bring the phone to my ear. "Yeah. Sorry. Just got the I'm-a-crappy-daughter text from my mom."

"Oh. Fix that one, sweetie. No one wants to be cross ways with her." She pauses and then gets us back on subject. "It would be best if we had a roadmap going forward before the grand opening in regards to Johnny."

"The press is already camped outside my carriage house. This morning I took an Uber the whole four blocks to work because I didn't want to be chased down my street like I was the last time my relationship was made public."

"Did they come to the store?" she asks with a hint of concern in her voice.

"Once I went inside, they waited for a bit and then left."

"I've a feeling that's not always going to happen." Cindy is almost apologetic for pointing out what's gnawing at my gut.

"I've had the same thought."

"Do you think you need a security guard?" This is the same question that I had this morning when I saw my sidewalk full of men and a few women all with their cameras trained on me.

"I don't know. Aaron and I will discuss over lunch."

"Are you doing okay, MK? I know you had a rough time with this before."

Sighing, I don't how to respond. "I'm doing okay. I have Aaron's support and a fence. That makes life much more tolerable."

"Hang in there," she replies before we both hang up.

Walking back to where everyone is working, I announce, "Ladies, lunch is on me today." Reaching into my wallet, I pull out my credit card and hand it to Bella. She gives me a concerned look, but I shake my head and flash her my big, pleading eyes. "If you get back here and there are reporters everywhere, come around to the back entrance to the store." I smile and add, "I'm super sorry."

Five minutes later they've cleared out, and No Pink Caddy is empty.

Pacing, I wait for Aaron to arrive. My finger, once again, discovers that the band aid is in place for a reason so I trace my star tattoo instead. My heart feels like it's going to beat out of my chest. Brushing my hair from my face, a handful remains in my hand. Staring at the loose strands I conclude that stress is going to indeed kill me.

I discard the hair in an empty box as Aaron's black SUV arrives out front with cars of reporters in tow. Because the store is such a short walk to my carriage house, I see some of the media running the couple of blocks. As the passenger door flies open, he ducks his head, and ignores the five reporters with cameras that have made it to the front of NPC. My door flies open with a loud whooshing noise, and the sounds of cameras clicking fill the air. Then, as it gently closes, their intrusive sounds go with it.

He takes a seat on one of the vintage stools that's in front of the kitchen island. His brow rises, and his smile is cocky. I flush at the memory of our morning. "Come show me how much you missed me."

My eyes dart back and forth. "I can't." I gesture to the sidewalk that is quickly filling up. "They'll take a picture through the windows. This is not how I want my fans to find out that we're back together."

His Adam's apple bobs up and down as he shakes his head. All cockiness is gone. "I know. How big of a problem are they?" The tone of his voice is worrisome.

I open the refrigerator and pull out some sliced deli roast beef and Havarti cheese. "Mayo or mustard?" Then I spot horseradish that I made yesterday. "Never mind." Resting all the ingredients on the marble, I grab a loaf of sourdough bread and slice two pieces. I spread the horseradish on both sides and extract a couple of slices of meat.

I don't know how to respond to his question. The paparazzi are a problem. When I saw them this morning, my heart raced so fast one would think I was being chased by a guy wearing a mask and carrying a chainsaw. The media doesn't want me dead. That's the positive.

"Put down the meat, MK," he demands. "Talk to me."

I look up and smirk. "Odd request from you, Mister Emerson. You normally like me touching your meat."

His solemn expression doesn't crack. "Answer my question."

Finishing the sandwich assembly, I put it on a plate and slide is across the counter. "I'm assuming you're asking professionally and not personally if they're a concern."

His left fist bangs on the counter so forcefully that I jump, and my eyes grow wide. "You're damn right I'm asking about professionally. Personally, Zed will be with you at all times. You're also moving to the New Orleans house."

"What?" My face crinkles while my lip curls. "I am not."

The *V* forms on his forehead, and there's a tick to his clenched jaw. "Zed sure as shit isn't sharing a one bedroom apartment with you."

My arms cross as my face relaxes. "Good point." I concede that one. Turning away, I gather up the food items I took out and put them in the fridge.

"You've told me what a problem those bastards,"—he gestures to the media outside—"were before. I will not leave you vulnerable again."

"I'll stay at your place until we can come up with a better plan."

He picks up the sandwich and takes a bite. "What're you eating?"

I shake my head. The thought of food is revolting. "I'll get something later."

Aaron stands and walks over to my fridge. Opening the door, he begins rummaging through it, placing the things I just put up back on the counter. "I felt your fucking hips, MK. You're too skinny. I'm making you lunch."

I could argue, explaining all the reasons that food is inconsequential right now, but I don't. Instead, I silently let him make a sandwich identical to his. He stands over me with a glare that could intimidate Satan himself. I take it from him and place it on a paper towel. "Happy?"

He nods. "Professionally, what are your thoughts?"

I gesture at my crowded sidewalk. "That certainly doesn't say 'welcome to No Pink Caddy.' I mean who would even want to come in here? I certainly can't film with them pressed against the windows. They're panic inducing. That's how big of a problem they are. Now, on the flip side, I'm sure Janet and Cindy are turning cartwheels. This is all an incredible promotion for *Burnt Sugar.*"

He takes another bite and replies around a mouth full of sandwich. "Security guards seem important. I'll have Zed get two for out front and then, I'll have one guy sleep in the store to make sure there's no funny business."

"Funny business?" I ask as I pick at the bread.

"Listening devices, cameras . . . that kind of shit." He says this like it's no big deal.

That never any occurred to me. It's like I'm teetering on the edge of a mental cliff. So far I've been walking the edge of sanity, and I think I've done a fine job of staying on the non-crazy side. But, that comment sends me diving head first into the rocky ravine below.

My heart races, and my stomach twists into such a tight knot that I might never eat again. My head swims. "Oh God," I gasp, standing and walking to the kitchen sink. I run the cold water and grab a towel, wetting it. Placing it on the back of my neck, I beg my body to cooperate. I'm so light headed that my knees buckle and bile comes up my throat.

He's by my side with his arm wrapped around my shoulders, supporting my weight. "It's okay, MK." He kisses my hair. "Leave this to me. You've got nothing to worry about, sweetheart. Zed and I will make sure that your grand opening goes perfectly without any interruptions from them."

I spit the nasty substance that's filled my mouth into the sink. Cupping my hand, I fill it with water and bring it to my mouth, taking a sip. The water does little to wet my dry lips and kill the horrible taste. Gripping the bullnose edge of the marble, I pray to stay upright.

"MK," he demands. "MK, look at me." He takes the washcloth and blots my forehead and cheeks. He has the saddest eyes. "I'm so sorry, sweetheart. Please forgive me. Trust me there's no amount of money I won't spend to make this better."

His fingers tuck the strands of hair behind my ears as tears spill from my eyes. I'm shaking so violently that it's hard for me to articulate words. "I can't have this be a failure. Do you understand that I've put everything that I have inside of me into No Pink Caddy?"

He takes my hands and leads me to the barstool he was sitting on. His jaw twists and spider webs form around his clear, blue eyes. "Hey," he says pulling out a stool and placing it next to me. "It's not going to be, MK. You've got to calm down, sweetheart."

Swallowing, I squeeze his fingers. "I'm trying." Taking a deep breath, I let it out. "They can follow me. They can camp out at my home, but you can't let them ruin my dream." I take his chin and with pleading eyes, I express the words that echo in my head every second, of every minute, of every hour, of every day. "If No Pink Caddy fails, it will kill me."

He pulls me into his chest and kisses my hair. "I know, sweetheart. I know how much this means to you. You're my number one priority."

Grasping his arm, I hold on for dear life. Slowly, I seem to gain control of my body, and I feel more able to deal with what's been heaped on me.

"What do you think of that out there?"

He leans back and meets my eyes. "I fucking hate it, but it's my life."

My hand rests on his thigh. "But you've stayed out of the spotlight for the most part. You said that's why you live in Austin. You spent a lot of time and money making sure Jude was not photographed. I want to know how you are." I emphasize the word *you.*

"I've been famous long enough to know that this will pass. There's always something more interesting and the world gets distracted." He sighs. "We just have to stay strong while we're the most interesting thing anyone has to talk about."

That makes me smile. "We're going to get through this together, right?" I ask because I need to be reassured that we're partners in this.

"Together, sweetheart." He takes my hand brushing his lips over my knuckles. Tingles pass through my body.

"Not to act like a mom, but remember stress makes the musician's dystonia worse."

Scoffing, he examines his right hand. "So far, so good."

Chapter Thirty-Five

Aaron
October

Music Times @MusicTimesMagazine
@RealJohnnyKnite stayed overnight at the home of @NoPinkCaddy

Music Times @MusicTimesMagazine
Sources confirm @RealJohnnyKnite and @NoPinkCaddy are officially an item.

MK Landry @NoPinkCaddy
@RealJohnnyKnite will you be my date to the #NPCGrandOpening party? #GirlCrush

Johnny Knite @RealJohnnyKnite
@NoPinkCaddy I'm so proud of you. Of course! #WhyAreWeTalkingViaTwitter

Jude Emerson @HorseGirl4Life
@RealJohnnyKnite and @NoPinkCaddy how come I find out y'all are dating again on Twitter. #ParentingFail

Natalie Van @SewingIsLikeCool
@NoPinkCaddy I've followed NPC for five years. Why did I find out you and @RealJohnnyKnite were together on the news?

"Don't tell, MK," I plead as I lie crumpled on the sectional in my house in New Orleans. My guitar rests on the hardwoods where it tumbled to the floor when the cramp happened. The pain is off the charts. It's hard for me to focus, and I'm so nauseated that I'm afraid to move.

Grace stares with fear in her eyes. "I've called Calvin. He'll be right here."

As if on cue, I hear the backdoor open and close with a slam. In seconds, Calvin is kneeling next to me. "Show me your hand."

I'm able to move my arm enough to pull my fist out of my stomach. An ungodly noise that I didn't know I could make exits from my throat. My hand is twisted in a grotesque way. My middle finger points at a forty-five-degree angle to my pinky, and my wrist is twisted perpendicular to my arm. "Do something," I groan.

My heart pounds against my ribs. All I can see are shades of red. I've never felt anything like this before.

"What's the pain level?" Calvin asks in a concerned, but controlled voice.

"Fucking crazy," I yell. "This makes the first attack look like nothing."

He pulls a needle from his bag. "I'm going to give you a shot for the pain."

I feel the stick of the needle and moments later all I can see is black as my body relaxes on the couch cushions. As I move into the darkness, my mind throbs with agonizing thoughts of just how bad this really is.

When I can open my eyes again, I'm lying on top of the comforter of my bed in the house in New Orleans. I have no idea how I got here, or why. Looking down, I'm completely dressed and it's still light outside. My head is filled with chaos. It's like I know where my nose is, but I can't seem to find it with my finger. I stagger out of bed so woozy I must use my hand against the wall for support.

That's when I notice the white cast on my right hand. It's not like when I was a kid, and I broke my arm falling off the monkey bars. The material is the same but my hand has been splinted as if I'm in the middle of playing a song on my guitar. My head turns, and I hear the theme music from *Alice in Wonderland* playing in my head.

"The fuck?" I yell as I stumble into the living room. It's filled with my bandmates, Doctor Odom, Calvin, Grace, and MK. *What's she doing here?*

MK rushes to my side. I drape my arm around her, and she helps me to a chair. When I'm finally able to study her features, her bloodshot eyes let me know that she's been crying. "What's wrong? What did those bastards do to you?"

She kneels at my feet and places her hand on my knee. "No one hurt me, Aaron."

Holding up my arm, I ask, "Why is this on me. Why do y'all look like someone died?" My eyes dart from Grace to Sam to the doctor looking for the answers.

Doctor Odom adjusts his glasses. I've come to think of this as a nervous tick. "You had another incident. Grace heard you screaming when she got out of shower. Apparently, you'd been playing the guitar, and it happened."

"I had my glove on." I have no memory of the attack. When I try to remember the last thing that happened before I woke up lying on the bed, it was leaving MK's store, then coming back here. I put the condom on my hand and was working on the new song on the guitar.

"Grace and I made the decision to splint your hand," he continues ignoring my comment.

"Why do I feel like I'm coming down from a really shitty bender?"

"Calvin had to give you an injection for the pain. Plus, we had to manipulate your hand into that position. That's not something you would have wanted to feel without the aid of a drug." His eyes dart to Grace.

Mine follow his as everyone in the room looks at my sister. She cracks her neck and says, "I'm sorry to tell you this, but we've postponed the rest of the tour indefinitely."

MK's grip on my thigh tightens, and I instinctively reach over and lay my cast on her shoulder. The inability to feel her through the thick material makes me crazy so I stand, offering her my left hand. She grabs it and joins me with her arms around my waist and her head against my arm.

"The show can still go on. I can sing, right? I won't have my guitar. We can issue some sort of statement saying I tripped over my shoelaces. Y'all were willing to let me do it a couple of weeks ago. What's changed?" They just can't decide to postpone my tour without my consent. What kind of bullshit is this? I'm Johnny Knite. This is my band and my tour. ACE are my initials.

MK turns, and I meet her concerned eyes. "Doctor Odom has consulted with others in this field. Grace, Sam, and I were on a conference call with all of them." She touches my pec. "Aaron, they were wonderful. You can truly say the world has come together to help you through this."

My right hand goes to my hair, and I'm quickly reminded that I can't use it to tuck the wayward strands behind my ear. "And?"

Her tongue swipes over her bottom lip. "And even though stress doesn't cause this, everyone believes that it does exacerbate it. You're going to have to take some time off and focus on getting better. Doctor Odom is going to work every single day with you. You're going to fly to New York with him and Calvin, and they're committed one hundred percent to making you better."

Stepping away from her, I walk to the corner of the room. It's like an out-of-body experience. This isn't happening. It's a bad dream that I can't wake up from. I can't seem to rectify this in my mind. I've never missed a show. I've played with a one-hundred-four degree fever, strep throat, and a broken ankle. I've played after finding out that the woman who birthed Jude killed herself. Now, they're telling me I have to walk away from this tour because my hand hurts. It doesn't seem believable.

"No." I turn around and face all of them. The fight or flight instinct has kicked in, and I'm fighting. "No. We aren't taking time off from the tour. Grace, undo whatever you did. Make this right," I yell.

MK walks to the middle of the room and says with such force that I'm shocked she has it in her. This is the girl who let me storm out of the restaurant when the band was being disloyal. This is the girl who chose my band over me. Her voice booms. "Go. He's upset. He's going to lash out at all of you. I'll handle him from here."

Sam attempts to interject, but MK cuts her off. "He's going to say stuff that he'll regret. Let me help him through this." Then in a pleading voice, she says, "Please just go."

Slowly my living room empties. I get lots of pats on the back and a few "so sorry, man." I can't look at my bandmates. My eyes stay glued to the floor. I've let them down. My weakness has hurt them. They're my family. They're my everything.

Grace is the last to leave. She says to MK, "Let me know if you need anything. I'll be in the recording studio."

MK nods and smiles. "Thank you for everything, Grace."

Once the backdoor closes, she asks, "Will you come sit on the couch with me?"

"No." I dig my heels into the worn, wooden floor.

"Okay," she replies and remains standing. "Here's the cold, hard truth, Aaron."

"Give it to me." I motion. "Tell me everything that I'm not going to listen to." My left hand balls into a fist.

Her arms cross over her chest. "If you don't take this time off and focus on you, there's a chance that you may never play the guitar again."

Her words are like a punch to the gut, causing me to double over. Now I know why she wanted me to sit down. She drops to the ground in front of me, but doesn't touch my body.

"You're getting worse not better. They can't do anymore Botox injections. The side effects will be worse than the dystonia. You can improve. Everyone believes that you can retrain your brain and get back on stage, but you have to walk away from this tour and focus on you and your health."

My head hangs. My brain reasons that every word MK has said is the truth, but my heart, well, that's another story. It's shattered. It's broken like when MK gave up on me, and I had to take that pathetic flight back to Austin alone.

I don't quit.

I don't disappoint.

I'm a motherfucking rock star.

"This is my fault." I laugh, but there's nothing funny. My casted hand tries to drag through my hair again. "I've got you, so my music career has to end." Standing up, I start pacing, laughing like a crazy man. "I can only have one good thing in my life at a time. That's the way the gods designed it. I just always thought I would lose you but not my music. Boy, was I fucking wrong."

MK leaps to her feet. "That's not true, Aaron. The doctor said that up to two percent of musicians suffer from this. Most are male, and it presents itself between the ages of twenty-five and forty. You're not cursed. Think of this as an on-the-job injury."

I hear her statics, but it doesn't penetrate my racing, chaotic brain. I yell to the ceiling, "I can't be happy. I can't find the balance that the rehab doc told me to find. My life only skews in one direction. Height of my success, the woman who birthed Jude killed herself blaming me. I write the best album of my career. I lose you."

Reaching my fists to the heavens, I yell, "Fuck you, God. Fuck you for cursing me with this life."

Body Count by Manslaughter screams in my head. Ripping a painting from the wall, I slam it against the corner of the coffee table. It rips apart like MK's cheek did.

She shrieks, "Stop it, Aaron."

Ignoring her, I pick up the discarded alcohol glasses that my bandmates left behind. One by one, I hurl them against the raw, brick wall with my left hand, delighting in the sound of them shattering. I scream how fucking unfair life is. I beg God to give me use of my hand back. I make deals, promises if this situation can be reversed.

After the last glass is in shards, MK places her hand on shoulder. "Don't do this, Aaron," she pleads. "Don't sabotage us because you believe in some stupid curse."

Turning around, I look at her with disdain. It's her fault that I can't play my guitar—maybe ever again. I want to inflict pain. I want her to leave so my hand will work again. "Is your store hiring? I can be the stock boy, or the greeter. Or pretty, little MK's washed-up, rocker boyfriend."

Her chest bows as her feet go into a fighting stance. With a glint in her eye, she says, "I know you're upset, and you're taking it out on me. I'll stand here and be your punching bag. What else do you want to hurl in my direction?" Black streaks of mascara slide down her cherry-pink cheeks. "Here. I'll help. You're under the kind of stress that contributed to this condition because I gave up on you when you used. This happened because I wouldn't marry you last November when you asked. I have my own career and can't be at your beck and call. You helped me paint. Because you fell in love with me, we're the number one trending topic on Twitter. Anything else? Or did I cover it all?"

"You forgot that I can't have my guitar and you." My lip curls. "Get out. I choose my guitar."

She rears back, biting the inside of her lip as her hand connects with my cheek. Fire blazes in her eyes. "Listen to the words that are coming out of your mouth, you fucking bastard."

Touching the side of my face, I feel the sting from her palm. It's the red-hot passion she has flowing through her Cajun-spiced veins for me, for us. She's still here, taking my verbal abuse, because she's committed to me. God, I love her for it. No one else in my life has ever cared enough to fight for me. This is me at my worst, and she hasn't bailed.

"You aren't pushing me away. I love you, and I recognize a wounded animal when I see one. What else you want to throw?" She picks up one of my Grammy awards and hurls it against the wall. Then, she marches back to where I'm standing. "What else you have inside that dark soul of yours, Aaron? Give it to me. I can take it."

There's no response. It's like I verbally expunged every bit of rage trapped inside. I tested her. I showed her my worst, and she's asking for more. I've never loved anyone this much. "I'm sorry," I croak around a lump in my throat. Dropping to the ground, I sit like a rag doll amongst the shards of glass and ceramic. My bones no longer support my body. The sting of salty tears burn my eyes. I haven't cried since Jude's birth, and I fight like hell to keep them from falling. MK lets me pull her to my chest as I kiss her hair. "I'm so sorry. You're right."

The music in my head changes to an Enya song. Her tears wet my shirt and after a bit, mine join in the mix of pure agony. Devastation is not an emotion that I'm familiar with, but right now we're becoming intimately acquainted.

We hold each other as the room turns from light to dark. Words are not exchanged. Sometimes quiet speaks louder. Her body is warm against my cold heart. Her light soul illuminates mine making it not such a dark abyss.

After my eyes have dried and her back has quit heaving, she says, "You need to talk to Grace. There are plans to be made."

"And you?" I ask feeling emotionally depleted. It's an open-ended question because I'm not sure how to ask what this means for us. Is she done with me? Did I push her away for good this time? Was my rage too much for her to handle? Has she seen the worst in me and decided she can't do this for the rest of her life?

She stands and I join her, hanging on to hear her answer, convinced it's the only thing keeping my heart still beating.

The tight bandage wrapped around my hand reminds me that swimming, my one lifeline to sobriety, is no longer an option. Will she still support me if I use again?

"I left the store and raced over here when Grace called. I need to finish a few things. Then I'll pack an overnight bag and come back here if that's what you want?"

"I'd like that," I reply as relief oozes from every pore. Stripping off my shirt, I toss it on the floor. The toe of my sock digs at an imaginary wood knot. "You're going to be here with me while I do this? Right? While I remap my brain."

Her hand goes to her hip and she gives me the smartass smile that I love. "I've already asked Doctor Odom if he can also fix your inability to properly use a towel and your obsession with sugary breakfast cereal."

As I follow her to the front door, I swat her ass. I say the words that my heart has been screaming. "I love you, MK."

She turns around, and her soft lips brush against my stubbly cheek. "And I you. Aaron, we're going to get through this and come out stronger on the other side."

"This is burnt sugar, right? Life not turning out how we planned." Leaning against the door frame I feel a tornado of emotions churning in my gut: heartbreak, devastation, anger, fright, passion, and hope.

With a slight turn of her head, she blows me a kiss. "It's the definition of burnt sugar, but we're going to use it to make something even sweeter."

Dear Reader,

Thank you for stepping into MK and Aaron's world. This is the second book in my new series ACE. I know how hard it is to wait for more of their story so I created MK's website www.NoPinkCaddy.com. You'll find pictures of the actual places in New Orleans that are featured in this book. I also share the recipes that MK prepares as well as some of my favorite Cajun inspired dishes. Oh! And did I mention there will be teasers for the next book? It's true. As you witnessed in *No Pink Caddy* and *Burnt Sugar*, MK has a difficult time staying off social media. You can follow her here:

Twitter www.twitter.com/NoPinkCaddy
Facebook www.facebook.com/NoPinkCaddy
Instagram www.instagram.com/NoPinkCaddy
Pinterest www.pinterest.com/NoPinkCaddy

As always, I so appreciate your reviews and recommendations. Most of all, though, I love hearing from you. Email me at Layne@LayneHarper.com or find me on Facebook at www.facebook.com/LayneHarperAuthor.

Until we meet again . . .

Muah,

Layne Harper

About Layne Harper

Layne Harper is the Amazon bestselling author of the *Infinity* series. Her first book, *Falling Into Infinity,* fulfilled her lifelong dream of bringing Charlie and Colin to life. The kid who grew up in a small town in Texas never dreamt that one day, people from six continents would read her words.

Layne is married to her college sweetheart. They have two young children who are so similar to their parents that it's a bit eerie, one perfect dog, one dog who really is perfect, a puppy, and a four-pound cat who runs the house.

When Layne isn't driving carpool, scratching book ideas on the kids' homework, or volunteering, she's watching sports, rooting for the Texas A&M Aggies, or listening to music while imagining what the stars' lives must be like.

Burnt Sugar is the second book in her new series, *ACE.*

Manufactured by Amazon.ca
Bolton, ON

15000384R00164